YOU'LL BE SORRY!

—

YOU LEAVE ME COLD!

The author, Samuel Rogers

YOU'LL BE SORRY!

—

YOU LEAVE ME COLD!

SAMUEL ROGERS

COACHWHIP PUBLICATIONS
Greenville, Ohio

You'll Be Sorry! / You Leave Me Cold!, by Samuel Rogers
© 2018 Coachwhip Publications
Introduction © Curtis Evans

Samuel Rogers (1894-1985)
You'll Be Sorry! published 1945.
You Leave Me Cold! published 1946.
No claims made on public domain material.
Cover image: *Kiss of Death*, Poubleno Cemtery, Barcelona
    © Thomas Lusth

CoachwhipBooks.com

ISBN 1-61646-459-3
ISBN-13 978-1-61646-459-2

DEATH'S CARNIVAL

The Crime Fiction of Samuel Rogers (1894-1985)

CURTIS EVANS

"Of course," Paul Hatfield stated, "it's a bad thing to have the murders in a straight detective story committed by a madman, because . . . [the murderer] might almost be anyone. . . ."

"Most of the time we move along complacently, and take our sanity for granted. But haven't you sometimes felt, when you've been sick or tired or worried, that sanity was like a tightrope strung across a great gulf, that you have to walk over it and if the slightest little adjustment should go wrong you'll topple off and never stop falling. . . ."

—from *Don't Look Behind You!* (1944),
by Samuel Rogers

I

American crime writing of the 1940s saw a fundamental shift away from the brainteasing, between-the-wars, clue-puzzle detective novel (most associated today with the mysteries of the bestselling British Queen of Crime, Agatha Christie) toward other, more visceral crime fiction forms, namely hard-boiled, noir, espionage, and psychological suspense, the latter of which concerned itself not so much with tangled railway timetables and ingeniously locked rooms as the puzzling conundrums presented by the human mind. While the hard-boiled and noir subgenres were dominated by men such as Raymond Chandler, Cornell Woolrich, David Goodis, and James M. Cain, women authors quickly carried the field of psychological suspense, producing such outstanding Forties mysteries as Margaret Millar's *The Iron Gates* (1945), Charlotte Armstrong's *The Unsuspected* (1946), Helen Eustis' *The Horizontal Man* (1946), Dorothy B. Hughes' *In a Lonely Place* (1947), Elisabeth Sanxay Holding's *The Blank Wall* (1947), Hannah Lees' *The Dark Device* (1947), Sara Elizabeth Mason's *The Whip* (1948), Ursula Curtiss' *Voice Out of Darkness* (1948), and Mildred B. Davis' *The Room Upstairs* (1948), the majority of which are in print today. Yet one male author from the Forties who achieved great heights in psychological suspense was Samuel Rogers, a well-regarded mainstream novelist and professor of French literature at the University of Wisconsin. Between 1944 and 1946 Rogers published a trio of psychological thrillers in which his series sleuth, Professor Paul Hatfield, solves some truly depraved slayings which take place in a fictional Midwestern state (clearly Wisconsin): *Don't Look Behind You!* (1944), *You'll Be Sorry!* (1945) and *You Leave Me Cold!* (1946). (To drive a sense of urgency home to his readers, Rogers punctuated each of the titles with an exclamation point.) All three of these crime novels were favorably reviewed at the time of their publication and the first of them was adapted in 1962 as a teleplay for *The Alfred Hitchcock Hour* (directed by John Brahm and starring Vera Miles and Jeffrey Hunter), yet today they are mostly forgotten by mystery fans. One hopes the reprinting of two of these novels by Coachwhip will bring greater attention once again to the unique and accomplished crime fiction of Samuel Rogers.

Aptly described by the novel's publisher, Harper & Brothers, as a "tale of mounting fear and horror," *Don't Look Behind You!* introduces readers to Samuel Rogers' series sleuth, Paul Hatfield, a chemistry professor and amateur birdwatcher at the fictionalized Midwestern college town of Woodside (clearly Madison, home of the University of Wisconsin). On his first appearance, made at a cocktail party given by fellow chemistry professor Terry Macfarlane and Terry's wife Jeanne, Dr. Hatfield is described as follows:

"A thickset middle-aged man appeared in the doorway. . . . [H]e gave . . . the impression of moving with exceptional quietness. His face might have been carved very sharply, very neatly, out of wood; his eyes moved perkily; his head was cocked like a bird's." Decidedly quirky in his personality and behavior, Dr. Hatfield is a true crime enthusiast who discourses cheerily about such terrifying real life mass killers and/or sadists as Henri Landru (Bluebeard), Jack the Ripper, Fritz Haarmann (the Butcher of Hanover), Jean-Baptiste Troppmann, George Joseph Smith (the brides-in-the-bath killer), Baron Gille de Rais, and the Marquis de Sade, and himself has rather an unorthodox marriage with his still sexually attractive wife, Wanda. (It is made clear that the couple has no physical interest in each other, though Wanda definitely takes rather a voracious interest in the male animal more generally and the professor for his part is not averse to the presence of pretty coeds.) All this marks the professor as a suspect in the first Samuel Rogers mystery, which concerns Ripperesque serial mutilation murders of young women around Woodside. In the event, however, we find that Dr. Hatfield is not the novel's frightful murderer but rather the insightful sleuth and a friend in need to Daphne Gray, a lovely nursing student imperiled by a maniac killer who deviously takes cover behind a gulling masque of normality.

American book reviewers roundly praised *Don't Look Behind You!* for its "atmosphere and mood and mounting horror" and its "carefully wrought" examination of "abnormal psychology." Most notably, Anthony Boucher, future dean of American crime fiction critics, in the *San Francisco Chronicle* pronounced of the novel: "Good talk about murder, some fine chilling moments and a uniquely brilliant psychological plot." Better yet, in my estimation, are Rogers' two follow-up novels, *You'll Be Sorry!* and *You Leave Me Cold!*, which succeed splendidly both as tales of creeping suspense and as trickily clued psychological puzzlers. (To me the secret in *Don't Look Behind You!* seems less well-hidden.)

You'll Be Sorry! is a tale of another menaced lovely young co-ed, Kate Archer. Summer has arrived at Woodside and Kate has been invited by an old school friend, June Gladstone (four years younger than Kate and still something of an awkward adolescent), to spend her vacation with June and her (really rather disturbingly odd) family at her wealthy father's rural retreat, Valley Farm. Kate also has received a threatening missive, penned in red ink, which bluntly warns: DON'T GO TO MR. GLADSTONE'S. YOU'LL BE SORRY IF YOU DO. Undaunted, the intrepid Kate goes to Valley Farm, where she finds, as she is plunged into a terrifying mire of mystery and sadistic murder, that she is sorry indeed. Fortunately a vacationing Professor Hatfield is at hand to expose a shockingly diabolical criminal scheme. "[A] plot of Jacobean murk and terror," enthused Anthony Boucher of the novel, "magnificently evil." He concluded of Samuel Rogers that the author was "developing a horror-suspense style of his own almost as chilling as [Cornell] Woolrich or [Elisabeth Sanxay] Holding." "Horror succeeds horror," noted the more squeamish Isaac Anderson in the *New York Times Book Review.* "The more horrible [the murders] are . . . the better [Samuel Rogers] likes them."

Covers for the first two mysteries

Horror mounts yet higher in the final Samuel Rogers mystery, *You Leave Me Cold!* Indeed, the reviewer in *Kirkus* deemed the story a horror novel first and a mystery second. I would prefer to classify it as a horrifying mystery novel, one of which that darkly imaginative master of mystery and terror, Edgar Allan Poe, would have been proud. In contrast with the first two Rogers mysteries, *You Leave Me Cold!* has a male protagonist rather than a female one, this person being John Frazer, late of the US Navy and the Pacific theater of war and, we find, the handsome young nephew of Professor Hatfield. Now enrolled as a medical student at Woodside, where there is a severe housing shortage, John is anxiously seeking a place where he can stay. (Inconveniently, the professor himself has closed his own house, Wanda Hatfield being away in California for the winter, and is baching it at the University Club.) In terms of its repellent weirdness the domicile which young John finds to take him in ultimately rivals such fearful haunts as Castle Dracula and the House of Usher. Anthony Boucher deemed the motive for the singularly awful initial murder in *You Leave Me Cold!* "the most shocking . . . in the history of the crime novel," a sentiment which was echoed by Isaac Anderson, who declared it "so macabre that few will be able to read of it without a shudder." One is sorry with *You Leave Me Cold!* to come to the end of Samuel Rogers' magnificently macabre series of crime novels, but how, one wonders, could Rogers ever have outdone this final fearsome performance in his fictional carnival of death?

II

At first blush there would seem to have been little in the life of Samuel Rogers to account for the gushing wellspring of gore and ghoulishness which one finds in his criminal trilogy of terror. The esteemed academician and author was born Samuel Greene Arnold Rogers on September 5, 1894, in Newport, Rhode Island, the eldest of four sons of Reverend Arthur Rogers, an Episcopal clergyman, and Cornelia Arnold (making him a close contemporary of Providence's H. P. Lovecraft, another, rather more famous Rhode Island horror novelist).[1] Samuel Rogers' family lineage was one of prominence in Rhode Island, his paternal grandfather, Horatio Rogers, having served two terms as Attorney General and a dozen years as an Associate Justice of the Rhode Island Supreme Court, and his maternal grandfather, the distinguished lawyer and historian Samuel Greene Arnold, for whom Rogers was named, having served as Lieutenant Governor, a U. S. Senator, and President of the Rhode Island Historical Society. Arnold additionally was the author of the two-volume *History of the State of Rhode Island and Providence Plantations* (1859-60).

Himself a highly literate and learned lawyer, Horatio Rogers served three years in the Civil War and as a colonel commanded the 2nd Rhode Island Infantry at the Battles of Chancellorsville and Gettysburg. Of the bloody carnage he witnessed at the latter engagement, he wrote memorably that "Death seemed to be holding a carnival." After leaving the Army in 1864, he was nominated by the Republican Party of Rhode Island as its candidate for Attorney General; the returned war hero was elected to the office with 96% of the vote.

Unusually for a politician, Horatio Rogers also was a noted antiquarian and bibliophile, and he authored several books, including *Private Libraries of Providence* (1878), which surveyed the book holdings of some of Rhode Island's most prominent citizens (including his own 4000 volume library), and *Mary Dyer of Rhode Island* (1896), a tribute to the fervent Quaker and religious martyr who was hanged in Boston by the Puritans in 1660. Of bibliophilia Horatio Rogers philosophized in the essay which opens the former work that "the extremes of society meet in appreciation of books. The lofty and the lowly alike are cheered by their presence, and solaced by their companionship. The conqueror will not be separated from them, even in his victorious career; and the simple artisan and the petty tradesman, after their humble labors, turn to them as to the sunlight of their existence." (He might well have been describing the remarkable social ubiquity of mystery fans in his grandson's day, when seemingly everyone from statesmen and ministers to "tired businessmen" and office clerks, housewives, typists, and shopgirls devoured detective fiction and crime thrillers.) Probably the most intriguing literary question today about

Horatio Rogers, however, is whether he might have been the actual author of one of the most revered and eloquent of Civil War soldier missives: the celebrated "Dear Sarah" letter ostensibly written by Horatio Rogers' friend Sullivan Ballou, who also served, until his death at the First Battle of Bull Run, in the 2nd Rhode Island Infantry.[2]

Although he was a Rhode Islander by birth, Samuel Rogers spent his formative years in West Chester, Pennsylvania, where his father in 1899 was appointed Rector of the imposingly bell-towered Holy Trinity Church. Rogers attended Delancey School in Philadelphia, Brown University, the University of Chicago, and the Sorbonne, though his advanced education was interrupted for a time by his service in France during the First World War, first in the American Ambulance Field Service and later as a private in the U. S. Army, in which capacity he was awarded the French Croix de Guerre medal. All four of the Rogers brothers served in the Great War, prompting the printing of photographs of them in the *Chicago Tribune Pictorial Weekly*, below the inspirational banner headline PATRIOTS—FOUR BROTHERS FIGHTING FOR UNCLE SAM. The brothers had proved themselves worthy not only of Uncle Sam but of their Grandfather Horatio.[3]

Paul C. Rogers.   Horatio Rogers.   Samuel G. A. Rogers.   Arthur W. Rogers.

FOUR BROTHERS FIGHTING FOR UNCLE SAM—The sons of the Rev. and Mrs. Arthur Rogers of 1501 Ridge avenue, Evanston, are in the service. Samuel, G. A., Arthur W., and Paul C. are members of the American expeditionary force. Horatio, who is only 17, is in Section 2, A. R. C., Italian ambulance service on the Piave front, unless he has passed the test and is in the Royal Flying corps. He cabled asking his father's permission to take the test some time ago.   (Photography by Tobb, Evanston.)

Chicago Tribune, April 21, 1918

After leaving military service Samuel Rogers in 1919 married Marion Richmond Gardner, daughter of Henry Brayton Gardner, an economist and Eastman Professor of Political Economy at Brown University. The couple had three children, all of whom were named for his and his wife's illustrious forebears: Cornelia, born in 1920, and, a few years later in 1923, a pair of twins, Henry Gardner and Lucia. Rogers joined the French Department at the University of Wisconsin, where he remained for four decades, until his retirement in 1960. (My parents were students at UW in the late 1950s, when Rogers was still an active member of the faculty.) During his years at UW he published a scholarly monograph, *Balzac and the Novel* (1953) and was awarded the Chevalier de la Légion d'Honneur, but outside of the groves of academe he was best known for his six mainstream novels, which he published between 1927 and 1942, and his three psychological suspense thrillers from the Forties. Artist Forest Ponder Rogers recalls that the wooded Tudor Revival house in Madison of her bibliophile grandparents "was like a time machine. There was a bookcase in a dark upstairs hall, full of storybooks illustrated by Rackham, Kay Nielsen, Dulac and others. I spent hour upon hour sitting on the floor exploring those shelves during Christmas visits. . . . I rummage the universe for my ideas the way I used to search for treasures in that house."[4]

Unquestionably the most critically successful and lucrative of Rogers' mainstream novels was *Dusk at the Grove*, a seemingly semi-autobiographical stream-of-consciousness story about a patrician Rhode Island pastor and his family which won the $10,000 Atlantic Prize for 1934. Rogers' novel, one out of over 13,000 manuscripts submitted for consideration that year, was the first by an American to win the prize. However, after penning two additional novels of acute psychological portraiture, *Lucifer at Pine Lake* (1937) and *Flora Shawn* (1942), Rogers became afflicted with writer's block. Like many another stalled mainstream novelist before and after him, Rogers turned to writing crime fiction, but the interest in aberrant psychology which so characterizes these later books had already been signaled by his earlier mainstream fiction.

As has been noted in a recent edition of the University of Wisconsin's alumni magazine, *On Wisconsin*, Rogers drew inspiration for his first crime novel from the university's Science Hall, a gloomily imposing Richardsonian Romanesque structure with "creaking, maze-like hallways, [a] bat-infested attic, [an] underground tunnel system and a basement that was once a morgue." In a 1973 oral interview, Rogers recalled that three decades earlier he had got to thinking "what a lugubrious place Science Hall was." UW Alumnus Tim Brady affirms that "anyone who's opened the heavy oak doors of the Romanesque Revival building, climbed the winding staircase—past the exposed brick walls bearing the ghostly signatures of students from long ago—to a tiny landing on the top floor where a pair of locked doors seem to lead nowhere, can appreciate [Rogers'] impulse." Creepier yet, the Hall had been home to the college's Anatomy Department and human cadavers once had "outnumbered the living" in the building. On the top floor "medical students were allowed 24-hour access to the cadaver laboratory in order to practice their surgical skills, and they disposed of dissected corpses by way of a four-story body chute."[5] In the dramatic climax of *Don't Look Behind You!*, Daphne Gray desperately attempts to evade a pitiless killer pursuing her through the darkness of the remote and lonely upper reaches of a fictionalized Science Hall. One is reminded of the climax of the suspenseful serial killer film *The Spiral Staircase* (1946), which followed the novel two years later, although that particular carnival of death takes place in a more typical old dark house.

Samuel Rogers' later years were darkened by a family tragedy that seems indicative of the sort of psychological maladjustment which so clearly engaged the author in both his genre and non-genre novels. In 1944 Rogers had dedicated *Don't Look Behind You!* to his 21-year-old son, Henry Gardner Rogers, a UW graduate who then was serving as an ensign in the U. S. Naval Reserve. (John Frazer, the protagonist in *You Leave Me Cold!*, may have been modeled after Henry Rogers.) After the war, during which he had risen to the rank of lieutenant, Henry attended Harvard University, where he also worked as a mathematics instructor. He later left Harvard, took up art professionally, married artist Lou Ponder, and with her moved to a wooded house he had built by the Connecticut River in South Deerfield, Massachusetts. (Among his paintings was, Van Gogh-like, an arresting self-portrait.) In 1958, not long after the birth to him and his wife of a daughter, who was named Forest after the trees which surrounded them, the 35-year-old Henry, who had for some time suffered from severe bouts of depression, drowned himself in the nearby river. His body, which was not discovered for nearly two weeks, was identified by his father.[6] How all this contrasted with the passing of Samuel Rogers' minister father, Arthur, whose life had ended peacefully two decades earlier at the age of 73. Reverend Rogers was laid to rest at Swan Point Cemetery in Providence, below a simple granite headstone upon which an etcher had elegantly inscribed these modest yet resolute words:

ARTHUR ROGERS
PRIEST
Son of Horatio &
Lucia Waterman Rogers
October 26, 1864
June 10, 1938
I have fought a good fight
I have finished my course
I have kept the faith

Having come to South Deerfield to assist in the desperate search for his missing son, Samuel Rogers, upon the dreadful discovery of the drowned body of his boy, received melancholy confirmation that in real life the problems of the human brain are far harder to unlock and decipher than any fiendishly sealed murder room from the Golden Age of mystery.

ENDNOTES

[1] In fine Puritan New England tradition (though in fact the family, in-laws of freethinking Rhode Island found Roger Williams, had long ago become Baptists), the maternal great-grandfather of Samuel Rogers was named Resolved Waterman.

[2] For the text of the "Dear Sarah" letter, which was made famous in 1990 by Ken Burns' Civil War documentary, see "Sullivan Ballou Letter" at http://www.pbs.org/kenburns/civil-war/war/historical-documents/sullivan-ballou-letter/. On the question of the missive's authorship, see Robert Grandchamp, "O Sarah! Did Sullivan Ballou's Famed Letter Come from Another Pen?," *America's Civil War Magazine* (November 2017), at http://www.historynet.com/o-sarah-sullivan-ballou-letter.htm and "'No, Sarah!' Did Someone Else Write the Sullivan Ballou Letter?," *John Banks' Civil War Blog*, 2 September 2017, at http://john-banks.blogspot.com/2017/09/no-sarah-did-someone-else-write.html. On Horatio Rogers' bibliophilia see Bachmann, "For the Love of Books," 13 February 2018, *The Shelf: Preserving Harvard's Library Collections*, at http://blogs.harvard.edu/preserving/2018/02/13/for-the-love-of-books/.

[3] Samuel Rogers' paternal uncle, Lucian Waterman Rogers (named for his and Arthur's mother, Lucia Waterman), also was an episcopal minister and he served for many years as the rector of the Church of the Redeemer in Chestnut Hill, Massachusetts. Lucian's son and Samuel Roger's cousin, Horatio Rogers, served with the artillery during the First World War. His wartime diary was later published under the title *World War I Through My Sights* (1978).

[4] Natalia Joruk, "Wild Abandon Between Here and Eternity: Interview with Forest Rogers," 1 September 2016, *Beautiful Bizarre*, at https://beautifulbizarre.net/2016/09/01/wild-abandon-between-here-and-eternity-interview-with-forest-rogers/.

[5] Tim Brady, "Scary Story," *On Wisconsin* (Fall 2018): 13; Joanna Salman, "Spooky Ghosts Possibly Haunting Science Hall," 12 November 2003, *The Badger Herald*, at https://badgerherald.com/news/2003/11/12/spooky-ghosts-possib/.

[6] A moving account of the marriage of Henry Gardner and Lou Ponder Rogers and his subsequent death, written by their daughter, who also is an artist, is found at https://forestrogers.typepad.com/about.html. Samuel Rogers successively dedicated his remaining pair of novels, *You'll Be Sorry!* and *You Leave Me Cold!* to his respective daughters, Cornelia and Lucia, and the husbands whom they had recently wed ("Keena and Carl" and "Lu and Hod"). One wonders what the daughters made of these grisly studies in morbid psychology. Perhaps Lucia, who at the University of Wisconsin majored in zoology and did a semester of graduate work in parasitology before her marriage to medical student Horace Kent Tenney III, son of a UW professor of pediatrics, was not shocked at all. Her sister Cornelia married future noted plant physiologist Aldo Carl Leopold, son of UW professor and influential conservationist and environmentalist Aldo Leopold, author of *A Sand County Almanac*, a "conservation classic" of which more than two million copies in 14 languages have been sold since its original publication in 1949. The two young women both must have spent considerable time on campus at Science Hall.

YOU'LL BE SORRY!

For
Keena and Carl

1

Kate Archer studied the strange note she had just been reading, wrinkled her forehead, and stooped to rescue the envelope from the basket beside her desk. She realized now that the stiff handwriting was actually printing, though this was not so obvious in black as it was in the red crayon of the enclosed message:

DON'T GO TO MR. GLADSTONE'S.
YOU'LL BE SORRY IF YOU DO.

What she felt, after her first moment of sheer surprise, was more than anything annoyance at the unreasonableness of her correspondent: here she was to be called for within the next hour; even if she wanted to, there would be no time now to change her plans. Then the next instant she was ashamed at having considered any change. "If he thinks a childish trick like this will have the slightest effect on what I do," she muttered to herself, "he's very much mistaken."

But who was "He"? Even an anonymous letter must be written by someone with a name. Who would not want her to go to Mr. Gladstone's? Of course Mother was disappointed; she had hoped that Kate would come East now, to spend the whole summer at Matunuck, instead of staying out here for another month, to visit in the Middle West; but it was absurd to think of Mother's writing this: Mother would never try to scare her, even in fun.

She caught herself up sharply and glanced about the quiet room. Whatever she felt it was not fear; she would not give "Him" that satisfaction! The envelope, she now noticed, was postmarked *Woodside*, and was dated June 14th; today was Thursday, the 15th; it had been mailed here in town yesterday afternoon.

Could it be one of the young men who had asked her to marry him during this last year at the university? She thought of her fellow students, of her lab instructors. Rejected suitors, she had discovered were apt to feel that in a way she had deceived them—not by any definite action but just by the fact of her own nature: each one had told her that at first she had seemed so "sweet," so gentle; they could not understand her growing bored, or even impatient, at their persistence. She never pretended—certainly she never tried—to be "sweet." If they thought she was, it was largely because of her appearance: her dark golden hair, her blue eyes, her fine skin and softly "classic" features; and for some reason boys seemed to think that that combination went with sweetness of nature; but it was also because she did hate to make people unhappy, because she couldn't help being kind and pleasant to them at first—and then suddenly they would be in love with her, and she had to make them understand that she was not in love with them. But surely none of those boys would stoop to such a petty revenge, even if in some way they had learned of her visit.

Kate continued to frown. She would have hated to think that someone she knew, someone she liked, had written this letter; and yet it would have been comforting to be able to place it, to lift it out of the realm of the mysterious. She looked once more around the small room, so intensely silent, where she had studied for so many hours during the past winter. All her things that had not been sent off earlier were now packed in the two big suitcases standing side by side near the door. The room looked unnaturally neat and stripped. There was nothing on the bureau, nothing on the table; the framed photographs, the brilliant van Gogh print, had gone from the walls. Afternoon sunlight streaming across the threadbare blue carpet seemed to touch it with strangeness, as if it were the carpet in some huge impersonal secondhand store: this silent place had withdrawn into itself; it was waiting for her to get out.

She glanced at her watch. It was quarter to three and Mr. Gladstone had written that she would be called for at three; but she walked over to the window and looked down through the box-elder boughs. Perhaps the car might be early. The short street was empty except for some boys playing ball in front of the apartment house at the corner. Kate wondered from which direction the car would appear, what kind of car it would be. Would Mr. Gladstone be driving it himself? And what would Mr. Gladstone be like?

DON'T GO TO MR. GLADSTONE'S.

For an instant she could see a pale fixed face that stared straight ahead at the road from under its hatbrim, that would not look at her until suddenly in a lonely place the car stopped, the driver raised his hands to the back of his head and she could see that his face was a mask. He was taking it off, he was going to stare at her now, but he had no eyes, no features. She could not bear to look.

YOU'LL BE SORRY IF YOU DO.

This was absurd, she thought angrily. How pleased the writer of the letter would be! But she could form so little idea of her month at Mr. Gladstone's that it was impossible to imagine its beginning, to picture a car turning one of these corners, to the left or to the right, and stopping there below in front of the house; just as sometimes when you wait at the telephone for a long-distance call, you can't believe that the voice you are expecting will actually break that silence.

Might the warning have been sent by anyone in the Gladstone household? But who could it be, when June, the only one she knew, was so terribly eager for her to come? She took June's letter, the first she had received from her in more than two years, out of her purse, and read it slowly once again:

Dear Katey,

It's crazy that you've been at Woodside for a whole year and I live only twenty miles away and we haven't seen each other. You bad girl, why didn't you write me you were there? I just found out by chance from a girl at school who says she knows your brother. Of course I've been away at school except for holidays so we wouldn't have had much chance to get together. But now I'm home for the summer and I want you to come and visit me for at least a month. Father says why should someone that's really grown up and finishing college want to bury herself out here with a schoolgirl like me, but he doesn't know about you and me, does he? I guess no one could understand that.

I bet all sorts of things have been happening to you since the old days at Miss Barstow's. Nothing at all has happened to me, at least nothing nice, just two other schools, after Miss Barstow's, and I hated them both just as much. I really hated them more because you weren't there, and I never found anyone else to be really nice to me the way you were. There's something wrong with me, Katey. You used to say there wasn't but I know there is, because I try to be nice to people but nobody likes me. It may be just because I'm so damn ugly and clumsy. I can hear you scolding me now for that "damn." It just slipped out. If you come I give you permission to scold me as much as you like, and I promise not to get mad the way I used to.

Honestly Katey, I can't tell you how much I want you to come. I'll be watching the mail every day for your answer, so be quick, won't you? I can't bear having to wait for things I want.

With loads of love,
Your bad "little* June"

* Only I'm not little any more. I wish I was.

Kate had replied affectionately but had said that she could not come. She had not seen June Gladstone in four years, and remembered her as a dumpy girl whom everyone ignored and who had seemed to go her way in rather morose indifference until the afternoon when Kate discovered her lying on the grass behind the summerhouse, her body shaken with sobs. It was because she was lonely, June explained, after Kate had coaxed her to talk, because everyone despised her. Kate had put her arm around her, had quieted her at last, and got permission from Miss Spencer to take her to Johnson's for a chocolate sundae.

After that, for the rest of the year, June had dogged her footsteps to an almost embarrassing extent, never talking much, never making any demands, but glaring like some fierce dark little animal at any girl to whom Kate paid much attention. Just before the end of the spring term she had been mysteriously expelled, and when Kate, who had come to feel rather responsible for her, had questioned the headmistress, Miss Barstow had explained that some "bad books" had been found in her bureau drawer. "To do June justice," she had gone on, "her family background, from what I can gather, isn't at all what it should be. I feel very sorry for her. I'm quite sure her parents are more to blame than she is, but there was nothing else to do, for the sake of the school."

Kate had smiled to herself, with some indignation, at the thought of poor little June's corrupting her so much more sophisticated schoolmates. She had thought at the time, and she still suspected, that the books, whatever they were, had been planted in June's drawer by one of the girls who disliked her, who were jealous of the way that Kate had taken her under her wing; but June had already gone, there would be no way of proving such a plot; and in the letters Kate and she had exchanged for the next two years, letters which had grown more and more scarce, neither one had ever alluded to the affair.

Kate had refused this summer's invitation chiefly because she was so eager to get home, to see Mother, to bask in the sun on the long white beach; but she had felt a little guilty and more than a little curious. June had never spoken a word to her of any sort about her family. During Kate's year in Woodside she had heard rumors of the Gladstone estate out by the river, and the "things that went on" there. A week after June's letter, she had received one from Mr. Gladstone himself, urging her to come; she had accepted then, though without committing herself as to how long she would stay, because she knew that if she refused, her conscience would bother her all summer.

She folded June's letter now, put it back in her purse, and took out Mr. Gladstone's, frowning a little as she tried to decipher once more the bold careless-looking script

Dear Miss Archer:

God knows I detest people who interfere with other people's business, and I think my record is pretty clear on that score. My excuse for writing you now is that you can tear this up, if you like, and not give it another thought. I'd be the first to sympathize with you.

The fact is, June is so desperately disappointed that you won't visit us that I said I'd see what I could do. Let me give you an idea of the general setup. We live in what might be described as the deep country, out by the river. There is no suitable person approaching June's age in the neighborhood, and she is terribly lonely and restless. I should mention, perhaps, if she hasn't, that she has an older sister, about your age. If June were different and if Clotilde were different, that might fix things up—but you know what families are. Or perhaps you don't. If not, you'll learn when you have one of your own.

I can quite understand that a month's tête-à-tête with a girl like June may not seem too exciting for a girl four years (so June tells me) older than she. Let me reassure you that in the first place it will not be a tête-à-tête. We're quite a little group out here, and if we're too old to suit a girl of sixteen,

I'm sure that some of us won't seem too senile for a young woman of twenty.

But if what June says about you is true, the inducements to dangle before you are not the things you may receive but the things you may be able to give. You can give June, I believe, a period of really intense happiness, which she will appreciate all the more because that is something, I'm afraid, that on the whole she hasn't known very much of. One of my reasons for urging you is no doubt that, as a father, I haven't been a startling success. If I haven't always done right by our June, naturally the easiest way to quiet my paternal conscience is to find a friend of hers who might to some extent compensate for my shortcomings. Since you have known June, you don't have to be told that when she wants something she wants it very much indeed, and I can truthfully say I've never known her to want anything so much as to have you visit her.

Sincerely (and hopefully) yours,
Norman Gladstone

It was a queer letter. She did not like it very well, but certainly Mr. Gladstone was eager for her to come. It would be wholly unreasonable to send her such a letter as this, and then follow it up with an anonymous warning to keep away.

A knock at the door startled her so that she dropped her letter on the rug. After she had picked it up, she glanced once more out of the window. An empty car was parked in front of the house, a magnificent grass-green convertible than which nothing could be less sinister. "I'm afraid I'm not meant to live alone," she thought.

She walked quickly to the door, opened it, and smiled at the man who stood in the doorway. He had a real face, there was no doubt of that; he was medium-sized, about forty, with blunt features, thin hair, and a neat brown mustache. As a matter of fact, everything about looked exceptionally neat—his dark blue suit, his black necktie, the very way he stood, easy and erect and somehow shipshape. His brown eyes looked softly and brightly into hers.

"Is this Miss Archer?" he asked, and his voice seemed to fit his appearance—gentle, firm, and efficient.

"Yes, it is," she said, "and I suppose you're Mr. Gladstone."

He smiled. "Far from it," he exclaimed. "I'm just the chauffeur, the gardener, the man of all work. My name is Felix Brownell."

Kate noticed now that his dark suit, his tie, had the suggestion of a uniform or livery. She felt embarrassed. "Oh I'm so sorry," she said, "Mr. Brownell."

"Don't apologize," he told her. "It's a compliment. As a matter of fact, I've been with the family so long I almost feel as if I was part of it. And by the way, of course you must call me Felix."

"Oh, well—yes, I will," Kate said still rather self-conscious. She suspected that for some time at least she would call him only "you."

"I assume these are your bags, miss?" He stepped into the room and picked them up easily. She was sure that he had added the "miss" simply to put her at her ease.

"I'm afraid they're very heavy."

"You should feel Mr. Gladstone's, or for that matter, Miss Clotilde's. I'll be taking them down. If you have anyone to say good-by to—"

"No, there's no one," she said. She took a last glance at the room, shut the door quickly, as if she were shutting her nervousness inside, and followed him down the stairs.

It gave her a luxurious feeling to step into the big shiny car. As she settled back on the dark green leather cushions it seemed to her that she could not imagine a more comfortable seat.

"If you'd prefer to sit in back," Felix said, "I can put up the top, but otherwise, I'm afraid, it would be too windy."

"I'd much rather sit here," she said—"that is, if you don't mind."

"Personally, I always prefer company when I'm driving," he said in a courtly tone. "Which reminds me: June said to be sure and tell you she'd have driven in with me, except that I left this morning right after breakfast. I've been doing the week's marketing, and selling stuff from the farm."

He started the car so smoothly and the motor was so silent that Kate was surprised to see that they were already moving. In ten minutes they were out of town, had skirted the end of the lake, and were driving westward through the rolling fields, the patches of oak forest, that surrounded Woodside. It was a lovely afternoon, with a few clouds softly brushing the treetops and the telephone wires. The air smelled of white clover and as the breeze touched her face she felt that it had still kept something of the remoteness of the farthest hills.

She was trying to think up a friendly remark to make to Felix, when he spoke himself.

"You know," he said, with his eyes fixed on the road, "I'm glad you're going to be visiting us at Valley Farms. June needs someone, some nice pleasant young lady like you, to keep her company. I hope that doesn't sound impertinent."

"Not at all," Kate said. "I'm glad you think I'll be of some use. Of course June does have a sister, doesn't she?"

For a moment he merely pursed his lips. "Clotilde is very attractive," he said at last, and Kate noticed that he had dropped the "Miss" before her name. "She's the beauty of the family, you know. But between ourselves, I don't think she's much of a help to June. You'll see soon enough. Of course they are only half sisters. You probably know all about that."

"No, I didn't know it," Kate said. "I never even knew June had a sister until I got Mr. Gladstone's letter. And who else is at the farm? I don't know anything about the family really. I haven't even met Mr. Gladstone."

"Well, there's Mrs. Gladstone, June's mother—everyone calls her Mavis, even the girls. And just now there's Mr. Green; he's Clotilde's fiancé. They're going to be married in a few weeks, I guess. I shouldn't be surprised if they ran off any time. And there's Jo, or I should say Mr. Martinez. He's Spanish."

"But who is he?" she asked. "What does he do?"

"He's a violinist. They say he's very good."

"But I mean is he a relation? Is he connected with the family?"

Felix hesitated again and again pursed his lips; Kate could see that he disapproved of Jo.

"No—he's not a relation," he said slowly. "You might say he's just a kind of—special friend."

For a long time neither spoke. It seemed as if the thought of Jo had dried up Felix's sociability; and Kate found that the breeze as it lapped around the side of the windshield, the monotony of woodland and meadow, were lulling her into a pleasant drowsiness. She did notice, however, that the hills were growing higher, the farmhouses somewhat less frequent. Now and then a spur of rock jutted out from the end of a wooded ridge like the prow of a gigantic ship. She noticed, too, how Felix always kept the car at exactly thirty-five miles, whether they were going up hill or down; she could imagine that she was floating through the sky, a summer sky endlessly blue and soft, floating above a region of green silent waves.

Then, without warning, the car stopped.

In a flash she recalled her imaginings in her room a little while ago, and glanced at Felix. But Felix was leaning out of the car and talking to a thickset middle-aged man, with sharp features and bright birdlike eyes, who was sitting on a bank, with a bicycle leaning against the turf beside him. They were near the top of the highest hill so far, and he had evidently stopped to rest.

"Well, Professor," Felix asked, "can I give you a lift? You look just about all in. Men our age oughtn't to attempt long bicycle rides in summer—especially with these hills "

Kate smiled at Felix's tact: this stranger must be ten years older than he.

"It's all very well for you to talk," the man replied in a precise voice, "with your boss getting gas for two cars, and then wangling a C card out of his ration board. I should think he'd be ashamed of himself."

Felix shrugged his shoulders and his flickering smile became for a moment almost a grin. "Well, there are no trains around here; there are no busses. And we have to get our produce to market. When I drove to town today the trunk was full of fresh vegetables. Mostly lettuce."

The man with the bicycle stood up and slowly shook one leg, then the other. "Well, if he can get away with it, who am I to object? There are worse things than that the matter with the Roosevelt regime. But as far as busses and trains go, they don't come any nearer me than they do you. And I'm farther from the main road."

"Perhaps they don't think your work out here is essential to the war effort," Felix suggested. Then turning to Kate, he explained. "Professor Hatfield spends his vacations by the river looking for birds."

"Wherever the gas comes from, I'd gladly accept a lift," Professor Hatfield went on. "But what about the bicycle?"

"We can fit that in behind," Felix said; and the next moment he was in the road and, rather to Kate's alarm because the car looked so spotless, he was lifting the bicycle into the back seat. In a couple of minutes he had arranged it so that it rested firmly propped, without a scratch to the paint or the rich green leather.

"But I haven't introduced you, have I?" he went on to Kate. "You must think I'm very rude. Professor, I take pleasure in presenting you to Miss Katherine Archer. Since she goes to the university, she's probably heard of you. She's coming out to visit June, and I hope she won't think me fresh if I say I can't imagine a more charming visitor."

Kate recalled Professor Hatfield's name, and thought now that she remembered having seen him about the campus. His eyes were fixed intently upon her; he cocked his head so as to get a clearer view, and for that moment he reminded her of a smooth, alert, but rather dusty parrot.

"June is very lucky," he said, "to have such a friend. I hope I won't crowd you, Miss Archer. At any rate I'm several pounds thinner than when I started out after lunch."

Kate was thoroughly enjoying herself; she was growing quite fond of Felix, now that he no longer surprised her, and thought she would like this friendly sharp-eyed gentleman.

"Are you an ornithologist?" she asked as the car slipped smoothly over the crest of the hill. "I always thought you were in the chemistry department."

"I earn my living teaching chemistry," he said, "and just now I'm doing research for our government. Birds are my vice. When I get a few days off, or better still a few weeks, I'm apt to sneak away from town and leave my good wife to her various social engagements. The bottom lands and the river bluffs are the best places in the state for bird life. Up here I see no one but birds and the unique Valley Farms household."

"You have a house near Mr. Gladstone's?" she asked. "How nice! Then perhaps I'll be seeing you."

"You'll be seeing me tonight at dinner," he said, "than which for me nothing could be nicer. But one can hardly call my little hide-out a house, especially when you compare it with Valley Farms which is almost a feudal estate. All I possess is a one-room shack near the top of a small bluff, overlooking the river. But there is a fine view, so perhaps you'll drop in on me sometime. I'm not more than a mile from the big house."

"I'd love to!" she exclaimed. "Perhaps I could bring June along."

"June too, of course," he said, "if she would care to come. She has never done me that honor so far. June's a rather queer child, I think Felix will agree, but I have never found her dull. I think your visit may be interesting, Miss Archer. I hope it may be happy—or at any rate profitable. Of course out here we're very remote; it's a little world of its own. I'm sure at any rate that it will be a new kind of experience for you."

"Now Professor," Felix exclaimed, "you're talking as if Miss Archer was about to bury herself in the African jungle. Don't let him scare you, Miss Archer. He's got quite an imagination, the professor has."

And suddenly Kate remembered the strange note that was in her purse. The nervousness, the doubt she had felt alone in her bedroom swept over her again with a qualm as of seasickness. Because in her room there was still time to retreat: she need not, after all, have answered the knock on the door; she could have written Mr. Gladstone that she had changed her mind; but now that she had started it was too late. She felt as if she were in one of the little cars on a roller coaster. It was slowly pulling her up the long slant to the dizzying take-off; at any moment the plunge would begin, and she could not get out; she could not stop the car: she could only draw in her breath and close her eyes tight, and swear never to get trapped in such a thing again.

Then she was glad this feeling had come back, because obviously the way to strip the note of its mystery was to tell Mr. Hatfield about it, Mr. Hatfield and Felix: it would be no longer a secret, no longer something buried in her mind, but a trivial objective fact of common knowledge.

"I've had a new experience already," she said. "Not very important but it sort of worried me a little. You'll probably think I'm foolish."

Professor Hatfield cocked his eye at her, and leaned forward as a robin might do if he thought he saw a worm. "I'm sure not," he said. "What is it?"

Kate opened her purse, took out the note and handed it to him. He stared at it for a long minute with his lashes drawn together. "Hmmm-hmmm" he muttered at last, in a tone that reminded her of Dr. Medway whenever he examined her teeth. "Have you told Felix about this?"

"I've told nobody. It arrived in the two o'clock mail this afternoon."

The reassuring laugh she had expected did not come: Professor Hatfield's expression remained thoughtful; and the beauty of these wild hills seemed all at once faintly poisonous, as if the region were enchanted.

"May I tell him about it?" the professor asked.

She tried to laugh. "Of course. Why not? You don't think it means anything?"

"Listen, Felix," Professor Hatfield said. "What do you think of this? DON'T GO TO MR. GLADSTONE'S. YOU'LL BE SORRY IF YOU DO. Sort of an ominous start for poor Miss Archer's visit, isn't it?"

"It looks to me," Felix said, "like some kind of a joke; but if it is, it's a damn poor one. You'll excuse my language, I hope."

"A joke? Hmmm . . ." The professor squinted as if he were peering into the future. "Well, very possibly. And now, Felix, if you'll let me out at the top of the next hill, I'll coast down the lane to the foot of my bluff."

In a minute the car stopped again and Felix was lifting out the bicycle as neatly as he had lifted it in.

"There's Valley Farms," Professor Hatfield said, pointing down the long steep hill ahead of them. "You get the best view of the estate from here. I'm over there to the left, beyond those woods."

"How perfectly lovely!" Kate exclaimed, and for a moment she forgot everything in the charm of the view.

Directly below them was a huge green bowl, checkered with woods and fields, and cut in two by the white line of the highway. To the left of the road there clustered a group of red-roofed buildings, surrounded by shrubberies, by gardens and lawns— the whole thing shining in the midafternoon light with a strange liquid clearness as if you were staring down at it through still water.

Professor Hatfield got out of the car and shook Kate's hand.

"I'll be seeing you tonight then," he said.

He took his bicycle from Felix, swung his foot over the bar, and turned back to give her one more of his shrewd glances. "Perhaps I should explain," he added, "that it wasn't just the wording of your note that interested me. Had it occurred to you that the red crayon might be meant to suggest the idea of blood?"

2

Kate waited on the front steps while Felix lifted out her bags. She had never seen a more charming house; its whole atmosphere was reassuring. It was of whitewashed brick long and low, with blue-shuttered French windows opening on to a grassy terrace. The lawn through which the driveway wound stretched for acres behind her, scattered with oaks, with birches, with huge pines, and beyond it, like a spectacular green wall, the wooded hills seemed to rise almost vertically to shut out the rest of the world. The air had a damp freshness down here which brought out sharply the smell of grass and leaves—perhaps because the river was so near.

She had noticed a whining and scratching from inside the door, and as Felix opened it a little black and white beagle dashed out, wriggled first around Felix's legs, then around hers, then flew circling over the lawn, its ears waving, its tail held high like a pennant.

"How perfectly darling!" she exclaimed. "What's his name? How old is be?"

"It's a young lady," Felix said. "Her name is Bobbie, and she's not quite five months old."

Kate watched her with delight as she stopped so suddenly she fell all over herself, grabbed for a large stick, dashed back to the door and dropped the stick at Kate's feet. Then with her chin on the ground between her front paws, her hindquarters raised, her tail wagging frantically, she looked up at Kate with dark liquid eyes. Kate could not resist stooping down. The little hound thrust its head between her outstretched hands, and Kate could feel through the silky skin the bones of her skull and jaw, as delicate and buoyant as those of a bird.

"I see you've made friends already," Felix said. "Bobbie certainly has good taste."

As Kate stood up she saw a woman in black with a maid's apron walking toward the door from the back of the wide hallway. She was middle-aged, with a weathered handsome face and thin brown hair pulled back from her forehead and temples.

"My wife," Felix explained to Kate. "Ruby, my girl, let me present you to Miss Katherine Archer. Quite an addition to the household, if you ask me."

"I didn't ask you," the woman said in such a fierce voice that it almost made Kate jump. For an instant she glared at Felix; then shrugged her shoulders and peered at Kate.

"That outburst wasn't meant for you, Miss Archer," Felix apologized. "It was meant for me, though I'm afraid you're partly to blame. Youth and beauty can be very disturbing as we grow older, can't they, Ruby, my love?"

Beneath the suavity of his tone there was a sudden hardness that Kate would not have expected: it seemed not so much Felix's own voice as a reflection of his wife's.

"Oh, shut up!" the woman said; then as she turned to Kate her face lost something of its belligerence. "I'm sorry, miss," she said. "But Felix is right. It wasn't meant for you. We're a queer household here at the farm, and you might as well learn it now as later."

"I'll take up your bags," Felix said. "Don't let Ruby scare you, Miss Archer. Her bark is worse than her bite."

Felix walked back through the hall to the stairway, and Kate looked over her shoulder to see where Bobbie had gone. At first she did not discover her; but then she saw her, through the still-open door, a small black and white object racing around a pine tree a hundred yards or more from the house.

"You better step in there," Ruby said, escorting her to a doorway on the right. "Mr. Gladstone wants to talk to you before you see June. He's lying down. I'll go call him."

Kate, who was apt to be critical of furniture arrangements, glanced sharply about the room. It was large and low-ceiled, its floor entirely covered with a sea-green carpet, which recalled her impression, as she had looked down from the hilltop, that the valley was under water. For its size, the room was sparsely furnished: there were several sofas and easy chairs; along the walls stood two or three carved chests like pieces she had seen in Brittany. Besides the three French windows opening on the terrace, there was a fourth one, at the further end, screened by a Venetian blind; and through the slats she could see another, smaller terrace, this one paved not with grass but with red tiles and strewn with wicker chairs and tables. Beyond it, in the sunlight, she caught the gleam of delphinium and scarlet lilies.

She thought of the grim woman who had just left her: perhaps Ruby, if she was as jealous of Felix as she seemed, had sent the note in a last effort to prevent the arrival of an attractive young girl in the house. "But of course Ruby had never seen me," Kate thought, and then smiled at her own conceit. And yet, in fairness to herself, it was not really conceit: she had learned by experience that most men found her nice to look at, and it would be crazy to pretend that she did not know it and did not thoroughly enjoy it, even if it was sometimes embarrassing. Or again, perhaps Felix had sent it himself, for the sake of domestic peace, suspecting that Ruby would resent her coming. She wished that either one of these explanations was true: then everything would be cleared up and she would feel free to enjoy this wonderful place; but she was not convinced. She couldn't believe it of Felix, and not even of Ruby. In spite of her dourness, she looked honest and only too forthright.

As she strolled toward the farther window, Kate noticed that a pair of feet was protruding from one of the wicker chairs whose back was turned to the house. They were small feet, wearing scarlet sandals with very high heels, and through the straps Kate could see that the toenails were painted crimson. Could that be Clotilde, she wondered: it was certainly not June. But then the thickness of the ankles and the flabbiness of the bare calves, daubed with sun tan, made her sure that this was an older woman. It must be Mrs. Gladstone, June's mother, though one wouldn't have thought it. A tall glass, empty except for a sprig of mint, stood on the tiles beside her.

Then as Kate idly watched, an extraordinarily pretty girl in gray flannel slacks appeared on the terrace from somewhere behind the house. She had a small head set on a long neck; she looked as composed, as beautifully made up, as the models in a fashion display; but the most striking thing about her was her hair, which floated down to her shoulders in waves of the glossiest, palest gold that Kate had ever seen. Kate thought regretfully of her own hair, which had had that almost silvery brightness when she was two or three (Mother had kept a lock of it), but which had darkened ever since. She suspected that she would not like this girl: she seemed far too smooth; but she did arouse Kate's sporting instincts. It would be interesting to see her fiancé.

"Well you owe me five dollars," Clotilde called to her stepmother (Kate was sure she had identified them both). "I beat him 6-4, 6-3."

"Anyone else but you," a throaty voice answered from the chair, "wouldn't feel right about taking the money. It's quite obvious that if you did beat him it was only because he let you."

The first thing that struck Kate about this voice was the fact that, with its drawl, the mannered way it lingered on certain syllables, it assumed the presence of an audience. Since they were betting, Kate felt she would be willing to bet even money that Mrs. Gladstone had once been an actress.

"You ought to know Ralph by this time!" Clotilde laughed, and her tone seemed exaggeratedly casual, as if she were trying to underline its difference from the older woman's. "He's not so damn chivalrous as all that."

"Chivalrous!" Mrs. Gladstone snorted. "Who said anything about chivalry? If he didn't bother to win, it was because he was bored, poor lamb, and God knows I don't blame him! You're not at your best, my dove, on the tennis court."

The voices came through the open window as clearly as if they were in the room. Kate did not know what to do: should she

cough, or pretend to adjust the blind? But it would be embarrassing to make her presence known now; and as far as Clotilde
and Mrs. Gladstone were concerned, she felt they would not care
in the least who might hear them. Clotilde had walked nearer
her stepmother's chair, and was gazing down at her with a fixed
irritating smile.

"Mavis, darling," she said, "I'm afraid what really worries you
is the idea, and I admit there's something in it, that it's I who am
growing bored with *him*."

"And why, pray, should that interest me?" Mavis sounded like
a duchess on the stage of a summer theater.

Clotilde lifted her fine eyebrows and drew her lips together in
an expression of innocence. "Ah, why indeed?" she asked.

"Darling, do you know what you remind me of?" Mrs. Gladstone went on after the slightest pause; and Kate was now aware
of a rasping note beneath the smoothness of her voice. "You make
me think of a mosquito, a very charming, slim mosquito—that
goes without saying—with lovely gauzy wings, but a mosquito
nonetheless. And I'm terribly afraid, you know, that Ralph is
beginning to agree with me."

Clotilde seemed to be having a very good time. "Let's see
what *you* remind *me* of," she said. "It's like that descriptive game,
isn't it, and you have chosen the subject of insects. Of course
it's very hard to think of you in such terms. If you had chosen
flowers, say, or nice things to drink, nothing would have been
easier. But if I had to describe you as an insect, I think I should
be inclined to choose a tick, one of those pretty, plump little
ticks you find on dogs."

Mrs. Gladstone laughed huskily. "I hope not a tick," she said.
"They can be quite dangerous, you know."

"Not unless you let them get under your skin," Clotilde replied.

Mrs. Gladstone's laugh died away in a kind of purring chuckle.
"I don't flatter myself that I could ever get under yours," she said.
"It's—shall we say too fine-grained? So you're perfectly safe."

Kate was amused but at the same time slightly revolted by
this scrap of conversation; she felt at least that she was beginning

to understand what Miss Barstow had meant when she said that June's family background left much to be desired. Then, the next instant, a young man in white flannels appeared on the terrace, and in her surprise and pleasure this malicious sparring seemed all at once unimportant. He was a solid straight young man, with chestnut hair, a brown skin, and deep-set brown eyes. His features were large; his eyebrows were almost ferociously dark and thick; but the general impression one gathered from his face was that of a somewhat detached and distinctly patient kindness. It was Ralph Green! There could be no doubt of it. What fun that he should be here! She remembered now that Felix had mentioned a Mr. Green, and of course Mavis had referred to "Ralph"; but it had not occurred to Kate to put the two names together. She had not seen Ralph for five years and she thought of him always in connection with the summer she had spent in Maine. She had been only fifteen years old and Ralph must have been twenty-one or two; but he had taken her sailing, he had coached her in tennis; he had been kind, even affectionate, never in the least condescending; and Kate during the last month of her stay had been more nearly in love with him than she had ever been with anyone since that faraway summer.

Of course, to him, she had been just a rather big little girl; he had liked her very much; she could realize that he must sometimes have been amused by her. She would always be grateful to him because she felt that he had given her a standard of comparison by which she could judge the series of younger boys who had begun that very winter to fall in love with her. She could hardly wait now to speak to him. She wondered if he, too, would be surprised; she even wondered if he would remember her. Then like a chill it came over her that Ralph was engaged to marry this awful Clotilde.

"I couldn't find the last ball," he said, and there was an edge to his voice, suggesting that even his patience had its limits. "I'm not going to waste any more time looking for it."

"Now really, Ralph!" Clotilde exclaimed. "They were very special ones. It's almost impossible to get them."

Ralph looked at her with a fixed and quite unrevealing smile. "You like things that are hard to get, don't you?" he said. "You like things made to order. I wonder if there's anything you'd enjoy, if you thought that the average person, the common run-of-the-mill individual, could get it just as easily as you could."

Ralph was standing very straight and yet he seemed quite relaxed; he had the surprisingly light stance and poise that you notice sometimes in even the most dignified and massive dogs. Kate watched him with keen curiosity. He was not so handsome as she remembered him; no actual young man could be that. In fact, she had to confess, he was not handsome at all; and yet it seemed to her that she liked his face more than ever. Its present impatience or irony, or even scorn, seemed only to emphasize what must be its habitual gentleness: You felt that he had learned not to expect too much either from himself or others, but that he was more inclined to be tolerant of others than of himself. Clotilde met his eyes.

"I haven't given the matter much thought," she said coolly.

"No, I expect not," he said. "Well, I'm going up to take a shower. See you at dinner."

He stepped out of sight toward the front of the house, and Kate felt with pleasure that he had snubbed Clotilde; already she had the sense that she was watching some kind of game and that the side she was cheering had just won a point. A moment later she could hear him opening the front door and running upstairs. She had almost gone out into the hall to waylay him; but then she thought it would be more fun to surprise him at dinner, and she would have hated to do anything that might have seemed like thrusting herself on his attention before he noticed her.

A faint noise made her look around, and she saw a large dark man in a Palm Beach suit, with a rose in his buttonhole—a man whom she thought she had seen somewhere before—coming toward her across the watery expanse of carpet.

"Were the girls out there putting on one of their little shows?" he asked in a deep voice with a slightly sardonic intonation.

Kate blushed. She felt like a child caught in a preserve closet. "Well, I don't know," she said. "They were talking and I'm afraid I couldn't help—"

The man grinned, and his teeth looked younger and more vigorous than the rest of his face. "Of course you couldn't and why should you? I only hope they kept the script clean."

He held out an enormous hairy hand, and as she took it she realized why he seemed familiar: in spite of the pouches beneath his eyes, the sag of his jowls, his nearly bald head, he reminded her of June. He had the same oblong face with its heavy chin and small rounded nose, the same swarthiness of skin, the same dark glance; and yet his face, at any rate when he spoke, had a kind of concentration, of liveliness, in spite of its air of fatigue, which June's had always lacked. He was an ugly man, but she could imagine that he might be interesting, even attractive.

"I'm sorry I kept you waiting," he went on. "All the more so, now that I've seen you. The fact is I was napping in my underwear, and I didn't feel I knew you quite well enough to appear as I was. June told me you were beautiful, but I knew she had a crush on you—in a perfectly nice way, of course—so I made considerable allowance. But my word!"—He looked her up and down with embarrassingly direct admiration beneath his bantering air. "It was really an understatement."

Once more she saw his lopsided grin. "You may give quite a jolt to Clotilde," he went on, "and poor old Mavis will be sick; but what a treat for Ralph and Jo, not to speak of my aged self! And I mustn't forget Felix. Felix was quite a lady's man in his prime, the rascal. Don't let that respectful manner fool you. I bet Felix was licking his lips!"

Kate felt that Mr. Gladstone spoke as if she were a choice morsel to be served up at dinner. She suspected that he was trying to tease her and determined to show no sign that she noticed it.

"I'm looking forward to seeing June again," she said. "She must have changed a good deal in the last four years."

Mr. Gladstone sent her a sharp glance. "The more, the better, eh?"

If she hadn't prepared herself against confusion, Kate might have blushed. "I didn't mean that at all," she said, "and I think you talk horridly for a father. I noticed it in your letter too."

He looked at her quizzically and as she met his gaze she had the feeling that he liked her all the more for her sharp retort.

"I know my appearance suggests one of the larger anthropoid apes," he said after an instant, "but that doesn't mean I don't have a father's heart. But wait a minute—"

He walked past her over to the window that opened on to the terrace. "You see, the theater had reversed itself," he explained. "We had become the stage in here, and Mavis and Clotilde had become the audience." He raised the blind and closed the casement window. "That's better," he said, "and now please sit down. I don't know why I didn't suggest it before. Let's say it was because I was dazzled."

Kate sat down in one of the big leather chairs near the fireplace; it gave her the same feeling of super-comfort that the seat in the car had done. Mr. Gladstone seated himself in an even larger chair on the other side of the hearth, leaned back and crossed one ankle over his knee.

"Seriously, Miss Archer, I'm damn glad you're here," he said. "But I'm not going to call you that. Katherine? Kate? Kate's what they call you, isn't it?"

"Most of my friends call me Kate," she admitted.

"Swell! Anyhow: to be frank, I feel just a little bit guilty about June, as I told you in my letter. Of course she's not much more decorative than I am, though I will say she has improved during the last year, and I suspect you can give her some damn good advice. You know, her clothes, her hair, and things like that. I think she's really a nice kid. Between ourselves, I think she's worth two of Clotilde. I confess I have a weakness for Clotilde, but I know damn well it's mostly because she's such a knockout to look at. Clotilde knows what she wants and she'll get it, regardless. It may be my fault for spoiling her, but her mother was very much the same type. When I was a young man I was a lousy judge of women, at least the ones I married. But to go back to poor June. I hope you will stay here for a month anyway; and if you can give her a little self-confidence and brighten her up a bit, you'll have done your good deed for the year. We're a pretty free and easy bunch out here, as you're probably discovering, but I think you'll live through it. If you can stand me, you ought to be able to take the rest of us, and you seem to be doing pretty well so far."

A scurrying in the hall made Kate turn her head in time to see Bobbie dash into the room, slide back on her haunches for a moment in the midst of her rush, to look around her, and then make for Kate's ankles with a series of little grunts and barks. Kate put down her hands to protect her stockings, and Bobbie, after a few growling charges, wheeled on her hind legs, her front paws waving, her ears swirling about her face like the curls of a ballerina, and dashed straight across the room for another armchair. Kate thought she was going to fling herself against it, but in the nick of time, without slackening her speed, she flattened herself out and half slid, half scrambled under the border of pleated chintz that touched the floor. Then almost at once her head appeared peeking from under the edge, her chin pressed close against the carpet, while her eyes gleamed up at Kate as if to challenge her to try to drag her out of this refuge.

"Bobbie, come here! Bobbie, where are you?"

It was June's voice, and the next instant she stepped into the room and came toward Kate with a smile that showed her large strong teeth. At the same time Bobbie's head ducked under the chair, and then she scrambled out, holding in her mouth a very dirty doll made of string, which she brought over and dropped at Kate's feet. But Kate had hardly time to notice her now, because she was so curious to see what June would be like as a "young girl."

June shook her hand vigorously, leaned toward her as if to kiss her, and then straightened up as if she did not quite dare.

"Kate!" she exclaimed in her rather deep voice, which had always been the most attractive thing about her. "It's the same old Katey! I was so afraid you might have changed. I was so afraid you might seem all grown-up and fancy, but you don't look any different."

It was not quite the same old June, Kate realized at once. Not only was she about a foot taller, several inches taller than Kate now, but she was far less stolid-looking. She still moved with awkward abruptness; her face was still too heavy, but it had a kind of intensity of expression, a liveliness at this minute of greeting, which suggested her father more than ever. Her complexion, too, dark and slightly oily, was at any rate much better than it had been. At present she was wearing too much lipstick of too pink a shade; her black hair fluffed in unbecoming wisps about her cheeks; and Kate who liked nothing better than fixing things over according to her own very particular taste, looked forward, as her father had suggested, to starting in at once on the reconstruction of her appearance. June, with a little tact and care, might be smart-looking, even distinguished. Kate was sure Mr. Gladstone had been right when he said she was worth two of Clotilde.

"It's great fun to be seeing you again," Kate said. "It doesn't seem as if it could be four years since we were together, except that you certainly have grown up, if I haven't. And this is such a lovely place! I've never seen anything like it. You must show me all around. I'm sure we'll have a wonderful summer, June."

"June, sweet," Mr. Gladstone said, with a touch of irony in his tone, which probably, Kate thought, had become so habitual that he was no longer aware of it, "I suggest that the first thing you show Kate is her own room. Felix took up her bags. And then she may doubtless want to be left in peace to unpack."

"I'd love to have June help me unpack," Kate said. "That is, if she wants to."

"You bet I want to," June said. "I'm crazy to see your clothes. You always had such pretty clothes."

"Well then, my little dears," Mr. Gladstone said, making only a token gesture as if to rise from his chair, "I'll be seeing you before dinner "

As the two girls walked upstairs side by side, Bobbie climbed ahead of them, putting first her two front feet on each step above her and then bringing up her hindquarters with a little bounce and jerk that made Kate think of a mechanical rabbit. At the top of the stairs they turned to the left along a pleasant hall, with green and white straw matting on the floor, and then turned to the right into another wing which led toward the back of the house.

Presently they reached the end of the corridor. "Here we are," June said. "Your room will be this one straight ahead, and mine is here to the left. They're next to each other."

Kate pushed eagerly through the door into her room, and then couldn't help smiling because she loved it so. On the floor there was the same green and white matting, whose damp smell reminded her of Matunuck. The chintz curtains had a pattern of cornflowers and poppies, and near the bed stood a luxurious chaise-longue.

"It's not so big," June said, "but I've always liked this room. I used to wish it was mine, but I couldn't have it because it was used as a guest room. Do you like it, Kate?"

"I just love it!" Kate said. "I can't imagine a nicer room."

She walked gaily across to one of the windows. "And what a pretty view!" she exclaimed "It looks so quaint and peaceful."

An oblong of turf, like a bowling green, stretched smoothly to a little house of white brick, with mossy red tiles and blue shutters like the main building; but this was as miniature and dainty as a cottage in a fairy tale. Behind it a wall of trees rose so steeply that she had to lean out of the window to look up at the sky. And from the little house she could hear the sound of a violin.

"I suppose that's Mr.—I suppose that Jo," she said. "Felix told me about him."

"Yes, that's Jo," June said, and if Felix's tone had suggested disapproval, June's expressed real dislike. "He lives out there so his practicing won't disturb us, but sometimes when he plays late at night it keeps me awake. Mavis, that's mother, accompanies him; she plays pretty well; but lately it's been mostly Clotilde. She plays too."

Kate smiled. "You don't think much of him, do you?" she said. "Felix didn't seem to either, not that he wasn't very polite. What's wrong with him?"

"Nothing's wrong with him really," June said after a minute, "except that he's a sponge. I don't blame him so much. He's no worse than the rest of them." And then her face darkened into a scowl, the kind of scowl Kate remembered when girls at school had bothered to tease her. "It's just that it's all so nasty. Everything's nasty around here. It's always been that way ever since I can remember. It's not fair for things to be so nasty!"

Her face suddenly lightened, and she looked with the new intensity of her glance directly at Kate. "That's one of the reasons

I wanted you to come," she said. "Because you won't mind it, I guess. It's not *your* family."

At that moment Kate was so sorry for her that she felt like putting her arms around her and kissing her, but it might be just as well not to start a precedent. She wondered if she were referring to any special things. Whatever they were, she was perhaps exaggerating.

"We can treat everything like an adventure," she said. "And we won't have to bother with people when we don't want to."

"But Kate," June went on after a minute, in a new tone of voice, no longer passionate but rather stilted and hesitant. "That's not the only reason I'm glad you've come. That's not the main reason."

"What is it?" Kate asked curiously.

When June spoke, her voice was almost a whisper. "The main reason is that I'm afraid."

Kate felt a crawling sensation inside her stomach, as if the roller coaster had begun its downward plunge, but she tried to smile incredulously. "Afraid!" she exclaimed. "What on earth are you afraid of?"

"You mustn't laugh," June said. "It's not my imagination. Listen, Kate. A week ago I was walking with Bobbie on the river bluffs. I walk around here a lot. I always have. That hill out there behind the little house is the start of a bluff. It rises for just a few hundred yards, getting steeper and steeper, and then there are rocks, and the bluff drops almost straight down into the river. It's quite wild all along the shore. The bluffs go on for miles, and there are lots of little nooks and caves. I guess nobody knows them all, unless it's Professor Hatfield. Felix said you met him on the way out here. Well, on one of the bluffs about a mile down the river from here, Bobbie started barking and barking. I thought it was at some animal so I began to explore. Over the crest in a kind of a steep place I found a little cave I'd never noticed, because a juniper tree spread out from the bank right smack above it. It was sort of hard to get down, but I'm a pretty good climber, and inside there was an old blanket and some whisky bottles and an electric torch and a kind of tin lunch box that I didn't look into. Bobbie was still yelping on top of the bluff, because she couldn't get down, and all at once I had the most awful creepy feeling that someone was near. I don't think I heard anyone. I didn't see anyone. It was just a feeling, but it was so awful I could hardly climb back around the juniper."

"I can imagine that," Kate exclaimed. "I'd have never dared climb down in the first place. I suppose it was just some camper. Or perhaps a hunter, if anything's in season."

"I don't think it was an ordinary camper," June said.

"But why not?" Kate asked. It almost scared her to feel such relief that June's fear was irrational: what had she been expecting anyway?

"Wait a minute," June said. "I'll be right back." And she hurried out of the room.

Kate wouldn't have believed how empty June's absence would make it seem. Even Bobbie lying beside the bed, her slim hind legs spread backward like a frog's, was scarcely a consolation. She could still hear the violin, but it only increased the silence of everything else. That wall of trees seemed now rather suffocating, as if it shut out the natural air and light. Thank heaven, at least, that Ralph was here! She gave a faint start as June came back into the room, just as she had started several hours ago (it seemed like an entirely different day) when Felix had knocked at her door back in town.

Then as June handed her a letter, her heart began to beat so violently that it was almost an agony to force herself to smile. Because she recognized that envelope, that printing.

"It came in the mail just two days later," June said. "That was five days ago."

Kate felt that she could not trust her voice. She took out the paper, and there printed in the same red crayon—blood-red it looked to her now—she saw the following message:

IF YOU GO ON POKING
YOUR NOSE INTO THINGS,
YOU'LL BE SORRY.
AND I MEAN SORRY!

3

When Kate looked out of her bedroom door at ten minutes to seven, she was glad to see that June's door was still closed. She had planned to start this very first night with June's hair, with a general reclaiming process, but the more she thought over this new red-printed warning, the more anxious she was to tell Ralph about it; and she would prefer doing this when June was not present.

Kate had not told June about her own letter; there had seemed to be no point in increasing her nervousness. Yet perhaps she ought to tell June: she had proof now at any rate that the writer of the notes was a person associated with this region; this second letter made the whole affair seem much more ominous, and she felt that she could not sleep tonight until she had asked Ralph's advice. She only hoped that she might have a chance to speak to him before June came down.

She had thought regretfully, as June showed her about the farm, how much she would have enjoyed everything if only the air had not been tainted by this clammy breath of the mysterious. It kept seeping in around the edges of her mind to ruin her pleasure in this beautiful, faraway place. It was like a symptom that you half suspect may point to some horrible disease, and that all the while your common sense tells you is probably of no importance: at one instant, desperately, you are sure that your life is threatened; at the next, you are merely annoyed with your jumpy nerves.

In spite of its name, Kate felt that Mr. Gladstone's home was more of a country estate than a farm. The buildings, like the

47

house, were of whitewashed brick; none of them was large, and among them were little graveled courtyards leading one out of another, with espaliered fruit trees trained in angular patterns against the white walls. June had shown her the two riding horses in the stable; then they had seen the garage, where Felix was polishing the green convertible, and the cow barn, where Olaf Larson, an old Norwegian, was milking a Guernsey cow. June took Kate to a cottage across the paddock to call on Emmy, his wife. Both of them had been on the place, June explained, since before her father went to college, and they still spoke with a Norwegian accent. Then June and she had walked through the formal garden, of which Kate had already caught a glimpse between the slats of the blind; they had skirted the tennis court and the truck garden, while Bobbie kept running off to explore and returning to bounce about their legs. A light at once blue and iridescent had begun to fill the shadows; and eastward, beyond the lawn and the fields, the wooded hills through which she had driven three hours ago looked, in their soft brilliance, more impenetrable than ever.

Kate was very much pleased with June. As this awkward girl felt the noses of the horses and stroked the sides of the cows, there had been a brusque grace and directness in her movements. She had seemed thoroughly at home with animals: no doubt she loved them more than she did people, although she had shown something of this easy manner toward Felix and the Larsons. This struck Kate as rather pathetic in its suggestion that she knew these workers about the place more intimately than she knew her own family.

As they were entering the house, by way of the kitchen, June said: "I'd have loved to take you up the bluff and show you the river. That's the nicest thing around here, but I don't know—I kind of felt perhaps we'd better not."

"It must be nearly dinnertime," Kate said lightly. There was no point in letting June suspect how much she would have hated just then to plunge into those woods behind the house.

She walked swiftly now along the halls, down the broad stairs and into the living room. It was empty, but the blinds at the end were drawn up, the French window was open, and she could see a man in a white suit standing alone on the terrace. For a minute she thought it might be Ralph, but then as she crossed the room she noticed that this man's hair was black: he must be Jo Martinez, the violinist.

She was hesitating in the middle of the room, wondering whether to join him or wait until someone else appeared, when he turned and saw her.

"Hullo," he called. "Come on out! Don't be afraid. I'm quite harmless." His voice was resonant and he spoke with a marked accent.

Kate came forward willingly: she was curious to see what this man was like. "You must be Mr. Martinez," she said, as she stepped out on to the terrace. "I'm Kate Archer."

"Kate!" he exclaimed. "One of those simple English names that can either be so commonplace or can be filled with so much beauty! Kate and Jo! My name is José but all my American friends call me Jo, and I'm sure—I was sure the first instant that I saw you, in a flash, like that!—that we should be friends."

"That wasn't very long ago," she said smiling.

Felix and June had prepared her for someone at once sleek and forbidding, but this man suggested neither a thug nor a gigolo. He was wiry, even darker than Mr. Gladstone, with shining hair brushed straight back from a very low forehead; his face, without being handsome, was aquiline and alert; the intensity of his eyes made her think of a Goya portrait.

"It seems already that for me a long time has passed since then," he said. "Or perhaps I should say the element of time is not involved. When the saints saw visions they entered a world that is timeless. Not that I am a saint—please don't let me give you that impression!"

"I'm sure you're far too young to be a saint," Kate said. "Perhaps you will be sometime."

The man beamed at her but shook his head. "Ah, ah!" he exclaimed. "And I thought you were so innocent, so artless, I who pride myself on reading human nature. Yet you have the wisdom of the serpent. You see at a glance that after I have exhausted

my passion for this world I might well conceive a passion for
the next; and you also put your finger on my leading vanity: the
desire to remain, to appear young, especially before beautiful
women. It's disconcerting a little, because you would not have
sensed that vanity if you had not also seen that I am not so young
as I should like to appear."

As a matter of fact, Kate guessed that he was in his late twen-
ties. It was pleasant and gay, at the end of this disquieting afternoon, to be talking nonsense with an attractive young man, even
if he was rather exotic. She realized that her comfortable sense of
having Ralph in reserve, as it were, made her feel more kindly toward Jo, whose strangeness might otherwise have faintly repelled
her. She was delighted that she had put on her white organdy
and that she had brushed her hair until it gleamed and floated
about her shoulders, almost as soft, though not so silvery, as Clotilde's. It was with Clotilde in mind that she had tried to make
herself appear as young as possible, that she had chosen such a
candid-looking dress and been quite sparing with her lipstick.
Since she could not hope to equal her sophistication, the best
she could do was to suggest by contrast that Clotilde was brittle
and overworldly.

"And you have put your finger on my weakness too," she said.
"I think I'm the one to be embarrassed."

"Then it must have been my little finger," he exclaimed, "and
it was quite by accident. What is your weakness? There are few
things I enjoy so much as having lovely women tell me their
weaknesses."

"I'm sure you must have had lots of experience in that line,"
she said.

He shrugged his shoulders. "What will you have? I'm humble. I'm sympathetic. I'm indulgent. If I could only behave myself, I would have made an excellent priest."

Before Kate could think of some phrase about her own love
of flattery, she was startled by a throaty chuckle from the living
room, and turning her head she saw a woman who surely must be
Mavis standing on the threshold of the terrace. Kate was intensely

curious to meet the person who went with the voice she had heard this afternoon.

Mrs. Gladstone was small, and not so much plump as baggy. She was wearing a kind of tea gown of cream-colored lace which trailed on the floor behind her but flared open in front to show her legs to the knee and attract attention to her feet, still stockingless, and humped into tiny mesh sandals with even higher heels than the red ones which Kate had seen. Across the room her face might still appear pretty, with the fleshy dated prettiness of a Sennett bathing beauty; but as near as this it looked as if it were made of wax which had been kept in too warm a place: the nose was beginning to spread, the cheeks and chin to sag, and about the eyes, the mouth, the throat, a network of wrinkles now filled with powder suggested to Kate the fine veins of a leaf. Her lips, painted rather crookedly, were wine-colored, her eyelids were cerulean blue, and a cloud of brassy hair stood out like a synthetic halo around her head.

"José," she exclaimed, with a guttural Spanish J, "did I hear you tell this poor child that you'd make a good priest? God pity the woman who trusted herself to your ghostly administrations!"

"Oh, I don't know," he said airily. "Even as a layman I've managed to bring comfort to some poor souls."

Mrs. Gladstone advanced toward Kate with a jerky sway that just missed being a hobble. "And so you're Kate," she said. "Poor little June has raved about you, and really I don't wonder. I hope this depraved and utterly decadent young man here hasn't been telling you some of his 'feelthy stories.'"

"Mavis, my love," Jo said, "I save those for ears that I think will enjoy them."

At this moment June and Clotilde stepped out of the living room, side by side yet certainly not together, with Mr. Gladstone close behind them. June was wearing a bunchy pink dress that made her look her worst, while Clotilde was in sleek pale-gray silk, the color of a sea gull's wing; her dress was so inconspicuous and yet so striking that Kate was sure it must be the work of some famous designer. Around her long throat was a string of pearls.

Mr. Gladstone grinned at Kate, with the left corner of his mouth pulled down as if it were holding an invisible cigar.

"Charming, my dear! Charming!" he exclaimed. "You strike a completely new note in our menagerie." And Kate felt a little as if a large and aged grisly bear, pressing close to the front of its cage, had shown signs of wanting to play with her through the bars.

"But you and Clotilde haven't met each other yet," he went on. "One can hardly expect two such beautiful girls to like each other, but that's no reason why you shouldn't be dear friends."

While he was speaking Clotilde had given her a level glance, and now she came forward with her hand outstretched and with a smile that even Kate had to admit was charming. If she had not heard her this afternoon with her stepmother, she would not have guessed how very unpleasant she could be—and perhaps with Mavis there was some excuse. She wondered if Ralph so far had caught a glimpse of Clotilde's other manner. Poor Ralph!

"I'm so glad you've come," Clotilde exclaimed. "For June's sake, and also for my own. I'm sure we can have lots of fun."

"I'm sure we can," Kate said; and as she took her hand, meeting her eyes with what she hoped was a look of spontaneous pleasure, she knew that Mr. and Mrs. Gladstone, that Jo and even June were all watching them. Inside her there was a small warm feeling of triumph, because she was sure Clotilde had come prepared to snub her, in a polite Park Avenue way, and then, seeing her, had simply not quite dared. This stranger, she must have thought, was too attractive not to be welcomed with complete friendliness: because any other treatment might be interpreted as an admission of inferiority.

Kate was glad, however, that just then Felix appeared from around the corner of the house with a large tray of cocktails and canapes. She would not have known what to say next to Clotilde; Clotilde showed no signs of speaking herself, and they could not have smiled at each other much longer. Then as Felix began passing the tray, Kate noticed Professor Hatfield walking toward them through the garden. Everyone was here now but Ralph.

An insinuating voice spoke close to her ear:

"A cocktail, Miss Kate? And how about a canapé? Those black ones are the best. I've sampled them."

Felix stood at her elbow with the tray. He was leaning forward, the picture of the well-trained servant, but his eye was raised to catch hers with a look that seemed almost of complicity, of encouragement, and she could not have sworn that his right eyelid had not flickered. She hoped people did not notice the smile she gave him, because it was so much more natural than the one she had given Clotilde.

Professor Hatfield came over to speak to her, but she hardly heard what he said, because at that moment Ralph stepped out of the house and started to pour himself a cocktail by the table where Felix had left the tray. He raised his glass, looked around him perfunctorily, and then as his warm brown eye caught hers it was as if a light had been turned on somewhere in the depths of his mind and was illumining his whole face.

"Kate!" he exclaimed. "Little Kate Archer! What on earth are you doing here? This is wonderful! I can't believe it."

As she met his straight glance, at once so bright and so deep, so gentle, and yet in the midst of all this strangeness so completely reliable, she wondered how she ever could have lost the sense of its special quality. It was like your first whiff of the soft salt air after you have been for months away from the sea. Then she blushed as she realized that everyone was staring at her.

"Do you know Ralph?" June asked, and there was reproach in her voice. "Why didn't you tell me, Katey?"

Kate tried to laugh. "I only discovered it was Ralph a little while ago," she said. "I hadn't seen him for five years, and I thought I wouldn't tell anybody until I was sure he remembered me. It was just my vanity, I guess."

Ralph crossed the terrace and seized her outstretched hand.

"Remember you!" he said. "Don't be silly! Do you think I could forget that summer of ours? As a matter of fact, I'm one of those stupid people that never forget anything. It's pretty much of a curse as a rule, because most things I'd much rather forget, but it does have its compensations. When something happens I really want to remember, I've got it tucked away for life. I always hoped I'd run into you again, but I never thought it would be around here. Of course I heard June talking about 'Kate,' but I don't think she ever mentioned your last name."

Clotilde laughed. "Perhaps we should all withdraw," she suggested, "and give these two old friends a chance to talk over their memories."

As Ralph glanced at his fiancée, Kate noticed again the fixed and blank smile with which he had faced her, out here, this afternoon.

"I'm going to do my best to see that we find plenty of chances," he said. "You can certainly count on that."

Kate was pleased by the finality in his voice: it was as if he were merely stating a fact that required no special emphasis. Then he continued to herself, but so quietly that only June and the professor, who were standing close beside them, could hear him:

"I might not have recognized you at that. In fact the more I look at you, the more surprised I am that I did. You were an exceptionally pretty little girl, Kate, but you've grown to be so beautiful! Or were you always that way and is it just that my taste has matured? How old were you at Hancock Point? Thirteen? Fourteen?"

"I was fifteen," she said with a pretense of indignation. "I'm sorry if I seemed such a child. I was only a year younger than June is now."

The other people had turned their attention elsewhere. Clotilde was talking and laughing with Jo; and Kate felt that she must bring June into the conversation.

"But June is so big," he said. "You were just a little thing."

"I'm not so terribly big," June said, and Kate could see that her feelings were hurt. "I've lost eight pounds in the last two months."

Kate put her arm around June's waist. "He only means that you seem quite grown-up," she said, "and when Ralph knew me in Maine I was just a skinny little girl."

If it was reassuring to find Ralph here, it certainly did not diminish her sense of strangeness: the nicer he was, the queerer and the more illogical it seemed to think of him in Clotilde's clutches. It was like the kind of dream in which you find that you yourself are engaged, or possibly married, to someone whom you cannot bear: you can't imagine how it happened; you are simply faced with the fact and there is no escape.

She had sipped half her cocktail, which tasted of absinthe, and she was sure it must be very strong, because already the voices seemed louder and more confused, the colors more intense. The garden was completely shadowed by the hill behind the house, but the larkspur, the iris, the poppies, seemed to glow each with its own inner brightness among the paths and the watery green edgings, while the upper sky, above the bowl of the hills, shimmered in a dust of light. She could smell the lilies from here, or perhaps it was the clove pinks; it might even be the perfume that Mavis or Clotilde was wearing. She chattered of she hardly knew what with Ralph, with June, with Professor Hatfield; and everyone's features—their eyebrows, their noses, their mouths—looked exaggerated and somehow fixed in spite of their mobility. Her own must have that same strange look, and she felt she must control her smile and make an effort to speak softly. It seemed all at once like the world through the Looking Glass, but a Wonderland in which Alice's dream might change without warning into a grotesque kind of nightmare.

They must have remained on the terrace for more than half an hour. She drank her cocktail as slowly as she could, but she had finished long ago and with difficulty prevented first Jo and then Mr. Gladstone from refilling her glass, before they began to move into the dining room. She was thankful she had taken no more, when Mavis seated her between Ralph and Mr. Hatfield. Perhaps during dinner she could tell Ralph about the letters.

At first, however, Mavis, who sat at his other side and whom Kate suspected of being quite tipsy, questioned him with vague repetitious innuendo about his former friendship with Kate. It was not until their soup bowls had been removed and Ruby had begun passing the chicken that Mavis turning to Jo, who was seated on her other side, gave Kate a chance to talk with Ralph.

He leaned toward her at once, and as she met his eyes, peering warmly into her face from under his pirate's eyebrows, she

had again the feeling which had come over her in the moment of
his first recognition: that he had somehow shut her off with himself in a world that excluded all the rest of these strange people.
Then, though his expression hardly changed, though his smile
continued, it was as if a film had been drawn across his clear
brown glance; they were once more, the two of them, breathing
the air of this candlelit dining room, the same air as Mavis and
Jo and Mr. Gladstone, an air that was at once too heavy and too
thin.

"Ralph!" she exclaimed quickly, in an effort to recapture her
sense of the instant before. "Tell me what you've been doing. Tell
me something about yourself."

He shrugged his shoulders. "What an unappetizing topic," he
said, "to bring up at the dinner table!"

Beneath the lightness of his tone, behind the deliberate blank-
ness of his eyes, she was suddenly aware of something tense, and
it seemed to her even tortured; she realized that to know Ralph
well one would have to be able, at times, to peer through the
most opaque of shutters. She could hardly resist the impulse to
place her fingers on his arm.

"I'm not just talking," she said gently. "I wouldn't have asked
what you've been doing, if I didn't really want to know."

"The over-all answer to your question," he said, "would be
'Nothing'—at least nothing of any consequence. As a matter of
fact, until a month ago, I was working in the Bell Telephone Laboratories in New York. I'm relieved from that now, just hanging
around for my navy commission to come through."

"How exciting!" she said, and hoped the interest in her face
might counteract the banality of her words. "Will you like being
in the Navy?"

"I think so," he said, "as much as anything. More than most
things, I suppose. You know, it's strange," he went on; and she
felt that his glance was growing transparent once more; there
was a queer eagerness in his voice, as if for a long time he had
found it impossible to talk, to talk as he would really like, to
anyone—"It's strange, but when war broke out, I was glad I
wouldn't have to go. I was willing to do all I could, of course. I

was no pacifist. But at the same time I felt I was very lucky to be in electronics. It seemed to me I could help the war effort most by staying just where I was. As a matter of fact, I think that was true. I'll probably make a lousy officer. I'll be doing a very special type of work, of course, but I think I could work better in a laboratory than on a ship."

"Then why did you want to change?" she asked him. She felt that some of the others, that especially Clotilde, might be watching them, might be wondering what they were saying; but the round table was large and dim; Mr. Gladstone, in jovial mood, was telling risqué stories to the general company. Ralph and she were talking in such low voices that at least no one could make out their words, and Kate just then, perhaps because of her cocktail, did not care what anyone thought.

"I hardly know why I changed," Ralph answered her. "Partly vanity, no doubt, and a kind of envy. When I read of what was going on in the Pacific and across Europe, when I got letters from my friends with the Army or Navy, frankly, I couldn't help feeling somehow that I was in a theater and much too far away from the stage. I wanted to grab one of the best seats, if I could. And then it must have been partly stubbornness. When I suggested to my boss that I give up my job, he wouldn't hear of it. The moment he told me I couldn't go, even if I wanted to, that made me want to all the more. We had a real fight about it." He suddenly smiled, but his smile was not gay. "And then I guess partly it was just what you might call a naïve romantic desire to escape, to get away as far as possible from where I happened to be—the feeling that if I could get into a nice new uniform I'd become a nice new person. It seemed to me then, in fact it still seems to me—" his voice became hesitant, as if he feared that she might laugh at him—"that there's something peculiarly clean in direct action, and most of all in action that involves a measure of risk."

"I think I see just how you felt," she exclaimed, "though I don't think I'd describe it in the same way. And I never thought of war's being clean, Ralph. Think of the trenches, think of the jungles, think of the smashed men and ships!"

"I'm sure war itself is foul," he said. "I'm sure it's just as hellish as it was in Sherman's time. Probably more so. I've no doubt I'll hate it. But there are different kinds of hells. I don't think for me, at least, that it will be the worst kind."

"What other kinds do you mean?" she asked softly, although she felt that she should not.

He gave her another long look, and once more the rest of the people were pushed far away. "Perhaps one of the worst," he said slowly, "is realizing the possible heavens you have missed."

This time she dropped her glance before his; and then swiftly, with a feeling that she was running away, she told him of her anonymous warning which just now seemed quite unimportant.

But it evidently didn't seem unimportant to Ralph. "Good God, Kate!" he exclaimed. 'You shouldn't have come!" And then he added: "Not that I'm not thankful you did."

"You really think it means something then?" she asked.

"I haven't the faintest idea," he said, "but I don't like it. Why on earth should anyone threaten you?"

"June got a warning too," she said. "I wasn't the only one."

"Look here," Ralph exclaimed, "does anybody else know about this?"

"I told Professor Hatfield about mine," she said. "That was on the way out here this afternoon. I didn't know then about June's."

"I'm glad you told him," he said. "The professor's the only person I trust around here." And Kate caught herself being surprised at the fact that she was *not* surprised at Ralph's excluding Clotilde from the people whom he trusted. "I think we ought to tell him about June's letter too. I think he ought to know everything that's going on."

Kate, strangely, now could feel almost glad that she had been threatened: if Ralph's face showed anxiety, it also showed a new alertness. It was as if a flame which had been smoldering in the tight prison of his inner mind had suddenly been offered an outlet, and now could give not only heat but light.

"I'd love to tell Mr. Hatfield," she exclaimed. "I like him very much."

She turned from Ralph toward the professor, and at the same instant he turned toward her, so that she half suspected he might have overheard something of her talk with Ralph. But if he had, his ears must be extraordinarily sharp.

Mr. Hatfield listened to her attentively, with the dry, ingratiating air which already she had come to know.

"I'm familiar with the cave June described to you," he said. "Some duck hawks nest in the cliff beneath that particular bluff."

"But what does it mean, Professor?" Ralph exclaimed. "The whole thing sounds crazy to me, but you expect things to be crazy around here. Does it mean that Kate—and June—are in any danger?"

"The only thing we know it means," Professor Hatfield said, "is that some stranger obviously is, or has been, lurking in the neighborhood. I think I will investigate that cave, though I suppose by now he will have moved out, that is if he had anything to do with June's letter. Of course we can't positively assume that he did. If he really did, it does seem to make it a rather more elaborate plot, doesn't it?"

"A plot!" Kate exclaimed. "Then you really think it is a plot?"

"That's just a manner of speaking," he said in his dry voice, which seemed at the same time so impersonal and so intimate. "If it's a joke, it's a more elaborate joke."

"If you ask me," Ralph said, "it's one hell of a joke! I'd like to get my hands on whoever thought it up."

"I hardly think it's a joke," the professor said doubtfully, "although there are several people around here who have perhaps what might be described as a perverse sense of humor."

"But what do you think it is then?" Kate asked. "There must be something behind it. What is it?" She tried to keep her tone calm.

"My dear Kate," he said, "—you don't mind if I call you Kate?—I only wish I knew. It interests me enormously."

"But what do you think I ought to do?"

"Hmmm—" He looked abstractedly at the sweet Williams in the center of the table. "You know, I don't think it would be a bad plan, if you have no objections, to spread the news to the assembled company. Perhaps there have been more letters. What do you think, Ralph?"

"By all means," Ralph said. "Let's bring it out into the open. Let's clear the air around here, if that's possible."

The idea startled Kate: it would focus so much attention on herself; and perhaps June would resent her having told Ralph and Mr. Hatfield. "You really think we ought to?" she asked.

"I don't see that it would do any harm; and it might—it just might—begin to clear things up. Will you give me permission to go ahead?"

"All right," Kate said rather faintly. She dreaded the next moment, and yet if everyone knew, it might, after all, be more comfortable.

The professor tapped on his glass with his knife, as if he were calling a meeting to order. Everybody turned to look at him.

"I've got a rather strange question to ask the company," he announced. He paused for a moment, as if he enjoyed the suspense; then in a matter-of-fact tone he asked: "Has any one of you within the last few days received an anonymous letter?"

June, directly across the table from Kate, sent her a startled look, and Kate leaned toward her. "I thought it was wiser to tell him about it," she said. "I got one too."

"An anonymous letter!" Mr. Gladstone exclaimed. "I used to get them occasionally—quite juicy ones. I always thought they were sent by jealous females, or sometimes possibly by husbands with whose wives I had become acquainted. But that was long ago—in my salad days."

"Perhaps I had better elucidate," Professor Hatfield went on, and precisely, neatly, as if he were analyzing an experiment before a class, he told them about Kate and June.

"But how perfectly thrilling!" Mavis exclaimed, leaning forward with a shudder and staring at the professor. "You're not just inventing it, are you, you terrible man? You're not going sadist on us?"

No one else spoke, and Kate followed Professor Hatfield's glance as it moved from face to face about the table.

"I take it then," he said, after nearly a minute, "that none of the rest of you has received one of these—I suppose I should call them warnings."

"*I* got one!"

Kate jumped, for the voice, loud and harsh, came from almost directly behind her. Then she realized that it was Ruby who had spoken.

Professor Hatfield glanced at her over his shoulder. "You say you received one too? May I ask what the message was?"

"Just about the same as June's. 'Keep your nose out,' it said. Something like that. The other night walking in the woods I heard the bushes rustling. I thought it might be Felix back at his old tricks, with some girl from one of the farms. So I charged, but they were too quick for me, whoever they were. To tell you the truth, I thought Felix might have written that letter. But you can take my word for it, Felix would never write a letter to scare away a young girl from here, not if I know Felix!"

"Ruby darling, we wives do have our troubles, don't we?" Mavis exclaimed, flinging back her head and looking archly over her shoulder; but Ruby paid no attention and continued passing the asparagus.

4

It must have been an hour after dinner, though Kate had lost all sense of time, that Mavis rose from her chair. She had drunk several glasses of cognac, which had been served with the coffee out here on the terrace, and now she tottered so wildly that she might have fallen if Jo had not sprung to her rescue.

"If you'll excuse me," she said, "all this charming company, I think I'll be going to my room. I don't feel quite up to par all of a sudden. In fact, if you ask me, I feel like hell."

She let her glance wander vaguely around the dim terrace, noticed Kate, and pulled Jo in her direction. Kate rose to say good night, and to her embarrassment, Mavis flung her arms around her neck and kissed her effusively.

"Good night, darling," she cooed, with a suggestion of a hiccup. "You're lovely, you're just lovely! You remind me of myself when my name was in lights not so many years ago. I can't ask you to come up to my room, because Jo, the foolish boy, would be so jealous, and I wouldn't be leaving you now, but it's this dizziness, this silly dizziness. Every so often the spells come over me, just like that! The semicircular canals, you know. It seems that mine are particularly semi."

And leaning against Jo, she wavered into the house. When Jo returned five minutes later, he paused for a moment on the threshold of the long, lighted window and shook himself delicately, like a cat who had just come in out of the rain.

"And now," he said, "that our dear Mavis is safely in Ruby's hands, why don't we all adjourn to my studio and have a little music? I often do not care to play after such an excellent dinner, but tonight I feel for some reason inspired."

Mr. Gladstone was not enthusiastic.

"My dear fellow," he said, "I'm sure it will be wonderful, but Ralph and I had rather counted on a game of chess before we go to bed, so perhaps you'll excuse us. How about it, Ralph?"

"By all means, let's play chess," Ralph said with decision if not with eagerness. Kate could gather that he, too, was not fond of Jo.

"I'm sure the music will be a treat for the professor and Kate," Mr. Gladstone went on, "and I know Clotilde always loves to play for you. More and more, Clotilde darling, isn't that so? More and more you like to play with José."

Clotilde laughed lazily and rose from her chair "Father dear," she said, "your first expression was more accurate—play *for* him, not play *with* him. I love to play for any good musician who will condescend to let me. Perhaps you wouldn't quite understand."

Mr. Gladstone shrugged his shoulders. "Does one ever understand one's children?" he exclaimed. "Come along, Ralph, let's you and I turn to the comparatively simple problems of chess."

Clotilde took Jo's arm, and Kate and the professor followed them around the corner of the house, through an herb garden, wonderfully fragrant in the soft night air, to the cottage which she had seen from her window.

When Jo turned on the light, the room looked so large that she realized it must be the only one, and that the divan covered with an old Navaho blanket must be Jo's bed. At the other end of the room stood a grand piano, and above the fireplace hung a stilted yet clinically detailed painting of St. Sebastian bristling with arrows. It made Kate rather uncomfortable to look at it, and she shifted her chair slightly.

Professor Hatfield had taken a chair close to hers, and June had slumped down on the divan. "Golly," she exclaimed, "I'm tired! You know, Katey, I was so excited about your coming today I woke up at four o'clock this morning."

The first thing Jo played was a Tartini sonata, and after a few bars Kate realized that he was a first-rate violinist. It interested her that his face, so mobile when he talked, became when he played as quiet as a mask. She had to admit, too, that Clotilde knew what she was about: she had a pleasant touch and followed Jo accurately, although in the final allegro she fumbled the passage work.

As soon as he had finished, Jo put his violin on the piano, and wiped his forehead and neck. Clotilde kept her seat on the bench. "And what about a Mozart?" she asked. "Let's try the C major, the one we did the other night."

"I'm afraid that would go better if you hadn't taken that second cognac," Jo said. "However, we can try."

Professor Hatfield rose quickly, almost furtively, from his chair. "If you will excuse me," he said in a deprecating voice, "I think I'll slip along. I find the early morning one of the best times for my observations. And also I hope I may track down an owl or two on the way home. That takes longer than you think. It was very nice, Jo, very nice indeed. Thank you ever so much. And Clotilde, you might thank your good father for me. I don't think I'll disturb them at their game. Good night all!"

He slipped noiselessly out into the darkness, and Kate felt that his last glance had been for her.

At the first bars of the sonata she recognized that it was one she had played often with her brother. She sank back in her chair and closed her eyes, to try to recapture the times when they had played it together at Matunuck, but the Mozart did not go so well: Clotilde was stumbling more and more. Kate looked up and saw that Jo was frowning. Suddenly he put down his violin.

"I think," he said, with an edge to his voice, "that it's no use to continue. You must excuse me, Kate, I should have liked to play you Mozart, but circumstances beyond my control—"

"You go to hell!" Clotilde exclaimed in a tone that reminded Kate of the way she had spoken to Mavis this afternoon. "You ought to keep your mind off your audience, Jo. I don't think this one's too damn critical, if you ask me."

She rose from the piano bench, opened her compact, and started to put on more lipstick.

Kate was so furious that she could feel herself trembling. She stood up quickly. "If you'd like to play the Mozart," she said, "I'd love to accompany you. I've played it with my brother. In fact we've done almost all the Mozart sonatas together."

Jo's glance was surprised and a little skeptical. "Splendid," he said. "Splendid! We'll try again. But Mozart isn't easy, as our beautiful friend here can testify."

"No?" Kate said, and realized that her voice was imitating Clotilde's. "I always thought he was."

She glanced at June to see what she thought of this audacity, and then smiled in spite of herself. Poor June was now sitting on the edge of the divan, her knees wide apart, her hands drooping between them; her jaw looked as if it would sag at any moment and her eyes seemed dead with sleep. She reminded Kate just then of some big homely puppy trying to keep awake as it stared into the fire.

"June darling!" she exclaimed. "It's too cruel! You must go right to bed. I hadn't noticed how exhausted you were. You don't have to wait for me."

June blinked and got up. "I guess I will at that," she said. "Good night, Katey. It's great you're here."

"Good night, little June," Jo called. "Happy dreams!" But June left the room without paying the least attention either to him or Clotilde.

As Kate sat down at the piano, she had to exert the greatest effort to keep her fingers from shaking, to fight off that helpless soft feeling in your arms and wrists that makes all control impossible. She knew that Clotilde would watch like a hawk for mistakes, for any clumsiness; she knew that Jo, no matter how many fantastic compliments he paid her, would be annoyed if she bungled. But she did know also that she played more musically than Clotilde, that she had a more finished technique; and she had the advantage of having taken only one cocktail before dinner and having refused the brandy.

She watched Jo out of the corner of her eye for his signal; then, incredibly, they had begun.

Clotilde was standing directly behind her, and it seemed to Kate that she could feel her eyes fixed on her back, trying to hypnotize her so that she would fumble or blur or lose her place. She did not dare let her eyes swerve from one measure to the next; but presently she began to find Clotilde's hostility stimulating— or perhaps it was simply Jo's playing. It was never arbitrary, never sentimental: like an expert dancer, he gave her the feeling that she could not help moving with him, pressing forward or retarding slightly as the music demanded. Soon she forgot Clotilde, and hardly thought of her again until the last chords of the finale.

Now she turned on the piano bench, doing her best not to look triumphant. To her amazement, Clotilde was not there.

Jo grinned. "She left," he explained. "She left in the first movement, as soon as she saw that you played so much better than she does."

Kate glanced around the room. It was as if she had stepped back into a strange lonely place from a beloved region where everything was beautiful and secure. She remembered suddenly that this was Jo's bedroom as well as his studio.

"I must go now," she said. "I loved the music. You were very good to let me play for you."

He shook his head, smiling vividly at her. "It seems a miracle," he exclaimed. "She's beautiful; she's wise; and then she turns out to be an excellent musician. But I mustn't try to keep you," he went on, "because in the first place I know I should be unsuccessful, and in the second place, between ourselves, I think the exquisite Clotilde wouldn't at all mind if the news spread that you had lingered here with me late at night—if it spread, for example, to Ralph's ears. In fact, I rather suspect that was one of the reasons why she left, counting on your innocence and my experience. But Clotilde does not know me entirely. I am more complicated than she thinks and also more simple. I am, after all, a romantic Spaniard. I divide all women into only two classes, the good and the bad. I love both kinds, but my feelings toward them are quite different. And now good night. I won't go with you. It is better not."

"Good night," Kate said, and hurried out of the cottage. She hardly knew whether to be pleased or angry or amused; she only knew that she had blushed.

She kept on hurrying across the turf, which felt very wet through her thin slippers. The herb garden was more fragrant than ever, but she did not linger there for a moment. When she turned the corner of the house, she saw that there was no one on the terrace, softly flooded by the light from the long window— no one, that is, unless somebody were crouching behind a chair. She nearly ran across the intervening grass, stepped up on to the tiles, and looked into the living room. The chessboard, with two or three men left on it, was still spread on a little table, but Mr. Gladstone and Ralph had gone: the big room was empty.

For some reason she shrank from walking through it, as if, once she stepped across the threshold, something would close in behind her and she would be trapped. This was absurd: she must get control of her nerves. She turned away and moved to the edge of the terrace. If she could lose herself in the beauty of this summer night, it should be easier for her to sleep afterward.

The sky was swimming with stars and as she gazed down over the garden she could see more and more clearly the pale windings of the paths, the pattern of the flower beds.

Through the quiet air she could hear a faint shrill noise: she could not decide whether it was the sound of crickets or frogs. Whatever it was, it must be far away.

She did not know how long she had stood there, but she had the feeling all at once that it was very late. It made her think of the times, years ago, when she would wake up in the night and wonder where Father and Mother were, and if they would answer her if she called. Then she would hardly dare to open her mouth, not so much because she was afraid they might scold her as because it would be so awful if no one answered her, if Mother and Father perhaps had died in their sleep, or been taken mysteriously away where she could not reach them. And suddenly this whole night seemed like a huge empty room from which she could not escape, from which no one could rescue her no matter how loudly she called.

There came a sharp rustling from the bushes at the edge of the garden, and she put her hand to her lips, as if to keep herself from crying out.

Then she saw a small black and white object scuttling toward her across the slope of turf between the garden and the terrace. With a gasp of relief she recognized Bobbie; this dear little creature was something warm and natural and friendly. The night was itself once more. She was ashamed of her panic.

She stooped down and called softly: "Bobbie, Bobbie, you dear little thing, come here! I think you ought to be in bed. We both should be in bed, you and I."

With a shake of her ears, Bobbie ran up to her and dropped on the tiles at Kate's feet something which she had been carrying in her mouth. Kate thought it might be the string doll she had been playing with this afternoon, and bent forward to look at it.

The glow from the window shone vaguely across the terrace. There was something a little queer about Bobbie's prize: as far as Kate could make out, the string, if it was string, looked finer, and silkier than she remembered, with an odd effect, in the diminished light, of being itself luminous.

She reached down in curiosity, picked it up, and realized with a chill of repugnance that it was hair, hair that might be either white or of the palest gold. At the same instant she felt something slimy and warm that slipped down into her palm like a small sluggish reptile. She tried to fling the hair from her, but a strand caught in a ring she was wearing, so that for a moment she could not shake it loose. Then the whole sky reeled, and she in deathly sickness was reeling with it; she heard in the distance a scream which she dimly knew had come from her own throat.

What Bobbie had brought in out of the night was a scalp lock, sticky and bleeding, cut or brutally torn from a woman's head.

5

It seemed to Kate that the next instant Mr. Gladstone was crouching beside her, lifting her head and shoulders, but as her brain cleared she suspected that she had been lying there on the tiles for more than a minute.

"My dear Kate," he exclaimed, "what happened? Did you see a ghost?"

This was the first time in her life she had fainted and Kate was ashamed of herself. "No," she said, and tried to smile. "It was only—it was that awful hair. Where is it?"

She drew in a trembling breath and looked to either side of her. The lock had disappeared, though Bobbie sat a few feet away, staring at her with lowered head and ears drooping forward.

"If you'll help me up—" she said. "I'm afraid I'm still a bit shaky."

Then as Mr. Gladstone raised her shoulders and she scrambled to her feet, she saw that the scalp lock had been all the time close beside her: when she had fallen, her dress had covered it. The rushing blackness seethed upward again and for a moment she thought she was gone; but this time she was able to control it.

"There!" she said, and pointed. "There! You see?"

"Good God!" Mr. Gladstone exclaimed. "Where in hell did that thing come from?"

"It was Bobbie," she said. "Bobbie brought it in from the bushes—from the woods, I guess, behind the garden."

Mr. Gladstone stared out into the night, and Kate, very close beside him, followed his gaze. The next moment she clutched his arm, as she noticed something moving along one of the farther paths.

"Who's there?" Mr. Gladstone called sharply.

"It's Paul Hatfield," a familiar voice answered. "Is anything wrong? Didn't I hear someone scream?"

"We've got something pretty to show you," Mr. Gladstone said. "Perhaps you know more about it than we do. It was brought in from the woods."

"You arouse my curiosity," Mr. Hatfield said, and paused a moment to stoop and greet Bobbie who had streaked across the grass and now was jumping about his legs.

"Was Bobbie with you just now?" Mr. Gladstone asked. "Did you hear or see anything strange?"

"Bobbie was not with me," Mr. Hatfield said, crossing the grass to the terrace, "and the only strange thing I heard was a scream. It gave me quite a start. I was on the track of a great horned owl, where the woods begin to rise toward the bluff. What's the exhibit?"

At that moment Ralph stepped up on to the terrace from around the front corner of the house, and a second later Jo appeared around the other corner, from the herb garden.

"Did I imagine it?" Ralph asked. "Or did some woman scream?"

"My dear Ralph," Jo said, "even my imagination could not have invented that scream—much less yours. Why Paul, you back again? And Kate, my dear child, you still up and about? Don't tell me it was you! Why wasn't I here to protect you?"

"Gentlemen," Mr. Gladstone announced, "a minute ago, just before you arrived, Paul asked me what the exhibit was. If you'll step over here, I'll be glad to show you what the dog brought in. It rather disturbed Kate, and I can't say that I wonder."

For a minute the four men stared down at the bloody disheveled coil in silence, and Kate, turning away, looked off to the black woods beyond the garden, and the veiled luminous spaces of the sky. She saw a bluish star which she recognized as Vega, but even its familiarity could not break through this dark enchantment. The faraway chirping sound once more filled her ears, and she wondered who else might be listening, from out of that thick shadow.

"But that looks like Clotilde's hair!" Ralph exclaimed suddenly. "It *is* Clotilde's hair!"

There was such a sharp note of anguish in his voice that Kate, to her bitter shame, felt for an instant a pang of disillusionment, which was swept away at once in her sense of horror. Without another word, Ralph turned and strode into the house, and as Kate watched him running the length of the living room, her horror became filled with pity.

"At any rate, it's obviously meant to give that impression," Professor Hatfield said after the briefest pause.

"What do you mean?' Mr. Gladstone asked sharply. "What makes you say that?"

"I only mean," the professor explained, "that since Clotilde's hair is such a striking color, it's natural to assume that any lock of the same color is hers; but Clotilde is not the only woman in the world whose hair is that shade of very pale gold."

"We'll soon find out," Mr. Gladstone said in a hard, strained voice. "Kate, perhaps you'll rouse June and Mavis, if Ralph hasn't. And Jo, you might go for Felix and Ruby, and even the Larsons. I think it might be well to get everyone together."

"An excellent idea," Mr. Hatfield agreed.

Kate ran through the big room, as Ralph had done the minute before. Jo was close behind her. In the lower hall she stopped for him to catch up with her.

"Which is Mavis' room?" she asked him.

"It's the door opposite the head of the stairs," he said. "Felix and Ruby have two rooms on the ground floor, in the kitchen wing, so unfortunately we must part company—unless you'd like me to escort you. I'd be delighted."

"No thanks," Kate said, and hurried up the stairs.

Though no hair could be more unlike June's than that awful sticky lock which she still could see in her mind, coiled like some living thing upon the tiles, it seemed to Kate that the nightmare whose presence she had felt that afternoon lurking in these cheerful rooms, saturating the quiet air of this damp green valley, had begun to manifest itself, and now there would be no stopping. June was the first to have been threatened; and in her eagerness to see that June was all right, Kate had forgotten any other fear.

At the top of the stairs she met Ralph. His face looked white and ravaged. "Clotilde's not in her room," he said. "She's not in her bathroom. She's evidently not up there."

"She couldn't be?—" Kate began, and stopped herself just in time.

But Ralph finished her question for her. "In Jo's room? Very possibly. That's where I'm going. And then I'm going to have a look around the gardens."

He brushed past her, and she hurried on until she reached June's door. It was locked; it must be locked on the inside, and that struck her as a good sign. Unless someone had climbed in the window—or through the transom.

She rapped violently on the white paneling. "June," she called, "June dear, are you there? Are you all right?"

She listened as she had never listened before, and presently she could hear something—was it a muffled groan?

"June," she repeated. "June, answer me. Can you let me in?"

"Katey," a sleepy voice called. "What is it? Is that you, Katey?"

With a rush of relief that almost took away her breath, Kate realized that the first sound she had heard had merely been the mumbling of someone aroused from sleep.

"Open the door," she said. "I have to see you."

In a minute the door opened, and June stood before her in white pajamas, her hair matted over her forehead and into her eyes like a sheep dog's.

"Get on some clothes," Kate said, "and go right downstairs. Something has happened. I must rouse your mother."

"But Katey—"

"You must do it," Kate said urgently. "I can't stop to explain. But I'm so glad you're all right, June."

Then impulsively, in her relief, she kissed June's cheek, and hurried back to the main hallway.

The door of Mavis' room was also locked. She rapped for at least a minute before she heard an answer, and then a querulous and sleepy voice called: "Do stop that awful noise! It's enough to wake the dead."

"Mrs. Gladstone," Kate answered, "I'm sorry to disturb you but something has happened—something pretty dreadful, I'm afraid. You must get up. You must come downstairs."

"What do you mean?" Mavis replied, and her voice sounded suddenly wide awake. "What has happened?"

"We don't know really, but perhaps— It looks as if someone has been murdered."

"Murdered!" Her voice rose sharply. "Someone in this house? Who is it?"

"It may not be as bad as that," Kate said. "We really know nothing yet. You'll be right down, won't you?" And she turned away from the door.

She was thankful to meet June at the top of the stairs, and took her arm as they went down side by side. When they stepped out on to the terrace, a minute later, neither Jo nor Ralph had returned.

"But Clotilde?" Mr. Gladstone asked sharply. "She wasn't in her room?"

"No, she wasn't in her room," Kate said. "Ralph's looking for her outside. Mrs. Gladstone is coming down."

"If Clotilde has been murdered!—" Mr. Gladstone exclaimed, and Kate was surprised, considering the way he had spoken of her, at the savagery in his voice.

"Let me remind you," Mr. Hatfield said, "that a scalping such as this is a comparatively minor operation. Painful and terrifying, yes, if performed without anesthetic; perhaps disfiguring, if the skin and flesh torn away encroach upon the forehead; but not dangerous. And I hardly see, if murder were involved, why anyone should bother with such a trifling addition."

Jo appeared again around the corner of the house, looked for Kate, and came over at once to stand beside her. He was followed on to the terrace by Mr. and Mrs. Larson, both of them in old flannel wrappers. A moment later Felix and Ruby stepped through the living room window.

Ruby had put a shawl and an apron over her nightgown; Felix was in his shirt and trousers, as if he had not been in bed.

"If you'll give me your attention—" Mr. Gladstone began.

He paused, and Kate, following his glance, saw Mavis hurrying toward them through the living room. Kate felt that she could gauge her curiosity by the speed with which she had appeared: her face was splotched with powder; she had smeared a daub of red on her lips, and her head was wrapped in a green silk scarf so that none of her hair was visible. She was wearing a peach-colored negligee trimmed with fur.

"What is it?" she exclaimed as she stumbled out on to the terrace. "Kate hinted at all kinds of horrors."

"If you will give me your attention," Mr. Gladstone began again, "I'll tell you why I've sent for you. A little while ago Bobbie deposited this scalp lock on the terrace. She brought it in from the woods behind the garden—at least from that direction. The hair is the color and texture of Clotilde's. Kate has just told us that Clotilde is not in her room. Ralph is now looking for her."

Mavis pushed her way between Jo and Felix. "Let me see it," she ordered. "It will probably make me sick, but I must see it. Where?—"

She bent down as she noticed that the lock lay on the tiles in front of her. She glanced dramatically around her, and Kate could picture her raising her finger to her lips; then pulling her negligee closely about her she leaned forward as if she were fascinated.

"Yes, that is Clotilde's hair," she said in a half whisper.

"You're sure?" Mr. Gladstone asked curtly.

Mavis stood up. "Of course I'm sure," she said in her natural voice. "It had begun to darken a few years ago and Clotilde had to have it treated every so often. I remember telling her only last week that the muddy natural tint was quite noticeable close to the scalp, and if you examine this, you'll see that I was right. You can tell the difference even out here."

Mr. Gladstone took a step toward her. "You hated Clotilde," he said threateningly.

"Yes, I did! I did!" she exclaimed in a rising voice. "Clotilde deserved anything, but you couldn't think that I— All this is too horrible. It's just come over me. It's really amusing it's so horrible!"

She threw back her head and began to laugh, drawing in her breath like a child with the whooping cough.

Mr. Gladstone gave her a hard slap on each cheek. Mavis shook her head and suddenly became silent.

"I'm sorry, my dear Mavis," he said, "but just now Clotilde, although absent, is the center of the stage."

"May I suggest," Felix said, breaking a moment's startled pause, "that it might be a good thing for someone to call the police. Or perhaps you've already done it, Mr. Gladstone."

"No, I haven't," Mr. Gladstone said. "I will." And he strode into the house.

Vega was still coldly shining in the depths of the summer sky. The air was faintly sweet, not so much, it seemed, from the flowers in the garden, as from the miles and miles of damp sleeping forest. As they stood here now on this dim terrace, waiting for Mr. Gladstone's return, Kate thought all at once of the hour before dinner, and the noise, the gaiety as they drank their cocktails; it reminded her of the second act of "Parsifal" when the magic garden is turned into a desert, except that here the spell was not broken: it had only grown darker and more ominous.

In a couple of minutes Mr. Gladstone returned, and with him came Ralph.

"Ralph has been looking everywhere," Mr. Gladstone said grimly. "He couldn't find a trace of Clotilde. And the telephone's out. I guess the wire has been cut."

"But that would mean someone has been up here near the house, wouldn't it?" Jo asked.

"Not necessarily. The wire is brought in from the road on half a dozen trees. Some of them have plenty of branches. You wouldn't even have to climb a pole to cut it."

"I always said we should have it put underground," Mavis remarked.

"Shut up!" Mr. Gladstone said savagely. Then turning to Felix, he went on: "Where's the nearest telephone? It would be at the Torgersons', wouldn't it?"

"If you would wait just a minute," Professor Hatfield suggested before Felix had a chance to reply, "an idea has occurred to me. It might possibly be well to wait a moment before summoning the police. They are easier to get hold of than to get rid of."

"But surely—" Ralph began.

"Hear what the professor has to say," Mr. Gladstone ordered. "What is it, Paul?"

"My idea is this," Professor Hatfield said. "You can take it for what it's worth. In the first place, this crime, whatever it turns out to be—"

"Whatever it turns out to be!" Mavis exclaimed. "It's obviously murder. Clotilde's murder."

"Will you shut up?" Mr. Gladstone rumbled, and Kate could imagine him striking her again.

Professor Hatfield cleared his throat. "I was going to say that the performance of the crime must have been upset by Bobbie's getting hold of the lock. All of us who know Bobbie realize that no one could count upon her neatly delivering it here—even if it were someone whom she knew well. With due respect to her owners, Bobbie cannot be described as a well-disciplined dog."

"Are you implying," Jo asked, "that this thing was done by someone whom Bobbie knew, some one of us?"

"I'll request nobody to interrupt the professor for any reason whatever," Mr. Gladstone said fiercely. "Now, Paul—"

"It might be well to state first," Mr. Hatfield went on, "that I'm implying nothing. I'm merely trying to explain what seems to me to have happened, on the basis of the facts we know. I think, then, we can take it that the schedule of the crime must have been upset by Bobbie's action. Undoubtedly the scalping was an important part of the crime. In fact, as far as we know, it may be the whole crime."

Kate noticed that Mavis was about to interrupt again, caught her husband's eye, and subsided with a shrug of her shoulders. As the professor continued talking, in his dry meticulous voice, Kate felt that she was attending a strange class in a nightmare. She glanced at the faces she could see: every one was concentrating upon his words; she could imagine a shadowy blackboard behind him; each sentence seemed clear and reasonable, and yet the whole thing, like the phrases in a dream when you try to remember them later, was fantastic.

"When I say, 'the whole crime,'" he went on, "I'm simply suggesting that we haven't the faintest proof Clotilde has been murdered. The criminal, however, we do know, cut the telephone wires. That was an added detail, an added risk. He must have realized that we could use another telephone, that we could reach one in a very few minutes. Since the police could not get here in less than half an hour, those few extra minutes couldn't make much difference to him. Why then did he go to the trouble of cutting the telephone wire? He must have felt, it seems to me, that if he could postpone our telephoning for only a few minutes, he might be able to persuade us not to telephone at all. He could only do that by providing us with some reason in consideration of which we ourselves might decide we did not want to telephone—in other words, some reason why we should prefer not to notify the police. If the crime had been allowed to take what I might describe as its due course—a course which we can now trace back as far as June's mysterious letter of nearly a week ago—I suspect we should have received some word, some warning to that effect, not later than our discovery of the crime itself. That was all I wished to say."

"In other words," Ralph remarked in a dry unnatural voice, "you're telling us you think the criminal is trying to do precisely what you yourself are doing at this moment: stalling us off from the police."

Professor Hatfield looked pleased, Kate thought; in fact he almost seemed to smile.

"Very neatly put," he said. "Very exact. I suppose I may be acting as a kind of providential proxy for the criminal. But if so, I'm acting not only in his interests but in our own as well. But I could hardly expect my tactics, however ingenious, to keep you from telephoning very long, unless something should occur to substantiate my hypothesis. In the meanwhile, since various ones of us, including yourself, I believe, Ralph, were out of doors at the time, it might be well if we'd each say exactly where we were and what we were doing. Who knows? One of us may un-wittingly have seen some trace of the criminal or observed some clue. I'll begin with myself. I was in the woods, near the foot of the bluff. I was looking for an owl I'd observed there only last night. Although I was in somewhat the same direction, apparent-ly, from which Bobbie appeared, I heard nothing out of the way or unusual until Kate's scream. I then came here with all possible haste. And now—" He turned to Mr. Gladstone, as if he were introducing the next speaker at a banquet—"perhaps you will question the rest of us, Norman. It will be simpler to have some kind of orderly procedure."

"I agree with you," Mr. Gladstone said. "I might say that I was in my study looking up some chess problems. When I heard Kate's scream, I came out here at once. Ralph and I had stopped our game a good half hour before. You said you were going for a walk, Ralph. Where did you go and what did you see?"

"I walked down to the main road, and then up to the top of the hill in the direction of town," Ralph said stiffly. "I heard an owl. I heard a whippoorwill. I saw a rabbit or two. That was all. Not a sign of a human being. No cars passed me. I was a hundred feet or so outside the gate when I thought I heard a scream." He paused, and for that instant Kate felt that he was shuddering. "I wasn't sure where it came from," he went on directly, "but I thought it was from the house."

Mr. Gladstone glanced around as if to decide whom he would question next. "And you, Olaf," he asked, "where were you?"

"I was asleep in my bed," Mr. Larson told him, with his Nor-wegian accent. "Emmy and I were both asleep. We were sleeping since nine until he came to wake us up."

"You couldn't have seen much then," Mr. Gladstone said, and Kate noticed that when he spoke to Olaf his tone was kinder than she had yet heard it. "What about you, Felix?"

"I was doing a crossword puzzle in my room," Felix said. "I may have heard the scream, but of course that's on the other side of the house, and it was so faint I didn't pay any attention. When I'm doing those puzzles, I'm just about lost to the world."

"And Ruby?"

"I was in my bed and asleep," Ruby said shortly.

"What about you, Jo?"

"Like several other of you gentlemen," Jo said, "I was taking a stroll. I had been playing. My emotions were a little disturbed." He paused, and Kate looked away as he sent her a meaningful glance. "I thought a walk on this lovely night would prepare me for sleep. I too heard the scream. I know so little of your night animals, I thought it might be one of them. Then I said to myself: 'That scream is horribly human. It is the scream not of an injured body but of a terrified soul. I'd better investigate'; so I turned back and found you here on the terrace."

Kate started, as someone behind her seized her arm. Looking around, she saw June who was staring across the garden, in the direction from which Bobbie had come.

"Kate," she whispered, "did you see anything move over there?"

"Where?" Kate asked. "In the garden?"

"Yes—yes! I saw it too!" It was Mavis' voice, with again a tinge of hysteria in its rising inflection. She had pushed in between Kate and Jo and stood in complete silence since Mr. Gladstone had spoken to her so fiercely. "Something dark and swooping!"

"Did you really see anything, Mavis?" Mr. Gladstone asked sternly. "If so, tell us what it was."

"I don't know," Mavis faltered. "I couldn't describe it. It was something that moved stealthily, over there, near the end of the garden, beyond the sundial."

Kate herself, as she peered into the shadows, could see no trace of movement anywhere; then she could imagine that the whole darkness was seething like live steam.

"It will do us no good inventing things," Mr. Gladstone growled. "There's enough that's real, without that."

But at that moment Bobbie ran barking down the grassy slope, not toward the sundial where everyone had been looking, but to the nearer edge of the garden, at the left, where one of the paths skirted some lilac bushes.

"What's that she's got?" Mr. Gladstone called. "Take it from her! Hurry!"

And Kate, with a dizzy feeling, saw Bobbie, not ten yards away, standing over some small white object, giving little playful growls and grunts, as if she would defend it with her life.

Ralph stooped, brushed Bobbie aside, and picked it up.

"It's a letter!" he exclaimed. "At least I think it is. It's an envelope and it's weighted—I suppose so he could shy it further." He handed it to Mr. Gladstone. "Jo! Felix!" He shouted with a kind of fierce exuberance. "Come along! Let's see if we can catch him!"

The next instant the three men had dashed across the garden and were plunging into the woods, with Bobbie yodeling at their heels.

"What is it?" Mavis eagerly asked of Mr. Gladstone, as he stepped back on to the terrace. "Who's it from? What does it say?"

"That I shall know presently, when I have read it," Mr. Gladstone answered her curtly, and slipped the letter into his pocket.

"Olaf," he said, "I see no reason why you and Emmy shouldn't go back to bed. And you too, Ruby."

"Good night, Sir," Olaf said, and he and his wife walked around the corner of the house into the darkness. Ruby, without a word, tramped back through the living room.

Mr. Gladstone drew out a large pocket handkerchief, spread it by its two upper corners, as if he were a magician about to perform a trick. Then he stooped, put it over the bloody lock, wrapped the linen carefully around it, picked up the small bundle, and followed Ruby into the house.

Kate caught herself guessing what he would do with it. Would he put it in a safe? In the icebox? In a bureau drawer? What would you do with your daughter's scalp? A question for Emily Post.

The lock, she noticed, had left a smear on the tiles, like the trace of some gigantic slug. She drew in her breath sharply. It required all the strength of her will not to start laughing hysterically, as Mavis had done; and once she had started, she felt that she could never stop.

Fortunately at that moment June put her arm around her and held her tight. "It's not fair!" she exclaimed in an intense passionate voice which brought Kate at once to herself. "I got you into this, Katey. It's all my fault. I brought you out here. You must go away tomorrow. I can't keep you here now. Clotilde didn't even get one of those letters, and look what they did to her!"

"I'm in no danger," Kate said. "No one's after me. How do you think I'd feel if I ran away?"

June's arm tightened about her with an almost savage energy.

"I want you to go!" she exclaimed. "I couldn't bear it if anything happened to you."

"You can't get rid of me as easily as that," Kate said, but she felt that her tone was shamefully fainthearted.

6

"If you'd only tell us what's in the envelope," Mavis urged. "Norman, you're positively sadistic, keeping us in suspense like this."

"I told you once," Mr. Gladstone said coldly, "that when Jo and Felix and Ralph come back, you shall hear all about it—not that I think it will give you much pleasure. In the meanwhile I'm in no mood for obscene female curiosity."

They had been sitting here in the living room, Kate supposed, for not more than twenty-five minutes, but she had the impression that there were infinite wastes of night behind her, all around her. On the drowsy fringes of her memory were hours when, as a child, she had waited in dentists' offices, waited so long, it seemed, that her fear had been drained of its living quality and simply lay on her mind like something inert and dead, an indistinguishable part of the boredom of prolonged suspense. Mr. Gladstone sat in a big chair near the fireplace, and the lamp on the table beside him emphasized the pockets beneath his eyes, the sagging of his jowls; as he glowered at the empty hearth, it seemed to Kate that he had aged in the course of the evening. Mavis, slumped in the chair opposite his, kept yawning nervously; her powder had settled into the wrinkles of her cheeks and gave her face a scaly appearance suggestive of leprosy. Kate was glad that at least June was beside her here on the sofa. At first they had talked to each other in low voices, but now June's face had stiffened into a sleepy mask. Only Professor Hatfield seemed to be content with the situation: he had picked up a copy of

Time magazine and was reading with every sign of interest, his head cocked to one side.

Kate hardly noticed it when at last Bobbie walked in from the terrace, her tongue lolling out, her head drooping so that her ears almost swept the floor. But the next minute Ralph and Felix entered, with Jo a few steps behind them. Their damp shirts clung to their bodies; a twig was still caught in Ralph's hair.

Mr. Gladstone raised his head without otherwise changing his position, and stared somberly at them. He reminded Kate just then of a corrupt and powerful Renaissance pope receiving a legation.

"Well?" he asked.

The three men glanced at each other. Then Felix spoke.

"I'm sorry, sir," he said, "but we didn't find a sign of anyone or anything. I went up to the left, to the top of the bluff through the woods, and Bobbie was with me. She carried on so at first, I thought we might be on the trail of someone. Then she left me and joined Mr. Ralph who was working along through the bottom lands. Mr. Jo says he went down toward the road and the open fields. Coming back, not five minutes ago, I thought I had some one sure, but it was only Mr. Jo and Mr. Ralph."

The smooth respect with which he spoke to his employer did not prevent, Kate thought, a tinge of irony in the "Mr.'s" that he attached to the names of Ralph and Jo.

"It occurred to me," Ralph said, "that it would be easy to get down the bluff to the river. If there was a small boat ready, a man, or a group of men, could be miles downstream by now. Or they could land on the other side. With the bluffs and the bottom lands going on for miles, a gang might stay hidden indefinitely."

"You seem to have given some study to the terrain," Mr. Gladstone said drily. "But now I should like to read you the interesting letter that was thrown into the garden. It is printed in red crayon which, Professor Hatfield tells me, seems to be quite a fetish of our correspondent—that is, if one assumes that all the letters were sent from the same source."

He spread open the folded sheets of paper, looked around at his audience for a moment, and began reading as if the message were of no personal concern to himself or anyone present.

My dear Mr. Gladstone:

In spite of the rather sensational way in which this has reached you, it is merely a routine business letter. My friends and I should like you to hand over fifty thousand dollars. Since we prefer it in cold cash, in bills no larger than $50, and since naturally you do not have that much on hand, we will give you until day after tomorrow, which allows you the whole of tomorrow to make arrangements. In day after tomorrow's (Saturday's) mail you will receive instructions as to where and when we should like it delivered. As you see, this is just the old kidnapping racket.

If there is any new twist to it, it is because we have noticed that kidnapping in the past has often failed because the kidnappers had either too little imagination or too much sentiment. They haven't put themselves in the place of the victim's family. Their threats have been unconvincing, and sometimes they have failed to carry them out.

I can understand the temptation on your part to call in the police. "How will the kidnappers know?" you say to yourself. "We'll take a chance on it." Mr. Gladstone, you may take a chance, but it is to convince you of the imprudence of such a course that we are sending you the scalp of your daughter, Clotilde. If we have the slightest reason to suspect that this affair is mentioned to the police, or to any living soul outside this immediate household, you will receive other, and more essential portions of your daughter's very lovely body, chosen in such a way that she may, by the grace of God, still survive.

You will be relieved to hear, I know, that the little operation does not seem to have affected her general health, but I'm sorry to say that her morale is definitely low. She's the type of girl who believes in taking chances, I guess, but I'm sure she would join me in urging you not to take this one.

Our real talking point, however, is not only what may happen to Clotilde. I say this so you won't feel inclined, at any time, to write her off as a total loss. When it comes to prying loose a sum of money, even such a trifle as $50,000, we believe the more leverage the better. So we're not just counting on the little surgical operations you might force us to perform on Clotilde, but on what will happen to June as well, if the cash isn't delivered without any monkey business. We are using Clotilde as a kind of sample or warning.

I must tell you that if any attempt is made to smuggle June out of this region, as a protective measure, we will finish off Clotilde in some appropriate manner, and also some of the boys would then count on having a little fun with her first. Also, I can promise you that sooner or later we'd catch up with the unlucky June.

For every reason then we suggest that you will comply with our demand. We know it is well within your means. We have taken care to be reasonable. Even a father's heart might hesitate to part with, say, $200,000. One sign of the lack of imagination in kidnappers is their failure to understand how much even the very wealthy—or I might say, most of all the very wealthy—hate to part with large sums of money. But $50,000—that is a small affair. We don't insult you by suspecting that you will hesitate. Come across, and everything will be all right except the little matter of Clotilde's scalp, and damage there can be hidden by the right kind of hair-do. Hold back, gossip, with a neighbor, call in the police, and you, and your two daughters, I do assure you, will be sorry.

At the mention of her name June had clutched Kate's fingers, and now in the moment of silence as Mr. Gladstone's voice stopped abruptly, Kate thought that she could hear June's heart thumping; or perhaps it was her own that she heard. The long bright room, the group of people, surrounded her like a wavering film that barely managed to keep out an abyss of darkness; the only real thing was the feeling of June's palm pressed tightly against hers, the hot grip of her fingers. For June's sake, for the sake of this child who trusted her, whose sole friend she was, she must keep her head. In this horrible time she must prove herself of some use.

"Perhaps you can guess my reason for reading you this literary effort," Mr. Gladstone continued grimly. "Among other things it's a proof of the intelligence of Professor Hatfield, to whom I'm deeply grateful." He gave a sharp glance from the corner of his eye at the professor. "I should certainly curse myself if I had got in touch with the police. And now I make to you all the absolute request that none of you, for any reason whatever, say a word to a living soul of what has happened. It may be just as well that the telephone is disconnected; though on second thoughts, perhaps not. You'd better get in touch with the company tomorrow, Felix, unless you find that you can fix the wire. It's conceivable that the kidnappers might want to call us up. As they state in their letter, their demand under the circumstances is moderate. I believe in taking chances for myself, but not for my daughters. If any of you, deliberately or accidentally, should spread any hint of the state of affairs, I'll hold him completely responsible for the results. And now, good night, everybody!"

He slouched heavily to the door; then, looking back, he added with a suggestion of his sardonic smile:

"I'm afraid it would be useless to wish you pleasant dreams."

7

As she stood in the sun, the next morning, on the grassy bank that skirted the front of the house, Kate felt it was lucky perhaps that she could not remember her dreams.

Mavis had not appeared for breakfast, and every now and then Kate had caught herself thinking of Clotilde, also, as lying comfortably in bed. This would remind her, each time with a new shock, of the unspeakable reality, and for a moment she could not force herself to eat. Ralph had greeted her with a fixed smile which made her think of the way he had looked at Clotilde yesterday on the terrace. For that was yesterday, of course: today was only Friday, though she could hardly make herself realize it. In spite of herself she could not keep a shade of reproach from her own glance as she returned his "Good morning." Certainly she had done nothing to make him feel that for her he must put on a mask. Then his smile had wavered. The mask was still there; but it was as if, through the painted cloth grown slightly transparent, she had caught a glimpse of distorted tense muscles, but so obscure a glimpse that she could not interpret their expression: it might be anguish, or shame—or terror. He had eaten hurriedly and excused himself before the rest. Even Jo had hardly spoken; but Mr. Gladstone had made a number of carefully trivial remarks: it was clear he intended that, so far as possible, life at the farm should proceed as usual today.

"June," he said after breakfast, "be sure you're back from your ride by half past ten. Felix is going with you. He's driving me into town at eleven, to the bank, and if you're late I'll give you hell."

When June had said she did not want to ride, he had flared up.

"You're going as usual," he said harshly. "Damn you, don't you see that if you once give in to this infernal business, you're lost!"

June had merely scowled at him; then she had turned without a word and gone upstairs. Kate had followed her to her room.

"He's right, June," she said, as June was changing into her riding clothes. "We mustn't give in." But June had remained sullen.

"It's all very fine for you to talk," she exclaimed. "He's not your father, the damn fool!" And Kate had made a pretense of laughing, as if it were a joke.

Now as she watched June and Felix, both very spruce and correct on their bay horses, trotting down the driveway, with Bobbie scampering beside them, she wondered what she should do for the next hour. June had promised that she would teach her to ride, but Kate was just as glad the lesson had not started this morning. The only person she could bear to see at present was Ralph; she felt that he would want to be left alone; so she avoided the house and walked around over the lawn to the garden.

As the sun glistened on the pink gravel paths, the turf edgings, burning up the dew that remained on the leaves and petals, it was hard to associate this spot with the shadowy terror of last night. A catbird alighted on the sundial and stared at her. The top of its gray back, the surface of each leaf, the spaces of lawn, the loop of the distant road, were all reflecting in their separate colors the shimmering blue sky. "I mustn't give in!" she repeated to herself. "I mustn't give in! I must take each hour as it comes and not let myself start imagining."

Nonetheless, when someone called her name from behind the hedge of junipers that separated the garden from the woods, she barely checked her impulse to cry out, before she recognized the voice as Professor Hatfield's.

"Kate," he called softly. "Listen to me, my dear. I'm sorry if I startled you. I've been in the offing for the last hour or so, hoping I could make contact with you. Walk to the arch that leads out of here. I've got several things I'd like to say to you."

Puzzled, and a little annoyed with him for the scare he had given her, Kate followed the path to the rose-covered archway that

led into the woods. As she stepped through it, out of the glare of
the garden into the damp shadow, it was like walking into a vault.
Professor Hatfield was waiting for her, standing with what struck
her as almost unnatural stillness at the foot of a hickory tree.

"I don't see why you had to be so mysterious, even if you did
want to speak to me," she said irritably. "What difference would
it make if anyone saw us?"

"My dear girl, I can quite understand," he said in a soothing
tone. "Naturally it's disconcerting to have your name called from
out of a bush, especially after what happened last night. And
very possibly there's no earthly reason why everyone in the house
shouldn't know of our meeting this morning, but I would rather err
on the safe side. Perhaps you can guess why I want to talk to you."

"I'm afraid I can't," she said, still a little coldly.

"Well," he said, as if eager to be quite fair, "that's natural too.
As a matter of fact, there are really several different reasons—
different though interrelated. In the first place, I felt I ought to
caution you."

"Caution me," she repeated, in uneasy surprise. "Against what?"

His thin lips smiled at her. "Well, let's say against coming out
into the dark woods, when somebody calls your name mysteriously from behind a tree, as I did just now. Especially if there is
no one else around."

Her heartbeats quickened unpleasantly. As she looked at him,
here in this deep-green shadow, standing with such almost furtive stillness under the tree, she could imagine that his unblink-
ing eyes which had yesterday reminded her of a bird's were instead the eyes of a snake.

"Don't be silly!" she exclaimed with somewhat forced impatience. "Didn't you want me to come?"

"Yes, my dear Kate, I did," he said, "and I assure you I'm
quite harmless. But perhaps someone else would not have been."

"I'd probably have run for the house," she said, "if I hadn't
recognized your voice."

"Ah, but that's the point I'm trying to make," he exclaimed.
"Just because you recognize the voice of someone doesn't necessarily mean that he's not dangerous."

Again, for a moment, her heart felt too big for her chest; it took an effort to breathe naturally. "You mean that someone I know—someone in the house—may be dangerous? You mean that someone in the house may be connected—with this—with Clotilde?"

"That's precisely what I mean," he said with a confidential drop in his voice, "and that's why I thought it might be just as well if no one saw that you and I were having this little talk. He might have suspected that we were up to something. It might have put him on his guard."

"But who is he?" she asked incredulously. "How can you know?"

"I don't know," Professor Hatfield admitted. "And even if I knew that it was some member of the household, I wouldn't have the slightest idea who. That's another reason why I wanted to see you. You are completely an outsider. It's obvious that you at least could have nothing to do with this. It would have been ironic should I have chosen the criminal to confer with. So I thought that you were the logical person to help me discover if possible who he is."

She shrank from this idea as if he had offered her some poisonous thing to eat.

"But it can't be anyone in the house," she exclaimed the next moment in relief, "because everyone was gathered on the terrace when that dreadful letter was thrown into the garden."

"Ah but," he said, "to abduct a young woman and hold her somewhere for ransom would obviously require more than one person. Two people, I should say, at the very least, when you consider the necessity for first-aid treatment. I'm merely suggesting that one of them, and it seems to me highly probable the guiding mind of the scheme, belongs to the household."

They had been walking slowly along a path through the woods and now they came to a small six-sided summerhouse of mossy latticework. A Virginia creeper covered one side of it and had reached from the top to the overhanging branch of an oak tree.

"We might go in and sit down," he suggested. "The chairs are comfortable and you look as if you had found the strain of the last twelve hours a little wearing."

He stood back courteously for Kate to enter first. The light in here was even dimmer and greener than outside; only a few intensely white spots of sun, piercing the leaves and the lattice-work, brought out as in a detailed drawing the grain of the old wooden floor and made the prevailing shadow deeper and more liquid. Once again Kate had the sense that this whole valley, like a lost region in a fairy tale, was buried under deep water—water that little by little would chill you to the bone and prevent your breathing.

"But why should it be someone in the house?" she asked with an effort, after she had seated herself in a low wicker armchair. "It's horrible, it's ridiculous, to think that someone here on the farm would do such a thing."

"Horrible, I admit," he said. "Ridiculous, no. Let me give you some of my reasons. How many people outside of this household, do you think, knew that you were coming here to the farm? I'm the only friend the family sees much of out here, and Mr. Gladstone hadn't even mentioned it to me. I doubt if anyone knew, unless he were purposely informed of the fact. The farm keeps very much to itself nowadays; it's a little community of its own, as I told you yesterday; and yet you received that warning letter. You can see that if there was any scheme involving June, a loyal friend who might be expected to be with her most of the time would be a major complication, but nonetheless that note was a mistake. If I had been arranging things, I never would have allowed it to be sent. And then there's the question of Bobbie. We know she must have been somewhere near when the abduction, and the mutilation, occurred. Had there been only strangers she would undoubtedly have barked, or rather howled, with that particularly piercing voice she has begun to develop; and even if it had been as far away as the main road we would have heard her. Whereas she would have slipped along after one of the household without making a sound. Then consider the actual technique of the crime. Clotilde was probably approached fairly near the house by someone who on one pretext or another lured her further away. It would be far simpler if this were someone she knew and felt completely at home with. It seems probable that she was engaged in conversation when an accomplice attacked her from behind, and knocked her unconscious or possibly drugged her. It seems almost certain, moreover, that whoever managed the affair was thoroughly familiar with the ways of the household. After all, there are a great many people around here."

"You needn't go on," Kate said. "I can see your point. But Professor Hatfield, why should they do such a thing? It wouldn't be just for that money, would it—especially if they had to divide it up?"

"I hate to think," he said, "how many crimes have been committed—brutal, hideous crimes—for far smaller sums. Various people in our little group, to start with myself, could gladly do with more cash. There's Felix, Jo, Ralph, Mavis—"

"Mavis!" Kate exclaimed. "You surely don't think that Mavis—"

"I'm only saying that Mavis, along with the others, could gladly do with fifty thousand, or even a share of it. Most of Mr. Gladstone's money came from his first wife, Clotilde's mother. Mavis didn't have a thing. She has to get along on what Norman gives her and she doesn't like it. But I think you're quite right in this case not to consider merely the money motive. I shouldn't be at all surprised if a good part of it were budgeted as wages for the outside help, whose responsibility and risk it will be to collect it. Though of course there may be a second demand, after the first is acceded to. It would be a piquant touch, for example, to ask for another fifty thousand for medical expenses."

"But then, if it's not the money," Kate asked wearily, "what other motive?—"

Professor Hatfield gave his dry chuckle. "I said not *merely* the money," he corrected. "Undoubtedly it entered into the scheme. But my dear girl, there is a whole tangle of plausible personal motives to back it up. Let's start with Mavis: as you no doubt have guessed she couldn't abide Clotilde. Clotilde has always resented her father's second marriage, and lately there has been the question of Jo. Jo belonged to Mavis. Mr. Gladstone who is not old-fashioned and who is perhaps a shade cynical did not object to the situation, and I think it rather amused him. But when Clotilde came back from New York this spring, Jo began to find her very attractive—much more so, I'm afraid, than poor old Mavis. Jo loves comfort but he also loves beauty. However, Clotilde was engaged to Ralph. She'd met him last winter in New York where he was working in the Bell Laboratories, waiting for his navy commission to come through. Apparently she took him by storm. Clotilde, to speak mildly, is a rather domineering, a rather spoiled girl, but she can be as smooth as silk when she wants to. She is used to getting whatever she sets her heart on. As Ralph came to know her better, to see her in her native habitat, he began to regret the situation—unless I've read the signs all wrong. All the more so, as Clotilde seemed to find Jo intensely congenial. Personally, I think she was only trying to hold Ralph by stirring up his jealousy. Now Jo is clever—more so than you might think; he's also fiery. It wouldn't be surprising if he realized that Clotilde was using him for a purpose, and that he would certainly resent. Clotilde, I regret to say, rather enjoys leading men on. Even Felix. Clotilde, at one time, deliberately played up to him in a fashion that almost suggested the Countess Julie, if you're familiar with the plays of Strindberg. It wouldn't be surprising if Felix detested her, and I know Ruby does. So you see—"

"Yes, I see," Kate said, and rose from her chair: she felt she had heard about as much as she could stand, and perhaps the worst thing of all was having Ralph involved. As she thought of his face at breakfast, it seemed, incredibly, as if he too might have been bewitched by the foul enchantment of this place. "But it sounds so fantastic!" she broke out. "Suppose everything is like that, you still can't make me believe that any of these people would do such a—such a ghastly thing, for any of those reasons."

Professor Hatfield got up also. "I quite agree with you," he exclaimed. "I said the motives were plausible: they are merely that, if one is considering normal individuals. I don't think any of those motives, even with the money added, would be enough in itself to account for this particular crime. It has an atmosphere of its own, a kind of gratuitous ferocity, of macabre though quite unoriginal fantasy, that points to a very special type of mind in the person who conceived it."

"You mean," she asked, "that you think he's mad?"

"It depends on what you mean by mad," he said. "In the usual sense, no. We had a case here in Woodside last summer of a man who really was insane, obsessed by a lust for killing; I had something to do with it myself—in fact, I had the honor to figure for a time as a suspect—" he gave his little chuckle—"and this, I think, is quite different. The lust killer, apart from his obsession, may be a sensitive and scrupulous man; his particular urge is too much for him, that's all. But the thing that marks our present man is his complete absence of scruple. He must be someone for whom the moral world, the world of kindly human emotions, of love, of pity, of altruism, simply does not exist, except perhaps as an intellectual abstraction. In other words, he must be what is sometimes called a moral imbecile."

"But I thought an imbecile," Kate said, "was the same as a feeble-minded person, only even less developed."

"Not a moral imbecile," he explained. "Such people are not infrequently intelligent and quite normal except that they have no sense of right or wrong. If they tortured an animal, it would not be so much through sadism, which implies a measure of sympathy, even if perverted, as through idle curiosity. They might choke a baby to death, if its crying annoyed them. They might wreck a whole trainload of people, if it seemed a safe way to kill off a creditor among them."

Kate shuddered and stepped out of the summerhouse on to the shaded path. Professor Hatfield's description seemed to her particularly chilling and revolting. It suggested a human being who was yet not human, a stranger, an outcast who lived in the midst of men and yet inhabited a cold dreadful world of his own. Then, across the years, she remembered once when she was a little girl standing with Mother in the Jardin des Plantes in Paris and watching the hyenas. Their hair was so rubbed off, so scanty, that she could see patches of pale pinkish skin on their tight bodies. It looked almost like coarse human skin, and suddenly she had seen them not as animals but as monstrous deformed people; she could imagine them rising on their hind legs and walking toward her, with their flat heads thrust forward, their mouths dripping; she could imagine them trying to talk to her, to call her by name; and the idea had terrified her so that she began to scream, and she could never bear to tell Mother why. This man seemed such a creature as they. And according to Professor Hatfield, she might be living under the same roof with him; she might have talked with him, have shaken his hand; today she might be seeing him again. For an instant she could almost smell a faint animal stench. The white spots of sunlight stabbing through the leaves danced before her eyes. She swallowed mechanically; and then she realized that she must look ill, for Professor Hatfield had taken her arm and was guiding her gently along the path.

"Perhaps you see now why I spoke to you," he said. "Such a man—such a mind—is dangerous; once he has begun a career of actual violence he rarely stops. You and June, who have received letters, have already attracted his attention. Frankly, nothing would relieve me more than to know he was safely behind bars."

"But what can I do?" Kate asked, and her voice sounded to herself far away.

"You can keep your eyes and ears open. You can notice anything unusual, even if it seems to you quite insignificant, and you can report it to me. But I see that you don't feel well. Perhaps it is too much to ask. Perhaps I should advise you to leave at once, to go home. In fact, my dear Kate, I'll drive you into town myself this afternoon, if you don't think you can bear it out here."

The possibility of escape dazzled her; it was as if she had been shot to the surface of the water, had filled her lungs with clean fresh air. But this lasted only for an instant: there was the question of June. She had come out here, really, to help June, and now the poor girl needed her a hundred times more than ever. If Ralph were not here, Kate felt, perhaps she could not have borne it, but with Ralph to rely on, strange and tortured though he seemed, there would be no excuse for running away.

"I'll stay!" she burst out passionately, half resentfully. "Of course I can't go now. It would be mean for me to go!"

"I admire your decision," he said, and gave her arm a friendly squeeze. "And you can think of this, my dear. If anything we unearth results in rescuing Clotilde a day, or even an hour sooner, it may save her life or her reason. Clotilde is not an entirely sympathetic character; but I've always felt sorry for her. Such an upbringing as hers is not calculated to foster one's finer qualities, and now she must be going through a particular kind of hell that I don't like to imagine."

Kate shuddered. "Do you think," she asked in a voice she managed to keep firm, "do you think they may be holding her somewhere near?"

"Who can tell?" Professor Hatfield said. "The bluffs and the woods continue through two whole counties on either side of the river. There are hundreds of square miles of wilderness at our doorstep. She may be out in some hut, or some lonely farmhouse or perhaps some cave; or she may be far away by this time in a closed room in a big city. But if we can once discover our man—"

His voice stopped as if it had been switched off. He stood quite still, and his pressure on her arm tightened. She glanced at him in surprise, and saw that he had turned his head, that he was listening intently. Then she, too, heard somewhere back in the woods a slight sound—was it a footfall, the brushing of a twig?

Almost at once the professor resumed his walk along the path, but he did not speak and she herself could not bear to say anything just then. In a few minutes they had reached the arch that led into the garden. There he paused and peered out blinking into the brightness. Beyond the flowers and the lawn, she could see June and Felix on their horses, trotting up the drive, with little Bobbie loping behind them. In the gay sunlight, with the sweeps of sky overhead, the hills in the background, they were like the figures in some old English print.

"I don't want to alarm you any further," Professor Hatfield said with soft preciseness, speaking close to her ear, "but I'm afraid now there's a new reason for you to be on your guard. I have a strong suspicion, my dear, that someone was listening to our talk."

8

Kate looked up with a start from the bench by the tennis court where she had just begun a letter to her mother, and watched Jo as he came toward her out of the shrubbery that divided the court from the herb garden. There was no reason to be alarmed: here it was broad daylight; if she called, her voice would be heard on the terrace, or for that matter in the living room; but since her talk with the professor this morning, she had tried to avoid being alone with anyone—with anyone but Ralph, that is; and Ralph, she felt, had for some reason been avoiding her. It was too horrible to think that among these people there might lurk the monster Professor Hatfield had described; and yet it was not so much fear that she felt as a kind of nervous incredulity. Just as a powerful electric charge may not injure when a weaker one would kill, so the very horror of the picture in her mind made it impossible for her to relate it, with real conviction, to any of these people, strange as they were, who made up the Valley Farms household.

She had lived through the day like someone walking in his sleep: she would catch herself thinking trivial thoughts, making casual remarks, smiling or even laughing, as if this were a day like any other; then half waking, as it were, she would be swept along by such a sense of pity and horror that she wondered how she could think, or speak of anything except Clotilde—Clotilde and the all-enveloping nightmare of which her mutilation seemed only one part, one definite and ominous symptom. A few minutes ago she had finished two sets of tennis with June, whose strenuous game had badly beaten her and exhausted her wind. June was now in the house reading *Little Women*. After their tennis Kate had mentioned as tactfully as she could the reform of dress and make-up that Mr. Gladstone had suggested. June, who she was afraid might resent it, had jumped at the idea; she had insisted on fetching Kate her writing things so she would not have to move from her bench, and they had arranged a "date" for a little beauty treatment before dinner. It was incongruous, perhaps, to consider such a thing today; and yet if you did not keep your mind well filled with trivia, if you let yourself wake up, you might plunge into a gulf, like the sleepwalker whom somebody disturbs as he picks his way serenely along eaves and over roof tops.

The shadow of the bluff, which had advanced across the whole width of the court, suggested already, so long before sunset, the furtive approach of evening. Kate could not bear to think that darkness once again would be crowding in from these hills, but as she watched Jo coming nearer she forced herself to smile. Her policy of avoiding people today had not been much help toward gathering clues for Professor Hatfield. She should really seek people out of her own accord. As she thought of the awfulness of Clotilde's position, she felt fiercely ashamed of her timidity.

"So here's where you are!" Jo exclaimed. "Hidden away behind the trees, and I must say they make a lovely setting. I wish you could have seen yourself just now, as you looked up when you heard my step. It's too bad people have written so much about startled nymphs, so that the phrase stinks with banality; because really, you know, as you raised your head and tilted it to the side, with the breeze blowing back your hair so that I could see your ear, with your lips just parted, and the green leaves all around you— But of course you think this is only my line—rather quaint, rather foreign, just a shade middle-aged, eh?"

He stood in front of her bench and stared down at her with a tight-lipped smile, his thick lashes so narrowed that she could hardly see the whites of his eyes.

She returned his smile. "Not middle-aged," she said. "Just quaint and foreign."

As he laughed, she noticed the smallness, the evenness of his teeth; his blue-black hair, his intensely swarthy skin, gave his smile the brilliance of an Hawaiian's.

"May I sit down?" he asked. "You wouldn't mind too much?"

"What makes you think I'd mind?"

"My dear Kate," he said, "you are innocent, yes, but you are no fool. You must have seen something of our situation here. You must have thought my own part was perhaps a shade equivocal; and it really was more than anything to explain my position that I was eager to talk to you today—as soon as I could."

"You mustn't feel you have to explain anything," Kate said coldly. "I don't think it's any of my business."

He sat down beside her and hitched up his white trousers so that she could see his finely knitted cream-colored socks.

"My little Kate," he exclaimed, "when you know me better, you'll realize that I never feel 'I have to' do anything. The phrase is abhorrent to me. I am a musician, an artist; I need congenial surroundings to do my best work. If I could improve my playing, I would pimp without shame for a house of prostitution. My art comes first."

"I've always heard," Kate said, "that too much comfort was apt to be a bad influence on an artist. It might make him lazy. It seems to me most of the great ones had quite a struggle."

"Ah, but I am also a sensualist," he said. "I love good food, good drinks, beautiful scenes and exquisite women. I love to receive pleasure; I love even more to give it, which is the refined essence of sensuality. If I can procure some passing joy for Mavis, in return for what she, and her most understanding husband, my good friend Norman, can offer me, who am I to hold back? But, as I told you last night, I make distinctions. Mavis, Clotilde are bad women, and it is not merely a question of physical chastity. You, my dear Kate, are a good woman; no matter what you do, even should you be dragged through the gutter, you will always remain one. Last night, you may remember, I virtually pushed you from my room. I would not even go with you out into the darkness. It was no lack of admiration—quite the reverse. It was my homage to the immaculate."

During his last words a chilling and incredible doubt had made it hard for Kate to maintain her smile: had Jo pushed her from his room yesterday evening so that he might be free to follow Clotilde into the shadows from which she had vanished? Had it occurred to him that his behavior, if Kate thought of it afterward, might arouse her suspicions? Had all this talk of his just now, this unfolding of his character, been merely leading up to an excuse for his impatience to get rid of her? She felt that she must say something quickly or he would wonder at her silence. Then, with intense relief, she noticed that Mavis, in peacock-blue silk, with a rose stuck in the brassy halo of her hair, had appeared from the herb garden, and was watching them from under her raised eyebrows.

"So there you are!" she exclaimed. "My dear Jo, I feel responsible for Kate while she is in my house, and I refuse to have her seduced before my eyes. Kate darling, don't listen to anything he says. The only time you can trust him is when he has his violin in his hands, and sometimes even then I think I should feel safer if he played the cello. But speaking of violins, Jo, my dove, I thought we were going to run through some sonatas before dinner. You've been playing so much lately with poor Clotilde that I'm afraid you are shamefully out of practice."

Jo rose briskly from the bench. "My precious Mavis," he said, "I was just coming to get you, but you can hardly blame me for lingering. A cup of pure spring water is delightful sometimes after even the choicest and oldest wine."

He glanced down at Kate and laughed, and his face for a moment looked startlingly young and unguarded. "Whatever else you may have learned," he said, "at least you will have gathered that I love to talk about myself."

Kate watched them as they disappeared into the shrubbery, and noticed with a faint feeling of repulsion how Mavis managed to give this breezy tennis court, the wall of shadowed foliage, the air of a stage from which she was making her exit. Kate glanced up at the sky to catch once more the sense that she was out of doors. White brilliant towers of cloud were floating upward in the blue; it was the kind of afternoon that makes you think of kites flying, of flags waving. There were still some hours before darkness.

Then as she turned to pick up her writing pad, she saw from the tail of her eye a man's figure gliding from one of the poplars directly behind her to another one a few yards away.

Before she had time to be scared she recognized it as Ralph's. For a moment she felt slightly sick: Ralph was the last person she could have imagined eavesdropping and then sneaking off into the shadows.

"Ralph," she called, "I see you. Won't you come here?"

He came slowly toward her through the trees. His lips were set, but not in a smile; his dark heavy eyebrows were drawn together, as if to divert attention, by their fierceness, from the rest of his stricken face.

"I've come," he said. "What did you want, Kate?"

"The first thing I want," she said with a kind of desperation, "is to know whether you are mad, Ralph, or whether its I. I'm beginning to feel that perhaps we both are. But certainly you were listening just now to Jo and me."

"Yes, I was," he said gruffly, "though I didn't hear much, if that's any consolation."

Kate was far too bewildered to be angry. "But why were you doing it, Ralph? I feel that everything and everyone around here is part of some plot, something confused and awful, the kind of thing you dream about, and now it turns out that you're in it too."

"It's just because I feel the same way," he said, "I mean that there *is* a plot, that I was keeping my eye on you, Kate. It is confused and awful around here. I trust no one, unless perhaps Professor Hatfield, and really I don't much care what happens to anyone, anyone but you, that is. Certainly not to myself. They can go as far as they like, but damn them, they're not going to touch *you!*"

"'They,'" she repeated. "Who do you mean by 'they,' Ralph?"

"I don't know," he growled. "I don't know a damn thing. That's part of the confusion."

He turned, sat down on the bench beside her, and buried his face in his hands. "Perhaps I am going mad," he said. "It might be a welcome change. What's that kind of madness people get as an escape from an impossible situation?"

All at once Kate remembered the tone of Ralph's voice, the look on his face, when he had recognized that awful sticky hair as Clotilde's; and it struck her that her own feelings were unimportant.

"Ralph," she said gently, "it's very kind of you to look out for me—especially now."

He raised his head from his hands and stared at her. "'Especially now'!" he exclaimed. "What do you mean, Kate?"

"I mean when you must be thinking so much of Clotilde. She seemed such a different kind of person from you, Ralph—you won't mind my saying this?—that I just couldn't realize you loved her so much."

His stare fixed her more intensely; then to her amazement he laughed—but his voice was so hard, so dry, that it did not sound like his. "You think I still love Clotilde!" he said. "After you've seen her in her native haunts, after you've heard her talk? Where did you get that quaint idea?"

Kate felt that she might have replied: At any rate, you *are* engaged to her, but she knew it would seem unsympathetic. If she was more bewildered than ever, there was now, she realized, a sense of relief and thankfulness beneath her wonder: it was as if poor Ralph, no matter how desperate he might feel, had been suddenly set free from some airless underground prison. "It's the way you looked when you recognized her hair," she said. "I'll never forget your face."

"I can well imagine that," he said quickly, "but do you know why, Kate? Of course the mere fact of its happening to anyone was hellish enough, but do you know why I felt a special kind of very personal hell? It was because during my walk yesterday night I was thinking how easy it would be for me to kill her. *There* would be action, I was thinking, and action of a most satisfying sort. In typical romantic fashion, I was mulling over ways and means when I heard that scream. Then when I learned it was Clotilde who had been attacked, it almost seemed to me as if I had willed it, as if my mind had cast a spell over her and now I

was confronted with what I myself had done. It was a queer feeling, hard to explain, but I can't get over it, Kate. I wish to God
I could!"

"I think I can understand how you felt," Kate said, "but
Ralph dear, the reason you felt that way was just because it was
something you couldn't possibly do. You'd never be able to commit a murder in this world: you're much too kind. You couldn't
deliberately hurt anyone if your life depended on it."

He gave her a long grave look. "You think I couldn't commit
murder?" he asked. "You know me as little as that?"

She met his eyes, and as she stared searchingly into them, she
saw that in their very gentleness there was something inflexible
that might be more deadly than any mere excitement or fury, just
because it would be always there. With a pang of terror, terror
that was all for him, she realized that Ralph could kill, not for
the sake of gain, not from fear or for revenge, but to exterminate
something he knew was evil. Her conviction was such a shock
that she felt actually faint; then, like fresh air pouring into a
gas-filled room, came the certainty that if Ralph might be driven
to murder, he could not be driven to cold-blooded cruelty; he
couldn't have arranged a kidnapping and written that terrible
letter; he could not have hacked off Clotilde's scalp.

Evidently he guessed something of her passing dread, for he
gave her a sad smile touched with irony. "You see?" he said quietly. "You might as well know the worst."

Kate still felt slightly dizzy. She glanced around her at the
limpid green shadows over the grass, at the walls of rippled foliage, and then up at the dazzling spires of cloud pointing one
above the other toward the deep free blue of the zenith. If only
Ralph and she could escape into that upper freedom and break
through the surface of the poisonous invisible water that filled
this valley, then perhaps once more she could draw a normal
breath.

"But if you feel that way about Clotilde," she said after a
pause, "then why did you ask her to marry you?"

"Why indeed!" he exclaimed with his bitter laugh. "You may
well ask. Because I'm a romantic fool. Because I can't see the

truth until my nose is rubbed in it. But to do Clotilde justice, she's very lovely to look at—that is, until you discover what's underneath that surface. She can be extremely charming and amusing when she wants to be. She can even be pathetic. When I met her in New York, some awful men were after her. She told me, with the most discreet wistfulness, about her family. She asked my advice. She could be touchingly gay and give me the feeling that really she was desperate, but oh, so plucky! She made me think of her almost as a poor little princess surrounded by ogres, which was very flattering to me, because then I became the brave and noble young prince who might rescue her. It makes me want to vomit to think of it!"

He paused, and for that instant he looked as if there were actually something nauseating in his mouth. "When I arrived at the farm," he went on "—it was barely a month ago, but it seems like years—I saw soon enough that if there were evil here, it was Clotilde's native element. By that time there were plans for the wedding and everything, but worse than that—and this is what I'm most ashamed of—she could still cast her spell over me at times. Oh, I wouldn't have gone through with it: I wasn't quite such a fool as that. I don't think she would have wanted to, herself. But she loved to torment me. The trouble was I let her know I wanted to back out. If she had thought I was still crazy about her, she most likely would have sent me packing."

He wiped his face with his hand. Again Kate glanced up at the clouds and noticed with a faint shiver that a hint of the palest gold-color had begun to stain their glittering whiteness. The sun, still high in the west, was slowly nearing the rim of these tufted hills.

"And then to see you!" he groaned. "To have you appear like someone from a past life, the dear little Kate I remembered, only now grown up to be so beautiful—to have you find me here in this—this sty, among the rest of the pigs! That was the last twist of the knife!"

Kate reached forward and put her hand lightly on his knee. She could not bear to see him so wretched.

"Don't, Ralph," she exclaimed. "You mustn't! Whatever Clotilde is has nothing to do with you. And whatever she has been, she's certainly paying for it now."

"That's just it," he said in a somber voice. "What am I going to do when she comes back?"

"What are you going to do!" she exclaimed. "You can go away from here and never see her again."

"If she's returned sound and well," he said, "of course that's what I'll do. But suppose she's crippled, permanently injured in some way. Suppose her nerves are all shot to pieces."

"I don't think that makes any difference," she said earnestly. "I don't think it could ever be right to marry someone you hate—no matter what. I can't imagine anything worse, or more unfair, for both the husband and the wife."

As he glanced at her with a slow smile, he seemed more like his natural self than he had been since yesterday evening at dinner.

"That's all very well for you," he said, "and I know you really think it, because you're fond of me. But unfortunately—or fortunately—I'm not very fond of myself, and so perhaps I can see the situation with more detachment."

"Detachment!" she exclaimed. "Is that what you call it? You *are* romantic, Ralph; that's the trouble with you. And if I can help it, you're not going to throw yourself away through some absurd notion of self-sacrifice. As far as I can see, it was just because Clotilde was clever enough to see how romantic you were, how you loved to rescue people, that she managed to get you in the first place."

"At any rate," he said, "I don't have to meet the situation until it arises."

Kate felt suddenly that she was blushing. Was it wrong of her, was it deceitful and underhand, for her to advise him in this way, when Clotilde was not here to defend herself? There was one thing at any rate that she could do: from now on she must devote herself to Clotilde; she must shrink from nothing that might help Professor Hatfield rescue her a moment sooner. Because only by acting thus, could she prove to her own conscience that, much as she disliked Clotilde, much as she liked Ralph, she was not in her advice being treacherous and selfish.

Then as she thought of Professor Hatfield, she recalled the unseen prowler who had been listening to their morning's talk.

"Ralph," she said, "a little while ago you said that you were keeping watch over me today. Was it you in the woods this morning, by the summerhouse, when I was talking with Professor Hatfield?"

"No, it wasn't," he said. "I only wish it had been. If anyone was spying on you, Kate—and I can well believe that somebody was—that only shows how careful you must be. You see that, don't you?"

She raised her eyes and again looked into his face, bent seriously toward hers. Then she saw his glance swerve, to pass over her shoulder, and realized that someone else had come from the house.

"There's June," he said. "I'm glad at least I've got something off my chest. You've done me no end of good, much more than you can know. I'll be leaving you now, Kate, but I won't be far."

He seized her hand and pressed it so firmly that it hurt. Then he strode off between the poplars, while Bobbie, who had been following June, tore after him, her stomach close to the ground, her head straining forward, like a tiny race horse. Kate couldn't help smiling as she watched her; and then with a new surge of dizziness, as if she had stepped too near the edge of a cliff, she found herself wondering what Bobbie might bring back from her romp in those dark woods.

9

As she stood behind June an hour later and experimented with her thick black hair, Kate felt that she was learning, with surprising success, to cheat her sense of reality. When you could observe yourself doing something so frivolous, working at it as intensely as if it were of major importance, you could push really important things—your bewilderment, your pity, your terror—into the dim outer regions of your mind where you could only hope they would not gain new strength from their banishment, to spring on you, at some unguarded moment, with even greater fierceness.

She had decided she would bring June's hair softly back from her brow and temples, since it was just long enough to knot behind her head. Then, just for fun, she shadowed June's lashes, but so slightly that no one would suspect. She wiped off every trace of her lipstick, and although none of her own was an ideal shade for June's dark skin, she did have a scarlet one which looked at any rate far better than the rose pink that June had chosen. June's dresses were discouraging; but Kate found a black one, ripped off some frilly white bows, and thus reduced it to something simple and inconspicuous. Then she stood off, by the door of June's room, and had June turn slowly around like a model, so that she could see the general effect.

What she saw was a young girl rather heavy and with plain features, but neither awkward-looking nor insignificant. You could see now the nice shape of her head; and her eyes with the help of Kate's handiwork were really striking and somber. Kate smiled, and could feel at least that under ordinary circumstances she would have been delighted with both June and herself.

"You look wonderful!" she exclaimed. "I just can't wait till they see you."

June smiled back at her, and the scarlet lipstick, the simplicity of her smooth black hair, gave her smile a brilliance it had never had.

"Oh, Kate!" she exclaimed. "Why didn't you come sooner? How happy we could be if everything wasn't so awful!"

"In a few days," Kate said, "perhaps tomorrow, everything will be over. And now, shall we go down?"

"Yes, let's. But there's something I think I ought to tell you first, Kate. You won't be angry with me?"

"How do I know," Kate said, "until you do? But I think you can take the chance."

"It's just that Mavis has been talking," June said slowly. "It made me angry, because it was about you and Ralph. When I came in from the tennis court she was talking to Father and Jo."

Kate turned her head so that June would not notice how she had flushed. "What on earth was she saying about Ralph and me?" she asked, and she had never tried harder to make her voice sound casual.

"She was saying—oh, horrid things. They were talking in the living room and I heard them from the terrace. I almost rushed straight into the room and told her to shut up, but I was afraid you mightn't want me to. Should I have, Katey?"

"I'm glad you didn't," Kate said. "But it makes me furious to think of it. What right has she to talk about us, I'd like to know, just because we're old friends?"

"I'm sure nobody believed her," June said. "It's just that she's jealous of anyone young and pretty. She'd be jealous of me if I wasn't so ugly."

"You're not ugly!" Kate exclaimed. "You look stunning tonight. Wait till they see you downstairs."

She went to June and put her arm around her waist; June had seemed so pathetic that it half diverted Kate from her anger with Mavis. After all, why should she be disturbed by the talk of an alcoholic and broken-down actress? She should have too much pride to let it bother her.

As the two girls walked downstairs, Kate thought of her afternoon's talk with Ralph; and the implications of something he had said struck her for the first time. If he had not been eavesdropping on Professor Hatfield and her, the list of possibilities had narrowed. She knew the professor did not believe the spy was a stranger. Who was he, then? It was not Ralph; it could not be Felix, because she had seen him the next minute a quarter of a mile away, riding up the drive with June. That left only Jo, Mavis, and Ruby, because she ruled out the Larsons entirely; and then, as June and she stepped from the living room on to the terrace, she noticed Mr. Gladstone. Physically, it would have been possible, no doubt, for him to be there; but such an idea was fantastic. She dismissed it at once.

"Well!" Mr. Gladstone exclaimed. "My dear June, you look amazingly smart. Is this Kate's doing?"

Kate could not help admiring the way his tone established at once the sense that this was a normal evening.

"It's a work of collaboration," she said.

"I don't see why you need sound so surprised," Mavis said. "Naturally one would expect a daughter of mine to have distinction. June is just beginning to grow up, that is all. You're emerging at last from the awkward age, aren't you, darling?"

But what pleased Kate most was the look Ralph gave her; and with Mavis in mind she deliberately sent him her most affectionate and brightest smile.

As soon as the flurry of their entrance had passed, however, Kate could not help comparing this scene with the similar one of yesterday evening, when Clotilde had appeared, so lovely-looking and smooth, in her gray dress. There was the same shadow across the garden, the same dusky glow of cloth and petal, the same fragrance in the air; only tonight there still towered above the woods the peaks of this afternoon's clouds, no longer white but stained with the palest rose. Bobbie lay sprawled on her back at the edge of the terrace; her front feet were drawn up to her chest; her hind legs spread limply. At most times, Kate could not

have resisted stooping and stroking the silky stomach, delicately
pink and marked with a few spots like the drops shaken at random from a pen; but tonight, here on the terrace, she could not
bear to: even poor little Bobbie had become part of the enchantment.

She turned her head as she realized that Felix stood beside her
with the cocktails.

"Congratulations, Miss Kate," he murmured, "you've done
a fine job. It's lucky, by the way, that you can keep your head,
because it seems that both our young men have lost their hearts."

She took a long sip of her cocktail. Her glance wandered
over the garden. Then, as she saw Professor Hatfield walking
toward them down one of the paths, she had the ghastly illusion
that time had been dialed back twenty-four hours, that presently
Clotilde would appear, that the two of them, each with her best
smile, would shake hands. She remembered how exquisitely silky
and smooth Clotilde's hair had looked in the early evening light,
and quickly drank the rest of her cocktail. Tonight she would
take two—or three.

Dinner was confused and seemed to pass quickly. She was
placed, this evening, between Jo and Mr. Gladstone and only
half listened to what they said. She decided that nothing would
induce her to go out on the terrace for coffee; and as they all
were strolling through the living room, she said good night, and
explained that she was going upstairs to write letters.

In the hall she was stopped by Professor Hatfield, who had
lingered behind the rest.

"Good night," he said. "I hope you'll manage to sleep," and
then he added, softly and clearly, though his lips hardly moved:
"Since our talk this morning was not private, I think it may be
safer for Clotilde, and for you, if we are not seen together. But
keep your eyes open."

It was a relief to get to her room and close the door behind
her. She turned on a lamp beside the chaise-longue and sat down
wearily, with her writing pad in her lap. She could hear again
the frogs from the river; and a whippoorwill was calling somewhere far away in the woods. She had never before taken so many

cocktails and she still felt dizzy and somehow distinct from her surroundings, as if she were enclosed in a wavy film which made breathing a trifle difficult.

She opened her pad on her knees and wrote: "Friday evening, June 16th. Dear Mother."

But how should she continue? What should she say? If she told Mother now what had happened she would scare her to death, and yet it was almost impossible to describe this place and these people as if everything were safe and normal.

After a long pause she made her pen write: "I came out here, as I'd planned, on Thursday, yesterday afternoon. I've been here now for hardly more than twenty-four hours, and yet it seems as if it had been days." That was true enough, but then what?

There was a knock at the door. She was sure it must be June, and was glad that she would not have to finish her letter, although she did not feel like talking.

"Come in!" she said, and the next instant dropped her pen in surprise, for it was not June who entered but Ruby.

"Why Ruby!" she exclaimed. "What is it? Can I do anything for you?"

For a moment Ruby simply stared at her, and Kate noticed what handsome eyes she had: they were a bright blue, very clear and piercing, and seemed to be coldly sizing her up.

"Yes, I think you can," Ruby then said stiffly. "That's why I'm here. It's for my own sake that I've come but if you'll listen to me, it may be for your sake as well. And don't think I'm meaning to be impertinent, because I'm not. I have nothing against you so far. But here's what I've got to say. Felix likes you. I know the signs. He used to be gadding about all the time, but lately he's settled down. I want him to stay settled. If he gets fresh with you, you put him in his place. Oh, I know you think you will. I know you think I'm insulting you by the very idea! He's a servant. He wears a livery. He's forty years old. Lots of girls have thought things like that about lots of men, and then it was all different. I know my place. I wouldn't come to you like this if I didn't think you were reasonable. I wouldn't come either, if Felix was just an ordinary fellow. But Felix is quite a man!"

Her voice had kept on at a steady level but with an effect of growing intensity, until at her last words it seemed charged with a strange passion and pride. Kate had been so amazed and then so impressed by her manner that there was hardly room in her mind for anger. While she was still wondering what she should feel, what she should say, Ruby turned abruptly and left the room.

10

The terrace extended in every direction as far as her eye could see, but it was not out of doors: it was an enormous hall or theater, with clouds painted on the ceiling. From far away on the rose-colored horizon a small black and white object was scurrying toward her; its chill green shadow reached out indefinitely before it and was already touching her feet. But this was no ordinary shadow: it was viscous, slimy, like the track of a slug; it glued her feet to the ground so that she could not move. She closed her eyes in agony; and as the softly scurrying feet drew nearer, the shadow, instead of passing her, rose within her body like the mercury in a thermometer, the green cold slime in a pond, that presently would reach her heart.

"Kate dear, you must play with Clotilde."

It was Mother's voice so she knew that everything was safe. Clotilde stood before her, a little girl of twelve, in a white lace dress; she was the prettiest girl at the party, prettier even than Kate. She shook her curls so disdainfully that Kate reached out her hand, although she knew it was very wrong, and gave them a sharp pull. The bunch of hair came right out of Clotilde's head; Kate was holding it, all bloody and sticky, between her fingers. She stared about her in horror. The only thing she could do was to fling it into the cage, and both hyenas started toward it. The tough pinkish skin on their long tight bodies twitched greedily, as if to shoo off flies. It wasn't a lock of hair, it was a small bloody animal that she had thrown to the hyenas. It was still half alive, it was trying to escape. She must rescue it, she must get it before they reached it. But how could she, for one of them, on its hind legs, was walking toward her, its head thrust forward, its dark mouth dripping and smiling. It was whispering slyly into her ear in its awful gobbling voice. She must scream as loud as she could so that she would not understand what it said; but the voice, gobbling and chuckling, grew louder and louder. She could not scream. She could not breathe.

Kate heard herself groaning and managed to fling back the sheets from about her face. Her nightgown stuck to her skin; she was still trembling. For a minute she lay quite still, her mind confused, trying to forget her dream. Then a sudden conviction startled her into wakefulness.

It had not been merely herself that she had heard: there had been some other sound.

She had no idea what it was or from what direction it had come—whether it was from near or far away, from inside the house or from out of the window; but she was sure that during her struggles to break out of her dream she had heard something.

She sat up in bed. A breeze stirred the curtains and lapped against her damp skin. The square of the window stood out vaguely in the light of the waning moon. She could hear a swish and ripple of leaves that reminded her of the sea, but that was all; even the frogs were silent; or perhaps it was the breeze that blew their voices away, across the river, into that wilderness of woods and swamps that Professor Hatfield had mentioned.

And then she thought of June. Could anything have happened to June?

She got out of bed, put on her slippers and dressing gown, unlocked her door and peered into the hall. The house was completely silent.

She walked through the thick darkness to the door of June's room, guided by the dim oblong of the transom. She could imagine that the straw matting crinkled ever so faintly beneath her feet. For a minute she listened intently, her ear close to the door, and then she could hear June's peaceful breathing. She tried the knob very gently, though she knew the door would be locked.

She had taken a few steps back toward her room when she stopped suddenly. There was that sound again, remote, indeterminate. It came now from below, from the ground floor—or perhaps it was a step on the stairs.

Kate felt a desperate urge to run into her room, to look the door, to spring into bed and burrow beneath the sheets; but she hesitated. This might of course be something quite normal: Mr. Gladstone might be coming up from his study, or moving around in the lower hall, although she knew by the moon that it must be very late—around two or three o'clock. But again, this might have something to do with the kidnapping, something to do with Clotilde.

Professor Hatfield had urged her to keep her eyes open for anything in the least unusual; and certainly it was unusual for someone to be prowling about the house at this time of night. Might this person, whoever it was, be choosing this hour to meet his accomplice—might he even be going out, with food perhaps, to the cave or hut in which Clotilde lay bound? She recalled Professor Hatfield's words: "If anything we unearth results in rescuing Clotilde a day, or even an hour sooner, it may mean the saving of her life, or perhaps her reason." She remembered her vow this afternoon when she had told Ralph that he should not marry Clotilde. Now was her chance perhaps to discover something: if she could only find out who this man was, it might be the key to the plot. It would do no good to tell herself that she would follow him outside the house: she knew that no matter how firmly she decided, her feet, her legs, at the last moment would simply refuse to carry her; but at least she could walk to the top of the stairs; she could investigate that far. Here in the house she would be safe, and to run back to her room now would be an act of pure cowardice that she could never forgive herself.

She turned, walked to the end of this little passage, and looked out into the main hall. There was no light, and no one was coming upstairs; so she moved as quietly as she could past the closed white doors to the head of the stairway. She stood there for a moment, with one hand clutching the banister, her throat and tongue so parched that she felt she could not make a sound no matter what happened. Someone, she was sure, was moving about in the dark near the front door.

He was fumbling with the lock, that was what he was doing. She caught her breath as a small flashlight went on; but it was not turned in her direction: it remained focused upon the lock. She saw a man's fingers turning the key, which apparently tended to stick; then the light was shut off, the door opened, and a dim figure slipped out and closed it behind him.

If only she had asked Ralph where his room was! But now if she were going to be of any use, she could not wait even a moment. The man had not looked up; he had not seen her; there was no possible danger. There was just a chance that she could make out who he was in the moonlight. She ran softly down the stairs, crossed the hall, and forced herself to open the door, which was now unlocked.

Slowly she peered out into the night. The air was so damp and chilly that it reminded her of shipboard. In front of her the lawn was blanketed by a white mist perhaps a yard deep, from which the scattered trees rose like huge feathery haystacks. Low above the hills a dingy crescent was dissolving in a streak of rust-colored sky. She looked in both directions along the façade of the house—and yes, there to the left, a man was skirting the wall, moving past the windows that opened from the living room.

She stepped outside the door but kept her hand carefully on the knob. In the moonlight and the fog she could not tell whether he was short or tall, dark or light. "Perhaps I should follow him," she thought, "I should track him down: that would be the brave thing to do; but I'm afraid I'm not cut out to be a heroine."

At the corner of the house the man paused, and she saw that he was looking back: he had noticed her. He ducked into the mist. Under that thick white cover he might be groping his way back; he might even, bent double, be running toward her over the silent grass!

In wild panic she clutched at the doorknob; and then occurred perhaps the worst thing that had ever happened to her: the barely opened door swung to, shutting her out. She heard the latch click.

For a moment her fingers were too weak even to try the knob. Suppose it were an automatic lock. It was all she could do to resist an impulse to plunge madly into the fog, to crouch hidden somewhere, like a small night animal, in the depths of some thick tree. But the knob was turning as she pressed it; she heard again that faint click, the white panel gave suddenly and she almost fell in upon the carpet. Then breathlessly she slammed the door.

Her heart was pounding so hard that she felt she might be ill; so she walked across through the darkness to the stairway and sat down on the bottom step, until she could breath naturally. For the first time it struck her that if she should arouse everyone, she might discover who the mysterious man was. But suppose it were Mr. Gladstone, who could not sleep and who had gone for a walk in the moonlight. Perhaps when he had seemed to stoop he had merely walked around the corner. Or perhaps, and this was more likely, the night prowler was Jo who had been with Mavis and had now returned to his cottage.

These thoughts reassured her. She rose from the step and walked upstairs, thankful that apparently no one had heard the door.

Then, just as she reached the top of the stairs, someone looming suddenly from the darkness, grasped her arm, and she gave a little choking scream.

"For God's sake, Kate, is that you?"

The voice was Ralph's, and she felt so relieved that for an instant she could not speak.

"What's happened?" he asked in a tone whose anxious sharpness made it sound almost fierce. "How did you get here? Did anyone come into your room? Are you all right?"

"Yes," she said with a half sob, "I'm all right. I'll be all right in a minute. It's just that you scared me so."

"Have you been outside?" he went on. "Kate, you shouldn't have gone, not for any reason. I was sleeping very lightly; in fact I wasn't really asleep. I heard a door slam. I thought it was the front door, so I hurried out here. Then I saw your figure coming up the stairs. I didn't know who it might be."

"I heard something too," she said. "That's why I got up." And she told him of the noise that had wakened her and the man she had seen. "Do you think he could have been going to Clotilde?" she asked. "Do you think he was part of the plot?"

"I don't know," he said grimly. "It might be. If it was Jo or Felix, either one of them could be back in bed and apparently asleep by now. But I do know this, Kate. You ran a terrible risk going out as you did. You must give me your word that if you ever hear any other noises in the night, you'll stay in your room. Of course you'll keep your door locked. And if you notice anything, when you're up and about, that seems suspicious or strange, you must tell me at once. Why didn't you wake me just now?"

"It seems to me that's what I did," she said, "even if I didn't mean to. I would have earlier, but I didn't know which was your room."

"It's the room corresponding to yours, at the end of the opposite wing. I wish it wasn't so far away. Now Kate, do you promise to do as I've told you, no matter what you hear? If not, I warn you, I'll spend the rest of the night pacing the hall outside your door."

"I promise that nothing will drag me out of my room again tonight," she said. "You needn't worry."

Her voice broke during her last words, and it was all she could do to keep from crying.

Without warning, he pulled her against him, and held her for a moment so close that she could hardly breathe. Then he let her go just as suddenly.

"This is a fine state of affairs," he said in a gruff voice. "Out of the frying pan into the fire, I should say. I won't apologize. You're forgiving enough to laugh it off. But now I'm going to escort you to your door, Kate. No more of this lonely wandering for you."

Kate hurried on ahead of him, shaken from so many emotions—fear, relief, and then surprise—that it never occurred to her to be angry or to pretend that she was. Presently they turned out of the main hall into the little side passage.

"Good night, Kate," he said, as they reached the end. "I'll wait out here until you put on the light."

But just then the light came on: they could see it through the transom. The door opened and June stood on the threshold, in pajamas and a pink wooly wrapper.

"Oh Katey!" she exclaimed, "I've been scared to death. I thought I heard you scream. I wasn't sure. You know how it is when you wake up suddenly. But I knew it was something, so I thought I'd go to your room, and then I found the door unlocked and went in, and you weren't there. I thought something awful might have happened to you. And then I heard a man's voice. Of course I see now it was Ralph's. So I turned out the light again and locked the door. I was just trying to get up courage to go out to look for you."

"I'm glad you didn't do that," Kate said. "But I don't wonder you were scared. So would I have been."

It occurred to her then that June would certainly think it odd to see Ralph and her roaming the house in their dressing gowns at this time of night; she remembered what June had told her about Mavis' gossip and found that she was blushing.

"I thought I heard a noise," she explained. "It was somewhere in the house. Ralph heard it too. We both started to explore to find out what it was and I ran into him in the dark. He scared me nearly to death. That's when you heard me scream." For every reason it seemed better not to tell June about the man she had seen.

"Well, good night," Ralph said. "Remember what I told you, Kate."

Kate left the door open until he had rounded the corner; then as she closed it she turned to June. "You poor thing!" she exclaimed. "I should have left a note. It never occurred to me that you'd wake up and come to look for me. Of course that was all on account of my silly scream."

"Oh, that's all right," June said, "now that you're back; but I wonder, Katey—would you mind if I slept in here, on the chaise-longue? Just for the rest of tonight? I think I'd feel easier somehow."

"I know I'd feel easier," Kate said. "I think it's a fine idea."

But she lay awake for a long time after she heard June's slow breathing, because each time she approached the threshold of sleep she felt that dreams were ominously lying in wait for her, like ghosts within the rooms of an empty house; and she would have to struggle back, with what was left of her strength, before they caught her and dragged her inside.

11

Kate did not wake up the next morning until after nine. June had left the room without disturbing her, and the blanket she had used as a covering was folded on the chaise-longue. The fact that she had not taken it with her suggested to Kate that June was perhaps planning to sleep here tonight as well; and Kate felt that for both their sakes this would be an excellent idea.

Before she got out of bed she realized that the air had changed during the early morning hours: it was quite still now, close and very humid; this would be a really hot day, the first of the summer.

When she stepped into the dining room, twenty minutes later, she found everyone just finishing breakfast—even Mavis. Kate wondered what could have brought her down so early; and then with a catch of excitement she remembered that today was Saturday: it was this morning that the letter should arrive with instructions for the delivery of Clotilde's ransom. Yesterday the mail had not come until after eleven, but her own feeling of tension made her realize why Mavis should have found it impossible to lie in bed.

"I'm sorry to be late," Kate exclaimed. "Of course nobody must wait for me."

As they all looked up at her, she wondered whether Mavis and Mr. Gladstone had been told of her night's experience. There was an empty place between Mr. Gladstone and Ralph, which Kate suspected Ralph had managed to keep for her; she sat down quickly and hoped that she did not look too exhausted and drowsy.

"Will you have your eggs boiled or scrambled, miss?"

She glanced over her shoulder at Ruby's impassive face, and as she thought of their strange brief interview in her bedroom the night before, she had the feeling that this was not a real breakfast, that Ruby was not a real servant, that this all was taking place on the stage. It was not even a real stage, though: it was a stage in a dream, one of those unpleasant dreams in which you find yourself in the midst of a theatrical performance and haven't the least idea what your next lines are supposed to be.

In a minute Mavis rose from the table. "If you'll excuse me," she said, "I think I'll step outside for a breath of air, if there's any to be had this morning. I rather doubt it. I've always found the sight of plates with egg drying on them peculiarly depressing. They give you such a very 'morning after' feeling, without the consolation of there having been a 'night before.'"

She lingered a moment, with her hands resting on the back of her chair. She was wearing a pale green housecoat of accordion-pleated chiffon, which gave the effect of at once clinging and bulging, and reminded Kate of the well-filled resilient skin of a tomato worm.

"Remember, Jo," she said languidly, as if the heat were already overpowering her, "we're going to do a little work on the César Franck presently. God knows, you need it!"

"In that case," Jo said, "I'll go and limber up my fingers. I didn't sleep very well"—he flashed a brilliant smile at Kate—"and I feel I'm still moving in a dream, a most delightful dream."

Mr. Gladstone also rose. "If your dreams are delightful," he grunted, "I envy you. But perhaps you enjoy them more highly seasoned than the rest of us."

June and Ralph both remained with her while Kate had her breakfast; then as they rose from the table, Ralph asked her to play tennis.

"Kate's going to play with *me*," June said. "Aren't you, Kate?"

She spoke so possessively that Kate might have resented it if she had not remembered that probably no one else had ever paid her any attention.

"I'd love to," Kate said, "but I won't guarantee that I'll hold out for more than one set, if the morning gets much hotter."

"I'll watch you," Ralph said, and the three of them went out together to the court.

Sunlight streamed down on the hard clay from a hazy whitish sky, and for the first time since her arrival at the farm, Kate noticed a flat faint smell of mud from the river or the bottom lands. By the end of the first set, which June beat her 6-1, strands of hair were clinging to her cheeks and forehead. She looked at her watch: it was quarter past ten; the mail might arrive in less than an hour.

"Come along, Katey," June called, "you'll do better next time. You just haven't got warmed up yet."

"Warmed up!" Kate exclaimed. "If I got much warmer I'd melt away."

She walked over to the bench where Ralph was sitting. "*You* ask June to play a set or two," she said in a low voice. "I know she'd love to play with you. You'd give her a much better game."

He made a slight face. "All right," he said, "since you ask me to. But I never feel comfortable with June. She embarrasses me."

"Don't be silly," she said sharply. "Get up and play with her. Quickly! Or she'll know you don't want to."

"Hey June," he called obediently, "how about taking on someone your own size?"

With a slight scowl, June glanced at him and then at Kate; Kate guessed she suspected that his offer was not spontaneous; but after an instant her face cleared and she called back: "Okay, if you want to. Two out of three."

Kate watched them for a few minutes and wondered how they both could move with such energy under this intense white sun. The green circle of hills seemed today not so much to be holding in the damp as shutting out coolness and life. The shadow was retreating from the bench on which she sat; so she got up wearily and walked through the shrubbery into the herb garden.

Here the sharp smell of mint, tarragon and sage gave one the illusion that the air was less stagnant. A man in a tight blue

jersey and black trousers was stooping over a border in the shadow of the further hedge. He stood up as she stepped out into
the sun, and she saw that it was Felix, with a pair of scissors in
one hand, a bunch of herbs in the other. He smiled and came
forward jauntily to meet her. After Ruby's warning, she thought
that perhaps she should not stay here, not so much because she
was afraid of him as because she stood in awe of Ruby; but she
felt more curious than ever to find out what he was really like.

She could see in this costume that he was certainly a fine figure of a man. She noticed for the first time how broad his neck
was as it widened to join his shoulders, how slim and yet powerful were his waist and thighs. He suggested in the easy control of
his movements a figure in a ballet, a sailor, or perhaps a Parisian
Apache, sure of himself, disdainful, and yet somehow sympathetic. His face was the only thing that revealed his age.

"Good morning," he said. "I guess you didn't know I was a
chef as well as a chauffeur and a butler."

"A chef!" she exclaimed. "I thought Ruby was the cook."

"Perhaps I should say an assistant chef," he went on. "Ruby
relies on me for some of the finishing touches. I make a specialty
of herbs and spices. Just smell this bunch. Now I claim that this
bouquet is better than any flowers you could mention."

He handed her the bunch of herbs, and she put her nose into
it. It was delicious, she had to admit, though rather too strong,
and in this hot sunlight it almost made her head go round. She
offered it to him again, but he shook his head and smiled.

"You keep it," he urged. "I'd be honored. Put it in water in
your room and the whole place will smell good enough to eat."

"Thank you," she said, and in spite of herself she felt flattered; then, almost furtively, she glanced at the windows of the
house to see whether Ruby were watching.

But the next moment her attention was attracted by the first
bars of the Franck sonata floating out, clear and soft, from the
open windows of Jo's cottage, beyond the herb garden and across
the green. It seemed to Kate that the musical phrase tinted this
heavy white air with a shimmer of iridescence, and gave it, for
the first time this morning, a suggestion of life. She realized that

of course Mavis must be at the piano, and was surprised at how well she played, far better than Clotilde, with an almost professional power and finish.

It gave her a quite different picture of Mavis and of her relation with Jo. Obviously somewhere within her there still lurked real energy and talent. It made her at once much more of a person, more to be respected, more to be reckoned with in every way.

"What did Mrs. Gladstone do when she was on the stage?" she asked Felix. "Do you know? Was she in musical comedy?"

"No," he said. "She was in real plays—legitimate drama. Shakespeare and all that. I guess she was pretty good. When she first came out here, after her marriage, she used to recite sometimes for friends in the evenings, but that sort of petered out."

"It must have been hard for her at first, to be so far away from everything," Kate said.

Felix looked thoughtful. "Well," he said after a minute, "I guess it was and it wasn't. You see when she was still on the stage she began to have those dizzy spells of hers." She glanced at him doubtfully, but his expression showed no trace of irony. "I know several times she couldn't appear. I guess her career was about washed up when Mr. Gladstone came along. He was crazy about her for a year or so, and afterward—well, he was always very understanding about letting her have her friends around for company."

"You mean friends like Jo?" Kate asked.

"Yes," he said. "That's the idea."

Now, for an instant, she did catch a suggestion of the invisible wink she had noticed night before last as he handed her her cocktail; yet she couldn't be angry, because she was almost sure she must have imagined it.

"She used to have lots of friends when June was a little girl," he went on. "Sometimes several at once. And Mr. Gladstone had *his* friends, too. Oh yes, we used to have pretty lively parties out here. It was all very free and easy."

Poor Clotilde! Kate thought. No wonder Professor Hatfield said her bringing up left something to be desired. And poor little June!

She glanced again at her watch. It was now 10:32. She would finish the letter she had begun to Mother last night, and take it down to the mailbox by the front gate.

She said good-by to Felix, went into the house and up to her room. The letter turned into the briefest note; but she promised she would write several pages the next time, and would probably have some curious things to tell: that might suggest that startling events were occurring, and yet it should not alarm Mother. It was now quarter to eleven. Perhaps the mail had already arrived; someone might have brought it in from the box. Her heart began to beat faster, as it did sometimes when she entered a doctor's office. What would the new message from the kidnappers be?

With her letter in her hand, she went downstairs and out of the front door. Here Bobbie joined her, her muzzle covered with dirt, as if she had been digging, and together they started down the drive to the road. The sun by this time had burned through the morning haze, and the zenith was a pale opaque blue. The wooded hill in front of her was at once dull and shimmering: in this hot light it had lost all individuality, all interest. It was just a sample strip cut at random from the thousands of miles of forest left over from the primitive world, when man had not yet come down from the trees.

As she stepped through the white gateposts and went to put her letter in the box, beyond the swath of clipped grass, she noticed Bobbie flattening out her body and wriggling forward with little friendly whines toward the group of cedars to the left of the gate. The next moment a voice called her from the shadow and she saw Mr. Gladstone sitting on the bank.

"It's a little early for the mail," he said, "but I just thought I'd be on hand. Won't you join me? It's as cool here as it is anywhere."

Kate went over and sat down on the grass beside him. She was glad of an excuse to linger. For the first time Mr. Gladstone, as he sat here waiting for the postman, with his heavy eyes turned to the stretch of road on which the car would appear, struck her as a pathetic figure.

"Sometimes he doesn't get here till noon," he said, "but God damn it, if he's late this morning—"

"I haven't had a chance to tell you," Kate said after a minute, "but I do realize how awful this suspense must be for you, Mr. Gladstone. When a thing like this happens, there's really nothing you can say."

"My dear Kate," he exclaimed, "your coming is the one bright spot in this living hell. If only I didn't feel so goddamn guilty!"

"Guilty?" she asked, surprised and touched, "why should you feel guilty?'

"I guess I didn't realize how much of the old-fashioned father there was in my bones," he said. "I remember in Sunday school they used to tell us you'd get caught up with, if you let things slide too far—and now look at this! Out of the clear sky! I keep thinking and thinking ever since Clotilde went, what chance has the poor kid ever had? Why didn't you come out here ten years ago and take them both on, June and Clotilde? Then at least I could feel— O hell! Mavis used to think it was cute when Clotilde came downstairs in her nightgown and some of the prime bunch that used to hang around would give her the cherries from their cocktails. I wouldn't put it past Mavis if she saw all along what it would do to her, and I never troubled to put my foot down. Mavis hated her because she was so much prettier than June, her own child; and she always was ashamed of June, because June was so much homelier than Clotilde." He gave a bitter rumbling laugh. "I'm afraid I can't get much credit for these moral qualms," he said. "I'm afraid they are just a proof I'm growing senile, a reversion to childhood. You wouldn't suspect my father was a straight-laced Baptist, and I had all the advantages of a strict upbringing. In fact, I'm damn sure I'm growing senile. Here I am talking to the prettiest girl I've seen in a coon's age, and all I can think of is what a fine friend she'd be for my daughters. I apologize, my dear. You should have known me earlier."

"I'm sure I like you better this way," Kate said.

He laughed again. "Yes, I guess you would. You're softhearted, and there's always a kind of romantic interest about a piece of old debris—you know, the old men that come to your door selling shoestrings; old broken-down dogs, old horses. If I wasn't old day before yesterday, I am now; and if you had met me at the height of my charm, I'm afraid you'd have seen through me."

Kate remembered her talk on the terrace, day before yesterday, with Jo; and wondered if all men whose main interest in life was women were obsessed by the idea of growing old.

Before she could think of anything to say, Mr. Gladstone was scrambling to his feet. "I hear a car," he exclaimed. "Don't you?"

Kate listened, and then realized that what had seemed merely the shimmer of the noonday heat was actually the sound of a faint throbbing; but it must have been at least two minutes before a small car appeared from beyond the curve in the road.

"That's he," Mr. Gladstone said, and his voice was now matter-of-fact.

Kate watched him tensely as he took three or four letters from the box and handed them to the postman. It seemed to her that no postman had ever taken longer to sort out the mail to be delivered; but at last he gave Mr. Gladstone a bundle of letters with a couple of magazines. Mr. Gladstone thumbed through them.

"Sorry," he said to Kate. "There's nothing for you."

Kate was disappointed: she had hoped to hear from Mother. Since tomorrow was Sunday, there would be no delivery; and now she would have to wait until the day after.

Mr. Gladstone picked out one letter from the pile and stuck the rest into his pocket. "I guess this is it, all right," he said, and his tone was as calm as when he had announced the postman. "If you'll excuse me for a minute—"

Kate watched him as he read it, his face impassive except for the faintest scowl. She could see that it was several pages long and printed in red on the same cheap paper as the others.

When he had finished, he folded it and stuck it in the pocket with the rest of the mail. He gave her a long thoughtful glance from under his dark lids but for the moment did not speak, and she hesitated to ask any questions.

"Kate," he said at last, "would you mind hunting up June, and then coming with her to my study? If you meet anyone else they'll be sure to ask you if the mail has come and if you know

anything about the letter. You can just say that for the present I
can tell no one what's in it."

They walked up the driveway together without speaking. Mr.
Gladstone went into the house, but Kate skirted off to the right
with Bobbie, and cut through the garden to the tennis court.
Ralph and June were still playing as vigorously as ever, though
they both looked intensely hot.

As soon as they had finished a game, Kate called June, and
June and Ralph both came quickly.

"The letter!" June exclaimed. "It's come, hasn't it? Do you
know what's in it?"

Kate shook her head. "Your father wants to talk to you in the
study," she said. "I think we'd better go right off."

"The letter has come?" Ralph asked.

"Yes, it's come," she admitted.

"Tell Mr. Gladstone," he said, "that if there's anything, of any
sort, that I can do—"

"Yes, I will," she promised, and she was grateful to him for
not asking any more questions or insisting on coming with them.

When they stepped into the study, a dark-paneled room with
hunting prints on the walls and not too many books, Mr. Gladstone characteristically did not move except to raise his puffy
bluish lids so that Kate and June could both catch the full force
of his stare.

"I think you girls will be interested in this letter," he remarked in a businesslike voice. "When you've heard it, you will
understand why I called you in. It's fairly long, so you'd better sit
down, and make yourselves comfortable—if you can!"

Kate sat down in a huge leather easy chair and June perched
on its arm, with her fingers touching Kate's shoulder.

> Dear Mr. Gladstone:
> Since you drove into Woodside this morning—
> that is, Friday, the 16th—I assume you were acting
> like the sensible businessman I have taken you to
> be and were collecting the little matter of $50,000
> which we had named as our fee. I know I can also

assume that you are intelligent enough not to have
marked the money in any way, or to have taken
down the numbers. When I specified only small
bills, I did this really for your sake, to save you
from too severe a temptation, because I know how
badly you would feel afterward, if any greedy desire
to retrieve your cash or any unchristian yearning
for personal vengeance, had led you to take a step
which would result in most unpleasant things happening to one or both of your daughters. Needless
to say, nonetheless, the bills will be very carefully
examined, as a sound business precaution, before
any steps are taken toward fulfilling our side of the
contract, namely the handing over of your daughter Clotilde.

Now as to the way in which we demand the
money shall be delivered. Wishing to spare your
feelings as much as we can, I warn you that at first
reading you may be slightly alarmed. You may even
hesitate to carry out our directions. As to this latter point, we have merely to say that if you vary
our specifications in the faintest degree, the whole
deal is off. As to the former, I think a little thought
will convince you that the course we have marked
out for you is not the result of idle whim, still less
of any mean desire to torment you, but merely a
sound and most understandable precaution.

To come to the point: we should like you to give
the money, wrapped in an inconspicuous brown
paper parcel, to your daughter June. She must start
at two o'clock tomorrow afternoon, the afternoon
of the day you will receive this, for the bluff about
two miles below your farm, opposite the old ferry
landing. Under the largest oak tree on that particular bluff—there is no mistaking the tree—there
is a flat stone a trifle more than a foot across and
roughly rectangular; under that stone she will find

a note directing her to some other place. You see it will be a kind of a treasure hunt, and I hope she will be able to take it in the spirit of a game. In the second hiding place she will find a second note, directing her still further. I will not say how many stations there may be, because in games of that sort part of the fun consists of the surprise, but in the final spot designated she will leave the package and will receive written directions as to when and where you are to call for Clotilde.

Since we realize that a jaunt of this sort may seem a trifle formidable for a young girl to take alone, she may, if she likes, take her young friend, Miss Katherine Archer, with her. You see, we are doing everything we can to make it easy for everyone. I assure you that June (and Miss Archer, if she cares to go) will be quite safe on their little hike so long as they obey the directions they will find, and so long as you yourself do nothing to endanger them. If we wished June any harm, at present, we certainly would not bother to lure her off into the wilds. You remember this was not necessary in Clotilde's case, nor would it be in hers. No, it simply occurred to us that this might be the simplest way of providing a hostage for your discretion until an hour or so after the money had been delivered.

N.B. On no account should the dog be allowed to follow.

One more word before closing. In our last letter, you may recall we criticized the methods of average kidnappers. It seems to us that in allowing only one chance to the bereaved family, as they so often do, they are unnecessarily brutal. Let me remind you, that if anything goes wrong, we promise you we will not kill Clotilde. Instead, before we touch June, you will receive next time perhaps Clotilde's hand. I say "perhaps," because although

we have talked over alternatives with Clotilde herself, we have not yet decided on the particular part
that might prove most persuasive. We very much
hope, however, in common humanity, that we have
persuaded you sufficiently already, and that you
will not require a second chance. In fact, we feel
we can count on it.

As Mr. Gladstone's voice stopped, Kate felt that these dark
walls were slowly revolving about her; it was as if the steady level
of his reading were the only thing that had kept them still; she
could feel June's fingers pressing into her shoulder, but she did
not dare to look up at her, she did not dare even to move, for
fear that she might burst out laughing or crying—or perhaps be
sick. From another world she could hear faintly the violin and
piano; the music no doubt had been going on all the time that
Mr. Gladstone was reading but she noticed it only now. She noticed, too, that Mr. Gladstone was again looking at June and her
with no change of feature.

"Well," he said at length, "I wanted you to hear it. I have no
comments to make. The only fair thing is to leave it up to you."

In the silence that followed, the room turned more and more
slowly and finally stopped with a faint and nauseating lurch.

Then she head June's voice: "I'll go," she said. "I'll have to go,
but Kate mustn't. I won't drag her into it."

"Of course I'll go. Don't be foolish!" Kate was relieved that
her voice had spoken for her so promptly, because she could not
have forced it just then.

"I think," Mr. Gladstone said slowly, "that there is no real
risk. As the writer of the letter suggests, there would be no point
in it. At least, I'm afraid the risk would be even greater if we
didn't do what he asked. However, this doesn't apply to you,
Kate. The letter doesn't require you to go, and you mustn't feel
you have to keep June company on a mission of this sort. June
has explored this region by herself since she learned to walk."

"You can't imagine my not going, can you?" Kate asked, and
now she felt that she had gained control of her voice.

"I'd have no right to think badly of you, if you didn't."

"I feel it's more important what I'd think of myself," Kate said.

"Very well then," Mr. Gladstone exclaimed briskly. "You're a damn good sport, and I'm not at all surprised. In the meanwhile don't mention this to anyone. Don't even let them know I've read you the letter. We want to guard against any well-meaning inter-ference which actually, I think, just now, is the thing we have to dread most. If you will both come back to this room at about ten minutes of two, I'll give you the package."

12

It was five minutes after two when Kate and June stepped into the thicket of trees beyond the tennis court on to a narrow steep path that Kate had not noticed before; and Kate felt almost at once that they had plunged into the midst of the wilderness. It was hard to realize that the farm, with its neat buildings, its lawns and its gardens, could not be more than a few hundred yards away.

The woods were intensely silent; only in the distance she could hear a drilling sound, which stopped, began again and stopped, and which she knew must be a woodpecker searching for grubs. The smell of leaf mold, of rotten bark, of fungus, hung in the air as in a closed room. Each leaf, each twig, was as motionless as if the whole forest were a huge "natural" background for a wild-life group in a museum.

The trail grew steeper and steeper; and in a minute they were scrambling upward, clinging to saplings and exposed roots, along the foot of a rocky ledge perhaps six feet high, from the top, of which a fringe of juniper branches jutted out like a line of broad green-black eaves. Kate found herself stooping instinctively, because this ledge reminded her of a picture in a fairy tale, a picture which always had scared her as a child, in which a young man climbed a path through a lonely forest, suspecting no danger, while just above him, on an overhanging rock, an ogre was crouching with a huge stone poised in his hands.

She was glad to step out a few minutes later into the glare on the top of the bluff.

June, who had been a few yards ahead, now stood still to wait for her. The package of money was in a knapsack slung over her shoulder, along with two bottles of Coca-Cola. When June, at the last moment, had gone back to the icebox to get these, it had seemed to Kate that on this particular excursion they would feel in no mood for drinking cokes; but already she was thankful that they would have something to drink before they reached home.

Kate climbed up through the sparse grass until she was standing beside June. By now her eyes were used to the brightness.

In front of her a series of terraces edged with yellow rock descended for a hundred feet or more to a group of gnarled junipers, which seemed from here to be hanging over a void. Below, sparkled the broad whitish-blue river, winding in either direction as far as the eye could see between bluffs whose bare tops protruded from a blanket of forest. Wooded islands, close to either shore, were rimmed with beaches of pink sand, along which at intervals there gleamed with the paleness of bone the trunk of an uprooted tree, washed downstream by the floods of past seasons. The whole landscape seemed to be trembling under the heat and glare. At first glance she could not discover a single house.

Then June pointed down to the left, where a small bluff, not nearly so high as the one on which they stood, stuck out into the river.

"There's where Professor Hatfield has his shack," she said. "Do you see it? About halfway up, just above those white birches."

"What a wonderful place to live!" she exclaimed. "But how does he ever get a bicycle up that hill?"

"He doesn't," June said. "There's a lane that leads in to the river from the main road. We'll be crossing it soon. He leaves his bicycle at the edge of the lane in an old piano box."

They followed now, much more quickly, the top of the bluff which kept on, rising and falling, for half a mile; then they climbed down into woods again, though the slope here was not so steep as it had been at first. In the hollow their path crossed at right angles a dirt wagon trail, raised above the marshy ground on either side. "That's Professor Hatfield's lane," June said.

Here in the bottom lands the air was teen heavier, and Kate had to keep brushing away swarms of small sticky gnats. She was glad when after ten minutes they began to climb once more, and presently came out on another bluff—a long dry ridge scattered with yellow verbena-like flowers that Kate did not recognize.

"There's the tree!" June said, pointing to a huge oak near the crest. "That surely must be the one."

Kate's heart beat faster as they walked up to the oak tree.

"Yes, there's the stone!" June exclaimed.

"It looks heavy," Kate said. "Don't you want me to help you lift it?"

"Never mind," June said, and sliding her strong fingers under the edge she moved it to the side without effort.

There, pressed into the close-packed dirt, was a piece of folded paper. June picked it up, unfolded it, and held it out toward Kate, so that the two girls might read it together. It was printed in the same red crayon.

"So far, so good," the note ran. "On the other side of this bluff you will meet a trail that leads toward the river. Watch carefully, because it's overgrown, and you might miss it. It would be unfortunate for Clotilde, and perhaps for you, if you didn't find it. When you reach the riverbank, walk downstream for fifty yards. There you will come to the top of a narrow island about twenty feet from the bank. Wade out to the island. On the spit of sand at the lower tip there is a tree trunk, half buried. Dig in the sand close to the exposed roots of the tree and you will find a wooden box. In that you will find your directions."

"I hope the water's not too deep," June said. "I'm wet enough already. At any rate it can't be awfully far."

Once again they plunged down into the undergrowth. The path here was really precipitous, and several times Kate asked June for her hand. The trail at the bottom oozed water as they followed it toward the river through a tangle of elderberries and briers; small spotted frogs jumped up from under their feet and plopped into the pools that soaked the roots of the bushes. By the time they reached the bank their feet were so wet that they decided it was not worth while taking off their shoes and stockings to cross to the island.

"The bottom looks as if it would be awfully slimy," June said. "You wait here. I'll go first and see how deep it is."

She started wading at once, and Kate, who had pictured their sinking into water waist deep, was relieved to see that it did not rise above June's knees. The water was warm and muddy; the island was a thicket of small trees bound together by wild-grape vines and brambles; they kept to the beach, and after they had gone thirty yards they found themselves on the spit which the letter had described. There, sure enough, was the dead tree, silvery white, with a network of twisted roots like a knot of snakes in some East Indian carving.

Both girls got down on their knees in the coarse sand and started scooping it up with their fingers. Kate was beginning to grow a little worried when her nails scraped something hard, and the next moment she uncovered a cigar box. She opened it hurriedly, spread out the paper enclosed, and again June and she read the message together:

"Go back to the main trail that leads from the river to the highway. Follow it in the direction away from the river for about half a mile. Then, to the right, before you reach the main road, you will see an abandoned house in an orchard. Enter the house, go upstairs, turn to the left and go into the front room. In a corner of the room there is a closet. Across the back of the closet is a deep shelf. On that shelf, in the extreme right-hand back corner you will find directions under a pile of loose plaster."

"That means we have to go back over that last bluff," June said. "Are you as hot as I am? What do you say we drink our cokes now? Then I won't have to lug the bottles any further."

They drank them sitting on the beach, with their backs resting against the dead tree. The bottles were lukewarm, and the brackish smell of the river seemed to flavor the drink, but even so Kate swallowed it greedily. The river slipped by on either side of them, washing bubbles on to the wet sand; two large herons pulled themselves up from another island, a hundred yards downstream, and flew with dangling legs across to the further bank to vanish among the trees. Where am I? Kate suddenly asked herself. What am I doing here? This strange errand has nothing to do with my life. And then, with a cold feeling about her heart, she had the conviction that she could never escape from this region in which she had been living—asleep or awake?—during the last few days, that she could never find her way back to the normal comfortable world she had always known.

"Gosh, I'm hot!" June exclaimed, as she put down her empty bottle. "What do you say we take a dip, Kate? The water would be cleaner on the offshore side of the island."

"Do you think we better?" Kate asked doubtfully.

"Oh, I only mean for a few minutes," June said. "We've sure made good time so far."

Kate stared at the sinuous current. Perhaps if she dove down through that shining water it would be like stepping back through the looking glass and she would find herself once more in the real world.

But it was just then that she heard a noise. It was so short that she did not know what it was—the crack of a twig, the swish of a branch, a footstep, from the thicket behind them in the center of the island.

"Listen!" she exclaimed under her breath. "Did you hear that?"

"What?" June asked.

"I don't know. But I think— It seems to me, June, that someone is on this island. Someone beside ourselves."

"It might be some animal," June said, but Kate could see her dark skin turn a shade less swarthy.

"Yes, it might," Kate said. "There! You must have heard it that time. It sounded nearer, I thought."

"Yes, I heard it then," June said. "Perhaps we better get going, after all."

Without speaking, they waded back to the shore, and as they hurried along the swampy path there was complete silence all around them. But after they had reached the top of the bluff, they heard the sound again, this time down to the right among the trees, as if someone—or something, a wild beast, perhaps— were furtively trailing them.

"I don't like it!" Kate exclaimed, and she realized that if she were not careful there might be tears in her voice. "I hate these faint sounds."

"So do I," June said in a half whisper. "But I guess the only thing to do is to keep right on."

"Of course," Kate admitted. "There's nothing else to do."

When they came to the trail at the foot of the bluff they could go more quickly, for although it rose, the slope was comparatively gentle and the ground was smooth underfoot. As they pushed on through the woods, Kate tried to pretend that she no longer heard the noises, just as you may almost convince yourself that you no longer hear some ominous sound in the motor when you are driving a car; but she knew that whatever it was, it still prowled beside them. The air was so breathless that even the faintest rustle called attention to itself, like a stone flung into a pool.

"There's the house," June said at last. "I remember I once explored it when I was little."

Kate felt that she could not have kept on much longer.

They climbed over the wooden gate, which was chained and padlocked, and waded through the long grass of the yard. It was a small house of yellow brick set among old apple trees; at one end a lilac thicket grew as high as the second-story windows. There were zigzag cracks in the walls, and the roof of the porch had fallen in. They had to climb over a litter of boards to reach the door.

The house was filled with hot green twilight like a sticky jelly. They could see no scrap of furniture. The floors looked rotten, and jagged bits of plaster lay everywhere.

"We must look out for the stairs," June said. "I'll go first. If they'll bear my weight, they'll certainly bear yours."

As she followed June cautiously up the steps, Kate thought what a perfect trap this would be.

In the upper hall they turned to the left, as directed, and entered what must have been the best bedroom. The door of the closet stood ajar. June went in, and Kate could hear the loose plaster falling as she brushed it aside; but all the time she was listening for some noise—the slightest creak of a board—downstairs. If she heard it she did not know what she would do: she must prepare herself not to scream. Or perhaps there would be no need for effort: her heart might simply stop beating.

"Here it is!" June said. "Gosh, I hope they don't send us much further."

When she came out of the closet there were pieces of plaster caught in her dark hair. This time the paper was not folded but crumpled into a tight ball, so that anyone discovering it would not suspect it contained a message. June spread it out carefully— there were three sheets covered with printing—and offered it to Kate.

"You read it to me," Kate said. If she were listening to June's voice, she couldn't keep straining her ears for noises downstairs.

"You have reached the end of your journey," June read. "Leave the parcel on the shelf where you found this. Be sure and cover it carefully with loose plaster. You are responsible for it until it is called for, so it would be most unfortunate if it was discovered by some tramp. As you know, you are now very near the main road, and you will be tempted to return home that way. Do not yield to that temptation. Go home by the trail through the woods and the river bluffs. There is no hurry. You can rest whenever you want to. We advise you to tell nobody where you left the money until Clotilde is returned. Of course you can use your own judgment, but if anyone, for any reason whatever, comes near this house while Clotilde is still in our custody, the deal is off, and your ramble will have been useless—not to speak of the money thrown away.

"*What follows is important:* tomorrow (Sunday) afternoon Mr. Gladstone and Mr. Green must drive into Woodside. At the square they are to turn left on State Highway 17. Keep on through Brookfield, Red Earth and Tuscoda. When they have driven twenty-one miles on 17 from the square in Woodside, they must keep their eyes open for a small road going down a hill into woods. It is about two hundred yards beyond a barn that has recently burned down. At the bottom of the hill, at the edge of the woods is a stream. Follow the current, on foot, for three hundred yards. At that point there is an abandoned cabin. In the cabin they will find Clotilde, resting, comfortably, we hope, on some straw. Don't be alarmed if she seems slightly drowsy. It has seemed more humane recently to keep her under the influence of a mild sedative.

"Be sure and obey the directions to the letter. It will take two men to carry Clotilde back to the road, and who are more fitting for this purpose than her father and her fiancé?

"We hope there will be no need for further correspondence."

June looked up at Kate, as she finished, and suddenly, before she could help it, Kate burst into tears.

"I don't think I can go back through those woods," she sobbed. "I don't think I can!"

June flung her arms about her. "We won't," she said. "We'll go back by the road. We've left the money. Why shouldn't we? Damn them anyway, the damn fools!"

"No, no," Kate said, as soon as she could control her voice. "This is crazy of me, June. It's just that I'm so tired. We must do exactly what it tells us to. And if that—that person hasn't hurt us so far, he probably won't. Perhaps he's gone away. Or perhaps, if it's one of them, he'll wait around for the money."

"I'm sure it would be all right to take the road," June said, but now Kate would not hear of it.

As they went downstairs, swished through the grass in the yard, and climbed the gate, there was no sound anywhere to disturb them. It was easier walking down the trail than up, and Kate was just beginning to be convinced that the prowler had gone, when suddenly, not thirty feet ahead of them, a man stepped out of the woods.

Kate drew in her breath hysterically and clutched June's hand, but then, with a sense of overpowering relief, she recognized Professor Hatfield.

"Hullo there!" he called pleasantly. "Taking a little walk? It's a pretty hot day for one."

"Yes," June said. "Kate and I have been exploring."

If Professor Hatfield suspected what they had actually been doing, he gave no sign of it.

"May I join you?" he asked. "I'll be going in your direction."

"Oh, do come with us," Kate exclaimed. "We'd love to have you."

She had been afraid that when they turned off the trail leading to his shack, he would keep straight on; but he did not leave them until they reached the top of the bluff directly above the farm.

"Perhaps I won't go down here," he said, "because it would only mean scrambling up again, but I'll wait a few minutes to give you time to get home."

"You weren't—" Kate asked hesitantly, "you weren't by any chance out on a little island earlier this afternoon? You weren't tracking us through the woods, were you?"

He chuckled. His small eyes peered at them quizzically.

"Dear me!" he exclaimed. "That sounds very sinister, doesn't it? Sort of like Red Riding Hood's wolf. No, as a matter of fact, I'd been tramping about across the main highway. It was a pleasure to run into you children. Remember, Kate, you promised to come and see me sometime, you and June. I realize that my house is rather remote, but I'd do my best to provide entertainment."

13

Kate stood at the door beside June and watched the green car, with Ralph driving Mr. Gladstone, move off between the trees to the gate, she could hardly realize that in a few hours the suspense might be over. Faintly, from somewhere beyond the valley, she could hear the sound of bells. Farmers were no doubt driving along the roads, on this quiet Sunday, to afternoon service in the little churches hidden among the woods. Clotilde was kidnapped on Thursday evening, she thought incredulously. "If they bring her back now, the whole thing will have taken less than three days.

June pulled out her handkerchief and wiped the sweat from her forehead. The afternoon was again hot. Masses of cloud lay along the rim of the hills, as if they lacked the energy to rise into the thick pale sky.

June yawned. "I think I'll go up to my room and see if I can take a nap," she said. "I hate to lie around waiting for them to get back, and there's nothing I feel like doing. I kept waking up last night. I guess you did, too, didn't you? You certainly were thrashing about."

"I *have* slept better," Kate admitted. "I'm sorry I disturbed you."

"It wasn't you that disturbed me," June said.

"You'd better go back to your own bed tonight," Kate suggested. "I'm sure it's much more comfortable."

"Yes, I guess I will," June said. "Damn this hot weather! I guess we'll have showers by evening."

June turned and went slowly into the house. Kate wished there were some chance of sleeping herself; but she knew that the most she could expect would be a stupefying half sleep that skirted the border of nightmare.

She strolled down toward the gate and wondered why she felt so lonely; but no—she did not actually wonder: she knew quite well. Now that Ralph had gone she felt that she had lost her one protector, her one link with the healthy world beyond this valley. Of course there was doubtless no longer any need for protection: the ransom had been paid, Clotilde would be returned, the whole cruel business would be finished; but Kate just now could draw little comfort from that reasoning. Nothing, she felt, could ever break the dark and poisonous spell that brooded over this valley.

She paused outside the gate, in the white road, and caught her glance straying to the junipers in whose shade Mr. Gladstone had sought refuge yesterday morning. It would have been some consolation to find him, if she couldn't have Ralph. She had felt, during their talk down here, that she was just beginning to know him; she was touched by his sense of failure. Poor Mr. Gladstone, he was certainly being punished.

As she started walking up the drive, she noticed a man and a woman coming toward her from the direction of the house, and in a minute recognized them as Mr. and Mrs. Larson, dressed obviously in their Sunday clothes. Sooner or later she must get to know them, because she was sure she would like them. June, who was such a friend of theirs, would help her in that.

"Hullo," she said now. "You must have lots of energy starting off for a walk in this heat."

"We're going to church," Mrs. Larson said with a suggestion of reproof.

Mr. Larson grinned. "Trust her!" he exclaimed. "If she lets me off in the morning, she gets me in the afternoon. She used to try to get me both times, but she's just about give that up."

Mrs. Larson allowed herself the faintest smile. "Now Olaf," she said, "don't you be fresh with the young lady. Don't you be acting like Felix."

"I'm coming to see you sometime soon," Kate said. "That is, if you will let me."

"Just tell me in time," Mrs. Larson said, "and I'll make some nice Norwegian coffeecake."

As she approached the house, Kate was half sorry she had met them: she had almost forgotten about them; she hadn't thought of their being around, but now she could not help thinking of their having gone away, like Mr. Gladstone and Ralph. Just now Kate would even have been glad to see Mavis; but Mavis had not appeared at lunch; she had kept to her room because, so Ruby announced, she had a "sick headache."

Kate skirted the front of the house, avoided the terrace, and walked into the garden. The sunlight was both harsh and veiled, and seemed to neutralize the tints of even the most brilliant flowers, so that the whole scene suggested a picture postcard. A small yellow wasp buzzed around her face, and she shook her head, not daring to brush it aside with her hand. From very far away, hardly louder than the buzz of the wasp, came the muffled growl of thunder. It might have been the caving in of huge vaults deep underground. Perhaps, she thought, when miners are trapped at the end of some close passage, the first crumbling of the shaft that blocks their escape to air and light sounds something like that.

She strolled back toward the terrace, then swerved and wandered through the shrubbery into the herb garden. She hardly knew whether she hoped or dreaded to meet Felix, as she had done yesterday morning; but Felix was not there.

It came as a relief when she heard a phrase on Jo's violin. It sounded like Mozart, but the sharp vaguely irritating smell of the herbs seemed to give it a hidden insistent meaning that had nothing to do with itself. It might have been an incantation.

She walked through the break in the hedge that led out on to the green in front of Jo's cottage. In a moment the violin stopped and Jo himself appeared in his front door.

"Wonderful!" he exclaimed. "You come as an answer to prayer. I was going through some sonatas with Mavis this afternoon, and of course she is ill, bless her soul, though I suspect she will be herself again tomorrow. Come in, do! You say you have played all the Mozarts. We will not practice. It is far too hot. We will simply read."

"I'd love to," Kate said. Nothing, it seemed, would make this dreadful period of waiting pass more quickly than playing Mozart sonatas.

They went through the long one in B flat, of which she was especially fond, and then tried the next one, in E flat. Kate did not feel so much at home in this one but on the whole it seemed to go well. When they had finished the last variation in the finale, Jo placed his violin on the piano, and wiped his face and neck with a huge handkerchief of orange silk.

"It is so hot!" he exclaimed. "I'm afraid I can't keep my mind entirely on the music, even on Mozart. A day like today we should dress like *him*, eh?" And he glanced up at St. Sebastian above the fireplace, bound to his tree, with a cloth about his loins, his body bristling with arrows.

"He doesn't look very comfortable," Kate said.

"I imagine," Jo said, "that in his ecstasy he could feel no pain. I could understand that. 'Love's arrows' is no mere pretty figure of speech. Like so many poetic figures that have come down through the ages, and so become meaningless to us, it is based on intimate personal experience."

Kate felt slightly uncomfortable. Jo was standing close behind her. There was a moment of silence, and again she heard, as far away as ever, the subterranean roll of thunder.

She got up from the piano bench and turned so that she could see him. He was staring at her with a fixed smile, his teeth tightly clenched.

"I have an idea," he said, as she walked away from him across the room. "A wonderful idea! It is too hot to play any more—at least to make music. Why not go swimming, you and I?"

Kate smiled with relief at this very normal suggestion, though nothing would have induced her to go swimming now with Jo.

"I'm afraid we'd get so warm climbing back over the bluff that it wouldn't be worth while," she said.

"Ah, of course, but we don't have to go over the bluff. If one follows upstream through the woods for about a mile this bluff peters out into nothing. There is a lovely little beach, and at this season the river is still cool."

"It sounds awfully nice," she admitted, "but I really haven't the energy this afternoon. And besides, I didn't bring my bathing suit out here. It never occurred to me."

"But I have no bathing suit either!" he exclaimed. "We would not need them. No one comes to that beach. This does not shock you, I hope, you who are an artist. It is a question of milieu. For grown men to go swimming in crowds in stuffy pools without even wearing trunks, the way your American men do, I find very distasteful. It always seems to me unpleasantly promiscuous and crude and at the same time slightly naïve. But for a young man in his prime, or hardly past it, and an exquisite young girl, to go swimming in a river, in the midst of the wilderness, to let themselves drift beneath overhanging boughs, to splash each other among the reeds—it would be very primitive and very beautiful and very innocent."

Kate would have laughed if she had not felt so uneasy. This suggestion was one of the things you make a note of to be amused at later but which at the time are anything but amusing. The smell of the herbs seeped faintly into this hot room; and as she noticed it, the odor seemed to vibrate with an effect of iridescence, so that at one moment it was mint she smelled, then sage, then tarragon. Jo was walking restlessly about.

"Well," he asked. "You'll come? Yes?" He stood and faced her, his head thrust slightly forward, the same tight smile on his lips.

"No," she said, and tried to smile naturally. "I certainly will not. I never felt less like a nymph."

"Ah," he exclaimed, "but I never felt more like Pan!"

He was standing between her and the door, and now he came slowly toward her, his arms outstretched, his black eyes fixed on hers, as if he would hypnotize her.

She looked desperately around, as if to decide which way to run, and then suddenly the complete assurance of his smile made her so angry that she did not even try to escape. Instead she waited for him to get within a yard of her, and then struck him sharply across his cheek.

"Ouch!" he exclaimed, and raised his hand to his face.

"Jo," she said fiercely. "Stop acting like a fool!"

He stepped backward, still rubbing his cheek.

"I hope my jaw doesn't swell," he said with an anxious air which was such a contrast to his manner of a moment ago that she had to restrain an hysterical giggle. "It would be very awkward holding the violin."

"If it does, it's your own fault," she said.

He looked at her with a tentative smile, as if he were testing his facial muscles.

"Yes," he admitted. "It was my fault. It was foolish. It was a lapse from grace, such as even the saints sometimes experienced. But this still close air, with thunder in the distance, I find it has a strangely aphrodisiac effect. It is some consolation to realize how quick my responses still are when subjected to adequate stimulus. Kate, my dear, you fierce tenderhearted virgin, if you will not come with me, then I must go by myself; and after I have soaked in that cold current for fifteen minutes you will find me once more as respectful as a worshiper before a Madonna. I hope this doesn't mean we can't have any more music together this month."

"Why shouldn't we have music?" she asked; but as she stepped out on to the green, she decided that after this she would be careful of the time she chose for it.

Ahead of her, from the direction of the big house, she heard Bobbie whining; she peered into the dense immobile shadow and presently discovered her, tied by a leash to a cherry tree near the back door. She went over to her, stooped, took her head, gracious and sleek as a young fawn's, between her fingers, and kneaded the folds of her throat. Kate would have liked to let her loose, but did not quite dare.

"Good-by, Kate," she heard Jo call, and looking over her shoulder, she saw him, with soap and towel in his hand, walking along the edge of the woods. "If I am drowned," he went on, "say a prayer for a lost soul."

He stepped into the fringe of trees and was gone.

Until the moment of his disappearance, Kate would not have believed that she could miss Jo; but now she would. have been glad to see him return. It was as if everybody were creeping away, one by one, according to some devious and furtive plan, as people might steal from a city at the rumor of plague. The whole farm, with its gardens, its great lawns, was beginning to take on the air of emptiness, of stealthy waiting, that had chilled her the other evening after she had played with Jo, and Clotilde had vanished. The harsh afternoon light seemed almost more treacherous than the darkness, just because it speciously appeared to be so frank. Again she heard thunder beyond the hills, and now it suggested a long sleepy growl from the depths of the jungle.

She felt suddenly that she must see June. Perhaps the music had wakened her; but even if June were still asleep, Kate would sit in her room, so that she could feel that someone, someone she trusted, was near. She said good-by to Bobbie, went in the back door, through the empty kitchen, and then hurried upstairs. Perhaps it would not be too selfish to wake June: she had been lying down for nearly an hour.

Kate hesitated by the closed door. Suppose it were locked, should she tap on the white paneling? But the door was not locked. She stepped into the room and looked at once toward the bed. The pillow showed a depression where June's head had lain, but June herself was not there.

Kate had to check a desire to burst into tears. Of course June might be in the bathroom across the hall. Kate went out quickly, tried the bathroom door: it opened to reveal another empty room.

But June might have gone downstairs to find *her;* June might have been walking through the living room, or the garden, at the very moment when she herself was coming in the back way and climbing the stairs. Kate ran along the hallway and downstairs once more: there was no one in the living room; there was no one on the terrace.

She stared out over the crude neutral brightness of the garden. "June," she called, "June, where are you?" and she realized that her voice was hushed, as if something that lay in wait in the thick depths of this breathless afternoon must not be allowed to hear.

She ran down, across the grass and through the poplars to the tennis court; then back through the herb garden to the green behind the house where she had started. Bobbie was still there, tied to the tree; but there was no one else.

Where was Felix? She must find him at once. Something awful, something that she could not bear to think of, might be happening to June. She went into the kitchen and looked around. It was somewhere back of the kitchen that Ruby and Felix had their rooms. Beside the refrigerator a door stood ajar. She peered into the room beyond: it was only a pantry, but beyond it there was another door, and this one was closed.

She knocked sharply and listened. After a minute, with a mixture of relief and dread, she heard someone moving about. The next instant the door opened, and she was standing face to face with Ruby, who was wearing an old kimono and who looked half asleep.

"Where's Felix?" Kate asked quickly. "I've got to see him."

Ruby blinked and stared at her suspiciously. "And just why have you got to see my husband?" she demanded.

Kate was too frightened now to get angry. "June has disappeared," she said. "I can't find her anywhere."

"What's the excitement?" Ruby asked. "June took care of herself all right before you got here. There's lots of places she could be."

"I know," Kate said, trying now to keep back her tears, "but don't you see, at this time, when this awful thing has happened to Clotilde, when June got that letter?—"

"If that's the way you feel," Ruby said, "why didn't you keep an eye on her yourself? I'm not paid to look after June. Neither is Felix."

Kate met Ruby's stony glance with a feeling of hopelessness. Then a wave of anger swept over her, carrying away even the realization of her terror.

"I won't argue with you," she said fiercely. "Tell me where Felix is, and don't waste any more time."

Ruby's glance did not waver; her expression did not change.

"If you must know," she said, "though I don't see it's any of your business, Felix has gone fishing."

"Whereabouts? Is he somewhere near?"

"He's somewhere along the river," Ruby said, with a trace of an ironic smile. "He may be upstream, he may be downstream. He may be near, he may be far. But let me give you one piece of advice. Not even Felix likes a woman along when he's fishing."

Before Kate could say anything else, Ruby had closed the door in her face.

For a minute Kate could only stand there, while her anger, her sense of injustice, rose within her like a searing hot geyser, shaking her body, bringing tears to her eyes; then it left her empty, for her sense of panic to rush back, to take possession of her trembling and make it its own. And mingled with her fear now, her fear for June and for herself which was one inseparable feeling, was a new sense of guilt. It was quite true: Ruby and Felix had not been paid to keep their eye on June; neither had she, of course; but in accepting Mr. Gladstone's invitation she had in a measure assumed that responsibility, and today of all days she had left her. Could Jo's asking her to make music with him be part of a cold-blooded scheme? Was it meant to keep her busy while June was spirited away?

She ran through, the pantry and the kitchen into the dining room. She called once more, desperately: "June!—June!" She could not bear to call again, because the house seemed so deathly still after her voice had stopped. Besides, what was the use? She knew June was not in this house.

But Mavis was. Even though Mavis was the last person you could count on, she must be told at once: she was June's mother. Kate remembered how beautifully she had played the César Franck; perhaps Mavis, after all, would surprise her.

Kate walked upstairs, tapping lightly on the banister with her fingers to break the silence, and knocked at the door of Mavis' room. No one answered. She turned the knob gently, the door opened, and Kate saw that the shades were drawn so that the room was filled with a sultry orange dusk. She could hear now an irregular stertorous breathing.

"Mrs. Gladstone," she called. "Mavis! I'm sorry to disturb you, but I simply have to."

The breathing paused for a second, and continued as before. Kate walked over to the bed.

Mavis was lying on her back, her head wrapped tightly in a towel. She had no make-up on, and her face was a uniform putty color, except for the flanges of her nose which Kate could see, now that they were bare of powder, were congested by a network of small veins. Her mouth lolled open. Even without bending over her, Kate could smell the stale stench of gin which coiled around her like an invisible fog. Mavis, too, in her own fashion, had gone away, like the others.

Kate turned from the bed. She must get out of this house at once. But where could she go? What could she do?

Then she thought of Professor Hatfield. He would be the one of all others to consult. He would know what to do, if anybody did. Fortunately she had seen just where he lived, and the bluffs, the woods themselves were not so terrifying as this empty house, the dull glare of these lawns and gardens. But even if the woods lay under the blackest enchantment, she must brave them now, because it was June she must think of—only of June.

She hurried downstairs, and in the hall it occurred to her that she could take Bobbie with her; that would be some company at least. But rather than go through the kitchen and perhaps run into Ruby, she went out through the living room, and around by the terrace and the herb garden. As she was untying Bobbie's leash, it struck her that perhaps Bobbie had been tied up so that she could not follow June.

With Bobbie straining at the leash, Kate hurried through the bushes to the tennis court and the wooded path that led to the crest of the bluff. If only Professor Hatfield were waiting at the top, as he had been yesterday when June and she had come down! Bobbie seemed to know the path well, for she went clambering ahead, stopping now and then to snuff the black leaf mold, to explore a juniper bush or a heap of pine needles. When Kate came to the overhanging ledge which she had noticed yesterday, she almost turned back; as she passed quickly under its fringe of

junipers she began talking to Bobbie to keep herself from thinking of what might be lurking above. The thunder was now almost
continuous but it sounded as far away as ever; she could imagine
its curdling this soggy green air among the trees, as it was said
to curdle milk.

When she reached the short grass at the top, Kate was out of
breath, and stood still a minute to look around her. The light
over the sprawling river, with its sand bars and islands, over the
miles of forest and bluff, was paler than yesterday; but straight
ahead of her the most distant hills, and the sky above them, were
a dense livid blue. As she watched that dark horizon, a pink-
white flame flared up for an instant and brought into relief the
volutes of nearer clouds.

She felt some small thing hit her ankles, and looking down
saw that Bobbie was digging in a patch of dirt and gravel about
a yard from where she was standing.

"Come along, Bobbie," she said, "we must be getting on."

She tightened the leash and gave it a little jerk, but Bobbie
paid no attention. She kept up her excited digging and scratching, her muzzle buried in the dirt, her paws sending up a steady
spray behind her.

"There's nothing there, Bobbie," she said. "That's not a rabbit hole."

But the next moment she leaned forward with an awful feeling
in her stomach and throat: there was something there—beneath
the dry yellow surface there was something clotted and dark, a
kind of red-brown paste that made an irregular stain more than
a foot across. She gave such a sharp pull on the leash that Bobbie
was lifted backward on to her hind legs, and almost fell over.

"Bobbie," she called. "Don't! Come here, Bobbie!" And she
dragged Bobbie along toward the rim of the first terrace from
which the bluff began dropping toward the river.

Then all at once Bobbie ran swiftly ahead, with excited whines
and barks. The leash did not quite reach to the little cliff, and
she strained and jerked at the end more violently than before,
her front feet pawing the air as if she were swimming against a
strong current.

"What is it?" Kate asked. "What are you after?" And as she stepped forward, Bobbie ran to the edge of the terrace and stretched her neck down as far as she could, with her same little whines.

Kate leaned over, herself. The crumbly yellow rock dropped almost sheer for about eight feet, and beneath was a grassy ledge a few yards wide, and then another miniature cliff.

"June!" Kate called breathlessly. "June dear, are you there? Are you hurt? Is it June, Bobbie? Is that why you're so eager?"

She looked along the top of the ledge to see how she could get down, and a few yards to the left she saw a half-dead cedar growing on the ledge below and reaching a few feet above the top of the cliff. It would be possible to climb down with its help.

Bobbie followed her in tense excitement as she walked quickly to it. "No, Bobbie," she said. "I can't take you. Its hard enough for me alone. You'll have to wait up there."

Then as carefully as she could she let herself down between the scratchy gray branches, and in a minute or so she was standing on the ledge below, and staring up at Bobbie's slim little head just out of reach.

Beyond the cedar tree the ledge narrowed swiftly and soon disappeared; but in the other direction it continued on a level around a curve in the main contour of the bluff. Kate walked in this direction, and when she reached the curve she saw that the cliff now overhung considerably, so that she would be invisible to anyone standing above.

Another cedar tree grew close to the rock, just beyond, and as she passed it she saw that she was standing at the entrance to a cave, one of the caves of which June and Professor Hatfield had spoken. But this was not a real cave: it was nothing but a stretch of grass, and then dirt, sloping steeply downward and backward for fifteen feet beneath the overhanging cliff; and even from where she stood, Kate could see something wrapped in a blanket lying on the ground at the bottom.

"June!" she called desperately. "June!" But she knew that if this was June she could not answer her.

She scrambled down the slope, knelt by the bundle, and pulled back the top fold of the blanket. As she did so, she noticed a faint smell, at once sweetish and nauseating, as if from the slime of some poisonous fungus.

The face she stared at was not June's; for the last instant she had known it could not be. If it were not for the clotted tangle of silvery-gold hair she would not have recognized those bruised and swollen features—that throat with the blackish grooves in the flesh, where strong fingers had pressed and dug into the larynx until death had come.

"Clotilde!" she gasped. "Clotilde!"

She drew in her breath sharply. The faint smell seemed to line her mouth and throat, to penetrate to the center of her brain. She must struggle or it would paralyze her thoughts.

Then she was aware that something had changed: a bar of shadow lay across the blanket where it wrapped Clotilde's legs. It did not move, and for an instant she tried to tell herself that it had been there from the first. But there had been nothing at the mouth of the cave to cast a shadow.

She forced herself, very slowly, to turn her head. A man's figure was outlined against the sky at the cave's entrance.

"No!" she called wildly, without thinking of what she said. "No! No! You mustn't!"

The man did not advance from where he stood. Only his head jerked forward to peer down at her, with a swift hyena-like movement.

14

"You seem to have discovered something." Not until he spoke did Kate recognize the man as Felix. His voice did not sound quite natural: its smoothness seemed hardly to conceal a kind of chuckle and snarl. He was stripped to the waist, and his whole chest and torso bristled with patches of reddish hair so thick that it looked as if his body might once have been covered with fur, like a wild beast's, and that the blotches of pale tight skin showing through were merely where the fur had worn off, or been eaten away by the spread of some scurf or mange. Even when she looked at his face, smooth and gleaming with sweat as it peered down at her, it was hard to think of this man as the debonair Felix she remembered.

She tried to tell herself that she should feel relieved, that it was all right, that there was no need for panic, but even so she could hardly force herself to speak. She must swallow; she must do something to overcome this paralysis of her throat and chest.

"Yes," she said finally, in a queer flat voice. "It's Clotilde. She's been murdered."

"Murdered? How can that be? Mr. Gladstone and your friend Green have gone to rescue her."

"But it *is* Clotilde!" she said. "She's been strangled. It must have been right away."

"Right away?"

"Right after she was kidnapped."

"What makes you think so?"

"Because—because she must have been dead for several days."

Felix lifted his head and sniffed the air. She had grown used to looking at him now, outlined against the light-filled sky, and she could make out his features more clearly; she could see that his eyes were half closed, that his nostrils moved like an animal's. She remembered that hyenas made their dens in cliffs and fed on carrion.

"Yes, perhaps," he said; and again his head jerked forward. As his eyes focused upon her once more, it seemed to her that he was smiling. "And so you think she's been strangled?" he asked. "That's a very brutal way to kill, but I suppose it's practical. Once someone has his fingers pressing against your windpipe, you can't make much noise. In fact there's not much of anything you can do."

"No," she said faintly. "No, there's not."

She drew in her breath once more and cowered backward as he took several steps down the slope into the cave; but after he had come a couple of yards he stopped and crouched on his heels on a ledge of stone that broke the steep incline, like a landing. Now that the sky was no longer behind him, she could see his red-brown eyes fixed upon her with a gaze that was at once soft and sly; she could see the faint rise and fall of his chest beneath its thatch of sticky hair. He had not threatened her; he had not suggested in any way that she could not leave the cave whenever she wanted to; but from where he was crouching he blocked the middle of the entrance, and she could not bear to take a step toward him, to try to get out of this place with its faint numbing stench of the grave, for fear of the awful moment when he would stretch out his arm to stop her. At least so far she could not be sure she was a prisoner; she knew that she could not be sure, because if she were, her heart would swell and swell until it filled her whole breast, until she could not breathe and would die of pure terror.

"Hasn't it struck you," he asked after a minute, "that it was a pretty dangerous thing to go looking for Clotilde? If the murderer left the body here, he must have hoped it wouldn't be found just yet. If he had caught you here, he might have felt he had to—well, shall we say, make some arrangements."

"I wasn't looking for Clotilde," she said, and although he was not more than ten feet away, she wondered whether her voice could reach him. "I was looking for June."

"That would be just as risky," he said, "and just as useless. If June is gone, I'm afraid there is not much you could do for her either."

"Where is June?" she asked. "Do you know where she is? I must find her."

This time she was sure he smiled. "Who knows?" he said. "She might be in another cave wrapped in a blanket. Let's hope that's not the case."

"Will you come with me, to look for her?"

An agonizing gust of hope fluttered for an instant in her breast as she stared up at him.

"I must cool off a little," he said, "before I do anything else. As you can see, I'm very warm. I've been exercising. When the air is as heavy as it is this afternoon, and charged with electricity, it's apt to be oppressive, or don't you think so? Of course it's exciting too. You kind of feel that anything may happen."

And now again Kate was aware of the soft persistent thunder, like some huge animal growling to itself as it thrust its muzzle deep into the warm entrails of its prey.

"It's too bad you didn't bring the herbs I gave you along," he went on. "We could have used them in here, couldn't we? Did you put them in a vase in your bedroom? I kind of liked to think that you would be smelling them as you lay in bed. I even flattered myself they might remind you of me. If the murderer found you here, it would have been sort of hard on him, poor chap, to find such a beautiful girl—to have to make arrangements for her. It would seem such a waste, wouldn't it? I think he'd try to get all the fun he could first. And then perhaps, who knows, if he was a well-set-up fellow, if he knew his stuff, there might be no need for final arrangements. That seems hardly possible, but you never can tell with girls, and he must be the kind of fellow that takes a bit of a risk now and then. It might be worth it. Who can tell?"

As he crouched on the small ledge, he had been balancing himself by the tips of his fingers touching the stone on either side of him; and now she noticed that he was slowly pushing himself up. His head stretched forward, swaying slightly, and the muscles moved in his arms and shoulders.

Then he sprang to his feet and looked around as Bobbie scurried, tumbling over herself, down the slope to the bottom of the cave and thrust her paws into Kate's lap, her tail wagging frantically. The next moment another shadow pointed downward across the dirt to where Kate was kneeling, and Kate staring up at the sky recognized Professor Hatfield.

"Well, well," he exclaimed cheerfully. "This is a surprise! I wondered why Bobbie seemed so excited."

"I'm glad you turned up, Professor," Felix said. "Miss Kate here has discovered that Clotilde has been strangled. She found the body. It's down there, she says, wrapped in that blanket. I was telling her it would have been a risky thing if the murderer had been hanging round the neighborhood and had trapped her here in this cave."

Felix had not moved from where he stood; the timbre of his voice had hardly changed; and yet he was once more the respectful though somewhat independent Felix she knew, the man who had driven her out to the farm, who had gallantly offered her the bunch of herbs. He was shaggier than she would have expected, but that was the only difference. For a moment it seemed to her that she had been imagining things or that the shock of finding Clotilde's body had unhinged her mind temporarily; but then as she recalled the soft insistent gloating of his eyes as his glance had moved over her body not more than a minute ago, she knew only too well that she had been suffering from no delusion.

"So poor Clotilde was murdered!" Professor Hatfield exclaimed gently. "I half suspected it."

He walked down into the cave past Felix, knelt beside Kate, and stared for a long moment at Clotilde's face. Then he bent still nearer, and Kate turned away her head as she realized that he was examining the awful dark grooves in the throat.

"Hmmm!" he murmured. "I can see a few shreds of black lint or something of the sort in the marks made by the murderer's fingers. It looks as if he had worn black gloves."

"I suppose now," Felix said, "there's no longer any reason for not calling the police. I didn't like to leave Miss Kate here alone, and she seemed so upset by what she had found, and I don't wonder, that I thought she better have a chance to catch her breath for a few minutes before she tried the path."

"That was very thoughtful of you," Professor Hatfield said. "Yes, I agree with you, we should certainly now get in touch with the police as soon as possible."

"Should we try to take the body down?" Felix asked. "I guess you and I could make it all right."

"I don't think it should be moved," Professor Hatfield said. "They will want to find it just as it was left."

"Well then," Felix suggested, "why don't I run right back to the farm and tell Mr. Gladstone, if he's got home, the poor man. If not, I'll call the police department in Woodside."

"An excellent idea!" Professor Hatfield said. "We'll be along shortly. I think Kate still feels a trifle uncertain, don't you, my dear? I'm sorry I haven't a good shot of brandy to give you."

Kate did not answer. It was such a relief to see Felix walk out of the cave that she was afraid she might burst into tears. She saw that Professor Hatfield had taken a small penknife from his pocket and was carefully removing what looked like a shred of black worsted from a crease in the swollen throat. She turned her head away.

"There's plenty left for the police," Professor Hatfield said with an air of apology. "But I thought I'd like to have a sample of this myself, just in case I should happen to come across a pair of black gloves. And now, my dear, if you feel strong enough, I think we might move at any rate out on to the ledge. This cave is not particularly inviting just now."

He helped Kate to her feet, and reached down to take the end of Bobbie's strap. "Don't be afraid to lean on me," he said. "You still look rather pale, my dear."

As Kate stepped out with him into the crude light on the ledge, she wondered if she would have a phobia about enclosed places for the rest of her life. She looked in either direction along the strip of sparse sunlit grass to make sure that Felix had gone.

"He's the man!" she then said tensely. "He's one of the murderers."

"You mean Felix?" Professor Hatfield asked.

"Yes. I'm sure of it."

"I shouldn't be surprised," the professor said. "But would you tell me why you think so, my dear?"

"The things he said. The way he looked. He all but admitted it. It was horrible."

"Under the circumstances," Professor Hatfield said, "I think it's just as well that I arrived when I did. But my dear Kate, how did you ever find the cave?"

"It was Bobbie really," she explained. "I came up on the bluff because I was going to your house, on account of June."

"June?" he asked. "What's the matter with June?"

"She disappeared. I've been almost forgetting it because I've been so scared myself. But June has gone. She went up to take a nap and I foolishly played some sonatas with Jo. Then Jo left to go swimming and when I went up to find June she wasn't there. Do you suppose—do you suppose that Felix has murdered her too?"

"I'm sure he hasn't," Professor Hatfield said. "I wouldn't worry too much about her now. I think you'll find she merely took a walk in the neighborhood. As a matter of fact, before I turned up a minute ago, I had been watching Felix for some time. He was down near the river, in a little thicket from which I've often watched aquatic birds. He had no idea, I might say, that I was watching him. What interested me was what he was doing. He was digging an oblong hole in the ground, which is rather loose and sandy just there. It was perhaps five feet-six or so long, a couple of feet wide, and when he left, it was a good four feet deep. You may be sure he's been busy since lunch time. No wonder he looked hot just now."

"Was it—was it a grave?" she asked.

"That's what I was following him up the bluff to discover," he said. "But since I still didn't want him to see me, I let him have a good head start. Then when I saw Bobbie up on top, I kind of suspected you or June might be around, and I thought I'd better make haste."

"But mightn't one of the others have gone off with June?" she asked, only half relieved. "One of the accomplices from outside?"

"I'm quite sure now there were no accomplices from outside," he said. "For the last day or so I've been coming more and more to that conclusion, and finding Clotilde's body here just about proves it."

"But I don't understand," Kate said. "I don't see that it proves anything."

"Let's go up to the top of the bluff," Professor Hatfield suggested, "where the air is a little fresher. Then you can sit down and rest for a few minutes, and I'll tell you what I mean. Once we get back to the farm the police will be arriving and everything will be in confusion."

"But what about Felix? Won't he be escaping?"

"You may be sure that Felix is not the kind of man to get in a panic and give himself away, just because he suspects you suspect he's the murderer. At the present moment he's probably telephoning the police. Or perhaps he's telling June, who no doubt was just as worried about you as you were about her, that you are in safe hands."

They had been walking slowly along the ledge and now they reached the old cedar which Kate had climbed down. Mr. Hatfield helped her up through the twisted gray branches, handed Bobbie to her, and then climbed up briskly himself.

As he seated himself beside Bobbie and her in the grass, he drew in a long breath. "That's better!" he exclaimed. "I shouldn't wonder if that storm reached us eventually, but perhaps not for an hour or so."

Kate saw that the band of blue-black cloud had climbed up the sky; in contrast to its darkness, the nearer woods, just beyond the river, looked brighter than before, shining with a brassy glow; and she could see chains of lightning forking down into the hills like the tongues of snakes. There was a slight coolness in the air, and the thunder reminded her now of the boom of surf.

"I can tell you very quickly how things happened," he went on, "and then you won't have to worry any more, for either yourself or June; because you may be sure even if it's impossible to

pin anything on Felix, and I think there's enough already to
arrest him, that he won't try anything more just now. You see,
my dear, he must have lain in wait for Clotilde somewhere near
the house, very likely in the bushes between Jo's cottage and the
terrace. He seized her throat from behind. The markings make
that quite clear: you can see the pressure of the fingers from
both hands on the windpipe. Felix is an exceptionally powerful
man. He could have grasped her throat so suddenly and with
such violence that she could make no sound. There were signs
of hemorrhage where his nails must have torn partly through the
fingers of the gloves and broken the skin, and that shows how
tightly they pressed into her throat. You and Jo were no doubt
still playing at the time, and even if there had been a slight gasp,
you would not have heard it."

Kate tried to suppress the tremor that ran through her body
as she thought that this had been happening to Clotilde at the
very time when she herself had been so sure that Clotilde was
standing close behind her, looking at the music. She still must
have been hearing the sonata, floating softly through the night,
when violence had sprung upon her out of the darkness and her
mind had reeled in a spasm of agony and terror.

"Once he thought she was dead," Mr. Hatfield continued serenely, "he must have carried her up here. For a man of Felix's
strength that would not have been difficult. The blood that Bobbie uncovered undoubtedly marks the place where he hacked off
her scalp. I hope that bleeding does not mean that perhaps even
then she was still alive. You remember I spoke the other day of
the type of mind that would do such a thing without a qualm. No
doubt he was rather proud of what fatuously must have seemed
to him his original idea; but it was mainly for practical reasons:
he wanted to scare Mr. Gladstone so much by this warning that
he would not notify the police and would deliver the ransom
in the manner specified. And you see, it worked. The hitch, of
course, was that he hadn't realized that Bobbie had followed him.
When she snatched the scalp, he must have been desperate. Probably what he had meant to do was to bury the body somewhere
in the bottom lands. He might have flung it in the river, but I

doubt it, because the current is apt to wash things ashore, and the water sinks so low in prolonged droughts that even a weighted corpse might come to light. No, I'm quite sure he was going to bury it, as he was starting to do this afternoon, and then the scalp lock would have been delivered at the same time with the note, perhaps flung into the window of Mr. Gladstone's study.

"But he realized then that Bobbie would probably run home with her treasure, that it might be discovered at once, and that he must not be suspiciously absent. So he dropped the body over this little cliff, still wrapped in the blanket that he must have had with him in his ambush, and shoved it down into the bottom of that cave until he could come back and put it permanently out of sight. And now you see why I'm sure there was no outside accomplice. If there had been, he never would have left the body here. When Felix went back to the farm, the other man would have disposed of it in some safe place. Perhaps Felix didn't think he could even wait to put it in the cave when he saw Bobbie running off. He may only have managed it afterward when he ran into the woods with Ralph and Jo, pretending to search for the mysterious man who threw the letter."

"I was going to ask you about that," Kate said. "You see there must have been another man. There must have been an outsider to throw that letter into the garden. You remember Mavis saw him."

As she had been listening to Professor Hatfield's even voice, talking of this crime with the mild detachment with which he might have discussed a problem in mathematics, Kate had felt herself growing more calm; she was even able now to look at that frightful waiting in the cave as a thing that had happened and now was finished, that could not happen again and so had lost something of its terror. Probably, she thought, this is the very best treatment anyone could give me to prevent that experience developing into some kind of complex, and she felt she would be grateful to Mr. Hatfield as long as she lived.

He smiled at her now, as if he were delighted at her objection. "Ah," he said, "that was just the impression the episode was meant to convey. It's a fine example of impromptu tactics, of taking immediate advantage of an unforeseen situation."

She could even return his smile, as she crumpled Bobbie's ears, and sniffed the coolness of the approaching storm.

"I must be very stupid," she said, "but I don't see what you mean."

"You say the letter was flung in from outside, by someone lurking in the shadows, but the fact is that none of us saw any such thing. All we saw was the letter lying in the grass just beyond the edge of the garden, at the foot of the little slope that leads down to the garden from the terrace where we all were standing. It might have been flung from any point of the compass."

"But if anyone had flung it from the terrace," she said, "somebody would surely have seen him do it."

"Ah, there's where you're wrong," he exclaimed, and raised his finger as in the gentlest reproof at such inaccuracy. "We were all so excited at that moment, and so confused, that he could doubtless have done it undetected at almost any time. He could have taken it carefully from his pocket, wrapped in a handkerchief to prevent fingerprints, and with a flick of his wrist, he could have shied it on to the lawn behind him. It was hardly twenty feet, you remember, from the edge of the terrace, and the envelope was weighted with a splinter of sandstone—no doubt to be flung, as I suggested a moment ago, through some window. But Felix was waiting for the perfect chance, waiting quite coldly, I imagine, but tensely too. And then when Mavis saw something in the shadows, something that attracted our attention, he seized the perfect opportunity."

"But Mavis saw a man," Kate said. "Do you think she was lying?"

"Mavis perhaps persuaded herself she saw a man," he admitted. "A man just then would be the most dramatic thing to see, and Mavis is not averse to dramatics, especially if she can play a leading role. But Mavis did not say she saw a man. I remember her phrase because it struck me at the time. She said she saw something 'dark and swooping,' and for the moment I thought of course she had seen one of the beautiful owls that I'm so fond of. But I was probably the only person who thought that, and I only thought it for a moment. Mavis pointed off to the right of the sundial. We were all staring in that direction, trying to see if we also could make out something moving in that darkness, which was, moreover, the general direction from which you said Bobbie had come. Then, the next instant, we saw the letter lying on the grass to the left, near the poplars that hide the tennis court. We then naturally assumed that the moving thing Mavis had seen must have been a man, that he had flung the letter the moment before Mavis had noticed him. In fact I recall thinking that it was perhaps the swift movement of his arm that she had seen which would account for the strange adjective 'swooping.' But during the minute or so that our attention was attracted to the far corner of the garden, Felix could almost have walked out on to the grass and placed the letter there by hand without anyone's noticing. As for shying it from behind him, there was nothing to it. It was child's play. Not that I have the least doubt," he continued with his dry smile, "that if the police question Mavis on the subject, she will swear that she not only saw the man, but saw him fling the letter, saw the curve it described in the air from the time it left his fingers to the second later when it landed on the grass."

Kate tried to recall the scene as accurately as she could but everything that had happened so soon after the shock of discovering the scalp remained a little confused, as if she had been half asleep.

"Yes," she said doubtfully, after a minute, "yes, I can see that it might have been that way. I'm sure it was, if you think so, because you see things so clearly. But then, what about the next night? If Felix was so nicely fixed— But of course you don't know about my experience."

"Yes, I do," he said. "Ralph told me. We've been sort of working together these last two days. That only helps to prove my point. Felix was nicely fixed for the moment, but he still had the problem of disposing of Clotilde's body. Even granting that it was improbable anyone would come across it for a day or so— although I quite well might have—it would be noticed before long by anyone who came to the top of the bluff. And that hot humid weather yesterday couldn't have made him feel any more comfortable. He didn't quite dare go out again that same night. He knew that people wouldn't be sleeping well. I doubt if Mr. Gladstone slept at all. And the next day was just as bad. If he had been gone from his work for several hours, people would have wondered. He chose the next night, or rather the small hours of the morning. Unluckily for him, you woke up. You heard something and investigated and I compliment you on your nerve. You see, your trip downstairs wasn't in vain, after all: if Felix had not been put off, Clotilde's body might never have been discovered. When he saw you watching him by the front door, Felix, you may be sure, scuttled around the house and in the back door to his room. For all he knew, you might waken everybody and the house might be searched. That was Friday night. I doubt if he would have started up yesterday, because by then he may have realized that he was being watched."

"Were you watching him then?" she asked. "Did you suspect him already?"

"I've been watching everyone at some time or another," he said, smiling. "I was watching you and June, and I'm afraid I gave you quite a scare, but after all it was for your own good. And Ralph was helping me. I'd sort of deputized him to keep an eye on Felix. I think Felix may have suspected what Ralph was up to, and that was why he specified that Ralph should go with Mr. Gladstone to call for Clotilde. And Sunday was a good day, too. He could go off fishing by the river without doing anything unusual. He probably felt pretty sure of himself at last. It must have been something of a shock when he found you in the cave, and still more of one when I walked in. The only thing he could do was to bluff, and I must say he did it admirably."

Professor Hatfield scrambled to his feet "I suppose we had better go down now," he said. "Mr. Gladstone may have got back, and in a little while we'll be having to answer questions from the police. I hope it won't be too much of a strain, my dear. I hope you feel a little better. Here, let me help you."

He took her hands and pulled her lightly to her feet.

"I feel much better," she said. "I don't think I'll mind the police. It's Mr. Gladstone that I can't bear to see."

They walked over the crest of the bluff, turned to take a last look at the storm, and then started down through the trees.

"The greatest relief," she said presently, "is to know who it is, and to know they will surely get him. The kind of things I hate most are things that happen mysteriously."

They had reached the little ledge of rock that skirted the path, and she felt that now for the first time she could walk under it without stooping or hurrying. But Bobbie, whom they had taken off her leash, had run ahead, and now was beginning to whimper.

Kate peered through the black-green shadow under the junipers to see what she was doing. The next moment, swaying, she reached backward and caught Professor Hatfield's hand.

Felix's body lay sprawled on its face, head downward, along the path, his skull split wide open so that through the mess of blood she could see the pale convolutions of his brain.

15

A gale had swept down into the valley, the thunder was banging among the hills, and the first drops of rain were beginning to fall, when between crashes Kate heard a car stopping in front pf the house. Professor Hatfield and she hurried to the door. It was not the police, whom the professor had notified half an hour ago, but Mr. Gladstone and Ralph; and Kate could hardly measure her relief when she saw that June was with them.

"Will you tell Mr. Gladstone about Clotilde?" she asked quickly. "I don't think I could bear to."

She had broken the news of Felix's death to Ruby, and she still was haunted by the sudden deadening of her face: it was as if her life's blood had frozen in that moment, to leave her a ghost, moving in a world of shadows.

"You say he's lying on the path to the bluff?" she had asked.

"Yes," Kate said gently, "but I don't think you better go there, Ruby."

"He belonged to me," Ruby said, "in spite of all of them. I've stood a lot from him. I guess I can stand this."

When Kate told Professor Hatfield where Ruby had gone, the professor had looked faintly disturbed. "I hope she doesn't change anything," he said, "though I think I observed pretty carefully how things were. I'm afraid she may get rather wet if she stays out there too long."

"I don't think she would mind that just now," Kate said. "I don't think she'll mind much of anything ever again."

And now as she watched Mr. Gladstone get out of the car, with the wind-lashed trees on the pale lawn behind him, with lightning shooting down into the hills and thunder rolling about the sky, it seemed to her that he too was a ghost.

"She wasn't there," he said, as he stepped into the hall. "There was no burned-down barn within miles. There was no stream and no cabin. The whole thing was a Goddamned hoax." He swept his hand across his face, as if to wipe off the rain that had splashed it. "It certainly looks," he said, "as if we'd never see her again."

Professor Hatfield took his arm and led him into the living room. Ralph, harassed and somber, walked after them. Kate seized June's hand and pressed it impulsively.

"At least you're all right!" she exclaimed. "Where were you, June? I was so afraid they'd got you too."

"I found I couldn't sleep," June said. "I might have known. So presently I came downstairs and looked for you. You were playing the piano with Jo. I didn't like to butt in, and I just couldn't sit still, so I thought I'd walk up the road toward town to meet Father and Clotilde. Father picked me up near the top of the hill. He's in quite a state. But I just can't believe that Clotilde is dead, Katey. Do you think they've taken her somewhere far away? Do you think they will send another note?"

"I don't think there will be any more notes," Kate said. She flung her arm across June's shoulder, and led her to the stairs. "Let's go up to my room," she went on. "Awful things have happened this afternoon, June dear, and I must tell you about them. Professor Hatfield is going to tell your father and Ralph."

When they stepped into Kate's bedroom, the rain was falling in such dense sheets that it almost wiped out Jo's cottage and the wall of tossing branches behind it. She wondered if Jo by this time had come back from the river. He had not been anywhere around when Professor Hatfield and she returned from the bluff, and just a few minutes before the car had driven up, the professor had gone again to his cottage to look for him. It occurred to her that it could not be much more than an hour and a half ago that he had left for his swim, though it seemed like yesterday.

He had said the beach was only a mile upstream, but perhaps in his eagerness to persuade her to go with him he had minimized the distance. And then, as she recalled that scene, pushed so far away by what had happened since, it struck her that, after all, he had not tried to persuade her very hard. Doubtless she could not measure the depths of masculine fatuity; but could even Jo really have thought that she would go for a nudist swim with him in the river? Perhaps again he had merely wanted to get rid of her. For what purpose? But she had lived through so many actual horrors today that she had no longer the energy to speculate on the unknown. In a sane world it would be fantastic to suspect Jo of such a brutal crime; but apparently the world was not sane—at least the world in this valley. Perhaps the only thing you could do was to cling with desperation to your own sanity. Meanwhile she had a task before her.

June had flung herself into the chaise-longue, and Kate sat on the bed. As Kate told her of the afternoon she did not once interrupt. It almost seemed as if she were too tired to take it all in; but when Kate had finished, June stood up quickly.

"Where's Ruby now?" she asked.

"I don't know," Kate said. "Perhaps she's still with Felix."

"I don't believe she'd stay out there in this rain," June said. "I'm going down to her room, Kate, to see if she's come back. I don't know what Felix has done, but she was crazy about him. I guess I'm her best friend around here. I guess I'm the only person she might like to see."

It struck Kate as a pathetic commentary on the Gladstone family that the person about whom June should show most concern was Ruby. However, the next instant she had to revise her impression, for June turned in the doorway, waited a moment for a peal of thunder to subside, and then said:

"I wish you'd go down to see Father, Kate. He doesn't say much but I know he likes you a lot. Clotilde's death will be a bad shock to him. If you'll be nice to him now, just at first, it will make it a little easier."

"And how about you?" Kate asked.

"I might be some help to Ruby," June said, "but not Father."

And before Kate could protest she had stepped out into the dark hall.

Glancing from her window, Kate noticed that now there was a light in Jo's cottage. The rain was falling more gently; the breeze had subsided, and she could see, scattered across the turf, a litter of torn leaves and twigs.

She walked quickly downstairs through the dusky house. She had seen, as she passed Mavis' room, that her door was still closed, and it gave her an odd feeling to think that Mavis even now knew nothing of what had happened. Kate suspected, however, that the thing she would most regret when she woke up would be having missed the thrill of the first disclosures.

The lights were on in the living room. Mr. Gladstone was sunk in an armchair near the fireplace; Professor Hatfield was leaning against the mantel. Each of them had a glass in his hand.

"My dear Kate," Mr. Gladstone said as she came in, "I must apologize for a certain lack of cheer about the house. My dear wife, who I'm told is still sleeping off a drunk, is probably acting more sensibly than any of the rest of us. Which reminds me, let me get you something. You look as if you needed it."

He rose from his chair before she could stop him. "No, no," he exclaimed. "It's still a pleasure to get a drink for a pretty girl—but that's about all I feel up to. Would you like Scotch or bourbon?"

"I don't really know the difference," Kate said. "I wish you wouldn't bother." There was something very pathetic to her in Mr. Gladstone's attempt, even now, to maintain his jaunty manner.

"I think Jo has come back," she told Professor Hatfield, as Mr. Gladstone went for the whisky. "I saw a light in his room."

"I thought he might have," Professor Hatfield said. "Ralph stepped out just a minute ago to see. I shall be curious to hear his adventures, if any, though I rather suspect his afternoon, from the time he left his room, will have been completely uneventful."

He cocked his head as if he had caught in the distance the note of some rare warbler. Then he walked quietly across the room and looked out over the lawn and the drive.

"It's probably as well Jo has got home," he exclaimed, "because here at last are the police. They will certainly want to question everyone. I'm afraid we may even have to disturb Mavis."

"Will the questioning be long?' Kate asked, not so much in alarm as in pure weariness.

Professor Hatfield smiled at her reassuringly.

"You and I will be the ones who have most to tell," he said. "It's a pity Mavis can't exchange roles with you. But I'm sure they'll be nice to you, my dear. I made the acquaintance of Inspector Waters last summer, and several others. In fact, they've done me the honor of consulting me once or twice, quite unofficially. They know I have a weakness for crime."

It must have been nearly eleven when Kate stepped out on to the dark terrace. Inspector Waters and the two men with him had gone into Mr. Gladstone's study, and one by one the household had been summoned for questioning. Most of them had remained only a few minutes, but Jo and Ruby had each been kept for at least a half hour, and she herself had been almost as long. As they sat waiting in the living room, trying to seem unconcerned, wondering who would be next, it had made her think of some lugubrious and endless game, the kind you used to have to play with children you hardly knew at birthday parties.

After dinner, which Emmy Larson had cooked and which had not been served until nine, Kate had taken two liqueur glasses of brandy, but this had had merely the effect of making her thoughts move around her in dark blurred circles. Mavis had hurried from the table in the midst of the meal and had not returned; Professor Hatfield had gone home; Jo had retired to his room, convinced, so he said, that he had caught pneumonia, and Ralph, more restless than ever, had gone for a walk. When she had stepped outside a minute ago, the only people left in the room were Mr. Gladstone, with the brandy still beside him, trying to concentrate on a chess problem, and June scowling to herself as she read *Little Women*. Kate thought there might still be policemen about the place, but she was not sure.

The air was sweet and cool after the storm. The sky was filled with stars, and she recognized Vega as she had done on her first evening. That was only three nights ago; and there was a whole month before her. Could she bear to keep on living here, in this valley, day after day, week after week? As she thought of the succession of events since Felix had knocked at her door back in Woodside, with their ghastly climax on that dark woodland path, it seemed to her that she had been groping her way through the narrowing circles of an inferno, walking down and down to an unimaginable doom.

She heard a step on the tiles behind her, and turning she saw that Ralph had just come out of the living room. She had never been so glad to see anyone in her life; but the next instant she felt more depressed, more lonely than ever, because she realized that of course Ralph would not be staying. There was no longer any reason why he should.

"Oh Ralph," she exclaimed. "I'm so glad you turned up! I couldn't bear it in the house. And out here I've been sort of drowning in all kinds of black, sticky thoughts. It may be just because I'm a little drunk. I hope so. But if this is what it feels like to be drunk, I must say I can't see the attraction."

He took her arm and led her toward the edge of the terrace. "And am I glad to see you!" he exclaimed. "You know why I went walking after dinner? Because I felt it wasn't decent to want to see you so much the very day I'd learned Clotilde was dead. But then I thought, why shouldn't I want to see you? It wasn't because of what I felt for Clotilde. I have no feeling for Clotilde any more. Not even hate. Not even pity, because she is not there any longer to be pitied. No, it was just a couple of words: I had been her 'fiancé'; we had been 'engaged'; and so the correct thing was to show a discreet display of bereavement, like going into light mourning. The hell with it! I guess I may be a little drunk, too. Come on, let's walk down into the garden. I've got some questions I want to ask you. First and foremost: What are you going to do now? You're certainly not going to stay here?"

"Oh yes I am," Kate said, and she was glad he had spoken, because it was so much easier to answer someone else's doubt than it was her own. "Why shouldn't I?"

"I should think you'd seen enough of this place already."

"I'm not staying as a vacation," she said. "I came out here to be with poor June. I feel now that she needs me more than ever."

"Do you realize that there's still a murderer at large?"

"He's probably miles away by this time," she said, "and at any rate, he's not after *me*."

"How do you know who he's after? Weren't you surprised when you found Felix had been killed?"

"Yes," she said, "I was. Please don't make me think of it now."

"I want you to think of it," he said fiercely. "I want to rub your nose in it, if necessary. I want you to realize that this is no place for you to stay."

They had stepped down over the wet grass into the garden, and now he was pressing her arm almost roughly as they walked up the central path toward the sundial.

"Well, really, Ralph," she said with a nervous artificial laugh, "after all, that's something I'll have to decide for myself."

"If you want to be a little fool," he exclaimed, "I'm going to stop you, whether you like it or not. Day before yesterday, by the tennis court, you told me I lacked detachment. Perhaps I did. It's hard to be detached about oneself. You talked about romantic self-sacrifice! Well, that particular problem was solved for me without my lifting a finger, which may have been just as well. It doesn't do much to boost my self-esteem, but I probably would have made a mess of it. The one thing that might have saved me would have been listening to you. Now you're going to listen to me. I'm not going to have you running any more risks, for all the Junes in the world. I know June much better than you do. She's quite able to look out for herself, believe me."

His voice, in its intensity, had grown louder; though Kate felt it was perhaps the brandy she had drunk that made it seem so loud, so all-enveloping. The night pressed softly about her. She felt a longing to give way before this urgent voice, to close her eyes, to let herself be carried far from this valley to a warm safe place where she could sleep. She must struggle against it.

"If only you would stay here, too, Ralph," she said; and she knew that this was a feeble compromise, that she must begin again.

But before she had the chance, Ralph was speaking.

"Do you think anything will drag me away," he exclaimed, "as long as you are here? But damn it, I keep forgetting I'm not a free man! The Navy may be calling me at any time. That settles it! If you don't tell Mr. Gladstone tomorrow morning that you're leaving, then I will."

"Of course I can't bear it here," Kate said, and in spite of her efforts she could not keep her voice steady. "You must know that, Ralph. But if I ran away like that and then anything happened to June, I'd feel horribly about it—just horribly—"

Then before she could stop herself she was sobbing violently; and Ralph had taken her in his arms and was kissing, just as violently, her wet cheeks.

"Kate," he said, when at last he could catch his breath, "Kate, dearest, I can't bear to see you unhappy. And this may be the worst of all, but I can't help it! I'll have had this anyway!" And once more she felt his lips on hers, on her cheeks, her eyelids.

She did not know how long it was before he was speaking to her again: "Kate, can't you stop crying? Kate, say something! Do you find this utterly repulsive?"

"No," she said through her sobs. "No, Ralph, of course I don't."

"Then you do love me, Kate?"

"I don't know," she said, and as she talked her tears kept rolling into her mouth. "I don't know, Ralph, I really don't know."

But she knew at least that in all the times young men had asked her that question, this was the first time she had not been quite sure that she was *not* in love.

Then, to her amazement, Ralph sprang away from her and plunged into the pitch blackness between the poplars.

She could hear him racing among the trees toward the tennis court; then he stopped; for a moment there was complete silence, and presently he was returning to her again.

"What was it, Ralph?" she asked, and although she did not feel especially afraid, her body had begun to tremble.

"There was someone among the trees," he said. "Someone spying on us, or perhaps he was hiding there for some other reason. If there had only been a moon, I might have caught him."

"Could it be anyone from the police?" she asked.

"Why should the police bother to run away? No, this fellow didn't act like a policeman."

"Ralph," she exclaimed, "I bet it's the same person that was listening to Professor Hatfield and me in the summerhouse. You remember, I asked if it was you."

For a minute Ralph did not answer, and she wondered what he was thinking. Then he said: "Kate, as a matter of fact, it couldn't be the same man, because it was I that was listening outside the summerhouse. Not exactly listening, but just hanging around in the neighborhood."

"But you told me you weren't," she said.

"I know I did. I was lying."

"But why, Ralph? Why did you do it?"

He took her hand and held it tight. "Because, as I told you when you caught me behind the poplar, I was going to keep an eye on you, and when you spoke of the summerhouse, I saw that you really seemed worried. I thought the more scared you were, the more careful you would be: so I decided I'd let you keep on thinking it was some mysterious stranger. I must say, it didn't do much good. It may seem perfectly outrageous, but I won't apologize. I'd do the same thing again."

He sounded so belligerent that it made her feel almost gay. "Ralph," she said, "if you can lie like that, how can I ever feel safe with you? I remember thinking how thoroughly honest you looked. I remember especially your eyes. They were staring straight into mine."

"Ah," he said, "my eyes *weren't* lying. They were expressing just what I felt. But now that I've told you the truth, Kate, you must promise me that you'll be on your guard every minute of the time until you get out of this valley. We'll have a talk with Mr. Gladstone tomorrow. Until then, do I have your word?"

"I already promised you," she said, "night before last. And I don't break my promises."

16

Kate sighed and turned over on her pillow, as the persistent voice continued, trying to break into her dreams. Sleep could change it momentarily into the rustling of leaves in a black wood, into the nipping of a small dog who was really Bobbie although her coat was mangy and red, but the voice kept on reasserting itself as a thing that could not be escaped.

With a start she realized that the voice was June's; that she was speaking urgently, softly, outside the bedroom door. Kate opened her eyes. It was broad daylight, but it must be very early.

"Katey—Katey, are you awake? You must wake up. It's very important. Open the door, Katey."

Kate sprang from bed and let June in. She was surprised to see that she was already dressed in a sweater and skirt.

"What is it?" she asked. "Is anything the matter?"

"Ralph says he knows who the murderers are," June said, speaking almost in a whisper. "We're in great danger, he says. Put on some clothes, Kate, but don't make any noise. He says we must get out of here before anyone wakes up. He's going to take us to Professor Hatfield's."

Kate blinked and tried to order her thoughts. "Ralph!" she exclaimed. "But where did you see him, June? Isn't it awfully early?"

"It's not six o'clock. That's the point. We must get out before anyone knows we've gone."

"But where did you see Ralph?" Kate repeated. "I don't understand."

"I've been up for half an hour," June said. "I woke up before dawn. I couldn't get to sleep and I just couldn't lie in bed any longer. I went downstairs and took Bobbie for a walk, and when I came back I ran into Ralph on the terrace. I think he'd been up all night. Most of the time he'd been keeping watch under your window, but he'd been prowling around too. He's discovered something. I don't know how. He'll tell us on our way to the professor's, but he said I was to come for you at once. If I hadn't turned up just then, he was coming up himself to wake us."

Kate had slipped out of her nightgown and was putting on an old woolen dress. "But who are the people?" she asked. "Didn't Ralph say who they were?"

"He just said I wouldn't believe him, but I know he'll tell you. He said you must remember your promise. I asked what that was and he said you'd know. But hurry, Katey! He said we must hurry, that everything depended on it."

Kate stuck her bare feet into her walking shoes. It was as if her dream were continuing, a desperate flurried dream whose setting was the pure still light of this early morning.

"Where is Ralph now?" she asked. "Where are we to meet him?"

"He's going to be waiting in the garden, or if he thinks it's safer he may go on to the summerhouse. Are you ready? Be awfully careful until we get outside."

Kate closed the door softly and followed June along the hall and down the stairs. The living room had never looked so large and clean. The sunlight streaming in the windows was as clear as the light over the yellow sand at Matunuck when you went in swimming before breakfast.

June opened the front door without a sound, and they ran along close to the house, through the drenched grass, just the way Kate had seen Felix walking through that white moonlit fog. It was easy now to move silently, because the singing of the birds was so loud that it seemed to ripple upward through the whole valley and break in a shower of spray along the rim of the hills.

They avoided the terrace and entered the garden through some bushes at the side. Kate looked around her but could see no sign of Ralph.

June seized her hand. "Somebody else must be up," she said. "Ralph must have seen someone. That means he'll be in the summerhouse. He's going to take us over the bluff by another trail. It starts from those woods. He thought it might be safer."

June was pulling her now swiftly through the garden, and in a moment they had gone through the arch, where Kate had met Professor Hatfield; and then Kate was following June along the dark little path.

"I feel safer now," June said. "We can't be seen from any of the windows."

They hurried along in silence for several minutes; and it was not until Kate caught a glimpse of the summerhouse around the last curve that June spoke again.

"I bet Ralph will be glad to see you," she said. "He's crazy about you, isn't he?"

"I don't know," Kate said. "I think he likes me."

"You know damn well he likes you," June said, and her voice sounded so much like her father's that it was startling. "He's in love with you."

"Perhaps he is," Kate admitted. "I haven't given it much thought."

"That's good," June said with a throaty chuckle, "because, Katey, you can take it from me, he won't be marrying you."

"I'd like to know why not!" Kate exclaimed. "Why shouldn't he marry me?"

"You wouldn't marry him unless you were in love with him, would you?"

"Well, suppose I am?" Kate said. "But honestly, June, I don't think it's any concern of yours just at present."

"Oh, I don't know," June said. "I caught him hugging you last night in the garden. He wasn't much of a watchdog, because I sneaked right back after he chased me off, and he never knew. I guess he must have been thinking of something else. I wonder what it was! And how about the other night, when you were bringing him back to your room? Too bad I was there to meet you, wasn't it? Too bad I didn't get out. I bet you were sore as hell when I stayed. I don't believe Father would think you'd be a good influence."

"June!" Kate exclaimed. "What on earth has got into you? What's the matter? Are you crazy?"

For a moment, in the shock of her surprise, she could not be angry; she could not even be scared. She simply could not believe that this coarse sneering voice was June's.

"Hush!" June exclaimed. "You don't want him to hear us talking about him."

They had reached the door of the summerhouse, and now June turned and seized Kate's arm. "You go in first," she said. "You're the one he really wants to see." And she gave Kate such a violent push that she fell on to the floor inside.

For an instant Kate was stunned. Then her first thought was Ralph.

"Ralph," she called. "Ralph, help! Where are you?"

June, who was standing on the threshold, had turned her back toward Kate. "Look behind the door," she said. "You may see something you don't expect."

With a sharp pang of terror, Kate picked herself up and peered through the shadow on to the mildewed boards which the open door had concealed. There was nothing there.

"What did you think you'd find?" June asked. "Ralph's body. Why should anyone want to kill Ralph? I'd hate to see that, because now that I'm in line to inherit Clotilde's money, he'll be marrying me one of these days."

"He won't! He won't!" Kate almost screamed, as if the sound of her voice might wake her up. "Let me out of here, June! Let me out of here at once!"

June turned in the doorway to face her.

"You don't think he'd marry a big ugly girl like me, do you?" she asked. "You make me laugh. Men like women but they like money even better, and when they have plenty of money they can get all the women they want. Just look what Father used to get, the dirty old ape!"

"Ralph loves me," Kate said frantically. "He won't marry anyone else, so you might as well let me go!"

"That's just it," June said with the same rough chuckle that Kate had noticed as they had come along the path. "Perhaps he wouldn't while you were still alive. That's your hard luck."

She took a step forward into the summerhouse, and Kate cowered away from her against the wall. While June had stood in the doorway, she had kept her hands clasped behind her; but now her arms reached forward, with their elbows raised as high as her shoulders, so that for an instant, as she moved nearer through the green twilight, she reminded Kate of some gigantic crustacean deep under the sea. And then Kate would have screamed if she could have moved her lips or her throat, because even through this dusk she could see that June's hands were covered by black woolen gloves.

17

Kate looked up from her copy of *Vogue*, as Mrs. Fulton, the pretty Nurses' Aide with the long eyes, opened the door of her room.

"Professor Hatfield's here," she said. "Do you feel up to seeing him?"

"I'd love to see him," Kate told her, and the next moment the professor, who must have been right behind her, stepped into the room, with Ralph at his heels.

"Well, I've come to keep my promise," Professor Hatfield said, "to tell you how it all happened, if you're sure you are comfortable enough."

"I feel fine," Kate said, "except that my throat's still pretty sore." She only hoped that Ralph wouldn't think the bulky bandage around her neck was too hideous.

Professor Hatfield smiled down at her. "You wouldn't have much chance to talk anyhow," he said, "unless to put in a question now and then, so I guess that needn't delay us. But I do feel sort of guilty about this young man. He insisted on coming. Do you want me to kick him out?"

"He can stay if he behaves," Kate said, and as she met Ralph's eyes, she had the same sensation that had come over her when he recognized her on the terrace at Valley Farms: the feeling that she had entered a beloved and special region, which she had always known and where she would be always safe; but now that feeling was so intense, so unimaginably happy, that her own eyes filled with tears.

"Did you notice that Nurses' Aide?" Professor Hatfield asked tactfully. "Daphne Fulton?"

"Yes," Kate said. "She's my favorite of all the nurses. Her husband's in Normandy, she tells me."

"She had quite an experience of her own around here last summer," the professor said. "You'll have to swap stories sometime. But of course you really don't know half of yours, and the part you don't know is the most interesting part—the inside part. It's the real story; and a terrible and evil one it is."

He paused for an instant, and Kate could almost have smiled at the gusto in his voice.

"Before I begin," he went on, "I'd better give you my sources, so you'll believe me. In the first place, I've talked to June several times. They let me see her whenever I want to; and I've succeeded in persuading her that it will be better for her if she admits everything. She's counting on her youth and on bad influences for her defense, and I'm sure you can trust her to put up a good one. Her father, by the way, has been most co-operative. Poor man, it was more of a shock than you might have thought him capable of receiving. He's going to testify to the way June was left to herself, to herself and Felix. He's going to describe the unhealthy and demoralizing atmosphere in which she grew up. His one relief just now, I think, is a kind of sardonic pleasure in painting himself as black as possible."

"And what about Mavis?" Kate asked.

The professor shrugged his shoulders. "Mavis will testify too," he said. "I'm sure by now she's looking forward to the trial. It will be a good fat part for her—a broken-hearted Mother, a Lady with a Past, a misunderstood Artist. Oh, it will be a brilliant comeback. She'll do her best to steal the show."

Kate smiled in spite of herself. "But you spoke as if there were more than one source," she said.

"Yes indeed. The other one is Felix's journal. The police are very grateful to me because I found it. It was hidden in the harness room. I must confess I made a complete copy of it for my files, before I handed it over. I'll read you a few excerpts presently. Unfortunately they will have to be short, because most of it is not suitable reading for mixed company, or any company except a group of hard-boiled scientists. Felix, as one could gather from his letters, rather fancied his literary abilities, just as Landru did—the famous French murderer, my dear. I had a hunch that something might turn up, so I poked around for a bit. Not that Felix ever committed himself on paper about the kidnapping or the murder. No, it was rather an account of his various—well, perhaps I might call them his romances, though that is hardly *le mot juste*. June knew that he kept a journal. That was what she was looking for in his room, late Sunday afternoon, when she told you she was waiting to console Ruby; but the only things she found were Felix's black gloves."

"But if there was nothing in the diary that involved June—" Kate began.

"There was a great deal that involved June," the professor said, "and June knew there must be. But let me start at the beginning, and then if any questions occur to you, don't hesitate to interrupt. That's what I always tell my classes," he said with his dry smile, "but they seldom take me at my word. The whole thing began with Felix, but what interests me most from the dramatic point of view is the way that June, little by little, took over, without his realizing it.

"You can open a page of his journal almost at random and see that Felix was just the kind of man I told you about—a kind of moral imbecile. He was clever in his way, excessively vain and quite inordinately sensual, but the most outstanding thing about him was his complete lack of any moral sense. He was too lazy to be terribly ambitious. I'm sure he derived a certain ironic pleasure from acting successfully the trusted and respected retainer. He had a comfortable well-paid job, and for a long time he contented himself with playing the local Don Juan, though I suspect, from veiled allusions in his journal, and from questions I've asked about the countryside, that he was responsible for the death of more than one infant. It is somewhat of an understatement to say that his sense of paternity was not particularly strong.

"I think I mentioned to you that Clotilde, when she came home from boarding school one summer—it was three years ago—had enjoyed flirting with him. Even then Clotilde, I'm afraid, was not quite so innocent as she might have been, and she could interpret quite well the way he looked at her. I gather that he felt he was sufficiently encouraged to make some unmistakable advance, and Clotilde just laughed at him. I'll read you his own comment on the episode."

The professor pulled from his inside pocket a roll of tissue-thin pages, and glanced through them with a serious and alert expression, as if they might be lecture notes.

"Ah yes," he said in a minute. "Here we are: *Clotilde, my fine young friend,*" he began reading, "*some day you may come crawling to me on your knees, and then it will be my turn. You're the first woman that ever laughed at Felix Brownell, and believe me, I won't forget it!*"

The professor looked up from his paper. "Felix didn't forget it," he said. "He was savagely humiliated. Clotilde had been playing a more dangerous game than she knew, but—one can hardly say in this case luckily—there was a way he could recapture his self-respect without touching Clotilde, at least just then. And this is where June enters the picture."

"But that was three years ago," Kate exclaimed. "June was only thirteen."

"Yes," Professor Hatfield went on, "it was the year after she came back from the boarding school where you had first known her and been, she told me so herself, about the only person who had ever shown her the slightest fondness or affection. Of course she was not a pretty girl, but Felix had reached an age when sometimes, for men of his sort, extreme youth is a greater attraction even than beauty, and June was Clotilde's sister, a member of the family If he could substitute June for Clotilde, his vanity would be satisfied, at least in part, and at the same time, to speak perhaps not quite accurately, his craving for romance. But June and Felix were a dangerous combination. It was when his cynical coldness and utter callousness were mixed, as it were, in a kind of chemical compound with June's passion and suppressed violence that crime, sooner or later, became almost inevitable."

He paused to clear his throat, and Kate was reminded of that afternoon a week ago when he had sat beside her on top of the bluff and explained about Clotilde's murder and the letter Felix had flung from the terrace.

"I've been talking so far mostly about Felix," he continued. "Now let's turn for a moment to June. Let's see how everything combined to enmesh the poor child, with none too good heredity to start with, and turn her little by little into something that might at first glance seem monstrous. You know the kind of household in which she was brought up, and a few years ago it was even more confused. One might describe it as—well, let's say a kind of high-class bordello, to put it crudely, only here it was the hosts that paid. I'm fond of Norman Gladstone. He has many good traits—generosity, good nature of a sort, an exuberant love of life—but chastity, temperance, or in fact restraint of any kind are not among them. It takes all sorts to make a world. June must have known, almost from her nursery days, precisely the nature of her mother's friendships with her succession of gentlemen guests—symmetrically balanced, one might say, by her father's special interest in the numerous lady visitors. Neither Mr. Gladstone nor Mavis was the type that bothers too much about closing doors, especially if there have been many cocktails, and you may be sure there always were. And if June had not suspected, I'm sure Felix would have told her.

"June has her father's violence and recklessness, and like her mother she craves the center of the stage. But in her youth, Mavis was very pretty; on the stage or off, she never lacked an audience; while poor June was ugly and awkward. Her mother was ashamed of her; her father ignored her—and so did everyone else, everyone except Felix, that is, and perhaps Ruby until she began to suspect how much Felix liked her. The only thing that might have been a good influence in her life was the Larson family, and June found Felix much more interesting and exciting, even before the—the association began. But not only was June ignored, and more or less made fun of (I don't think Norman ever realized how much she was hurt by the somewhat ironic

manner he adopted toward her, whenever he noticed her at all);
that would have been bad enough, but she had an older sister, as
you know, a half sister, who was exceptionally charming to look
at, whom everyone spoiled, and who regarded June with amused
contempt. To make it worse, Clotilde, as everyone knew, was
an heiress, while June soon learned, very possibly from Felix,
that she would have next to nothing. I don't think one could
be surprised if a less emotional, a less violent child than June
had allowed herself, under the circumstances, to be corrupted
by such an evil genius as Felix. I've known some bad ones in my
day, but even for me, as I read through his journal, I could feel
at times the breath of the pit. For it was a deliberate system of
corruption, a long éducation sentimentale, quite hellish in its
thoroughness and its depravity. The fact that it was interrupted
when June would leave for school only added to its piquancy
during the holidays and the long summer vacations. I'll read you
a few lines, written just about a year ago, which will give you
some idea of how Felix had come to think of the relationship;
and then you'll see in a minute how completely blinded he was
by his egregious vanity.

"*Felix, my lad,*" he read, "*you're a lucky dog! Talk about devoted
slaves! Well, I guess that just goes to show the value of education. I
trained her myself, brought her up by hand, you might say—especially made to order for Felix Brownell, Esquire, like those girls they
prepare for the harems of oriental kings.*

"And then just one more entry—the final one. It was written
last Christmas Day, when June was home for vacation. Its only a
few sentences, but it's the most revealing in the whole journal. A
new possibility had dawned, which I'll speak of presently. After
that he evidently did not dare trust himself to paper, for fear no
doubt that he might give himself away without realizing it. Here
it is:

"*Well, Felix, I think you may be in for something good. If I say
half a word, no one will ever marry her. I've set my brand on her,
and she knows it. I've got her just as surely as if she was behind bars.
My lad, you can do great things if you set your mind to it. Nothing
venture, nothing win.*"

"That entry is even more ominous than it may sound," he said. "June told me just the other day what his plans were."

He rolled up the manuscript and shoved it back into his pocket.

"And now, my dear," he went on briskly, "now that you have had a glimpse of the characters, viewed as it were from behind the footlights, we can get on to the drama of this spring. In a way, it was quite literally a drama; I think June always thought of it as such; because if she inherited her mother's craving for attention, she inherited also her flair for acting. In fact I rather imagine that June is a better actress than her mother ever was."

As he paused again, Kate had a vision of Felix standing half naked at the entrance to the cave. It was almost an hallucination: she could see the sweat sliding over his tight pale skin between the patches of sticky hair; she could see his head thrust forward, hyena-like, his eyes softly gloating. But it was not herself at whom he stared now: it was June, who stood there, heavy and expressionless, a lost soul unaware of its damnation. Kate shuddered and drew in her breath so sharply that it hurt her throat; but the vision was gone, and mercifully a quite trivial memory floated into her mind.

"And I thought at first that she was young and inexperienced for her age," she exclaimed. "I remember being surprised that she was reading *Little Women*."

"You must not forget," Professor Hatfield said, "that if she did have much experience that, very luckily, most girls never go through, she also lacked many of the happier and more normal experiences of childhood. June is an odd mixture of the crafty and the naive. I rather doubt whether *Little Women* was merely a theatrical prop. I shouldn't be at all surprised if she really enjoyed it and found in it a kind of dream world that delighted and even touched her, just because it was so very far away from her own. But to go back to this spring, which marks the beginning of the tragedy in which you, my poor Kate, were involved, and which also marks the emergence of June as the leading partner in the concern. As I look back upon the whole thing, I can almost see her as a somber young Catherine de' Medici, pulling strings and balancing combinations which even Felix did not suspect until near the last, and which took no one else into account—neither Clotilde, nor Felix, nor you who were her one real friend; which considered nothing in the world but the feeding of her own sense of power, the assuaging of her own passion.

"The thing was set in motion by a letter from Clotilde in New York announcing that she was engaged and was planning to be married this summer. June insists that it was Felix who first called her attention to the fact that if Clotilde married, her mother's fortune would definitely go out of the family. I have an idea, however, that June did not need much prompting, and I suspect that the germ of the plan for Clotilde's murder originated with her; not that Felix would have shrunk from it: he didn't; but simply that he wouldn't have been so apt to imagine it. He still hated Clotilde, but his hatred, I'm sure, was nothing to the intensity of June's feeling. They devised the kidnapping plan in detail; so far they were working together, hand in glove. But then Felix made a mistake. He did not realize that June had grown up during the last three years. He had done his best to help create the depraved lonely being she had become, but he did not suspect that like Frankenstein, he had produced a monster that would turn upon himself. Felix was not satisfied with the $50,000 ransom that would be his. His wonderful plan, which at first he mentioned to June as if it were merely a joke, was in the course of the next few years to murder Ruby, and Mavis, and Mr. Gladstone, so that the whole fortune would be in June's hands by the time she was twenty-one, and then he would marry her. What shocked June, what makes her angry now when she thinks of it, was not the wholesale cruelty of the scheme, not the fact that it involved the murder of both her parents, no: it was Felix's presumption that he, a servant, should think she would ever be his wife, and let him share her fortune. Already she had grown restive under his dominance; she had begun to resent his hold over her, and to be mortified by it. No doubt this feeling was increased by her seeing other girls of her own age and social position at the various schools to which Mr. Gladstone sent her.

But she knew Felix too well to let him suspect this. And then Clotilde arrived about a month ago with Ralph."

Professor Hatfield paused again, and gave Ralph a keen side-wise glance, like a parrot in the zoo, not quite certain whether to accept or to reject the cracker that is pushed between the bars.

"I don't know whether you realize, Ralph, that from the first moment she saw you, June fell desperately, passionately in love with you."

As Kate glanced at Ralph she saw him blush beneath his tan until he was almost copper-colored.

"I did notice at first," he said, "that she was always tagging after me. She used to brush against me sometimes, as if she was a great big dog. I never liked her; in fact she sort of repelled me. I hated seeing Kate with her. Whatever June felt for me, Professor, I don't think you could call it love."

"Call it what you will," he said, "she wanted you more than she had ever wanted anything in her life; she wanted you for keeps; she wanted you as her husband. I spoke of her strange naiv-eté: here's an example of it. She was convinced that if Clotilde was out of the way and she became an heiress, she could persuade you to marry her. Perhaps it was not so naive, after all: she was only judging you on the basis of her own experience of people which was not a fortunate one, although undoubtedly part of your charm was the fact that you were quite different from any-body she had ever known.

"As soon as she had made up her mind that the thing she wanted most in the world was to be your wife, she began making plans to accomplish her desire. This new scheme would coin-cide at first with the one she had worked out with Felix: Clotil-de must be got rid of, and as quickly as possible, because June was afraid you might elope or Clotilde might make a will. It was barely possible that Clotilde had done this already, but she would have to take that chance. But once Clotilde was out of the way, her plan differed considerably from Felix's little scheme, the main difference being that Felix himself must be disposed of; because she knew she would not be safe as long as he lived.

He would probably not murder her; it would not be worth his while; Felix would kill only for profit; but he would be sure to blackmail her."

"I can see why she wouldn't want me around," Kate said, "but then why did she invite me to come, and then get her father to urge me when I refused?"

Professor Hatfield beamed at her. "My dear," he said, "it's at this moment that you enter upon the stage: the good character who comes in fairly late, when the play is half over, to emphasize by contrast how very bad the rest of them are."

"You include me in that?" Ralph asked.

"I should consider you one of the more neutral characters," Professor Hatfield said judicially, "but on the whole fairly sympathetic for a young man placed in a rather awkward position. But now to answer Kate's question: June quite definitely did want you, my dear, and that was where she made her fatal mistake, as she realized only too soon. Although she was pretty confident that a million dollars or so, for I think it amounts to that, would be enough to purchase Ralph, she wanted desperately to be as attractive in his sight as possible. She knew that she couldn't dress, that she couldn't arrange her hair, that she couldn't choose the right cosmetics. I'm sure Clotilde's sarcasm would have told her this, if she hadn't guessed it without. Like many ugly hearty-looking people, she was terribly sensitive about her appearance, and that sensitivity was increased tenfold now that she had a special reason for looking her best. She remembered how kind you had been to her at school, how beautifully you had dressed and how nice you had always looked. She felt, and I'm sure she was right, that with your help she could be made, herself, far more smart and attractive."

"But then why did I get the warning to stay away?" Kate asked.

"Ah, but you recall that now we have two people to deal with, whose interests are opposed. Naturally June couldn't tell Felix why she wanted you to come. Naturally enough Felix could only see that you would be a nuisance, an added complication, and June had to pretend to agree with him. However, she did get the warning delayed until the last minute, and if it had scared you off, I think June would have written another pathetic letter to try to persuade you. Well, you arrived that Thursday afternoon, and for the first few hours June was delighted. She had great hopes, and also I think that her kind of friendship for you was the one glimmer of disinterested affection she had ever known in her life. She told you about the note she had received, which was of course a red herring, partly to divert suspicion from her but most of all to suggest that sinister strangers were prowling in the neighborhood, strangers who would naturally be blamed for the kidnapping. Ruby's letter was genuine. Felix knew her jealousy and wanted to scare her if he could, so that she wouldn't be in the way when the time came to dispose of Clotilde. But it must have been a severe shock to June when she found out that you and Ralph were old friends, and I think she began to suspect that very first evening that Ralph was falling in love with you."

"I remember that she did urge me to leave," Kate exclaimed. "It was while the men were searching the woods, right after Felix flung the letter into the garden. She was quite passionate about it, but I thought it was all for my sake."

"Hardly that," Professor Hatfield said. "If she had been surer of how you felt, she might have been ever more insistent. Though she probably wouldn't dare to say too much: it might have looked suspicious. And of course she hoped that you might not respond to Ralph's charms. Apparently she soon lost that hope, though I'm in no position to say why. Perhaps because she couldn't conceive that anyone could resist him, if he tried to make himself agreeable. The actual murder of Clotilde, that Thursday night, occurred as I described it to you. June swears that she did not herself help Felix, and I don't think she did. She would avoid that risk if she possibly could. We know how Bobbie upset the smooth working of the plan.

"This of course disturbed Felix, who was already beginning to suspect from June's manner that something was wrong. He had seen the way she looked at Ralph and doubtless noticed her growing jealousy of you. She told me that she found you talking with Ralph by the tennis court, Friday afternoon, in what seemed to her a rather intimate manner, and to use her own expression, it just about burned her up."

"Just a little while after that," Kate interrupted, "when was fixing her for dinner, she told me that she had overheard Mavis talking scandal about Ralph and me. I suppose she was just trying to keep us apart."

"No doubt of it," Professor Hatfield said. "Mavis, as you may suspect, is not averse to talking scandal, but here is one instance when I'm sure she was maligned. It was that Friday night—the night after the murder—that Felix came up to June's room. That was nothing new, except that now you were sleeping in the room next to it. He threatened June to let Ralph know of their relations, if she had any idea of backing out, or turning against himself. June was furious, and it was their quarreling voices that wakened you, Kate, that and Felix when he left to go downstairs. I'd sort of wondered at first how Felix could have roused you if he had come directly from the kitchen, and also why he had used the front door. I think it was his coming to her room that night, when June definitely did not want him to, and daring to threaten her, that determined her to get rid of him as soon as she possibly could. It had both frightened her and made her very angry; and June's anger is no laughing matter.

"The whole arrangement for leaving the ransom was excellent, I thought. I don't know which of them deserves the greater share of credit for it. Of course the notes had been put in their hiding places several days before, and June never took the actual ransom money with her. She slipped it to Felix and got from him in exchange a dummy package which she put into her knapsack. That must have been Saturday, after lunch, just before you started out together to deliver the money."

"But she couldn't have given it to Felix," Kate said. "I was with her when Mr. Gladstone put it into her hands, and she never left me for a moment afterward until we left the package in the mined house."

"Think carefully," Professor Hatfield said. "She must have."

And suddenly Kate remembered. "Of course!" she exclaimed. "Just as we were about to start, June said it would be nice to take some Coca-Cola along and ran back into the kitchen to get it out of the icebox. She was only gone a couple of minutes."

"That would be quite enough," Professor Hatfield said, "and June was justly proud of the arrangement about leaving the package, so neither Felix nor she would have to go after it; because of course if it were found there later, it would arouse suspicions. When she went into the closet, she thrust it through a hole in the plaster beneath the shelf, so that it fell down into the wall."

"But tell me one thing," Kate said. "If June was so eager to get me out of the way, why didn't she choose to do it that afternoon? She'd have had plenty of chances."

"There were several reasons," Professor Hatfield explained. "In the first place, it's possible that she hadn't quite made up her mind. Perhaps something happened afterward that precipitated matters." He glanced from Ralph to Kate and then continued in his confidential voice: "But the main reason is that she didn't dare to while Felix was still alive. If Felix already suspected how things stood, she knew that this would be a giveaway. If she wanted Ralph enough to kill you out of jealousy, Felix would know that he couldn't count on her for himself. And also it would take some skill to explain what had happened, to prevent suspicion falling on her. Perhaps though, if she could have been sure to make it seem an accident, so sure that even Felix would be duped— On the whole, I'm rather glad that I was in the offing. Of course, as you know, I'd been keeping my eye on you. When I saw you, on the top of the bluff from my shack, that same Saturday afternoon, I thought I'd tag along. I was a little nervous when you sat for such a time on the beach, at the top of the island, because from where I was hidden I couldn't see you."

Suddenly Kate felt once more that kind of shiver she had known so well a week ago.

"When we were sitting there on the sand bar," she said, "June suggested going in swimming. Do you suppose she thought then that she might drown me?"

"It's quite possible," Professor Hatfield said. "She certainly may have toyed with the idea. Of course when you left the island it was clear that you knew someone was tracking you, and June could do nothing then even if she had wanted to. I think she was as much startled as you were. The thing that must have scared her most was that it might be Felix and that he was going to strike in some way himself before she could strike first. But she overestimated him, or rather perhaps he underestimated her. She knew that he was going to bury Clotilde's body the next day. You recall how on Sunday afternoon, with Ralph and her father sent off to rescue Clotilde, she said she was going to take a nap. But her plan from the first was to slip away to the path if she could. That low ledge above the path, with the junipers overhanging, makes a perfect ambush. She told me she had hidden the ax there several evenings before. It was simple enough for a husky girl like her to split open Felix's skull from that point of vantage. She had seen you go up the path some time ago. She suspected you were looking for her, but she knew you were out of the way; so she ran along the base of the bluff, keeping just out of sight of the house, in the woods, and joined the road after she got beyond the barns. Then she simply sat down and waited for the car with Ralph and her father. I guess that about clears everything up, doesn't it?"

Kate thought for a minute: it was hard to believe that Professor Hatfield was talking of a place where she had actually lived herself; it was rather a region she had read of long ago, in some dark fairy tale.

"There's one thing more," she said. "Suppose you hadn't turned up so early Monday morning, suppose June had succeeded when she lured me to the summerhouse, wouldn't it have looked suspicious to find my body there?"

Professor Hatfield smiled. "After your midnight trip to the front door," he said, "I think it would have seemed quite natural. Doubtless June thought of that when she made her plans. She would have come quietly back to the house, gone to bed again, and you would not have been missed for several hours. When you were discovered, people would have assumed that this time you had gone even further, actually out into the night, and that the unknown man who had killed Felix had afterward killed you."

"But how did you suspect that June was that unknown person? You're so wise, I just take it for granted, but you must have had some reasons."

"I had two very good reasons," he said, "but it wasn't very wise of me not to think of them sooner. They only occurred to me about three o'clock Sunday night—or rather Monday morning—and then I realized how dangerous your position might be. If there had been no outside accomplice, there obviously had been no mysterious blankets and whisky bottles tucked away in a cave in the cliff; and yet June had described them to you to explain the reasons for the warning note she had received. The fact that she lied to you about it was pretty good proof she knew the note was a fake. And then I remembered that it wasn't Mavis but June who first called attention to the figure moving in the dark, on Thursday evening, just before Felix threw the letter into the garden. June mentioned it to you, and Mavis overheard. June had taken care that she should. She knew her mother wouldn't let slip any chance for a bit of drama. Of course I couldn't be completely certain, but I thought I'd better not risk going back to sleep. It's just as well I didn't."

Ralph rose from his chair, came over to the bedside, and gazed down at her.

"Kate," he said, "you told me out at the farm that I loved to rescue people, and yet you see I didn't even have the luck to rescue you. I'd been prowling around all night, and when you were in the summerhouse with June, I was keeping an eye on Jo's cottage. That's why I didn't reach you until after the professor. I seemed to be doomed to stand on the sidelines and just watch things happen."

Though his tone was serious, his effort to make it sound bitter was not too successful. Kate felt that the look with which she had greeted him must have given her away, but that Ralph, characteristically, to spare her embarrassment, was pretending he had not understood.

"Perhaps before long," she said quickly, "when you're on your ship, you may be rescuing soldiers and marines, and that's much more important."

Suddenly he smiled. "Who's being romantic now?" was all he said; but his glance was so direct, so ardent, so tender and so amused that Kate blushed to her eyes; and for the first time in her life she did not mind it.

Professor Hatfield rose also. "And now, my dear Kate," he said, "I must run along. You can flatter yourself that you have been involved in an exceptionally lurid case. As it stands, it should rank with the affair of Constance Kent, or of Madeleine Smith. Constance was a sixteen-year-old English girl of excellent family, who beheaded, or just about, her small half brother and threw his body into a cesspool. Madeleine was also most respectable, and very attractive, they say. She was accused of giving her lover arsenic, not because he would not marry her, but because he insisted on doing it. But I can't help thinking what this case of ours might have grown into, if it had been allowed to develop. It was really your fault, Ralph, for throwing a wrench into the gears. You say you just stand on the sidelines and watch things happen. I should say that in this case, at least, you were the center pin around which everything revolved. If you hadn't been engaged to Clotilde and come to the farm, June couldn't have fallen in love with you. In that case she might have been finally induced to agree with Felix's plans; and then not only Clotilde but all the rest of her family would have died, very naturally, I'm sure, in various ingenious ways. On the other hand, Felix might have been spared—but I don't think you need feel too badly about that. Felix and June were a wonderful team to create a really magnificent example of mass murder, though I suspect that, sooner or later, one of them would have finished off the other. Still, they could have accomplished a lot first."

He shook his head and his tone was almost wistful.

"I've learned one thing at any rate," Kate said. "If I ever get another anonymous letter, I'll do exactly what it tells me to. Felix and June gave me fair warning. They said that if I went to the farm, I'd be sorry."

"I hate to sound unsympathetic," Ralph said, "but frankly, all things considered, I'm damn glad you did."

The professor, with his hand on the door, turned toward him. "You're not coming with me?" he asked.

"No," Ralph said. "I'm staying."

YOU LEAVE
ME COLD!

For
Lu and Hod

1

While Professor Hatfield telephoned from his swivel chair, John Frazer glanced around the study. His uncle had a lot of books, even for a professor; the room was lined with them on shelves that reached from floor to ceiling. You could see the wall in only one place, a square panel opposite the desk, and that was nearly covered by four color prints of large and small owls which seemed to preside over the room. As he spoke gently and precisely into the receiver, his head cocked, his eyes fixed on nothing, his Uncle Paul himself suggested an owl; or no—he was much too sharp, too alert for that: he was more like a dusty and self-contained old parrot, full of friendliness and wisdom.

Professor Hatfield hung up the receiver for the fifth time. "There's nothing at the Jones's either," he said. "It's too bad. They have such a pleasant house. Well, I'll try once more."

John rose from his chair and walked to the window. Icicles, dully gleaming, hung like a fringe of stalactites from the gutter just above it, and John gazed through them across the snowy garden to the lake beyond. Skaters were skimming and circling over the ice. Their sweaters and scarves looked gay but cold. There were many uniforms. John smiled as he noticed a brown Spitz dog running to keep up with its master, and now and then having to sit down as its feet slipped out from under it. Woodside ought to be a pleasant place to stay.

When John had arrived here this noon and reported at Science Hall as a medical student in the U.S.N.R., he had been told that because of a mix-up with the Army all available dormitory space

was occupied by soldiers. The small group of navy men would
be given a subsistence allowance and would have to find quarters
for themselves. They had been handed a list of rooms, and John
had spent a couple of hours tramping through the windy streets,
only to find everything taken except for one or two rooms so
dismal that he preferred to keep searching.

Then he had thought of his Uncle Paul whom his mother
had told him to be sure to look up: perhaps this unknown uncle
would take him in; but Professor Hatfield had informed him,
with expressions of the most solicitous regret, that since his wife
(John's Aunt Wanda) had just left for California, he himself was
closing up his house and moving the next day to the University
Club. He had insisted, however, upon himself finding a place
for his young nephew, and for the last twenty minutes had been
calling up acquaintances and rooming houses.

As he put back the receiver once more, he pushed the telephone to the side of his desk.

"It's too bad," he exclaimed, "but the fact is the town is
crowded just now to overflowing, what with Clinton Field and
the powder plant at Tuscoda. I've tried all the obvious places, but
I'm sure there must be something. . . . Hmmm. . . ."

With his elbows resting on the arms of his chair, the tips of
his fingers touching, the professor stared across at the owls, and
it seemed to John that a film had been drawn over his eyes, like
the film that protects the eyes of birds, so John had read, when
they gaze into the sun.

"As a matter of fact, a place does occur to me," he said after
a full minute of silence, and a new note had come into his voice:
it was cautious, tentative. "The trouble is, John, I don't know
whether it would be quite . . . quite fair of me to recommend it."

"I'd promise not to get drunk and break the windows," John
said. "If you'd endorse me as a roomer, Uncle Paul, I'd guarantee
to curb my natural tendencies to raise hell. I'm sure I shouldn't
disgrace the family."

"My dear boy!" Professor Hatfield exclaimed in muted con-
sternation. "You completely misunderstand me. I'm sure that
wherever you are, you'll do the family, and the Navy, credit. Your

mother wrote me of your record at Brown. Brilliant! And I don't believe you ever raised hell—what I should call really raising hell—in your life. You're not the type."

His uncle gave John a glance both sharp and meditative: as if he were at the same time deciding under what letter he should be catalogued, and also, for the sake of accuracy, trying to determine an objective and fair definition of raising hell. His expression struck John as so very professorial that he couldn't help grinning.

"Well, if you think I'll pass, Uncle," he said, "what's the hitch?"

"I meant I didn't know whether it would be quite fair to you," Professor Hatfield said. "And to your dear mother. And for that matter, to the U.S. Navy." For an instant a smile played neatly about the corners of his lips; then serious once more, he leaned toward John with the air of a benign conspirator. "Of course, if I were in your place," he said, "I'd rather have a room just now in Dr. Chardwicke's house than in any other in all Woodside. I'd go there myself in a moment if I thought he'd let me in, but I'm sure he wouldn't."

"Let's by all means try Dr. Chardwicke's then," John said. "What's wrong with it?"

"I wish I knew," Professor Hatfield said thoughtfully. "I'd give a great deal to find out."

He blinked, moved his shoulders, and when he went on, his tone had recaptured its quality of dry precision. "Of course the room itself, if they took you in, should be comfortable. The situation is excellent. It's a big old house on the lake, like this one; in fact it's only a few blocks down the street. But the atmosphere. . . . You would surely find it strange. You might even find it very depressing. When the Chardwickes rent rooms, they insist that their roomers board in the house; so you couldn't help seeing a great deal of them."

"But if *you'd* like to go there so much . . ." John began.

"Ah, but you see," Professor Hatfield cut in gently, "I have most peculiar tastes. Some people even describe them as macabre."

"Macabre!" John exclaimed. If he was curious about the mysterious Dr. Chardwicke, he was even more curious about his own Uncle Paul. "Why's that? I thought your hobby was birds."

"Birds are one of my hobbies," his uncle said, "but I have another. Just look in that bookcase there to the left of the window."

John turned his head and glanced at the tightly packed shelves. *Mental Abnormality and Crime*, he read; *Homicide Investigation; Responsibility in Mental Disease; Mass Murder*. One whole shelf was nearly filled with *Famous British Trials*. Books on abnormal psychology rubbed bindings with mystery stories; there was a queer mixture of the serious and the frivolous, of science and fiction; but as John's eyes strayed from shelf to shelf, every book, so far as he could see, had something to do with abnormality or crime, with the strange dark twists of the human mind.

"Why Uncle Paul!" he exclaimed. "Don't tell me you're an amateur criminologist!"

John stared at his uncle with new interest and a shade of amusement. He had thought of him merely as a middle-aged professor, a research chemist, with a painstaking interest in birds. This new hobby made him seem more romantic, more original, though possibly a shade childish.

"A criminologist, no," Professor Hatfield said. "In a humble way, perhaps, a kind of field psychologist. I confess that when I suspect that something dark is going on, something queer or involved or devious, it's hard for me to keep my nose out of it. Why even among my respectable colleagues on the faculty, I've discovered enough in the course of the years to live in luxury for the rest of my life, if I cared to dabble in blackmail. But the life of a blackmailer, if thrilling at first, is bound soon enough to become humdrum, and then of course it *is* antisocial."

John thought his voice contained a hint of regret, and glanced at his face to see if he was joking; but his uncle returned his gaze inscrutably. The steely cloud beyond the window seemed to dilute and chill the brightness of the red Bokhara rug.

"I take it then," John said after a minute, smiling though slightly puzzled, "that you think there's something dark or devious going on in Dr. Chardwicke's house, and that's why it interests you. That's why you mention it to me."

The professor raised his finger. "Ah, but I didn't mention it until I'd tried almost everywhere else," he said, "and when I did

I warned you against it. I'm still warning you. Of course there's a good chance there will be no empty room there either. That would settle things once and for all."

Suddenly John laughed. "Uncle Paul," he exclaimed, "don't think I don't see through you! I bet you'd be disappointed as hell if I didn't get into that house."

The professor smiled faintly. "I must confess I should be," he said, "though I might be equally relieved if you couldn't get in. But don't think it's just my curiosity. I have what you might call a personal interest in it. I can't help feeling that if I had some kind of agent in the house, I might be able . . . I might be able to prevent. . . . Hmmm . . ."

"To prevent what?" John asked in surprise.

"I haven't the slightest idea," the professor said. "That's what makes it so baffling. Or rather I have a number of ideas, but I feel that each one of them is fantastic."

"You're sure you're not thinking in terms of your mystery library?" John asked, and realized he was trying to cover up a slight uneasiness.

"Very possibly," Professor Hatfield said, not in the least offended. "By all means let us hope so! But my dear John, I'll tell you what the setup is, and then you can judge for yourself. Dr. Chardwicke used to be a member of our medical school faculty, and a very distinguished bacteriologist, until some ten years ago he had a nervous breakdown. As you know, that rather polite and vague term may cover a number of conditions which are, to say the least, distressing. Within a few months he recovered his health sufficiently to go back to his house, but he resigned from active work on the faculty. He still has a tiny laboratory of his own, however, near the top of Science Hall, where he carries on his research, which of late years, I believe, has been nothing spectacular. Since of course he gets only a fraction of his former salary, Mrs. Chardwicke and he take in a few roomers to help things along. I confess that the house and its inmates have always had a certain rather bleak fascination for me.

"Then last September a really delightful boy came to live with them, and him I got to know very well indeed, because he's been doing confidential research under my direction. His name is Ronald Travers. He had been rejected by the Army because of a heart condition, and he graduated from Harvard last June. As a matter of fact, he's rather your type, John, physically at least; that was what reminded me just now of Dr. Chardwicke's house, in connection with you. He's tall and slim and blond, just as you are, though he hasn't your out-of-doors look. He's a trifle more on the ascetic side, I should say; but he has a fine mind, and as I told you a good deal of personal charm. He informed me, after I got to know him, that he has no immediate family, that Dr. Chardwicke is his nearest relative and his guardian, and will be until next month when Ronny comes of age."

The professor paused and fixed John with his probing eyes.

"And you don't think the doctor's an ideal guardian?" John asked. "But after all, you say it's only for another month."

"Yes, only for another month," his uncle said. "A great deal can happen in a month. But to get on with my story: sometime before Christmas he became engaged to Dr. Chardwicke's niece. Frances Maitland her name is. She was a biology major in the university, and now I believe she is doing Nurses' Aide work. She lives in the house, too. Wanda and I had them to dinner. I found her one of the most delightful and beautiful young women I've ever known. It's too bad she's engaged, John, though possibly the heritage is not of the best. There's another young girl in the house—a cousin, I think, of Mrs. Chardwicke's. She's a pretty little thing, though I'm afraid she's too young to interest you. And then there's a medical student, Douglas McFean, a handsome husky devil. I don't know why he's not in uniform. He seems like a nice fellow, though. Ronny brought him around once or twice. There may be others. But to get back to Ronny.

"About two weeks ago I noticed that he seemed rather listless at his work. I asked him if he felt all right and he said he did; but the next day it was clear to me that something was wrong and I told him he'd better go home that afternoon and advised him to see a doctor. I haven't laid eyes on him since. Last week I called up and unfortunately I got Dr. Chardwicke. I asked to speak to Ronny, but he said he was resting. I asked if he'd seen a doctor, and Dr. Chardwicke said that he'd examined him himself, that he was a bit run down, but that there was nothing really wrong. He wasn't even staying in bed; he was up and about the house. Well, unless I'm very much mistaken, something is wrong, but what could I do? After all, Dr. Chardwicke is an M.D.; he's still a registered physician, even if he doesn't practice; and what pretext have I to go butting in? The next afternoon, however, I called on Ronny at the house. It was Frances who came to the door. She said he was sleeping again and that Dr. Chardwicke had said he mustn't be disturbed. Well, he might have been; no doubt he was; but I'm sure Frances was profoundly worried—not only about Ronny, that would have been natural enough, but frightened of something else. She kept glancing over her shoulder, not actually perhaps, but that was the impression she gave me, as if she thought someone might be eavesdropping, someone of whom she stood in dread. All I could do was leave the house, with a message for Ronny, and then two days later I got this note. It might interest you."

The professor opened his top drawer, took out a sheet of note paper, and leaned across the desk to hand it to John. Even before John began to read, he was struck by the sensitive and individual handwriting.

Dear Professor Hatfield, [he read]
I want to tell you what a joy it has been working under your direction. It was very kind of you to call on me, and if I felt like seeing anyone just now it would be you; but at present I do not feel up to seeing even my dearest friends—perhaps my friends most of all. If there was anything you could do for me I should not hesitate to ask you, but there is nothing to be done. Nothing. For every reason it is much better so. Just now even my work seems unimportant.

This is to say good-bye to you.
Your grateful student,
Ronny

John handed the letter back to his uncle. It gave him a queer impression of having come from very far away and not from just a few blocks up the street.

"Well," Professor Hatfield asked, "what do you think of it?"

"It sounds to me," John said, "as if he knew he had some incurable illness, and wanted to be alone, at least for the time. I can understand that."

"Quite possibly," the professor admitted slowly. "Quite possibly that may be it."

He put the letter back in the drawer, rose from his seat and walked around his desk to stand near John beside the window. His gaze seemed to pass over the lake, with its swirl of skaters, and fix itself upon the clouds that stretched, miles away, along the top of the slate-blue hills.

"It's going to be cold tomorrow," he said. "Very cold!"

Then he turned once more to John, with his smile that seemed at the same time so dry and yet so friendly. "I should think from what I've been telling you," he said, "you might decide you'd prefer any other room in town."

"Far from it," John exclaimed, "if you think I could possibly do anything. . . ." And then, as if to break a tension, he gave a rather strained laugh. "When you hold out the prospect of meeting two beautiful young girls . . ." he said.

"My dear John," Professor Hatfield cut in, his face suddenly grave, "there's one thing you must promise me. Suppose you should decide to ask for a room at the Chardwicke's and suppose they give you one—well, if they do, that in itself would suggest that there's nothing very wrong, nothing unnatural, that is, and I'm letting my fancy run away with me. In any case, I don't see what could happen to you, going in there as a perfect stranger. But the Chardwickes, as you may have gathered, are a peculiar family; and the human mind, once it is ever so slightly thrown off the track, may wander far astray in dark and dubious regions. So you must promise me this: if I should say the word, you must quietly collect your things and leave the house at once."

2

Just as sometimes you can recall your first glimpse of a new acquaintance and later find it hard to believe that the person you saw then was actually the same one as the very different individual you have come to know, so John Frazer was always to remember Dr. Chardwicke's house when he saw it first in the dusk of that January afternoon, as a place which had no connection with the grim background of his terrible adventure.

It was a tall brick house with a wooden porch, a number of balconies, and a cupola. The snow clinging to the porch railings, to the scrollwork above the windows and about the eaves, suggested the designs of frosting on a birthday cake. Behind it, as it stood apart from its neighbors between its black elms, the sky was scattered with tiny clouds, each one detached as if hung by a separate wire and lighted, it seemed, by many candles burning just beneath the horizon. With its gleaming slits of windows, it reminded John of a transparency to be placed before a lamp at Christmas, and he felt that as he stepped inside he would be entering an innocent and cozy world.

When he reached the door, he was surprised to see that the bell was an old-fashioned metal knob, to be pulled instead of pushed. He gave it a tug and there was an interval of silence before he heard a ring from somewhere in the depths of the house. He must have waited on the wide dim porch for more than two minutes; then he pulled the bell again. Although he had walked only a quarter of a mile down the street from his Uncle Paul's, his ears were beginning to tingle, and he was rubbing them with his bare hands to restore the circulation when the door suddenly opened.

A young woman stood on the tiles of the vestibule peering out at him. Her features might have had a voluptuous appeal if her face had not given him the idea that it had been slightly pushed in: the end of the nose looked flattened, and the broad cheeks seemed to crowd upward toward the eyes to prevent their fully opening. John couldn't help being disappointed in his uncle's taste. Then as he noticed her short black dress, it occurred to him that no doubt she was the maid.

"Is this Dr. Chardwicke's house?" he asked pleasantly, but she did not return his smile.

"Dr. Chardwicke lives here," she said. Her voice was thinner than he would have expected, and without resonance.

"Do you suppose I could see him?"

The girl stepped back into the vestibule and partly closed the door.

"What do you want to see him about?" she asked. "You're not trying to sell anything?"

John chuckled. "No, I'm not," he said. "As a matter of fact, I'm in the Navy, and they discourage peddling."

"You're not in uniform," she said suspiciously.

"That's true," he admitted. "The stuff hasn't come yet. There seems to be something of a mix-up, but the doctor can investigate me, if he wants to."

John felt her eyes appraising him. He knew that he didn't rate as well as he would have done if he had been twenty pounds heavier and two inches broader; but the glance she gave him, at once direct and veiled, suggested flatteringly that she had seen worse.

"I want to ask the doctor about a room," he went on. "They told me at the medical school that he sometimes took in roomers." Professor Hatfield had warned him not to mention his name; and as John told his harmless lie he felt with a fillip of amused interest that already he was entering into a plot.

"If you ask me," she said, "they've got as many people as they can handle right now. Still, you never know. Step in, and I'll go speak to Mrs. Chardwicke."

As he followed her through the tomblike vestibule into the hall, John began to realize how misleading his first impression of the house had been. The hall was very high and lighted by a single bulb in a bronze chandelier which had evidently once been used for gas. The walls were papered in a kind of inky green embossed with tarnished gold figures. But what was most disillusioning was the smell: of mildew, of dust, of antiquated plumbing, the indescribable smell of old houses that have not been kept up, sharpened here by a disquieting hint of carbolic. While he watched the girl going upstairs, John noticed the swaying of her hips, and wondered if they would have swayed quite so much if he had not been there.

He had heard what he thought was one of Chopin's preludes which had broken off the moment he had stepped through the inner door. It had come, he was sure, from the room that opened into the hall on the right; and after a moment he walked over to the doorway and looked in between the threadbare portieres of crimson plush. It was a large long room and blocking one of the further corners was a square piano; but he could see no one. Wide doors, also draped with crimson, led into another, smaller room, what must once have been called the "back parlor." He took a few steps into the front room, and as far as he could see the other room was empty also. This surprised him, because of its two doors one opened into the rear of the hall where he had just been standing, and the second, which was of glass, with colored panes around its edge, evidently led out into the yard or on to a back porch.

His first impression of the room in which he stood was that in spite of its size it was crowded with furniture—huge Victorian pieces, with gold arabesques on their woodwork, with knobs and scrolls, with inset rows of tiny balusters, with fringes brushing the brown-and-purple carpet. The wallpaper in here must have once been crimson, like the portieres, but you could hardly see it except in the space directly beneath the ceiling because the walls below were covered by pictures of all sizes and shapes, most of them in massive and contorted gold frames.

Then suddenly from the back parlor he heard a sound, as if a book had been dropped on the floor. He stared once again into every part that he could see of the further room. If anyone was there, he must be deliberately keeping out of sight in one of the nearer corners. Remembering his uncle's request that he keep his eyes open for anything the least bit strange, he walked the length of the room and peered around the edge of the portieres, directly into the face of a girl who was standing behind a table piled with music.

She looked so young and so startled that John felt completely at ease. He didn't know what he had been expecting, but it was not this.

"Hullo there," he said. "I'm afraid I interrupted your playing."

She glanced from side to side, as if she were considering running away; but she was more or less cornered behind the table, and presently realized no doubt that John did not look very formidable.

"Oh, I was just reading through something," she said. "It wasn't meant for anybody to hear. Lots of the notes stick."

"It sounded all right to me," John replied. He noticed a piece of music on the floor near his feet and stooped to pick it up.

"Thanks," she said, and, as he stepped back to allow her space to come out of her corner, he saw that a desperate look was again clouding her eyes. This time, he suspected, however, it was merely because she was trying in vain to think of something to say.

"I guess I sort of barged in on you," John said, smiling. "I've come to see Dr. Chardwicke. I'm looking for a room."

He was realizing more and more how pretty she was and felt a shade guilty at having doubted his uncle's taste a few minutes ago. Her light-brown hair curled thickly about her cheeks; her eyes were deep blue, and her whole face had a freshness, a softness, a rather veiled glow that made him for some reason think of the word "downy." During his college years John had seen little of girls. He had enjoyed his work; he had worked hard, and had made a few excellent men friends. It had begun to seem to him that, like the boys he knew, he ought to be falling in love, if only slightly; and he had formed a habit of appraising girls he met as possible prospects. He was sorry this girl was so young—sixteen, or at most seventeen. Yes, it would be robbing the cradle. His rejection of the possibility of romance, however, made him feel all the more friendly and at ease.

"I have a sister about your age," he went on. "She's apt to run away too, when she hears callers coming. That is, unless they are *her* callers."

"I wasn't running away," she said. "Well yes, I suppose I was. It's just that I hate being caught."

"And I caught you, didn't I?" he exclaimed. "Well, I promise not to eat you."

He turned and walked back into the front room and was glad to hear her following him. "Are you a boarder here?" he asked after a minute, as she did not speak herself. "Or are you one of the family?"

"I guess you'd call me one of the family," she said, and he thought there was reluctance in her admission. "Mrs. Chardwicke is my cousin. She's really my mother's cousin."

"And you go to school here?"

"Yes, but I live here too. I mean I live here all the time."

There was such sudden desolation in her voice that John was sure her parents must be dead. He glanced at her, hardly knowing what to say, and then, almost before he realized it he had asked: "Do you like it here?"

From the fierce look that darkened her eyes he knew what her answer would be. "I hate it!" she exclaimed in a low voice. "No one knows how much I hate it!"

John would have liked to pat her shoulder, as you would a child's, to soothe her and comfort her; but the next moment her face showed only embarrassment and a kind of shame.

"I shouldn't have said that," she muttered. "It's just that you look so kind. And then I almost feel as if I knew you, because you remind me of Ronny."

"Ronny?" John echoed with a specious artlessness that made him feel most deceitful. "Who's he?"

"He stays here too," she said. "Dr. Chardwicke's his guardian."

"I'll be curious to see him," John said, "if you think we're alike."

"He's sick now," she told him; and again there was silence.

"If he's sick, it must be nice for him to have you around," John said at last.

"Oh," she said quickly, "I haven't seen him for a week. They hardly even let Fran see him."

"Fran?" The question in his voice made him feel guilty once more. He was afraid he was not meant to be a detective.

"Ronny and she are engaged, but that's not why she lives here of course. She's Dr. Chardwicke's niece. She's a wonderful person. I wish we were really related, but we're not. It's only by marriage."

"Have the Chardwickes any children of their own?" he asked.

"Oh no!" she exclaimed, as if she couldn't imagine it.

"It seems to me then that they're pretty lucky to have three young relatives living with them—you and Fran and Ronny."

The girl looked doubtful. "I don't know how much they like it," she said. "It's a way for them to get some money."

"I'm sure *I'll* like it," he exclaimed, "if they will take me in!"

"Did you say you were looking for a room here?" she asked, as if it had just dawned on her.

"Yes, I did. Would you mind me as a housemate?"

"Listen," she said quickly. She came quite close to him and her voice was lowered. "Generally I can't talk to people. I'm awful that way. But you seem like a nice person. I don't feel afraid of *you*. And you mustn't stay here, really you mustn't."

He looked at her in amazement. "Why not?" he asked.

"Because it's not a nice place," she said hurriedly. "You wouldn't like it. I know you wouldn't like it!"

"Ellen!"

The name was spoken quite without emphasis, as if it were released automatically and must reach its destination by the force of its own weight. They both glanced over their shoulders toward the door into the front hall, and John felt that of the two he doubtless looked the more embarrassed.

A woman stood in the doorway. She was tall and gray-haired. Her face was somehow a little empty, a little lopsided, a little vague. It made John think of an amateurish drawing, a portrait of a woman who must resemble her, but whose real likeness, whose characteristic expression, the artist had failed to catch.

"Perhaps this young man can decide for himself," she said.

Ellen gave John an earnest look, to re-enforce what she had been urging; then with flushed cheeks she walked out of the door, past her elderly cousin, as if she had not seen her.

"You mustn't mind Ellen," Mrs. Chardwicke said. "I'm afraid she's a little overwrought. Her parents were working in London with the Red Cross. They were killed by the same bomb."

"Good Lord!" John exclaimed. Then he added with energy: "I like her very much."

"The doctor lets her live here out of the kindness of his heart," Mrs. Chardwicke went on, "although she's no blood relation of his. I must say she's a help about the house, and perhaps you can't expect gratitude from one so young."

John felt that while she was speaking, Mrs. Chardwicke's large pale eyes had been thoroughly taking him in.

"Dorothy tells me you're looking for a room," she said.

"Yes, I am," he said. "Have you got one vacant?"

"We don't think of this as a regular rooming house," she said. "We only take in one or two people and we're very careful who they are. Perhaps you will tell me something about yourself. Sit down, won't you?"

Her voice was still so expressionless that he almost hesitated to obey. However he did sit down in a bumpy rocker upholstered in horsehair and explained to her his position with the U.S.N.R. Mrs. Chardwicke seemed to listen carefully though her face kept its queer vagueness.

"You seem like a fairly quiet kind of young man," she said when he had finished. "The doctor insists on quiet. He's very sensitive. Noise gets on his nerves. The only room we have free is a small one on the third floor. It's hard to heat up there, and I hadn't thought of renting it. I should explain that we make a point of our roomers boarding with us also. Would you object to that?"

"I should like it very much indeed," he said. Then feeling it would be wise not to seem too eager, he suggested: "Perhaps I could have a look at the room."

"Of course," she said. "I should expect that. Would you care to take off your overcoat?"

"No, I won't bother," he said; for he realized now that he had got over the first feeling of warmth on coming in from outdoors that the house was chilly.

John followed Mrs. Chardwicke out into the hall and up the steep stairway. She walked swiftly, and he could see that she must possess a great deal of physical energy. A light was burning in the upper hall in a bronze chandelier like the one downstairs; the hallway was long and dim and he had the impression of many doors, all closed. Up here the smell of phenol was even more pronounced.

At the top of the stairs she had kept on toward the rear of the house, and in a moment they entered another, very narrow corridor, itself unlighted. At its end was a stairway not wide enough for two people to walk abreast; and at the bottom she turned a switch that lighted the third story. As he followed her up the bare wooden steps, the air grew colder and colder.

"Dorothy sleeps up here," Mrs. Chardwicke explained, "and there is the little room I'm going to show you. The other rooms we use for storing things. The real attic is most inconvenient."

She opened a door, pressed another switch, and John looked into a room just large enough to hold a three-quarter bed of black walnut, a chest of drawers and one kitchen chair. It was hard to distinguish the brownish roses on the wallpaper from the stains made by dampness. John walked to the window, peered out through the frosted panes, and was glad to see that the room overlooked the lake.

"We could fit in a small table," she suggested, "for you to do your work on. There's a good view, if you like such things. Of course the room won't be nearly as cold as this. The radiator's been off all winter. But I won't guarantee it will be as warm as downstairs."

"It will suit me fine," John said. "I'll take it, if it's not too expensive."

"I ought to tell you," she said, "that there is no bathroom up here. There are two on the second floor and I'll show you which one you're to use. But an active young man shouldn't mind that too much. And now before we discuss terms and you make a down payment I want you to meet the doctor. He always likes to see people before we agree to take them. But I think he'll take you."

As she spoke the last few words, her voice, so neutral until now, took on a faint and momentary hint of color: was it bitterness, irony? He could not tell. Had he imagined it? It was not even remotely reflected in her face.

Intensely curious, John followed her down the stairs, through the narrow corridor, and then along the length of the second-story hall toward the front of the house. She stopped at one of the many doors, and then, rather to his surprise, she knocked.

"Is that you, Althea?" a man's voice called. "If it is, come in. Don't stand on ceremony." In spite of its request, the voice struck John as being somewhat pompous.

Mrs. Chardwicke opened the door and John followed her into the room. The thing that impressed John most, in contrast to the rest of the house, was its warmth and brightness; radiators were sizzling and a fire blazed in a black marble fireplace. With its book-lined walls, the room suggested his uncle's study, except that this was much darker and taller. Along the top of the shelves stood a row of plaster casts: the "Discus Thrower," the "Dying Gaul," the Young Antinoüs, and Bourdelle's "Heracles the Archer." The doctor was seated in an armchair beside an enormous desk. He was wearing a dressing gown of black and blue plaid; a book lay open in his lap, and as he glanced up at John he removed a green eyeshade.

"So this is the young man who'd like to stay with us," he exclaimed. "Sit down, young man, and tell me about yourself."

John seated himself near the door, on the end of a sofa, and as he repeated to the doctor what he had already told Mrs. Chardwicke, he examined him curiously.

Ds. Chardwicke must be at least ten years younger than his wife. He was a florid man, with curly yellow hair, protruding eyes, and the start of a double chin. At first glance his head appeared distinguished: it might suggest the bust of a Roman emperor; but as John looked at his features one by one he was not so favorably impressed. The rather pursey mouth, the prominent eyeballs, reminded John so much of a fancy goldfish that he had to make an effort not to smile.

"So you're in the Navy!" Dr. Chardwicke exclaimed. "It's always been my favorite branch of the service. I tried to get into it myself in the last war, but they wouldn't take me unfortunately, because of my heart."

"You know you never could have stood it," Mrs. Chardwicke said.

Dr. Chardwicke gave his wife an annoyed glance, and as John followed it he was struck by Mrs. Chardwicke's change of expression: it was as if in her husband's presence she had come to life, as if her vague features had suddenly found their focus. While she watched him hungrily from where she stood near the doorway, John felt that no Roman emperor had ever kindled in his subjects a more fanatical devotion.

"Of course I shouldn't dream of turning away a navy man," the doctor went on. "I should consider it unpatriotic, and I always prefer to take young men. They are much less trouble. They are reasonable and accept things without fuss. We have a charming fellow with us now. He's also a medical student—a handsome virile chap, Douglas McFean. I'm sure you'll get along together. I should explain perhaps that I never thought we'd be taking in boarders and I'm afraid we're not cut out for it. Frankly, I very much dislike having strangers in the house, though I realize quite well it's not their fault, and I hope you won't think that sounds unhospitable. As it is, we try to avoid a bourgeois boardinghouse atmosphere. I like our meals to be family affairs as much as possible, and as a matter of fact we have at present two young kinswomen staying with us, charming girls, both of them. By the way, Althea, what room did you say you were giving John? I shall call you by your first name, my dear boy; you don't object?"

"The little back room upstairs," she said. "It's the only one available at present."

"Yes, yes, of course," he exclaimed. "Too bad it has to be so small."

His lids drew together over his eyeballs; his pursed mouth broadened into a smile, and for the moment he looked less like a fish than a plump sleepy lizard.

"Do you think it's safe," he asked, "to put a hot-blooded young sailor like John up there on the third floor with Dorothy?"

Suddenly his smile disappeared; he opened his eyes wide, and stared at John with a most solicitous expression. "You mustn't mind what I say," he said. "Of course I was only joking. When would you like to move in?"

"I'd like to move in right away," John said. "If it's not inconvenient, I'd like to have dinner here tonight. I have to get my things at Science Hall, but that shouldn't take me very long."

Dr. Chardwicke beamed again.

"Fine!" he exclaimed. "There's the energy of youth for you! No sooner do you make up your mind than the thing's done. I was never much drawn to the Hamlet type. Give me Hotspur any day, or even Prince Hal, the young rascal! And now Mrs. Chardwicke and you can talk over business arrangements. All that is quite beyond me."

John rose, said good-bye and was just crossing the threshold after Mrs. Chardwicke, when the Doctor called him back.

"I was thinking," he said, "that a much more attractive room, a room on this floor, may be vacant soon, and then of course you can move down here. I shouldn't be at all surprised if it were free by next week."

3

"That's odd!" Professor Hatfield exclaimed, as John finished his swift account of what had happened in Dr. Chardwicke's house. "I called up the doctor not half an hour ago, to inquire about Ronny. It must have been not long after your interview. He seemed most cheerful and said Ronny was getting along fine. He even thought he might be back in the laboratory by next week."

"But perhaps it wasn't Ronny's room he meant," John said doubtfully. "Or if it was, Ronny may have told him that as soon as he's well enough he's going to move out."

"Perhaps," Professor Hatfield murmured. "Still, if Frances, his own fiancée is hardly allowed to see him, he can't be very spry. You know, John, it would be an excellent thing if you could get in touch with Ronny tonight; and if you can do it without anyone's knowing, so much the better. In fact, any suspicion of your purpose might make its accomplishment impossible. If you succeed, tell him that you're my nephew, that you come from me. Try to get him to talk frankly with you. Everything may be quite as it should be. As I said before, the fact of their taking you is in itself reassuring."

"But how can I find him?" John asked, so disconcerted at this task thrust suddenly upon him that he almost regretted having dropped in just now to tell his uncle of his success with the room. "And even supposing I learn where he is, if the doctor doesn't want him to be seen. . . ."

Professor Hatfield's sharp face seemed to twinkle.

"I'll leave that to your ingenuity," he said. "After all, you're a nephew of mine. And of course there is such a thing as entering the wrong door by mistake—especially in such a big old house. It's lucky that you have to come down to the second floor to the bathroom. If you can't make it, John, you mustn't feel badly. I probably shouldn't even be asking you. But if you do, well, it might. . . . Hmmmmm!"

With that ambiguous sound, the professor bade him good-bye.

As John pressed on through the cold darkness, with the stars caught like Christmas tree ornaments among the boughs of the elms, he knew that his uncle would not blame him if he failed. But he also knew that if something dreadful happened and he had not at least made an attempt, he would not forgive himself. You could laugh the whole thing off as a romantic fancy of his uncle's, which it probably was, but John was beginning to feel a kind of brotherly interest in this young man, this Ronny whom he had never seen. Suppose, just suppose that in some way he were caught, held captive. . . . John hardly knew what he meant. He was still brooding, half reluctant, half eager, when he pulled Dr. Chardwicke's bell.

It was Dorothy again who let him in.

"They've sat down to table," she said. "You better get a move on or the doc will be sore. He's got to have things just so. Still, at that, he may not mind, since it's you."

John put down his bag, hung his coat on one of the knobby horns that served as hooks on the coat rack and pushed his way between the portieres through which Dorothy had just disappeared into the dining room.

"I'm sorry to be late," he exclaimed. "I hope you'll excuse it, Mrs. Chardwicke."

"Never mind, my boy," Dr. Chardwicke said. "Once isn't a habit and you had quite a way to go. This young lady is Frances Maitland, my niece. That handsome rascal over there is Douglas McFean. My wife tells me you've already made the acquaintance of our little cousin Ellen."

The only light in the room was from four candles around a shabby poinsettia in the center of the table. The table itself, dimly reflecting their flames, could have seated twice the number of people without crowding; this destroyed whatever warmth and coziness the candles might have produced, and gave a strangely formal effect. But as soon as John really noticed Frances, seated across the table at the doctor's right, he lost his awareness of everything else in the room.

He had never seen anyone at once so beautiful and so self-contained. Her blond hair was drawn in antique fashion back from her temples, though her face was rather too broad to suggest the Greek ideal. Her features were clear-cut and might almost have looked sharp if it had not been for the lovely serenity, or perhaps merely the remoteness of their expression. Her whole face, through the candlelight, seemed bathed in a pale glow which made John think of the planets Mercury or Venus still burning, just before sunrise, in the pool of the eastern sky.

He realized that he was staring and forced his gaze to move on to Douglas McFean at her left. John had to struggle not to resent him: because he was seated beside her, because they must know each other well, and also, absurdly enough, because Douglas looked very much the way John would have looked if he could have chosen his own appearance: solid, swarthy, vigorous, and completely sure of himself.

"I hear you're a med student with the Navy," Douglas said. "They certainly give you a wonderful break. Free training, living expenses, a commission. . . . There's where I'd be if I could have made it."

Although John knew the remark was meant to be friendly, it annoyed him.

"After all, when I'm through," he said, "I'll have to go where they send me."

"Oh, the war will be over long before that," Douglas exclaimed; and John thought bitterly that airy and optimistic predictions were very easy to make for people whom the war did not affect.

John was quite aware of his jealousy and of how absurd it was; this McFean was not Frances' fiancé. And yet John felt strangely that if he had been, it would have been all right: Douglas and he then would have been on quite a separate footing; Douglas would have every right to look at Fran with that dark and ardent gaze. It was almost as if John were jealous not so much for himself as for Ronny whom he had never seen. If he were sick, John felt, he would not want his girl to be going around with such a handsome, such an obviously passionate young man. "Going around with!" There he was again. Frances could not help the way Douglas looked at her; and as for herself, she seemed hardly to notice his presence.

John felt that for his own soul's good he must try to make friends with Douglas.

"Perhaps you'll show me about the school in a day or two," he said, "and give me a line on some of the professors."

"Sure, any time," Douglas said. "Be glad to!"

"Most of the medical faculty," Dr. Chardwicke remarked with slightly ponderous graciousness, "are old friends and confrères of mine. Say the word, my dear boy, and I'll present you to any that you like. In big classes like ours, it does no harm if your teachers can sort of place you, set you, as it were, against your background . . . that is, if it's the right kind of background."

Dr. Chardwicke implied so clearly that acquaintance with him was the best background possible that John smiled to himself. Then he realized that in his preoccupation with Fran and Douglas he had until now ignored poor little Ellen.

"What class are you in, Ellen?" he asked, for want of something better to say.

"My last year in high school," she answered after a moment.

Her tone was so somber that he turned to glance at her more directly. In the candlelight she looked prettier than ever; the ruddy warmth of her face made moreover a charming contrast with Frances' pallor; but just now she seemed almost as distant as Frances herself. John recalled regretfully and a shade guiltily the sudden almost childlike confidence with which she had spoken to him that afternoon. Through the rest of dinner (such a well-cooked and plentiful meal that John was sorry there were so many things to distract his mind from the food) she did not say a word except to make the briefest answers to direct questions;

Mrs. Chardwicke and Frances hardly spoke either; and although Douglas and John tried to carry on their part, it was Dr. Chardwicke who did most of the talking. He made erratic and optimistic predictions about the war, though he criticized the strategy of the generals; he reminisced jovially about the pranks of his youth; and it was he, not Mrs. Chardwicke, who made the move to rise from the table.

"I should explain to you, my dear John," he said, as he pushed back his chair, "that after dinner the family congregates in the parlor for coffee. It's one of our local mores. I hope you will always join us."

"I'm going up to my room," Ellen said. "I've got some studying to do."

Dr. Chardwicke smiled good-naturedly. "I should think the studying, though I'm sure it's *most* important, could wait for a few minutes, my dear," he said. "Especially tonight, when we have a new addition to our household."

"Well, it can't wait," Ellen said.

As she hurried to the door into the hall, John walked beside her.

"I hoped we were going to be friends," he said.

Ellen, however, did not glance at him. "I have very few friends," she said shortly; and as she ran upstairs into the darkness above, he thought she looked very small and young.

John had been afraid that Frances too might disappear; so he was greatly relieved when she crossed the hallway with Mrs. Chardwicke and pushed through the crimson curtains into the parlor.

"I've got to run up to the lab in a few minutes," Douglas told him, "and get in a few licks on my cadaver. She's a wonderful old girl. I bet she's been around a lot in her day, I call her Gertie. Would you like to come along?"

Douglas' tone was so cordial that John felt his antagonism disappearing. Douglas, he admitted, was no mere handsome brute, the kind you saw photographed in their underwear in the advertising pages of the slick magazines: his wide brow, his boldly aquiline nose, gave a sense of energy and power. Perhaps he could be unscrupulous, even mean; John was not sure; but he was certainly friendly and good-humored. If John had not been so eager to talk with Fran, be would have been glad to go along now with Douglas.

"Thanks a lot," he said, "but I've been sort of rushed today. I think I'll stay at home and go to bed before very long."

"I hope you don't freeze up there," Douglas said. "There's almost no heat on the third floor. But you'll find out soon enough."

As John sipped his coffee, seated in the horsehair armchair from which he had talked with Mrs. Chardwicke this afternoon, the cluttered old room took on for him a kind of charm. A coal fire was burning in the grate. The ends of the room, with their long-curtained windows, were in shadow; the chains of bronze ivy that festooned the chandelier cast confused patterns on the ceiling, patterns more and more distorted as they merged into the general gloom. The place called up memories of John's childhood when his father had taken him to see elderly aunts and cousins in Providence or Wickford. Mrs. Chardwicke now, as she sat so stiffly on the sagging sofa, might be just such a vague aunt, an aunt whose face you couldn't quite remember even while you were staring straight at it, because it was so dim, so much a part of the room; and Dr. Chardwicke, with his pipe which he had to keep relighting, might be a benevolent if rather foolish uncle, the kind that chucked you under the chin and embarrassed you because he expected you to laugh when he did.

Douglas finished his coffee and put his cup back on the tray.

"Sorry to leave you all," he said, "but I'm going to pay a call on Gertie. She gets kind of lonely in the evenings."

Dr. Chardwicke smiled indulgently. "It's all right, my dear fellow. We've got nothing here to compete with Gertie. You're quite sure, though, you young rascal, that you're going to confine your attentions to the dead?"

"Quite sure," Douglas promised, "unless dear old Gertie should revive, and then I won't guarantee what might happen. That's not likely though, because most of her bowels have been removed."

As he spoke, he fixed his dark eyes on Fran who, seated beside Mrs. Chardwicke on the sofa, gave no sign that she heard him; and John fancied that his jaunty manner was bravado.

After Douglas had left the room, John asked for a second cup of coffee. He felt that he must approach the subject of Ronny and his illness; and quite apart from the strange task his uncle had set for him, he would have been disappointed if he could not talk a little with Frances, and begin to break through, however slightly, her reserve.

"I'm sorry to hear that your fiancé is ill," he said. "I hope it's not serious."

For the first time Fran gave him a long straight look. Her eyes were green-blue, very clear and very sad. "I'm afraid it may be," she said. "But Uncle Clarence says there's no danger."

"Ronny?" the doctor exclaimed the next instant, so sharply that John stared at him in surprise. "How did you hear about him, if I may ask?" His tone sounded annoyed, almost suspicious.

"Ellen told me about him this afternoon," John said, and hoped that this would not get her into any trouble.

"Told you about him?" the doctor repeated, in his same querulous voice, which reminded John of a startled and indignant old woman. "What do you mean? What is there to tell?"

The doctor's childish fluster irritated John just enough to destroy the hesitation he had felt in referring to Ronny. He was now quite at his ease.

"She only told me that you were his guardian," he said, "that Miss Maitland and he were engaged, and that he has been ill."

"And all of it is quite true," Dr. Chardwicke said, "even the last of it, unfortunately." His tone was calm once more and half-apologetic. "I just couldn't imagine how you'd heard of him," he explained, "because so far as I recall he wasn't mentioned at dinner. As a matter of fact, the poor boy has a rather troublesome type of food poisoning, and so far he hasn't been able to shake it off. It occurred to me that if you had heard anything of the sort it wouldn't be the best kind of recommendation for Mrs. Chardwicke's cooking. Let me hasten to say that it was *not* acquired at our table. Ronny always loved Chinese cooking, and used to go down to a very dingy little Chinese-American restaurant, though I often warned him against it. I'm sure that's where he picked up the infection."

"But if that's what caused it," Frances said, "I don't see why I didn't get sick too. I used to go there with him. You're sure it *is* that, Uncle? You don't think there is anything else?"

This time John could see Dr. Chardwicke's face actually growing red, and was reminded of the flushed wattles of a turkey cock.

"I *know* it's not anything else," he pronounced tartly. "How many times must I repeat it? After all, my dear Fran, you presumably didn't always eat out of the same dish, and even if you had, there is a wide range of natural susceptibility. Ronny has been delicate since he was a child. I suppose in the course of my practice I've run into a dozen cases exactly similar."

"You don't think even so," Fran suggested very gently, "that it might be well to consult some other doctor? It's not that I doubt your skill, Uncle Clarence . . . but. . ."

"*I should hope not!*"

The sharp interruption came from Mrs. Chardwicke. She frowned as she turned her pale eyes toward Frances; yet she did not look so much angry as deeply shocked. "You may count yourself lucky, Frances, that if Ronny had to be taken ill, it was in this house. He could receive no better treatment anywhere in America, or anywhere in the world, for that matter. I should think you'd feel like apologizing to your uncle."

Fran shrugged her shoulders wearily. "I didn't mean to hurt your feelings, Uncle Clarence," she said. "I'm sure you're giving Ronny the best of care. But after all, in cases of severe illness, there often *are* consultations . . . and I don't see what harm it could do."

"Doctors sometimes call in consultants, or suggest that they be called in," Dr. Chardwicke said, "when they are in doubt as to what should be done. This, for me, is the simplest kind of case. I am not in the slightest doubt. I know just how it should be treated. I am legally Ronny's guardian and I consider him as I should my own son. I don't intend to have his life endangered by the possible bungling interference of local practitioners who have not been following the case."

Fran bit her lips. John noticed that she drew in her breath as for a sigh, though he heard no sound. He was convinced that this was not the first time she had made such suggestions to Dr.

Chardwicke, and that she felt quite helpless. As he watched her seated there on the sofa, as lonely and desolate as if she were perched on some rock in the midst of the sea, all his reserves and hesitations melted away: from now on not even Professor Hatfield could be more eager to investigate Ronny's situation, and to save him, if he needed saving.

The next moment Fran turned to him.

"I'm particularly sorry that Ronny is laid up just now," she said, "because I know he would like you and I think you would like him. And that means more than you might imagine. Ronny is very reserved. He has almost no intimate friends; and so on the rare occasions that I see someone I think would understand him, it makes me very happy."

John hoped that his flush was not too obvious. His pleasure was not only because Fran thought he would get on with Ronny: it was even more because her remark showed that from the first she must have been noticing him, she must have been sizing him up, and not without sympathy. From another girl such a statement might be part of a "line"; but not, he would stake anything, from Fran.

"I'm glad you think we'd get along," he said eagerly, "and I hope he'll be well enough for me to meet him very soon."

"When you do," she said, "I know you won't be disappointed. He's a quite exceptional person."

She rose from the sofa. "If you will excuse me, Aunt Althea," she went on, "I think I'll go up to bed. I haven't been sleeping very much these last few nights."

"In that case," Dr. Chardwicke suggested, "a mild sedative would not seem out of order. I'll go with you, my dear."

John watched her as she left the room with her uncle; then as Dorothy came in for the coffee things, he turned to Mrs. Chardwicke.

"I think I'll be going to bed too," he told her. "It was a wonderful dinner, Mrs. Chardwicke. You certainly are a swell cook."

For the first time since he had met her she smiled, though the smile was gone so quickly that he could almost have taken it for a brief nervous contortion of her mouth.

"The doctor is very particular about his food," she said. "He looks robust but his health has always been fragile. He requires the best of everything to build him up. You may have thought I charged you a good deal for room and board; but I believe that people are glad to pay a little more if they can have the best. Of course Dorothy is a help. In fact I couldn't have done without her during these last few days since Ronny has not been quite so well. The doctor and I have spent hours in his room, in case he should require anything. Personally, I don't quite see the need of it, but the doctor is so conscientious! I've had to leave the cooking entirely to Dorothy, so it's she who deserves your compliment. Of course she did use my recipes and follow my directions. We have breakfast at eight, and we like people to be punctual, though the doctor does not usually come down. I hope you sleep well in that cold room. Would you care to have Dorothy knock at your door in the morning?"

"That would be very nice," John said. "Good night, Mrs. Chardwicke."

4

When John reached the top of the stairs, he caught a glimpse of Ellen, in a blue dressing gown, hurrying across the hall and entering the room behind the doctor's study. He had glanced through the half-open door of the room back of this one, which must be Ellen's, on his way to meet Dr. Chardwicke this afternoon, and had noticed a pair of trousers flung across a chair. That room, therefore, was probably Douglas'; and since there seemed to be only three bedrooms on each side of the hall, John could ignore that half of the house in his search for Ronny.

Climbing the stairs to the third floor, with his suitcase bumping against the walls, he felt as if he were on a ship and would presently step out into the spaciousness of an upper deck; but when he entered his own bedroom, its musty indoor smell was as different as possible, in spite of the cold, from the pure ocean wind. In the dark he stared down over the lake to the red lights of two radio masts on the further shore. A train whistle came to him faintly, long-drawn-out, trailing off into a tingling silence. It had the effect of making the whole house unreal: it was as if this were not actually happening but was rather something he remembered not too distinctly from long ago. He was now reliving it in a queer kind of dream.

He turned the switch and sat down on his bed to make plans. There was no reason to feel excited. The worst that could happen to him was embarrassment: he would have blundered into the wrong bedroom and would retreat at once with confused apologies.

Even if the doctor asked him to leave the house, he would at any rate have something to report to his uncle.

If Ronny was confined to his bed, the chances were that his door would not be locked. It should not be too hard, with his present knowledge, to locate the room. No doubt Dr. and Mrs. Chardwicke slept in the other front room, across the hall from the study: these two rooms must be the two largest, the real "master bedrooms," and John could not imagine the doctor choosing any other. That left, if he could rule out one whole side of the hall, only two rooms, which must be Ronny's and Fran's, with the bathroom he was to use between them. There were several narrow doors opening on to the passage that led to the third story, but John was pretty sure they were the doors of cupboards or linen closets, a "sewing room" perhaps, and the back stairs down to the kitchen.

An idea occurred to him of which he felt even his Uncle Paul might be proud. The porch, he recalled, extended around the west side of the house, which was the side he must explore; if he climbed out on to the porch he could peer in through the windows. Since they were so high up and in such a big yard, there was a good chance they would not be covered by shades or blinds. His own bathroom window, as he remembered it, was big enough to climb through, if a storm window did not make this impossible.

He must wait for a while because now people would be moving about the hall on their way to and from the bathrooms; on the other hand, he must not delay too long, until all the lights were out, so that he could not distinguish one room from another. He would hate, too, to rouse Ronny after he had gone to sleep for the night. It was only quarter of ten. He would give himself exactly one half hour.

He undressed, because it would be more natural, if he were seen, to be in a dressing gown so long after he had gone upstairs, and propped against the pillow he tried to read *Cakes and Ale*; but tonight he simply couldn't follow Maugham's sentences. It was lucky he did not like soft beds, for he had never felt one so hard. Well, he should grow used to that in a few nights. He heard steps outside his door, and Dorothy called: "Good night, sailor! Writing to your girl friend?"

"Writing to all of them," he answered. "Good night!"

During dinner he had noticed that Dorothy, as she passed the dishes, had kept staring at Douglas in very much the way that Douglas stared at Fran; there was not only disease in this house, there was also more than a hint of crude passion; no wonder poor little Ellen hated it so. He could hear mice scurrying overhead in the attic; at intervals a branch would scrape against the eaves. He looked at his watch: it was already half past ten.

He got out of bed, put on his shoes over a pair of woolen socks, tightened the cord of his dressing gown, and stepped into the pitch-dark hall. He must be careful not to stumble on the stairs: they were very steep and there was no railing. When he came out into the second-story passage, he could see that the light, around the corner, was still burning.

At the end of the passageway he stopped to investigate. The long dim hall was empty. The bathroom door, on the far side, could not be more than twenty feet away; if the bathroom was occupied he would just have to go back to his room and wait a little longer.

Trying to look unconcerned, he walked down the hall and felt the knob tentatively. To his relief the door opened at once. He went into the bathroom, drew the bolt, and turned on the light.

The smell of carbolic was so sharp in here that it forced itself again on his attention. As he glanced into the blue-and-white porcelain bowl, he saw a centipede, over an inch long, resting motionless near the drain; with a feeling of revulsion he took a piece of paper, crushed the insect with a swift dab, and threw it into the toilet. Then he looked at the window.

As he had hoped there was only a single sash. It stuck a moment when he pulled up on it, no doubt because of the ice, and then opened with a rush to let in a blast of bitter air. Sticking out his head, he could see that the porch roof was only two feet below the sill, and though the slates were covered with snow, there was a bare strip about a yard wide close to the house; the snow when it fell must have been blowing from the other direction and the protruding eaves would offer some shelter. John climbed through the window and stood shivering on the roof.

The first thing he did was to lower the sash, leaving just enough room at the bottom to stick in his fingers when he should want to raise it again; otherwise there would be a noticeable draft under the door. The half moon hung between the branches of an elm tree. Far away, along the lake shore, pinkish lamps projected a disk upon the ice, like the ring of a circus, and he could see the figures of skaters moving round and round as in a slow dance.

The cold seemed to climb up his legs no matter how tightly he pulled his dressing gown about him: he must not loiter here or he would freeze before he was done. He moved carefully along toward the front of the house, his shoulders brushing the rough brick of the wall, and in a minute had reached the edge of the next window.

Lace curtains were drawn across it, but he could peer through them. From where he stood he could see no one in the room; but the dressing table was evidently a woman's, and he noticed a pair of high-heeled slippers on the floor near a flowered armchair. It struck him unpleasantly, for the first time, that he was now in the exact position of a peeping Tom.

He was about to step back when he saw Frances in a silvery-white kimono appear from the left, like a figure on a stage, go over to the door and open it. For a minute she seemed to be talking to someone who stood outside in the hall; John could not see who it was, for the door was not opened more than a foot, and she stood blocking the entrance. Then she took a step backwards and closed the door swiftly. She turned away, and for the first time looked toward the window: she had raised her hand and was pressing it against her mouth; her fine eyebrows were drawn together, and on her face was a look of the sharpest repugnance, as if she had been shown something unclean. Disturbed and ashamed of himself, John moved back, close to the wall of the house, past the bathroom, until he had reached the window which he now felt almost sure was Ronny's.

No curtains were drawn here but the light inside was so dim that at first he could make out very little. Then he could see to his left a heavy walnut bed and a table on which stood a green-shaded reading lamp. Its light was concentrated upon a pitcher of water, a tumbler with a glass tube in it, and a bottle of some red medicine. He left the window, hurried along the roof, and climbed back into the bathroom. He had learned at any rate which was Ronny's room: it would be the next door to the left.

He listened a minute before stepping out into the hall, in case anyone might still be loitering; but when he looked, there was no one there, and in half a minute he had reached the door of Ronny's bedroom. He tried the knob, pushed gently, and the door opened.

"Ronny," he said as he stepped inside, "you don't know me, but I've come from Professor Hatfield. I'm his nephew. He's been worrying about you."

A boy, a young man, with matted yellow hair, was lying in the shadowy bed. The cheeks were terribly flushed, as if rouge had been dabbed on, with no attempt to blend it into the pallor of the surrounding skin; the lips were cracked; the eyes were sunk so deep beneath the blond eyebrows that John could imagine they had been sucked in by some vacuum at the center of the brain. But what shocked him most were the wrists and hands which, exposed to the chill of the room and possessed, it seemed, by an independent life of their own, were continuously plucking at the bedclothes, with the restless, jerky and nonchalant persistence of a monkey picking fleas from another.

As John approached the side of the bed, the eyes, after wavering for a moment, became fixed with an anxious look upon his face.

"Who are you?" the boy asked, and his voice seemed to come from far away, from the depths of some exhausting dream. "Are you a student of Professor Hatfield's? Are you a friend of mine? Or perhaps you're just myself. Are you Ronny?"

5

"No, I'm not Ronny," John said, trying to smile. "You must be Ronny. My name is John Frazer."

The young man looked at him vaguely, and then his eyes seemed to focus: it was as if he had been staring at a broken reflection in a pond—an image that slowly took shape again as the ripples subsided.

"John Frazer?" he repeated. "Yes, of course. How stupid of me! I must be pretty sick."

John hoped his own smile did not look as constrained as it felt. "You never knew me," he said, "but you may have heard Professor Hatfield mention me."

For an instant Ronny smiled himself, and in spite of his fever his face looked very pleasant.

"Professor Hatfield's a fine man," he said. "I was doing some work for him. At least I did once."

"He wanted me to see you," John said earnestly. "What is it, Ronny? What's the matter with you? Do you know?"

Ronny's smile disappeared and it was hard to imagine it had been there on that ravaged face. "I get into those hot empty rooms," he said. "That's what I mind most. There are lots of people but they aren't real. I know they are not real because my mother was there, and she is dead. That made me think I was dead too, but I guess they were dreams, sort of. I suppose you're a dream too, aren't you?"

"No, I'm real, all right. I want to be your friend. That's why I've come to live here."

"You say you live here?"

"Yes, I just moved in this afternoon."

"I came here a long time ago. I'm afraid I don't remember when. I'm very absent-minded. But I was well when I came here."

His eyes wavered; it was as if the reflection in the pond were once more ruffled; John had the sensation that Ronny had withdrawn into some other place—a place moreover that must be very peaceful and happy; but then a look of revulsion appeared in his eyes; his pupils moved from side to side as if to escape, to dodge something he knew was unavoidable.

"It's not foam," he said in a blurred hurried voice. "I thought it was foam. It looked so cool and soft, like the ocean. But it's dry. It's like hot rubber. It's covering me all over. It's sweeping me back into that awful cloud that keeps swirling me round and round and makes me so tired . . . so tired and sick. Give me some water, won't you? Quickly please. Some cool water."

John poured some water into the glass he had seen through the window. He bent over Ronny carefully and put the tube between his dry stained lips. For a moment. Ronny sucked greedily and then he seemed to forget that the tube was there; so John took it from his mouth and placed the tumbler back on the table.

Ronny's face took on a troubled expression, like a disturbed child. "You mustn't live here," he said suddenly, in his hurried voice, and his tone was more intense than it had been. "You must run away. Quickly. While there's still time. You're my friend, aren't you? It would be too bad if you got caught like me. Thanks for the water, but you must run away."

John leaned eagerly toward him. "Why must I go, Ronny?" he asked. "What must I run away from?"

Ronny's face grew even more troubled; his eyes looked helplessly about the room.

"It's bad here," he said after a minute. "I can't quite remember. You say you're John but you may be Ronny, and just don't suspect it. The names sound alike. It would be easy to get them confused."

"Do you think anyone has poisoned you?" John asked. "Is it Dr. Chardwicke? Or would it be someone else? You can say anything to me. And then I'll go away. I promise you to run away."

Ronny shook his head wearily. "I'm sick," he said. "That's why I can't remember. I'm sort of delirious. You must think I'm mad."

"I know you're not mad," John said in a firm voice. "You're just as sane as I am. This will all go when the fever goes."

Ronny merely shook his head with the same restless exhausted motion. Then the look of horror that John had already noticed, once more appeared in his eyes.

"They've come for me again," he said in a barely audible voice. "They're dead, that's why. Because I'm dead too. They don't want me to remember so that I can tell you. If I could only stop that swirling, just for a minute. . . . Because you're still alive. You're my friend. You mustn't go down there."

Ronny's eyes were fixed so intently that John could himself almost feel the muscular effort of his struggle to concentrate. His chest, his stomach, must be taut and strained, as if he were struggling up a long flight of stairs with a killing weight on his shoulders.

Then suddenly it was as if a veil had been removed from his face: every feature seemed to grow sharp and fixed; and in his eyes was a look, no longer half hidden but now glaring forth, of such horror and despair that John felt it would burn through his body like the beams of an X ray.

"John!" he screamed, for John knew it was meant to be a scream though it hardly carried across the room. "Run away, quick! I remember now. I remember what was in the cloud. Run away, or it will be too late. You don't believe it! You don't believe there's a hell. I didn't either. But it's true. I swear it's true!"

John saw that the whole body beneath the bedclothes was twitching and straining. Ronny's head raised itself from the pillow, fell back, and then was raised again; and suddenly with a twist of his shoulders Ronny sat up. His arms reached forward as if to seize John's hands.

"You mustn't!" John exclaimed. "I don't think you ought to sit up. Can I bring you anything?"

But Ronny still strained forward and his face now expressed nothing but the stubborn intensity of his effort.

"I'll take you, John," he muttered in a voice that John could hardly understand. "I'll take you out myself, if you've lost your way."

Then before John could protest again, Ronny's face was contorted by what must have been a spasm of the sharpest physical pain. A groaning cry came from his lips; and as he fell back on the bed, John knew that some swift incredible suffering had brushed from his mind all recognition, all memory, even all dreaming, to leave nothing but itself.

6

John bent over Ronny anxiously. "What is it?" he asked. "Do you feel much worse?"

Ronny made no sound except for the sighing of his breath. The flush had gone from his cheeks as if it had been wiped off with a sponge; his eyes seemed to have been drawn still deeper into his head, and in their pupils was the look of a cornered animal.

"I'm going to get some help for you," John said. "I'll be right back."

He hurried out into the hall and was starting toward the front room where he thought Dr. Chardwicke must be sleeping, when he stopped suddenly. Douglas was a third-year medical student: it might be well to have some check on the doctor. So John crossed the ball and knocked at the door opposite Ronny's.

"What is it?" Douglas asked sleepily, after a minute. "What do you want? It's not morning, or is my watch crazy?"

"May I come in?" John asked. "It's John Frazer. Ronny has had some kind of crisis. He looks very bad."

And without waiting, he pushed open the door.

As John entered the room Douglas switched on a light beside his bed. He had raised himself on his elbow and his black hair was matted into his eyes. "John!" he exclaimed. "For God's sake! What in hell's the matter?"

"I was just leaving the bathroom," John explained, "when I heard someone cry out. It seemed to come from the next room, and it sounded so desperate I went right in. It was Ronny. He looks to me as if he is dying."

Douglas sprang from bed and reached for his dressing gown.

"Have you routed up the doc?" he asked.

"I thought I'd speak to you first," John said. "I thought it would do no harm for you to be around too."

"Good idea!" Douglas exclaimed. "It's an understatement to say that my confidence in the doc's professional skill is not unbounded. Especially in an emergency. That poor kid Ronny didn't have a break, but what could you do?"

"I suppose I'd better go after him now?" John said.

"Sure. Run along. I'll be with you in a minute. It's the front room to the right."

John had to knock several times before there was an answer; and then it was Mrs. Chardwicke who spoke, not her husband.

"What is it?" she asked. "Unless it's something really urgent, there's no excuse for rousing the doctor."

"It is something urgent," John said. "I think Ronny's dying."

"What? What's that? What did you say?"

This time it was the doctor's voice, nervous, sharp, almost breathless.

"I said that Ronny's in a very bad condition."

"Wait there! Don't go away! I'll be right there!"

But it must have been at least five minutes before the bedroom door opened and the doctor appeared in a black-and-blue dressing gown, his usually florid face looking now strained and yellow. Behind him stood Mrs. Chardwicke in a gray wrapper.

The doctor peered at him with puffy eyes. "What's all this about Ronny?" he demanded. "And may I ask how *you* happened to be on hand? Ronny is my patient. I haven't been allowing anyone to see him for the last few days . . . anyone but Mrs. Chardwicke who's been acting as nurse."

In a sentence John told him the same story he had told Douglas.

"You should have come to me first," the doctor said severely. "Such symptoms are to be expected. They are doubtless not so grave as the layman would imagine. You haven't roused anyone else?"

"I spoke to Douglas," John told him. "I thought he might be of some help."

"In my professional work I don't require help," Dr. Chardwicke said. "Particularly the help of amateurs and students. It was inexcusable of you to speak to Douglas before coming to me."

After the pity and horror he had felt during his talk with Ronny, it was a relief to have someone to be angry with.

"Nevertheless," John told him calmly, "I'd do just the same thing again. When a man is dying, Dr. Chardwicke, I don't stand on etiquette. It will do no harm to have another opinion, even from a medical student."

John had expected an explosion from the doctor, but instead Dr. Chardwicke merely stared at him an instant and then lowered his eyes.

"At any rate, it's too late now," he grumbled, with a hint of apology, "and as you say, it will do no harm."

He glanced over his shoulder at his wife. "You go back to bed, my dear. There's no need for you to undergo what may be a painful experience."

"I'm going with you," she said. "If Ronny is really dying I certainly shall pay him my respects. My respects to the dead."

"Doesn't it seem to you," John asked impatiently, "that you ought to be hurrying, Dr. Chardwicke? The case is an emergency, and we've been standing here for five minutes or more. I'm thankful that Douglas is with him."

"Yes, yes," the doctor said quickly. "Yes, yes, of course."

And he bustled down the hall toward Ronny's room, with John walking beside him and Mrs. Chardwicke following.

The door was ajar, and Douglas came to meet them on the threshold.

"He's in a state of collapse," he said. "I forced a little whisky on him, but I guess there's nothing much to be done."

John stepped into the room after Dr. and Mrs. Chardwicke and stared through the greenish shadow at Ronny. He could notice a change even in the few minutes since he had left him: the skin now looked corpselike; the eye sockets reminded him of a skull, and he could hardly see the eyes themselves. As he watched, Ronny's breathing was interrupted by a kind of quivering groan; his body twisted beneath the covers.

"Do you think he's conscious?" he asked Douglas. "It looks to me as if he was suffering damnably."

"I doubt it," Douglas said, "but a shot of morphia would do no harm. How about it, Doc?"

"Precisely what I was going to do," Dr. Chardwicke said. "I'll leave you in charge of the patient, Douglas, while I get my hypo."

He left the room, closing the door behind him, but Mrs. Chardwicke remained near the foot of the bed, staring down at Ronny.

As she stood there, gaunt and still, with her lopsided face, her thin hair pulled back in a braid, John thought that a few centuries ago she might have been burned as a witch; not that she suggested the crones that ride on broomsticks, but rather some prophetess or sibyl standing in her cave, her own spirit absent or asleep, as she waited for the moment of divine, or perhaps demoniac possession.

Ronny's body shifted once more. John wished Dr. Chardwicke would return, but it might take a few minutes to sterilize the syringe. Then an idea occurred to him—a memory from the medical reading he had done for his own interest.

"Douglas," he asked, "you don't think this could be typhoid by any chance?"

"Good boy!" Douglas exclaimed. "That's just what I've been thinking ever since I laid eyes on him. Typhoid would do it; perforation, of course, probably multiple, along with exceptionally severe hemorrhage."

"But if it *were* typhoid," John suggested doubtfully, "wouldn't he show more signs of emaciation?"

"Not so early in the game," Douglas said, "and not the way they treat it nowadays. A generation ago they used to starve it, but that's out of date."

"Ronny has certainly not been starved," Mrs. Chardwicke said coldly. "He's been served the most nutritious, if simple, diet, and what's more the doctor has insisted on his eating it. But the idea of typhoid is absurd! The doctor would of course have recognized it."

"He probably would," Douglas said. "He has had plenty of opportunity, which is more than the rest of us have had."

"The doctor has told us that Ronny is suffering from food poisoning."

"Yes, I know," Douglas said. "That's what makes it interesting."

John glanced at Mrs. Chardwicke but her face showed no expression. The next moment the doctor came back into the room, carrying a small white tray.

No one spoke as he leaned over the bed, pushed back the sleeve of Ronny's pajamas almost to the shoulder, swabbed the flesh, and inserted the syringe. John was thankful that now Ronny need feel no more suffering.

"Clarence," Mrs. Chardwicke said abruptly, "these smart young men have just been saying they thought Ronny had typhoid fever. I told them the idea was preposterous."

"Typhoid!" Dr. Chardwicke exclaimed, and the shrillness in his voice did not give the effect, John thought, of assurance. "How in heaven's name could he get typhoid around here? You don't just pick it up in the street, my dear fellow."

"As I was saying a minute ago," Douglas remarked, "that's what makes it so interesting. You don't pick it up in the street, but you might pick it up in a lab." John saw through the gloom that the doctor turned even paler.

"Are you implying," he asked huffily, "that I would be so careless with my cultures, my bacteria . . . ?" Then his face brightened. "As a matter of fact, you may recall that there were two cases of typhoid in the hospital last September, the first we had had in years. They were workers in the Tuscoda plant who had come up here from somewhere in the South. It was only diagnosed after they had been in the ward for several days. That was when I insisted that Fran, as a Nurses' Aide, should have her typhoid shots. Of course Mrs. Chardwicke and I have had them at regular intervals. Personally, I'd no more think of going without them than I would without vaccination. Since I work with germs myself, I've always taken every conceivable precaution, and I resent your implication that I've been careless. I demand an apology."

"Of course I remember those cases," Douglas said, ignoring the doctor's strained pompousness. "However, they were several months ago. You may or may not have been careless. Perhaps you weren't. Though when you were showing me around, it struck me you were a little on the casual side, considering the dynamite you were handling—t.b., sleeping sickness, tetanus, not to speak of typhoid. But I am suggesting that you've been very generous in allowing people to visit your laboratory. You don't mind, to put it mildly, displaying your dangerous little protégées to the lay visitor. Every person in this house has been there more than once, except John, and you haven't had a chance with him yet."

"Really, Douglas! Your tone is outrageous. I can only explain it by the way you feel, the way we all feel, about Ronny. I should like to call to your attention that if I have shown a few people my collections, and explained a little of my work, I've always been there to see that everything was quite secure."

"Granted, granted!" Douglas said. "But I'd like to remind *you* that with the way you leave your keys around the house, anyone—even Dorothy, if the mood struck her—could doubtless have gone to your lab half a dozen times without your being any the wiser. Doesn't that strike you as perhaps a shade careless?"

"I confess I'm rather absent-minded," Dr. Chardwicke said. "Perhaps it's a carry-over from the days when I was a professor." He gave a dismally perfunctory smile. "But after all, my cultures, though I value them for the purposes of my own research, are not of general interest to the uninitiated except as I explain them. I can't conceive why anyone in this house, or anywhere else for that matter, should want to tamper with them."

"Unless to induce a nice deadly case of typhoid fever," Douglas said. "Because seriously, Doctor, you've been following this case. You've been seeing Ronny every day. And you can't deny that this may be typhoid. If you do, as a friend of Ronny's I should feel I had to call in the health officer. The faintest suspicion of typhoid would certainly warrant a complete investigation, from the public health point of view."

As he spoke, Douglas kept his bold dark eyes fixed on the doctor; and John could feel almost sorry for Dr. Chardwicke's embarrassment. He blinked and cleared his throat; his face which had been, for him, so pale, flushed a deep red.

"Yes," he admitted with nervous pettishness, "of course it may be typhoid. I won't say it's probable but it's not impossible. I told you it was food poisoning, didn't I? Well, isn't typhoid a kind of food poisoning? The idea occurred to me a few days ago, and since then I've been treating the case with that possibility in mind. As you may know, Mrs. Chardwicke was for years a registered nurse, and I can guarantee that Ronny had, to say the least, as conscientious care as he would have had in the hospital; much better, as a matter of fact, because the hospital is so overcrowded and so short of help. But Douglas, my dear fellow, let me make you a confession. You said just now I was careless about my lab, which I categorically deny. But I happen to know that several of my former colleagues begrudge me the space in Science Hall that the university allows me. There has been a whispering campaign on foot. They say that I am insufficiently responsible. Of course it is only spite and jealousy, but I was afraid if it were rumored that a case of typhoid had developed on my own premises they might seize that as an occasion . . . an occasion to kick me out of the building."

"Yes, they might," Douglas said. "And in the meanwhile there is not a damn thing we can do for Ronny. I suppose if we were at the hospital they might try a transfusion, wouldn't they, Doc? But I'm sure now it wouldn't do a bit of good."

"No," Dr. Chardwicke said with a faint return of his assurance, "nothing would do any good, and it's too late to move him now. At least the poor boy is unconscious. He's not suffering."

For a time no one spoke. John's eye was caught by the medallions on the wallpaper; their patterns suggested the stained cross sections of microscopic animals; his glance followed a line upward as they rose, dimmer and dimmer, toward the ceiling, and he had to resist an impulse to count them. Frost sparkled around the edges of the long window. He could imagine this room detached from the rest of the house, detached from the living earth, and suspended in some dream limbo of starlit and frozen space.

But he knew there were rooms on either side, and in one of those rooms Frances was sleeping! Frances was engaged to marry Ronny, and Ronny was dying. John walked to the door.

"I'm going to call Frances," he said. "She ought to be here!" Without waiting for any comment he slipped out into the hall.

He knocked at her door at first gently, and then, as she did not answer, louder and louder. All at once he remembered that

Dr. Chardwicke had offered to give her a sedative, and he was debating whether he should try the door and open it if it were unlocked, when he heard a sound behind him, and turning his head saw Ellen peering from the door of her own room.

"What's the matter?" she asked. "Hasn't there been a lot of talking and moving about? What is it?"

"Ronny is very ill," John said. "He's dying. The Chardwickes and Douglas are with him. I'm trying to wake up Frances, but I guess she took something to put her to sleep. Would you go in, Ellen, if the door's not locked, and rouse her?"

"Yes, yes," she said, "I will."

Her head disappeared, and in a moment she came out in her blue dressing gown.

Fran's door, he was glad to see, was not locked. Ellen hurried into the room; he could hear her calling Fran's name; there was a murmur of voices, and then Fran and Ellen joined him where he was waiting outside Ronny's door. Fran looked very white, but she smiled faintly when she saw John.

"I'm glad you came for me," she said. "I'm so glad you came."

When they stepped into the sickroom, Dr. Chardwicke was bending over the bed. He straightened up and turned as he heard them.

"My dears," he said solemnly, "it's all over. It was remarkably quick. For his sake, it was much better so."

Without a sound Fran walked to the bed and stared down at Ronny. John's eyes followed her glance. Relaxed in death, Ronny's features had taken on a sensitive and tranquil beauty; they no longer suggested illness: nothing but youth and a kind of trustful innocence. John looked up in sympathy at Fran. A quiver as of unbearable pain twitched the stillness of her face, and she raised her hands to press them against her eyes. Then she turned away swiftly, crossed the room to the window, and gazed out into the night.

Ellen took a step as if to follow her; but she stopped, drew in her breath with a kind of sob; and as John reached forward to take her hand she turned like some small rosy savage on Dr. Chardwicke.

"You killed him!" she cried passionately. "You killed Ronny! That was why you wouldn't let us come near him, so we wouldn't suspect. You killed him to get his money. Because if he'd lived a month longer you wouldn't have got it! Ronny told me. He was so generous, so sweet, that he wanted to give me some, because he knew when Mother and Father died I didn't have any. But he said he had to wait until he was twenty-one, because you managed it all until then, because it went to you until he was of age, and you could do with it what you liked. I wouldn't have taken any, because I had no right to it, but he wanted to give me some. He was the kindest, nicest person I ever knew, and now you've killed him!"

"Ellen!" Dr. Chardwicke almost shouted. His cheeks and jowls seemed to swell; and again he made John think of an outraged and furious old woman. "Ellen, I forbid you to say another word. Do you hear me? Not one more word for your own sake. Do you want us all to think you're mad? Oh, I know you and Ronny were as thick as thieves before Fran came along. I'd assumed it was perfectly innocent or I shouldn't have allowed it, but I'm beginning to have my doubts. I remember very well how you moped and sulked when you saw he was in love with Fran. I can see quite clearly even now the way you used to stare at him with those big reproachful eyes. I thought it was just a case of calf love and let it go at that. But now I'm not so sure. The jealousy of adolescents is quite unpredictable. No one can tell how far it will go—especially when they are unbalanced, as you have certainly proved yourself to be. Everyone knows I was devoted to Ronny! Althea, you can vouch for that."

"Yes," Mrs. Chardwicke said in a deliberate voice, "I can vouch for that. Everyone must have seen the fatherly interest you have taken in the various young men who have come to stay in this house. I think, Ellen, you had better leave the room."

No one spoke for a minute, as Fran turned away from the window and walked back to where she had stood beside Ronny.

"Perhaps we'd all better leave," Douglas said. "I'm a godless heathen myself, and I'm all for being free and easy, but even I feel a little embarrassed watching a cat and dog fight over a corpse. Especially when it happens to have been a friend."

Then, with an agility that made John think of a professional wrestler, he sprang forward and caught Fran, just as she was sinking to the floor in a dead faint.

7

Neither Fran nor Dr. Chardwicke appeared at breakfast next
morning. Ellen was subdued and hardly spoke, but it seemed to
John that she no longer felt the aloofness which had made her
so silent last night at dinner. Douglas, though he did not talk
much, seemed gripped by a kind of excitement: his keen eyes
kept glancing about the room and John thought he was eager to
be through with his breakfast so that he would not have to sit
still. He excused himself before John was finished and rose from
the table. Dorothy followed him into the hall; and when she
returned a moment later, after he had left the house, she looked
decidedly sullen.

Mrs. Chardwicke's manner was the most curious of all, simply because, so far as John could see, it showed not the faintest
difference from what it had been yesterday evening. When she
spoke, which was not often, her remarks were the flattest of com-
monplaces.

"The doctor told me to tell you," she said to John in a businesslike voice, as he was putting on his overcoat, "that if you find
you can't take lunches here on certain days of the week, because
of your classes, I should make some reasonable reduction in your
charges."

John thanked her and stepped out into the sunlight and the
long blue shadows of the morning with a vast relief. In spite of
the intense cold, he had never enjoyed so much the glitter of
the snow, the sight of healthy people hurrying along the street
about their everyday business. He was eager to inform his uncle of

Ronny's death, but when he stopped at his house no one answered the bell; and when he asked for him at the University Club he was told that Professor Hatfield had not yet arrived. Perhaps he was at work in his laboratory, but John had now just time to get to his first class. At noon he went again to the club but still the professor was not there.

Dr. Chardwicke and Fran both came down to lunch. The doctor looked harassed, though he had recovered his normal color; Fran seemed so exhausted that John felt she should not have left her bed.

"I should tell you," Dr. Chardwicke proclaimed as soon as they were seated, "that Dr. Gibbons, the health officer, will be here this afternoon. I notified him this morning of Ronny's death, told him that there was some suspicion of typhoid, and he agreed with me that there should be an investigation. In the first place we must have a further examination to make sure of the diagnosis, and if it *is* typhoid, why then of course we must try to trace its origin. I shall suggest that each one of you be examined to make sure that there is no carrier in the house and of course the plumbing will be thoroughly looked into."

He glanced around the table with a look of such conscious efficiency that John could hardly keep from smiling: to hear Dr. Chardwicke now, one would have thought that the whole idea of summoning the health officer had been his own and not Douglas', that he was even insisting upon it in the face of possible protest.

"I might add," Dr. Chardwicke went on, after he had taken a sip of water, "that even if it does prove to be typhoid, I shall be very much surprised if it was acquired in this house. Men have been coming here for the Tuscoda plant from all over the country. We know that two of them did develop typhoid fever after their arrival. They have been eating in our restaurants and so, on many occasions, has Ronny. The restaurants, as you know, are crowded and understaffed; dishwashing is doubtless inadequate, especially, I'm sure, in places like the Chinese eating house that Ronny was so fond of and of which I always disapproved. Under the circumstances, another case of typhoid in our town would not seem to me in the least surprising. In the meanwhile, you should not delay getting inoculations, those of you who have not had them. I could give them easily myself and of course that would be the most convenient way, but after Ellen's amazing remarks last night, I prefer that you go to the hospital."

He sent Ellen a dignified and consciously tolerant glance, as the aged Louis XIV, in a forgiving mood, might have looked at some indiscreet young courtier. Ellen flushed and did not raise her eyes.

"As I told you last night," the doctor continued, "Mrs. Chardwicke and I have both had them recently; so has Frances; but so far as I know neither Douglas nor Ellen has. I suppose, John, that you have been inoculated by the Navy?"

"No, not yet," John told him. "They haven't got around to giving us our shots so far. Everything seems a little mixed up, but I suppose we'll get them sometime this semester."

"I should think it would be very necessary," Frances said. "What shots do they give you, John?"

"Oh—typhoid, paratyphoid, tetanus, diphtheria, I guess, and of course vaccination against smallpox. There may be others."

"I shall insist then," Dr. Chardwicke said, "that you get your first typhoid shot today. It's especially important for you, John, as a defender of our Country. I've made tentative arrangements for the funeral to take place day after tomorrow at four o'clock. Of course it will depend on the post-mortem, but by that time everything should be cleared up. I hope that as members of the household you will all see fit to attend."

As John was starting back to his afternoon classes, Douglas joined him before he reached the street.

"If you'll come by the hospital now," he said, "I'll get a friend of mine to give you your first shot. In that way you can avoid Navy red tape. You can make it easily before your one-thirty."

John would have liked to see his uncle before classes but he decided the sensible thing was to go with Douglas. It was a great relief, however, when just after five o'clock, as he stopped at the club for the third time that day, the girl at the switchboard told him Professor Hatfield was in his room. "You go right up," she said. "It's number 312. Just turn to your left at the top of the stairs. It's one of the front rooms on the third story."

John took two steps at a time and a minute later was knocking at his uncle's door.

"Is that you, John?" Professor Hatfield said. "Come in!"

As John stepped inside, he noticed how much the professor had already recreated the atmosphere of his own study, even though in this room there could not be more than a few dozen books. But the same currant-red Bokhara rug was on the floor, and two of the owl prints, a magnificent horned owl, and a pair of screech owls, one brown, one gray, hung on the paneling opposite his desk.

"Your ears and nose look cold, my boy," Professor Hatfield said. "Since you're in the Navy now and are no longer an undergraduate, your mother will perhaps forgive me if I offer you a drink of something. Do you think you could do with a little bourbon and water?"

"I certainly could!" John exclaimed; and as he lolled back, a minute later, in a leather armchair, his glass in his hand, and looked at his uncle across the flat-topped desk, he felt as if he were just about to talk with a famous doctor who was also a trusted friend.

"And now, John," the professor said, "let's hear it. Don't omit a thing. Tell me everything that happened, in so far as you can recall it, everything that anyone said or did, from the moment you entered that house, for the second time, at about six-thirty yesterday evening. Tell me not only what happened but your own impressions, your inner comments. Much of it will no doubt be irrelevant, but unfortunately, just now, neither you nor I can have the slightest idea what is relevant and what isn't."

"In the first place," John said, "I must tell you that poor Ronny is dead. He died sometime before midnight. I've been trying to get you all day between classes, but I couldn't find you."

The professor did not move, except that his lashes drew closer together over his sharp small eyes.

"I'm sorry to hear it," he said after a moment in a voice somewhat slower than usual. "Very sorry indeed. I was fond of that boy. He should have had a fine future. The work he was doing for his country was invaluable. This makes it all the more important,

John, for you to rack your brains and tell me everything—*everything*. It's important for two reasons: if his death is really natural, or accidental, we don't wish to cause trouble and create scandal; but if it's not . . . if it's not. . . ." The professor paused, and his eyes had taken on a sharply-focused hardness. "If I have reason to believe that Ronny's death was caused deliberately and cruelly, I shan't rest until I get to the bottom of the whole thing and see that the guilty person receives his just punishment."

Professor Hatfield took a sip from his drink and settled himself in his chair.

"And now, John," he said, "imagine that you have rung the bell and someone is opening the door. Was it Dorothy this second time?"

"Yes, it was Dorothy," John said; and closing his eyes, he tried to recall the whole picture, somber and confused as it was, of the evening and the night.

His uncle listened almost without moving; only now and then he shifted the angle of his head or asked a brief question. He seemed particularly interested, John thought, in his account of Ronny's warning, and made him repeat the half-delirious words several times. It was at this point that John interrupted his narrative to rid his mind of one special thing that had been troubling him all day.

"Uncle Paul," he said, "I can't help feeling that I was the immediate cause of Ronny's death. If he had not made such an effort to sit up, to push me out, the perforation and the hemorrhage might not have occurred."

"We're not even sure yet that that is what happened," Professor Hatfield said. "And in any case, John, you have not the least thing to reproach yourself with. You were acting strictly under my orders for Ronny's best interests. If there is any responsibility, it is mine, and I gladly assume it. I confess that I feel a certain sense of guilt, because I didn't go there myself—and go sooner. I shall find it hard to forgive myself for not insisting on seeing Ronny, no matter what anyone said, for not breaking into the house, if necessary. However, it is easy to be wise after the event. And then what did you do, when Ronny collapsed? You aroused Doctor Chardwicke?"

"I spoke to Douglas first," John said, and went on with his story.

After he had told of Ellen's outburst and the doctor's angry reply, Professor Hatfield got up and poured him another drink. "You deserve it," he said, "for the admirable account you have given. I assume that was all . . . I mean until the morning?"

"No," John said, "it wasn't quite all. Something rather queer happened later. I was just coming to it."

"Let's hear it," the professor said, and refilled his own glass.

"I woke up," John continued, "at a little after two o'clock. I think it was the cold that woke me. I had opened the window wide and there weren't enough blankets on the bed. I couldn't go to sleep again. I got to thinking and thinking about poor Ronny and the whole setup, and grew more and more restless. I felt that I never would go to sleep unless I was warmer; so I made up my mind I'd go down into the front hall and get my overcoat. The second-story hall was dark but I noticed a light under Ronny's door. I was going to keep on down, but then I decided—I don't know exactly why, but I guess I thought it was what you would do—to go over to the door of Ronny's room. I could hear a faint noise inside. I have no idea what it was. Then, on the spur of the moment, I turned the knob, and found that the door was locked. And this is the curious thing: the moment the knob moved the noise stopped, and the light inside the room went out. I waited there for perhaps a couple of minutes to see if anyone would come to the door, if I could hear any further movement, but there was nothing—absolute silence. The whole business seemed kind of furtive and underhand, but that may have been just because my nerves were pretty much on edge."

"I don't think so," Professor Hatfield said. "Your impression was quite natural. Hmmmmm! Did it occur to you, by any chance, that the person in the room might be looking for something, something that might be revealing, some piece of evidence? If Ronny's death was expected, it was probably not expected so suddenly. And afterwards no one was alone in the room for even a minute. Either there were several people, or after Fran's fainting spell, when you all scattered to your rooms, presumably for the rest of the night, there was no one."

"I had thought it might be something of the sort," John said, "but what on earth could they be trying to find?"

"That," the professor said thoughtfully, "is what sooner or later we must see if we can figure out."

He took a long sip of his drink and continued in a brisker voice: "But all this, of course, is on the assumption that there has been foul play. As I said before, we can't be sure of that. Dr. Chardwicke's explanation of why he kept Ronny's illness so mysterious, so secret, is certainly plausible. I know there has been talk of taking away his laboratory. It's not impossible that what he said is at least partly true. It wouldn't be so very surprising if he half guessed that Ronny had typhoid but deliberately preferred, for his conscience' sake, not to know."

"But isn't that in itself more or less criminal?" John asked. "It seems outrageous. . . ."

Professor Hatfield raised his hand soothingly, as if to check the outburst of a well-meaning but unreasonable child.

"My dear John," he said, "we can none of us be sure of Dr. Chardwicke's motives. The facts, as we know them, are simply these: he admits that for several days he suspected the possibility of typhoid. Since it is almost unknown in this town, it's quite reasonable that he should have been doubtful. A mistaken diagnosis, or a failure to make a diagnosis, is no crime. If it were, most doctors would at one time or another be criminals. We have no proof that he would not have notified the health authorities the moment he became actually convinced that he had a case of typhoid on his hands. I share Douglas' scepticism of his professional skill; but he is a registered physician. Mrs. Chardwicke, before she married him, had the reputation of being one of the best trained nurses in town. I've no doubt that, as he claims, Ronny did have adequate care. We certainly can't prove that he did not. Of course if it is suspected that a doctor has been grossly negligent, some member of the family can bring suit against him; but in this case who would do it? Dr. Chardwicke is himself Ronny's guardian. Fran possibly, as his fiancée? But I can scarcely picture her doing such a thing; and even if she did, I'm certain she would lose. As you relate the circumstances to me, there wouldn't be the shadow of a case."

As John thought over what his uncle had been saying, an idea occurred to him.

"Listen, Uncle Paul," he said eagerly. "A minute ago you said the doctor's own explanation of why he wanted to keep Ronny's illness so mysterious sounded convincing. Mightn't the doctor have figured on that very thing? Mightn't he have calculated that if anything went wrong, people would reason just the way we've been doing. You see, he'd have, as you say, a most plausible explanation ready to hand."

"Good work!" Professor Hatfield exclaimed, with his dry smile. "You'll be a detective yet, my boy. That is certainly to be considered. The doctor might be very sly indeed. No doubt he has the peculiar slyness of the neurotic. But also, if he were quite innocent—innocent, that is, except of possible carelessness in his laboratory—somebody else might have realized that the doctor, suspecting perhaps it was his own fault, would do his best to cover things up, and what's more, that he had an obvious motive: to inherit from Ronny. If anyone else were considering putting Ronny out of the way, this would have been an ideal time, because after his twenty-first birthday that motive would no longer be valid. But what convinces me most that the whole thing is not just a deplorable accident is the warning Ronny gave you. Unless, that is, you think it was all sheer raving; but I gather that you do not."

"No," John said, "I could swear he was trying to tell me something . . . something that because of his fever, his wandering mind, he couldn't quite recall . . . something that he thought put me in danger. And then I think, though I'm not sure, that he did recall it, and that was enough to send his brain reeling once more."

"If it was not a figment of his delirium," Professor Hatfield said gravely, "it may have been so terrifying that his sick mind simply could not face it, and forced it down into his subconsciousness. I'm inclined to think, John, that perhaps you had better move out of Dr. Chardwicke's house now. You've already given me more information than I could have hoped for in so short a time, and Ronny at least, poor boy, seemed to think there was real danger if you stayed."

John did not reply for perhaps a minute, and during most of that time he met his uncle's eye squarely.

"Uncle Paul," he then said, "I can see that you might want me to leave, because you feel responsible for my having gone there in the first place. I'm going to stay, but it's purely on my own responsibility. You just said you wouldn't rest easy until you found out who had murdered Ronny, if he was murdered. If it was mere accident, then there is no danger for me. If it was a crime, then I'm as eager as you are to see that it's caught up with. Besides, if there were any risk for me, there might well be for the others. In fact, I should think that I, as a newcomer, would be the least exposed. I should hate to leave Fran just now, and poor little Ellen, to the mercy of whatever . . . whatever evil forces there may be in that house. Even Mrs. Chardwicke seems rather helpless, for I can't see that the doctor, if he *is* innocent, could be much protection. Not that I see at the moment exactly what use I'll be, but at least I can keep my eyes open and do my damnedest."

The professor nodded. "I know how you feel," he said. "Undoubtedly if a warped and evil mind is at work in the house, everyone there may be in some measure threatened. But on the bright side there is this to be considered: when Ronny warned you, if my impression of the scene is correct, he was at least partially, in his delirium, confusing you with himself. It was as if Ronny the victim were seeing you as the unsuspecting young man he himself had been when he entered that house. It was perhaps even more his former self he was warning, in the light of later knowledge, than it was you, a stranger. It's true of course that Ellen also in a way warned you; at least she discouraged you from staying. I think, John, that one of the most helpful things you can do to start our investigation is to try to talk with Ellen, to find out just what she meant, and if her remarks were based on any special knowledge. Also it would be well to learn, if possible, just how she felt about Ronny, and what their relations were."

"I'm sure she wouldn't confide in me," John said quickly.

The professor smiled. "She seems to have liked you at first," he said. "Of course you would have to win her confidence."

"But Uncle Paul," John protested, "I'd feel so cheap, so insincere, trying to worm myself into her confidence cold-bloodedly."

"It wouldn't have to be cold-blooded," Professor Hatfield said briskly. "Ellen, I'm sure, is lonely and unhappy. It's common kindness to pay her some attention. You say she's an attractive little thing. Just be nice to her, and let nature take its course. Don't feel you must hurry too much. Better be slow and sure than ruin our chances by undue haste. It may very well be that anything you can learn from Ellen will be for her own safety and protection. Needless to say, whatever you can learn about the others in the house, and the tensions that may exist, will all be so much to the good. Remember, you will be betraying no one's confidence except that of the guilty person; and that, presumably, you would not object to doing."

"Well," John said, "I'll try my best, Uncle Paul. And now, I suppose, I should be getting back to the house for dinner."

He got up from his chair reluctantly and his uncle rose too.

"I don't have to urge you to be careful," the professor said. "I may not be to blame for your staying, but I was to blame for your going, and if you hadn't gone you naturally couldn't have stayed. The funeral, you say, is to be day after tomorrow. I shall call on the doctor tomorrow to express my sympathy. I shall let him know that you are my nephew and under my surveillance. If it puts him, or anyone else, on his guard, so much the worse. Otherwise, I should not feel right."

"I don't see why anything should happen to me," John said, as he was putting on his coat.

"You mustn't forget Ronny's words," the professor told him gravely. "He didn't believe in hell, but he found out that for him, at least, it existed."

A minute later, as John hurried along through the snow, past men in uniform, past groups of students talking and laughing together, he felt that he was set apart from them all, like a pilgrim bound on some extraordinary quest: if there was a hell, its entrance might be within the musty rooms of Dr. Chardwicke's house.

8

Ronny's funeral was held in the chapel of an undertaking establishment on the day Dr. Chardwicke had arranged. The autopsy had revealed that Ronny had indeed had typhoid fever; but the house itself, and all the people in it, had been given a clean bill of health. If Dr. Gibbons questioned Dr. Chardwicke about his laboratory, it remained a secret between the two men. Obviously in a region crowded with war workers from all over the country, it was not impossible that John had picked up the infection from some carrier—some transient perhaps—in a restaurant. No one attended the service except the Chardwicke household, half a dozen friends of Ronny's who had worked with him in the laboratory, Professor Hatfield, and John. After the ceremony the professor asked John if he wouldn't walk with him for a bit along the lake. The intense cold had broken; the winter dusk was gray and still, and the air smelled of snow.

John thought his uncle seemed depressed. He hardly spoke until they had reached the edge of the campus.

"I told you I was going to see the doctor this morning," he said as they were passing Science Hall. "His laboratory is up there somewhere on the fourth story. I asked him if he had noticed anything disturbed or missing. He said he had not; but he did admit the room was very crowded and not in the best of order. From the way he spoke, I imagine the place is a mess and that almost anything could be taken without his being much the wiser. You may be sure, however, that after my remarks, it will be difficult for anyone to get in there now, unless the doctor admits him—for some time, at least. I confess that it relieves my mind, since you are staying in the house. You may ask 'What about the doctor himself?' but you know, John, I'm nearly convinced that Dr. Chardwicke is innocent of murder. He was no doubt careless, he was stubborn, he was muddleheaded; but those qualities he shares with many of our most respected citizens."

"What did he say when you told him I was your nephew?" John asked.

"I could almost swear that it didn't startle him, as I suspected it might," the professor said. "I was watching him very closely, though I trust not obviously. And I think on the whole he seemed pleased that I should have recommended him as a landlord. In fact one of the things that convinced me he is not our man, if such a one exists, was the way he received that piece of news. He might have been putting on an act, but I've known him for a long time, I was fully prepared, and I think I should have seen through it. He was terribly upset when he spoke of Ronny, full of excuses and self-justification. Once or twice he was on the verge of tears. I should say that he was in a thoroughly neurotic state, but I do think he was telling the truth. It goes without saying that I may be wrong."

"Do you know much about his breakdown?" John asked. "You said he had one ten years ago when he gave up his teaching."

"As a matter of fact, I know a great deal about it, at least about what led up to it. Quite a number of people in town did too, unfortunately. The breakdown was largely the result of a near scandal. I needn't go into it. It was a very sordid affair. I don't think the doctor was wholly to blame, poor fellow. He comes from an unbalanced stock. His sister, he told me once, committed suicide. I suppose she would have been Fran's mother. His younger brother, a brilliant lawyer and a charming man, without any trace of the doctor's pompousness, ended his days in an asylum. One of the most regrettable things about Dr. Chardwicke's mix-up was that it was Mrs. Chardwicke who first spread the news. She went around to various influential women, faculty wives, and even to one or two of the doctor's colleagues, telling each one, of course in strictest confidence, her suspicions, and asking if someone would interfere and speak to the doctor himself. Naturally each woman to whom she confided told many others; they had a regular field day. You may be sure Mrs. Chardwicke's stories didn't lose in the repeating, and they were of such a nature that the outcome was far more drastic than she had planned. The doctor came within an ace of being run out of town. Luckily the whole business remained unofficial, but the doctor collapsed completely and had to spend several months in the Brookfield Asylum."

"I shouldn't think the affair would have tended to create the pleasantest feelings between him and his wife," John said.

"Once the scandal had broken," Professor Hatfield said, "Mrs. Chardwicke, to do her justice, was admirable. Of course it was her jealousy, based on her fanatical attachment to her husband, that had started the row in the first place; and when she saw what she had done she rallied to him one hundred per cent. She even went around to the people to whom she had spoken in the first place and said that she had been telling lies. Ever since the doctor returned home she has done all she could to protect him and make him comfortable. In fact, as you must have noticed, she has thoroughly spoiled him."

"She's a strange woman," John said. "I can't make her out. I wonder how he ever happened to marry her. She must be much older than he."

"Twelve years, I believe," the professor said. "Everyone was surprised at the marriage. They had assumed Dr. Chardwicke was a born bachelor. I think I can understand it, though. Mrs. Chardwicke had taken care of the doctor through a long illness; and I rather imagine her being older than he, was if anything in her favor: it made it easier for her to take the place of his mother. I've no doubt he's extremely fond of her, and always has been; though his feeling, I'm sure, is of a quite different character from the possessive passion with which she seems to regard him."

"Yes, they're strange people," John said. "I think I feel sorry for them both."

It was now quite dark. They had left the lake and were walking back across the lonely campus. As they passed the first arc light, John realized that there was mist in the air: the branches of

the trees around it seemed prolonged in straight diverging lines
by their own shadows cast upon the wall of moisture. It was impossible just now to guess their true shape or direction; and to
John this fog seemed all at once a symbol of the darkness through
which, with his uncle's help, he was groping his way.

This darkness showed no signs of clearing during the next ten
days. Luckily for John, his classes kept him busy and did not give
him much leisure for brooding. He rarely ate his lunches in the
house; so that almost the only time he saw Dr. Chardwicke was
at dinner and afterwards as they took their coffee in the shadowy
overcrowded parlor; but he came more and more to agree with his
uncle that the doctor was innocent of deliberate crime. In fact,
very often it seemed to John that in spite of Professor Hatfield's
suspicions there had been no crime at all. It was impossible for
him to convince himself emotionally, as he glanced about the table,
that any one of these people had done such an awful thing. It
would seem to him then that his uncle was a well-meaning crank,
that Ronny's words were the purest delirium, that the whole idea
was fantastic; but he knew the relief this rejection brought with
it was in the nature of a mirage. The very eagerness with which
he clutched at it made him aware of the nervous strain from
which he was seeking an escape—a strain that increased day by
day as he felt himself more intimately a part of this tense group.

He had heard gossip around Science Hall that Dr. Chardwicke, as he had feared, might have to give up his laboratory at
the end of the semester. The doctor must have heard it too: he
was more talkative, more fidgety than ever, trying no doubt to
hide his anxiety beneath a genial and overconfident manner. Mrs.
Chardwicke remained taciturn; and John would have placed her
as an efficient but somewhat negative person if it had not been
for the intensity of the gaze she fixed upon her husband: there
was passion there, he felt, there was tragedy, but there was also a
kind of adjustment, obtained at he did not know what cost. If he
did not actually like Mrs. Chardwicke—she was almost too aloof
for that, and his liking might merely have embarrassed her—he
began to look at her with real respect.

Fran seemed still to be moving in a daze. Evidently she had not yet recovered from the violence of the first shock, though she had insisted, in spite of Dr. Chardwicke's advice, on returning to her work at the hospital. John tried to talk to her as much as he could, and even came to feel, in optimistic moments, that she would rather talk with him than with anyone else. Her manner was always calm; she rarely smiled, but when she did her face would take on a look of tenderness and sweetness that John found quite heartbreaking. Nonetheless it was that look for which he was always angling, because only then, it seemed, was she aware of him or in fact of the outside world.

"I'm glad you're here," she told him one evening as he was bidding her good night at the foot of the stairs. "It's a strange thing, John. You're the only person in this house that did not know Ronny, and yet of them all you are the one whom I think of as his friend."

"That's just the way I feel myself," he exclaimed, "that I was Ronny's friend, and that I'm your friend, too, I hope, Fran."

"Mine, of course," she said, and he was surprised how happy it made him.

Meanwhile he had grown really fond of Ellen, though at times he thought she seemed to avoid him.

He would have tried to see more of her, if his uncle's suggestion that he win her confidence had not made him feel self-conscious and hypocritical. If the time should come, before too long, when he could question her naturally, of course he would do it; but he could not lay deliberate traps for her. A fierce sad little thing, she would often sit through meals with a somber and completely closed expression. He knew that she hated Dr. Chardwicke, that she disliked Douglas, and regarded Dorothy with the utmost contempt. This last, John thought, was because it became more and more clear from her sullen manner that Dorothy detested Fran; and Fran, John could see, Ellen almost worshiped.

"If I could look like her," she told him once, "if I could only half look like her, I'd give anything in the world!"

"It seems to me there's nothing wrong with you the way you are," John said smiling.

"I hate my looks!" she exclaimed violently. "I just hate them! I'm all chunky and brown, with thick ankles and horrible lamb's eyes. I don't blame anyone for not wanting to look at me."

"But I love to," he protested. "I always like to watch you. What makes you think I don't?"

"When Fran's around," she said, "naturally no one likes to look at anyone else. I can understand that." And she had left him quickly.

But of all the household the one who puzzled him most was Douglas. He seemed still to be living in a state of barely controlled restlessness or excitement. It was clear of course that he was in love with Fran; it would be hard for anyone to live in the house with her and not feel her charm. Perhaps his behavior showed merely the frustration of a young man used to making easy conquests; for John, with an inner sense of triumph, could see by now that Fran completely ignored him. Certainly he had been drinking a great deal, and when, ten days after Ronny's death, he asked John to come up to his room for a drink before going to bed, John accepted eagerly. This was something at least that he could do for his uncle. "Just steep yourself in the general atmosphere," Professor Hatfield had told him when John had apologized for not having made more progress. "If we are to discover anything, it's not, I'm sure, merely a question of unearthing facts but rather of getting to understand individual temperaments."

This was the first time that John had been in Douglas' room except for the moment when he had roused him, in the middle of the night, after Ronny's collapse. Douglas had tried to liven it up by putting several garish railroad posters on the walls, but these only increased the air of shabbiness and gloom. Half a dozen medical books were sprawled upon a table beside the window, and used socks and shirts and an old pair of trousers lay about on the red carpet. As Douglas went to the closet to take out some whisky and a syphon, John saw a collection of bottles tucked in among shoes and notebooks.

Douglas poured a couple of highballs, tossed a shirt from an armchair so that John could sit down, and seated himself, propped against a pillow, on the big walnut bed, his feet up on the quilt.

"Well, Johnny," he exclaimed, "here's to your good health! In this house somehow that old conventional toast seems to take on a real meaning."

John could see that he had already been drinking today. No one but Douglas called him Johnny; and although John did not care what he was called, he felt that the nickname showed on Douglas' part not so much friendliness as a hint of condescension.

"Here's to yours!" John said. "The place certainly does have an air of its own."

"Just about as cheerful as a morgue, if you ask me. Whenever I want to be really hilarious I have to go up and have a little séance with Gerty. It's bad enough with a fairly decent room, but I don't see how you stand that icebox of yours up there on the top floor."

"I'm going to move down into Ronny's room day after tomorrow," John said. "The doctor wanted to air it out for a week or so after the disinfection, before I went in."

Douglas gave a sardonic chuckle. "Well, seeing what's happened there," he remarked, "I shouldn't think that would be any too cheerful either."

He took several gulps of his drink, and John could see that his black eyes were watching him carefully.

"The fact is," he went on after at least a minute, "I'm rather surprised that you stay here, John. Frankly, I am."

"What about you?" John asked as casually as he could.

"Oh, I'm pretty used to it by now," Douglas said. "I was here before any of the rest of them—Fran or Ronny or Ellen, or Dorothy, for that matter. And then, since you ask, there are other . . . what I might call personal reasons."

"Oh?" John's tone was polite but not especially encouraging.

Douglas finished his drink and, without getting up, fixed himself another from the marble-topped table beside the bed, where he had set the bottle and syphon. "Are you ready?" he asked.

"I haven't finished my first," John told him.

"You're a careful cuss, aren't you?" Douglas said. "You go your own way. You mind your own business. Admirable qualities! But you must have seen my reason for hanging around. It may prove that I'm a damn fool, but there's nothing mysterious about it. What do you think of Fran? I hope you don't mind answering a direct question."

"Not at all," John said rather stiffly. "I think she's one of the most beautiful and charming girls I've ever seen."

"A coincidence!" Douglas exclaimed with a grin which seemed quite unrelated to his probing gaze. "So do I! So did Ronny! Ronny was a nice fellow, a damn nice kid, but he was not the man for her. Too intellectual. Too much brain and not enough brawn, if you get what I mean. Has anyone told you you're just a bit like him yourself? You're a damn sight huskier than he was, to be perfectly fair, but still you're what I'd call the intellectual type. Now Fran is quite a girl. Don't let that quiet manner deceive you. She's temperamental as hell, though you mightn't think it. For her own sake she needs someone who can manage her, someone just a little hard-boiled. . . ."

"Someone like you?" John asked; and he felt that he was bristling all over.

"Well, to be frank, yes," Douglas said, "and you can spare your irony. I'm not so conceited as you think. I know quite well what Fran thinks of me now, but I'm a persistent bastard. I'm willing to bide my time. You must have noticed all this. That's why I brought it up. The hell of it is you won't believe I'm disinterested when I give you a piece of advice. You ought to get out of here, Johnny, before anything happens."

John's surprise, his curiosity, prevented his feeling angry.

"What could happen?" he asked.

Douglas reached in his pocket, pulled out a cigarette and lit it before answering. "Well," he said slowly, as he watched a widening smoke ring, "you know what happened to Ronny."

John stared for a minute at Douglas' impassive face: that fixed glance might be gazing through the smoke at some distant and involved drama.

"If that's a threat," John said at last, "somehow it leaves me cold."

Suddenly Douglas laughed. "That's just how I hope you won't be left," he exclaimed. "Believe it or not, that's why I'm speaking to you now. Don't worry, Johnny. I'm not going to poison your whisky. It's against my morals."

"But you think someone else might?" John said. "Is that it?"

"Oh, I shouldn't go as far as that," Douglas protested, "but I have a kind of hunch, Johnny, that this house isn't very healthy. And I don't mean the drains."

"What *do* you mean?" John asked, hoping that he did not sound too eager. "I'd be curious to know."

"If you hang around long enough," Douglas said, and for the first time it seemed to John that there was something savage in his voice, "you may have a chance to find out. You're sure you won't have some more whisky?"

"Quite," John said drily. He got up from his armchair, put his empty glass on the bureau, and walked toward the door.

"You musn't take me too seriously," Douglas called softly, without moving from his bed. "That bottle was full at five o'clock this afternoon, and look at it now."

As he walked back through the dim hall, John tried to remember every word that Douglas had said, so that he could report them to his uncle. He was turning into the passageway when the door of Fran's room opened, and she beckoned him from the threshold. She was wearing her silvery kimono; her face looked tense.

"John," she said, "may I speak to you for a moment before you go upstairs?"

"Of course!" he exclaimed, and as he hurried to her his surprise was mingled with a warm flush of triumph.

"Has Douglas been talking to you about me?" she asked. "I suspect he has."

"Well, yes," John admitted in sudden embarrassment. "We were talking a little about you."

"I just want to tell you," she said with a strange controlled violence, "that there is nothing between me and Douglas and never could be. You must wonder why I'm telling you this. It's because I know the way he talks and because I don't trust him. It's abhorrent to me that anyone could think even for a moment that . . . that he, that a man like him could have the slightest claim upon me. And now, good night."

There had been in her voice, on her face, as she spoke of Douglas, a repulsion that was almost horror. It reminded John of the look he had seen when he watched her through the window the night of Ronny's death; and he was all at once convinced that Douglas was the unknown person to whom she had been talking. Had he tried to make love to her while Ronny lay ill? Did she suspect that Douglas had murdered him?

Before he could collect his thoughts, she had stepped back into her room and closed the door.

9

The next morning being Sunday, breakfast was not until nine o'clock, and Dr. Chardwicke, contrary to his custom, appeared at table. He seemed to be in almost playful mood. For the first time John lingered over his coffee with his host and hostess after the others had gone. As he was leaving the dining room, the doctor, just behind him, grasped his elbow and gave it a friendly squeeze.

"My dear boy," he said, "it's occurred to me that you haven't seen my laboratory. I thought I might go up there and fool around a bit this morning. I wonder if you wouldn't like to come with me."

"Thank you, sir," John said, pulling his elbow free of the doctor's fingers. "I should like to very much indeed." He had planned, before anything else, to report to his uncle; but this chance he should not let pass.

Dr. Chardwicke smiled at him mischievously, and glanced backward over his shoulder into the dining room, where his wife was giving instructions to Dorothy.

"In that case," he said, "I'm going to make a rather strange request. You'd better let me start first, and then in a few minutes you can follow without mentioning your destination. Mrs. Chardwicke has been such a help to me in my work that she's rather inclined to be just the tiniest shade jealous when I do the honors of my little sanctum without her presence."

John stared at him in surprise and then found himself, like the doctor, glancing at Mrs. Chardwicke. To his embarrassment, he caught her eye.

"If that's the case," he said, "why not ask her to come too?"

"Oh, my dear boy, it wouldn't be nearly so cozy. You know what women are. And then I'm sure she's busy with her household duties."

"Clarence!" Mrs. Chardwicke's voice sounded cool and dry. "I know what you're talking about."

The doctor looked startled but he winked at John. "You do, my dear?" he said affably. "Then you must have very sharp ears or you must have been flattering us with the strictest attention. I assumed that you were occupied with Dorothy."

"I know you did," she said.

"I was merely suggesting to John that he drop in at my laboratory later on this morning."

"Yes, that's what I thought."

"You have no objections?"

Mrs. Chardwicke crossed the room to stand beside them before she answered his question.

"You know quite well, Clarence, what my ideas are on the subject," she said.

"On what subject, may I ask?"

The doctor had lost his bland air: his tone, which had tried for dignity, was merely pettish.

Mrs. Chardwicke met his eyes coldly. It was the first time John had seen her stand up to him in any way, and he found it most unpleasant to be the cause of a domestic tiff.

"I think you've taken far too many people to see your laboratory already," she said. "After all, it's a workroom, not a place for display or for anything else. I should think especially that now, after what has happened, you would hesitate more than ever. Of course you will do as you please."

The doctor looked at her as a plump old rooster might stare at an interfering hen.

"You're quite right, my dear. That is precisely what I shall do."

"Remember," she said, and her colorless voice took on an undercurrent of meaning which sharpened it strangely, "it doesn't always work."

At that instant John noticed Ellen coming downstairs in her sealskin cap and brown woolly jacket.

"As a matter of fact," he said quickly, "I shan't be able to go with you anyway, Dr. Chardwicke. I just remembered something I have to do." And delighted to have escaped from the argument, he ran up the stairs to meet Ellen.

"Where are you going?" he asked softly.

"Just for a walk," she said. "Just somewhere to get out of this house."

"Fine!" he exclaimed. "I'll go with you. Do you mind?"

"No," she said, "if you really want to come. But I don't see why you should."

"Lots of reasons," he said gaily, and hurried down the stairs ahead of her, to put on his navy overcoat.

The doctor, he noticed, was still standing in the dining-room door, flushed and disgruntled. Mrs. Chardwicke stood beside him, and although she had won her point, she did not look triumphant.

"Till some other time then, John," the doctor said. Then with a sudden rallying of his spirits, he called after them as they were walking through the vestibule: "You young rascal, I might have known you'd be on the track of some pretty girl. Remember, this one isn't out of school yet. 'Jail bait,' I believe, is the modern term to describe her. So don't go trying any of your navy tricks!"

John almost slammed the door. He felt angry and embarrassed. Poor little Ellen crossed the porch and walked down the path so quickly that he had to run a few steps to catch up with her. She was scowling and he did not blame her. He tried to think of some comment to make on the doctor's tasteless remark, but then he decided he had better let it drop and wait a minute for the air to clear.

The morning was damp and not very cold. It had snowed enough during the last two days to cover the soiled drifts between the sidewalks and streets; snow lay in the crotches of trees and outlined the tops of branches. Through the relaxed air John could hear the grate of a shovel on cement as an old man scraped his front walk.

"It's nice to be outside, isn't it?" he said at last. "I'd like to get into the real country this morning. How about you?"

"Yes," she said in a muffled voice which made him think she was struggling to control tears. "I'd like to get far away . . . from everything."

They walked along past Professor Hatfield's house, past the gymnasium and the great red hulk of Science Hall, to the drive that skirted the lake. A group of sparrows rose from about a feeding platform in swift oblique lines like the fragments of a bursting shell. Nowhere was anything very bright but neither was there anything very dark, not even the wet tree trunks, the blackest centers of the spruces. The sky cast no shadows. It was the dead level of midwinter; and John had the feeling that it marked a pause, a breathing spell before—he did not know what.

"You know the country," he said presently, "so you must be my guide. I'll follow wherever you want to take me."

"There's a lovely quarry near the end of the lake," she said, "but I'm afraid we won't have time to get there and back before lunch."

"That's easy!" he exclaimed. "We'll take our lunch with us. We'll cut right across the campus to Main Street. There must be some stores open today, and I've got a half a dozen red tokens in my pocket I forgot to hand over to Mrs. Chardwicke when I gave her my ration book."

"There is a nice little store," she said, "if you think we really dare."

"Of course we dare! Who's going to stop us, I'd like to know?"

They crossed the campus to a store near the edge of town, where John bought some wieners, some buns, and a quart of milk. Then, after walking a few hundred yards along the main highway, they turned into a road through the woods. You could see now the position of the sun by a silver blur in the clouds. Ellen's face, her blue eyes, her hair about the rim of her cap, looked very bright and clear. He thought that she must feel the same kind of relief he did—that perhaps for the first time since he had found her in the back parlor she was really happy.

"I'm so glad it's still early!" she said suddenly. "I'm so glad we don't have to go back to that house for a long, long time!"

In half an hour they came out of the woods on to a bare hillside. Just off the road, cut deep into the slope of the hill, was the quarry, like a stone amphitheater facing the town a couple of miles away. Ellen and he scattered to look for sticks; and when John, ten minutes later, had started their fire against the protecting cliff, the sun burned through the clouds, the snow grew so dazzling they could hardly look at it, and the whole country, just now so uniformly pale, became scattered with indigo shadows.

John had about decided that he would not spoil Ellen's day by asking any questions; but after she had finished her first wiener and was roasting another, she said suddenly: "You must have wondered about that first afternoon, John, when I told you not to stay. You must have thought it didn't sound very friendly."

"On the contrary," John said, "I thought it sounded most friendly. It was a kind of warning, wasn't it, and I don't believe you'd have given it to just anybody."

"Of course I wouldn't," she exclaimed. "But right afterwards I felt I shouldn't have spoken to you. I didn't know what you'd think."

"As a matter of fact," John said smiling, "I didn't know quite what I should think. Perhaps I don't even now. Just why didn't you want me to stay, Ellen? I've sometimes wondered about it."

Ellen's face grew so somber that he felt this sunlight and this dazzling snow were hardly more than a mirage which was hiding for a moment the gloom of those tall rooms. Then a deep blush rose from her cheeks to her forehead.

"It was because . . . I liked you so much," she said hesitantly, "and I was so ashamed for you to see my family. I mean Cousin Clarence, of course . . . because Ronny told me some things about him . . . how the students have a nickname for him . . . he wouldn't tell me what it was . . . and I thought you'd hate living with us, just the way I did. I'd feel sorry for Cousin Clarence if he wasn't so mean to me. You heard the things he said. They weren't true. They were none of them true. It made me feel so awful just to think of them, as if he'd covered me all over with something black and sticky, like the oil from ships that gets washed up on the beach and smears all over your legs and feet after you've been in swimming. Of course I loved Ronny, but I was never in love with him. He seemed like a nice, kind, older brother, and I'd never had one, and with Mother and Father dead. . . They were in England, you know, working with the Red Cross. I was so lonely, because I didn't like Cousin Althea, though I guess she does what she thinks is her duty; and I hated Cousin Clarence. Why when Ronny came last fall, I was just a child. I was terribly young. I never went to parties like other girls. I hated the idea of growing up. I never even thought of being in love with him . . . the way Cousin Clarence meant."

"Do you feel very grown up now?" John asked with a smile. "After all, you're not so very much older."

"I feel *very* much older," she said gravely. "I guess it's because there's been so much awfulness."

"What awfulness do you mean?" he asked, and he felt guiltily that for the first time today he was not being himself but his uncle's secret agent. "Were you thinking of anything special?"

She shook her head and her eyes filled with tears.

"It's the whole house!" she exclaimed. "At first it was because Cousin Clarence was so horrid about me and Ronny. He was always making mean little smirking remarks. You could see he hated it that Ronny liked me so much. And then when Fran came. . . . It was only about a month after Ronny, last October. Fran's mother is dead, you know. Fran had been living in Washington with her father. He's a colonel and Fran came out here when he was sent to Europe. . . . Well, then it got much worse, because Ronny fell in love with her at once and she fell in love with him. And I was glad, honestly I was glad somehow, because they were both so lonely; and then Douglas got all mixed up in it. He's a horrid person, I think. He tried to kiss me once, but he never tried again, that's one thing! That was before Fran got there, because of course as soon as she came he fell in love with her too, and I know Fran hated that. Perhaps she knows the way he carries on with Dorothy. That's what's so disgusting, because if he's in love with Fran, how can he look at anyone like Dorothy? And Fran and Ronny were so happy together, if only they could have been left alone! I'd have done anything for them, anything! I wouldn't have cared what happened to me. And now . . . and now!"

They were sitting side by side, close to the fire, on a log from which John had brushed the snow. Suddenly Ellen flung her face forward into her hands and broke into sobs. John put his arm lightly about her shoulders.

"Ellen," he exclaimed, "my dear little Ellen, you mustn't!" It reminded him of times when he had discovered his own young sister in moods of temporary despair: the only thing to do was to wait sympathetically and hope that it wouldn't last long. "It's not as if you were to blame for anything. I'm sure you were always wonderful to Ronny, and to Fran too, and they are the only ones that count, aren't they?"

Then as poor Ellen's sobs continued, an idea occurred to him so terrible that he could hardly admit it to himself. Could Ellen perhaps, lonely and passionate and loyal, goaded on by the doctor's teasing and afraid that he was plotting against Ronny and Fran, could she, in some adolescent crisis of daring and desperation, have seized the chance to put the doctor himself out of the way? If so, might not her plans have gone wrong and Ronny taken the infected food which had been meant for his guardian? At any time Ellen could have gone to the laboratory if, as Douglas had said, Dr. Chardwicke was always leaving his keys around and everyone knew what they were. She could have stolen a test tube or poured a little of the culture into some kind of small container, and then put it into what? A glass of milk? A glass of water? A bowl of soup? Anything which she thought Dr. Chardwicke would be drinking. And how easy (in her desperation she would not have thought of that) for someone else to have taken the poisoned drink! For a week, two weeks, she would have waited, perhaps regretting this impulse of half-mad violence, hoping against hope that the germs would not take effect, or possibly watching with a grim sense of triumph for the first signs of the disease that would kill the man she so hated and despised. Imagine her horror when she saw that it was not he but Ronny who was falling ill, who would probably die!

One could even understand how, in the first shock of his death, she could say it was Dr. Chardwicke who had killed him: because no matter how much she might blame herself, she would blame the doctor too, as the prime cause.

As John patted her shoulders, and her sobbing grew calmer, this idea seemed grotesque, like the gothic fancy in a nightmare; but the whole atmosphere of that house was grotesque: existence there was not the real existence of the outside world; it was the blur of a subdued delirium that might at any time break out once more into violence.

"Ellen," he asked and he tried to make his tone as kind as possible, "you didn't really think Dr. Chardwicke killed Ronny, did you?"

"I did just at first," she said in a voice that was still not quite firm. "Because he kept it all so mysterious. He shut up poor Ronny almost like a prisoner in a dungeon. And I knew how triumphant he must feel. I knew how he hated Ronny to be in love with Fran, and I knew he'd get the money. I just couldn't help breaking out that way. But as soon as I'd spoken I didn't believe it any more, and I felt so ashamed; and then he turned on me like some great poisonous lizard and I thought I'd die, and all the time I was ashamed, too, that I could let anything else matter, anything that concerned me, when Ronny was dead."

John gave her shoulder an affectionate squeeze and stood up. A load had been taken from his mind: either Ellen was a consummate actress or his whole idea had been mad; and he would stake his life just then that Ellen was utterly sincere and truthful.

While they had been talking, the sky had thickened again; but the disk of the sun was still visible, high up, like a creamy moon, beyond blown curtains of mist.

"I'm afraid we should be starting back," he said. "I've got some studying to do, unfortunately. And Ellen dear, you must try not to be so sad. I can't take the place of Ronny, I know, but you can act with me, too, just as if I was your brother."

"I spoiled our picnic," she said sorrowfully. "You'll never want to take me on one again."

"Oh, yes I will!" he exclaimed; but he felt a touch of remorse, because at that very moment, as he took a last glance around the quarry, with its wall blackened by years of picnic fires, he had been thinking how he would love to bring Fran out here.

The next instant a suspicion entered his mind, even more shocking, because more plausible, than his thought of Ellen's guilt. Ellen was no actress, she could not hide her feelings; but what about Fran? Suppose he shifted his idea from Ellen to her? From the first he had never known what she was thinking; he had been sure only that she was always sad. She had the poise Ellen lacked. No more than Ellen would she hesitate to protect a person whom she loved and whom she thought was threatened. She worked in the hospital; she had been a biology major; it would be easier for her than for Ellen to go to the laboratory, to take what she needed, to carry the whole thing through. What denouement more truly hellish in its perverse symmetry than to have her beloved, for whose sake she had committed murder, fall victim to her own device! Or again! Why must the intended victim have been Dr. Chardwicke? John remembered the repulsion, perhaps even the terror (it was hard for him to interpret the looks that crossed her face) with which she had spoken to him of Douglas. Might Douglas perhaps even have attacked her? Stolen into her bedroom at night and found her sleeping? Might there in that house have been, not only murder, but rape? Nothing seemed impossible within those musty rooms. If it was Douglas she had meant to kill, the irony would be if anything sharper; and if she had confessed it all to Ronny before his death, he might well, in his fever, have felt plunged into the nethermost depths.

"John, are you very cross with me? Are you ashamed of me for being such a baby?"

"Of course I'm not," he said, and took her hand as they walked along.

They had turned into a little road that led down through the fields toward the lake, and he realized that he had not said a word for several minutes. The first shock of his suspicion had spent itself. No, after all, when he looked at the thing sanely, from the outside, he could no more believe in Fran's guilt than in Ellen's; or for that matter, really, in Douglas'. Thank God, he had his uncle to talk to! But he would try to talk with Fran first—this evening, if he could find a chance.

"We'll have to go on a lot of picnics," he said, "and perhaps Fran would like to come too."

"I'm sure she would," Ellen said, "because she's fond of you. I can see that. But I'll always remember this one, because it was our first."

They stopped a few minutes on the lake drive to watch the skaters: sailors and soldiers, girls in bright sweaters or jackets. A sergeant and his wife were pushing a baby carriage along over the gray ice; a man with a green scarf floating behind him swung by dragging a child in a tiny white sled. It all looked so comfortable and natural that John could hardly bear to move on and take Ellen back to Dr. Chardwicke's house.

As soon as they stepped in through the vestibule she ran upstairs; and while John was taking off his coat Mrs. Chardwicke appeared from between the portieres that led into the dining room.

She looked at him with one of her rare smiles, which never quite seemed to fit her face.

"Did you have a nice time with Ellen?" she asked. "I'm glad you took her out. I'm afraid she finds this house rather gloomy. She needs diversion, poor little thing. She'll be a fine woman, though, in no time at all. And it might be good for Frances, too, if you could turn her thoughts away from Ronny. I feel quite proud of my young relatives. I think you'd have a hard time laying your hands on a pair of prettier girls. Of course Frances is very reserved, but you mustn't let that put you off."

John looked at her in surprise. He agreed with every word she said, and no doubt she was only meaning to be kind; but as she met his eyes with her fixed dim smile, he found himself thinking of some elderly bawd.

10

Dinner that evening seemed to John particularly oppressive by contrast to the brightness of the day. Dr. Chardwicke was in a bad humor.

"It seems simply idiotic," he said snappishly, when Fran asked John what they had been doing, "to picnic at this time of year. Today was cold enough for the air to be raw and warm enough for the snow to melt. If you want to do it yourself, well and good, though I don't advise it. After all, I have no control over your actions. But it's quite different with Ellen. I haven't the slightest doubt that her feet are wet through, and if she escapes with chilblains she'll be lucky. If she comes down with flu or pneumonia, I tell you quite frankly, John, I shall consider you responsible."

He had piled his plate with spaghetti, and now he put into his mouth a forkful whose dangling ends he sucked in noisily, leaving a smear of sauce on his tight lips. It was almost as if he were being deliberately boorish, to show the company that he could ignore their presence. Douglas, to whom Dorothy was by this time passing the dish, heaped his own plate quite as high, and John fancied that his action, too, was deliberate: that, just to annoy the doctor, he would not allow him the childish pleasure of feeling that he had taken the lion's share.

"Let's hope she doesn't!" Douglas exclaimed with a grin. "It would be unfortunate if two people in this house should die of bacterial diseases within so short a time."

"I don't know what you mean to imply," the doctor said. "Naturally it would be unfortunate. From the way you spoke, I

291

must say, anyone might gather that you'd rather enjoy it. I consider your remark in Fran's presence, or at any other time, for that matter, in the worst of taste."

Douglas looked at Fran; there was ardor but there was also suffering, John thought, in his restless eyes.

"I'm sorry, Fran," he exclaimed. "You know, I trust, that I wouldn't do anything in the world to hurt your feelings. But sometimes, damn it, when I look at you, or rather when you look at me, it's sort of hard to imagine that you have any to be hurt."

Fran did look at him now, and John admired the starry coldness of her glance.

"I'm very thankful," she said, "that whatever my feelings are, it's quite beyond your power to hurt them."

Dr. Chardwicke wiped his mouth and turned toward Ellen. "I warn you, Ellen," he said, "if you do come down with something, I'm going to pack you right off to the hospital. I'm still not fully rested from all the hours I spent sitting up with Ronny and giving him my personal care. And what did I get for it? Merely hysterical accusations and implied criticism."

Ellen pushed back her chair and hurried to the door. Then she stopped, clutched the portiere, and looked over her shoulder at Dr. Chardwicke. "Cousin Clarence," she exclaimed, "you don't think I'd stay here another minute, do you, if I had anywhere else to go!"

She ducked through the crimson curtains, and John was sure that the moment she was out of sight she burst into tears. He would have followed her if he had not thought it would only make the situation worse.

Dr. Chardwicke glanced around the table as if for sympathy. "There's gratitude for you!" he exclaimed. "My dear Althea, I hope you haven't any more orphaned cousins that you'll expect me to receive into my house."

"You know I haven't," Mrs. Chardwicke said. "But if I had, Clarence, you'd be the first to want to take them under your wing. If Ellen is not grateful to you, I am—profoundly. You can't expect gratitude or understanding from youth."

When they left the table Douglas went up to his room; so that Dr. and Mrs. Chardwicke, Fran and John were the only ones to take coffee in the parlor. The doctor talked with his usual air of authority about the war, and, considering that Fran's father was in Germany, spoke most tactlessly, John thought, of how dangerous Europe must be for the American invaders.

In about half an hour Mrs. Chardwicke rose from the sofa.

"You do look tired, Clarence," she said. "There are pouches under your eyes. You'd better come upstairs and let me give you a good massage. I'm sure John and Frances will excuse us."

The doctor stood up and coughed into his handkerchief.

"People should be more thoughtful," he said. "If once a cold gets into this house, it's sure to go the rounds. Whenever I get the slightest infection I suffer agonies with my sinuses."

He held out his hand to John. "I didn't mean to be cross with you," he said with a suddenly benign smile. "My dear boy, I'm quite aware that the picnic was Ellen's fault. You were caught and you couldn't escape."

"But that's not true," John exclaimed. "If anyone's to blame for the picnic, I'm the one. I suggested it. I insisted. It was Ellen who was doubtful."

The doctor's smile broadened. "You believe that, I'm sure," he said. "Because you're an innocent and chivalrous young man. You haven't learned the wiles of the daughters of Eve. Read your Shaw, my boy. Read *Man and Superman* and beware?"

Frances and John had risen also. As she started toward the door, he asked: "Why must *you* go up so soon!"

"Why do you?" Mrs. Chardwicke exclaimed. "I'm going to tell Dorothy to bring each of you a glass of sherry. If John got chilled today, it would be very good for him. Why don't you stay and keep him company?"

"Oh, thank you very much," John said eagerly. "You will stay, won't you, Fran? You don't want to turn me into a solitary drinker!"

"I don't think there is much danger of that," Fran said with the faintest smile. "But of course I'll stay, if you'd like me to."

When the folds of the portieres had come together after Dr. and Mrs. Chardwicke, John felt a sudden constraint: he could only think of how awkward he must look as he stood here in front of Frances, not knowing what to say.

"Do you realize, Fran," he asked abruptly, "that I've been here for nearly two weeks and this is the first time I've seen you without someone else around?"

"Not quite the first time," she said.

She must, John knew, be referring to their scrap of conversation last night beside her door, and he felt clumsier than ever. How could he ask her ingenious questions? How could he play the detective now? It had been hard enough with Ellen: with Fran it would be quite impossible. In this dim Victorian room, with the light from the bronze chandelier shining across her wide forehead and filling her eyes with shadow, she might be the heroine of a Brontë novel, the sadly radiant inspiration of a poem by Byron or Shelley. But her dull-blue dress could belong to any age, and his pulse quickened as all at once he pictured her naked —the remote white goddess of some antique legend.

"Let's go into the other room," he suggested. "It seems a little more cozy somehow."

In here there were glass-fronted bookcases containing standard "sets"; a fire screen cross-stitched with red and blue parrots stood in front of the hearth, and above the mantelpiece hung the portrait of a young woman in a scarlet shawl. For the first time John noticed that the blond coloring, the shape of the face, suggested Dr. Chardwicke.

"That's my grandmother," Fran told him, "but they say it doesn't do her justice. She had the reputation of being a beauty."

"I can well believe that!" John exclaimed, with more enthusiasm than he had intended; and he was glad that just then Dorothy appeared in the doorway with two glasses of wine on a tray.

She gave them a knowing glance as she set it down.

"At first I didn't know where you two had gone," she said, "but I guess this is more private, if that's what you're looking for. Don't let me cramp your style. I'm going up to bed. But if you think of it you might leave the dirty glasses in the kitchen."

This interruption was so incongruous as it broke the train of John's thoughts that for a moment he was angry; then he laughed.

"I guess we're not favorites with Dorothy," he exclaimed.

Fran had seated herself on a small yellow satin sofa. He took the glasses from the table, handed her one of them, and sat down beside her. Dorothy's brief appearance, which might have constrained him still further, had made it, to the contrary, much easier for him to talk.

"I'm afraid I asked you to stay under false pretenses," he said.

She looked at him curiously. "What do you mean? I was very glad to stay."

"I mean I asked you for a special purpose," he explained. "I mean something more than just wanting to be with you, although that would be purpose enough. I wanted to find out something."

"What is it?" she asked. "I'll tell you anything I can, but I can't imagine what it is."

He sipped his sherry. It was so good that he knew it must come from the Doctor's private supply.

"I sort of hate to do it," he said slowly, "because it's about Ronny. Because it may be a shock to you, Fran."

For a long moment she fixed her eyes on his face. "You needn't hesitate," she said. "I've withstood many shocks. And you're one of the few people with whom I could bear to talk about Ronny just yet. You're one of the few people I absolutely trust."

"Fran," he said earnestly, with only the briefest pause as he wondered whether his uncle would have approved, "I'm going to confess something to you. The night Ronny died I saw him for a short time. I talked to him before he collapsed and he talked to me."

Fran looked at him without speaking; she did not appear surprised. Then she said: "I'm glad at least that you talked together, John. I like to think that you didn't pass each other by completely in the dark. Would you feel like telling me what he said?"

"He was convinced that something horrible had happened to him, something which he could not quite remember because of his illness. It's an awful thing to say, Fran, but I can't help feeling that Ronny was murdered."

Her expression did not change: it was still serious and calm, with the peculiar look which he could only describe to himself as "clarity," which he had noticed the instant he saw her, and which he had seen on no other face.

"I've thought so all along," she said quietly. "If you think so too, that makes it much more probable."

"You've thought so!" he exclaimed. "And you've never spoken of it! Or perhaps you have to others."

"No," she said. "I've spoken to no one. I told you that you were the only person with whom I could bear to talk of Ronny. You, and perhaps little Ellen; but she was so fond of him that I didn't have the heart. I didn't dare speak of it to any of the others, John, because I was afraid I might be talking to his murderer."

"And if I hadn't spoken to you first, you wouldn't have mentioned it to me?"

She passed her hand across her forehead as if to brush away some fatiguing dream. "I don't know," she said, and her voice was almost a sigh. "Perhaps I might have sometime; but when I thought of speaking of it, it would always seem so utterly unreal. And it could do no good. It could not bring Ronny back."

"But what made you think of it?" he went on eagerly. "Did you have any special reasons?"

"What made it first occur to me," she said, "was the fact that I'm sure, just as you are, that Ronny suspected it himself. Uncle Clarence let me see him very little and almost never alone; but once or twice he said things to me, too—very strange things. At first I thought they were only his delirium. But at night, as I've lain awake, they have come back to me, and now I'm not so sure."

"The strangest thing about our talk," John said, "was the kind of warning he gave me. He seemed to think I was in danger, that I was somehow threatened by whatever had destroyed him."

Fran leaned forward and for the first time her face showed surprise. "Did he tell *you* that?" she asked. "That's just what he told me. I think he would have told me more, because at that time his mind was fairly clear, but Aunt Althea came into the room and he stopped suddenly. The next day when Uncle Clarence let me see him for a few minutes, he was half out of his mind and hardly recognized me."

"But Fran," John exclaimed, "you should have let me know! I've come to believe there really is danger in this house. I don't think you should stay here."

Fran smiled. "What about you?" she asked. "I shouldn't mind very much what happened to me, but with you it's different. It's you that shouldn't stay here, John. Just now this is my home; but there's no reason why you should live with the Chardwickes."

"I think there's reason enough," John said. Then, as she seemed about to protest, he continued swiftly: "But tell me, Fran, you said just now you were afraid you might be speaking to Ronny's murderer. Have you any suspicions? Have you the least idea who it might be?"

"No," she said, "I simply can't imagine it."

"You don't think it could be your uncle? You remember what Ellen said that night."

"Uncle Clarence is a silly, vain man," she said. "He's a frustrated man. But I can't believe he would do such a thing. I don't think Ellen really believed it. As a matter of fact, Ronny had very little money, and Uncle Clarence, though he dislikes me, wants me to take half of it. I've refused. It belongs to him by law, and I should be glad if Aunt Althea and he could be more comfortable as they grow old. But it wasn't just a gesture. He really meant it."

"You don't think that might have been his conscience?" John asked.

"If his conscience didn't prevent his killing Ronny," she said, "I hardly think it would prevent his taking a few thousand dollars that might later have come to me. No. Uncle Clarence can be very difficult. He can be selfish and childish. He loves his own comforts. But he is also genuinely kindhearted. I've no doubt he was relieved when I refused, but his offer was real."

John finished his sherry and wished there were more.

"Fran," he said, and hesitated for a long while, "you don't think it could be Douglas, do you? Douglas, I'm sure, is very much in love with you . . . in his own way."

Fran paused even longer than he had done before she answered him; and he noticed her fine eyebrows drawn slightly together.

"No," she said at last, "I don't think it's Douglas. As I told you, I don't trust him. If he does love me, it is, as you say, in his own peculiar fashion, which is certainly not mine. If it had to be someone in the house, I would rather it were he than anyone else, but I can't think it is, John. I've come to know Douglas pretty well, far better than I should have chosen. In some ways, I'm sure, he's without scruple, but I can't believe he's a murderer."

John raised his head with a start as the door into the back hall which had been slightly ajar now opened and Douglas himself appeared. He stared from John to Fran with a sardonic grin.

"Thanks for the kind words!" he exclaimed. "It's nice to know your friends don't think you're a killer. I'm grateful for small favors."

Fran stood up, and John wondered how her face with so little change could suddenly express such scorn.

"Since you were spying on us," she said, "I hope you also heard me tell John that I didn't trust you and didn't like you."

As Douglas' eyes met Fran's across the room, John could not help feeling that Douglas and she made a splendid pair of antagonists in the concentrated fixity of their passion.

"If you care to believe me," Douglas said, "which you probably don't, I was not spying on you, though I've no doubt you gave me a fine character. I happened to run into Dorothy upstairs. She said you two were down here drinking together. It sounded convivial, so I thought I'd join the party. I confess when I heard my name mentioned, I paused for one instant but it was quite involuntary. And after all, even if I had been listening, what's a little eavesdropping among friends, that is if they have nothing to conceal?"

John's first impulse of anger against Douglas was blunted by the thought that if anyone in this house could be described as a spy, it was not Douglas but himself; and even the knowledge that his motives were disinterested could not make him feel comfortable.

Fran turned to him now as if Douglas were not there.

"Good night, John," she said. "I've enjoyed our talk. I'm only sorry it had to end like this. But there are very few things, I've discovered, that something does not spoil."

"Good night," he said. "I'm sure there *are* things, Fran, that nothing can spoil."

The two young men stood where they were as she walked out through the front parlor and between the portieres into the hall. Douglas smiled again; but now, it seemed to John, that his smile was no longer ironic, that it was even almost friendly.

"I don't blame you," he said. "You're a nice kid, Johnny. After all, it was only to be expected. God knows, the last thing I wanted to do was to fall in love until I was set up in practice. But I'm a realist and I suspect you're not. I can stand a good deal of knocking around if I think the end is worth it. You remember our little talk last night. I still think you'd be a lot more comfortable—shall we say?—if you looked for another room."

"I remember it very well," John said, "and you see I'm still here. It may interest you to know, Douglas, that you are the fourth person that seems to think I should move out; and one of them, if it's any consolation, is Fran. Such a lot of interest makes me feel quite important. I'm staying."

"Okay," Douglas said. "After all, it's your funeral. If you want to start upstairs, I'll turn out the lights down here."

11

John walked up the stairs, he remembered watching rats in a maze as part of his work for a course in experimental psychology. They would start out confidently in quest of the food they smelled; they would run into a blind alley, turn, scurry back, to set forth time and again, until he could himself feel something of their nervous frustration. Certainly for him the situation in this house was a labyrinth: hidden somewhere in its depths must be the knowledge he sought—the knowledge of mysterious and horrible death. It was lucky for him that he was an excellent student, because it was almost impossible to keep his mind on his work. Tonight he must try to catch up with some of his reading, and tomorrow afternoon he would go to see his uncle.

His little room now looked more cheerful. Mrs. Chardwicke, as she had promised, had given him a table which John had stacked with books. He had put photographs of his parents on the bureau, and a china greyhound his father had brought back to him from France when he was ten years old; he thought of it as a kind of mascot and, almost as much as the photographs, it reminded him of home.

He had been studying for more than three hours when he heard a step in the hall outside his door. For an instant he thought it might be Dorothy going down to the bathroom, but he realized the steps were walking toward her room and not away from it: it could not be she, therefore, because when he had come upstairs he had heard her moving about in her room. In contrast to the doors in the rest of the house, the third-story doors were flimsy, and he knew that if she had gone downstairs in the meanwhile he would have heard her.

He waited for perhaps two minutes, then turned out his light, opened his own door cautiously, and stepped into the black passageway. Dorothy's room was across from his but nearer the front of the house. At first he could hear only the scraping of the elm against the eaves; he had grown so used to it by now that even when there was a wind, as there was tonight, he rarely noticed it. The darkness swarmed around him. He could imagine that just by standing there, so still, he would grow dizzy, or that if he closed his eyes and suddenly opened them he might find himself in some quite different place.

Then, without a doubt, he heard whispering. It was very faint but it brought him back with a slight shock to the sense of his being here in this frigid passage. Of course his Uncle Paul would tiptoe to the door and listen. John had almost made up his mind that he would too, if only for a moment, to find out who was there, when it occurred to him that it must be Douglas. The way Fran had attacked him tonight might have had the effect of making him seek consolation for his hurt feelings; and John remembered Dorothy's sultry glances. Certainly, John felt, he could not spy on a love tryst. He might walk along the hall, taking care to be heard, and then knock at the door; but what could he say? He would merely have put himself in an absurd position.

Then, to interrupt his thoughts, there came a quite different noise and from a quite different quarter: it seemed to him like an intermittent tapping, as if someone, perhaps, in the shaft of the stairs, were sending signals in code. This at least he could investigate and he felt his way toward the stairhead. At the top it was closed by a narrow door, and as he put his ear against this, he could hear it distinctly: *tap . . . tap, tap, tap . . . tap, tap. . . .* He stepped back from the door, suddenly flung it open, and started down the nearly vertical stairs as fast as he could without risking his neck.

He had seen a light which went out so quickly he was not sure whether it was from a flashlight or from the bulb in the second-story corridor. There had been a scrambling down the lower steps but by the time he reached the bottom and turned on the light the corridor was empty. He ran along to its junction with the main hallway, but even before he touched the switch he could see by the spectral glow from around the corner that here too there was no one.

He had been so close on the heels of the fugitive that John was sure he would not have had time to run along the big hall and go into one of the bedrooms without John's seeing at least the shutting of the door behind him. As he glanced over his shoulder along the passage, he noticed that one of the doors here stood ajar. Impatient at having lost time, he hurried to it and found that it opened on to the back stairs; and he thought, yes, he was sure, that he heard a sound come up out of the darkness, as if someone had stumbled against a chair or table. There was a switch just inside the stairway. When he turned it, a light went on below in the kitchen. Then he leaped down the stairs several steps at a time.

The kitchen was empty. There were swinging doors covered with green baize, that led into the dining room; but if anyone had passed through them within half a minute (and John could have taken no longer to get down those stairs) they would still be swinging slightly; and they were quite motionless.

The kitchen was as large and dingy as the other rooms in the house. A huge coal stove was set into the wall with a hot-water boiler beside it that looked as if it was made of brass; there was also a small electric stove, a zinc-topped table, and a quantity of shelves crammed with boxes and tins and jars. Besides the doors into the dining room, there were four others.

The one at the end of the room, in an alcove or vestibule beside a wooden icebox, must lead out into the back yard, and even from here he could see that the bolt was fast. But next to it, just inside the main part of the kitchen, a door stood open perhaps an inch. The other two were closed.

As he passed by the table on his way across the room, something jumped at his foot. He leaped to the side with a startled "Christ!" and saw that he had sprung a rattrap baited with a piece of chicken entrail. The pounding of his heart and his feeling of relief made him realize the tenseness of his nerves.

The door that was not closed led to the cellar. As he peered down the stairs, he could see that in some far recess a light must be burning. He looked over his shoulder, noticed a poker in the coal hod beside the stove, and crossed the kitchen once more to take it. It was long and heavy, with a hook near the end, so that it suggested a goad: at least if he were attacked with anything but a gun he would be well armed.

He opened both the other doors and glanced into two deep closets filled with barrels of flour, of potatoes, with a dim confusion of mops and brooms. When he returned to the top of the stairs, the light still burned in the cellar, which struck him as strange until it occurred to him that whoever was down there must realize that to put it out, once he had seen it, would be a complete giveaway. If it were left, he might think it had been forgotten from the evening.

As he started down the steps, the damp and stagnant cold, the smell of mildew, almost sickened him: it was as if he were entering a vault. He had never felt less like going anywhere—even into Ronny's room; but now the chance had come to find his way, perhaps, to the center of the maze. There was nothing else to do than to go ahead, to search every corner of the cellar.

At the foot of the stairs he paused and glanced back. He had not realized how many steps there were and how steep. He remembered as a boy judging from the ground the height of a diving board and thinking it wouldn't be too daring to take a dive: he had climbed the ladder to discover that it looked at least twice as high from the top as it had seemed from below. Now he had just the opposite feeling: those long straight stairs, with cobwebs hanging from the beams, with old bottles, with rags stuck into the crannies along the side, reached up and up like the stairs in a dream to the lighted kitchen indefinitely far away.

Down here he stood in a thick gloom. The light was hidden behind a wall of masonry some ten yards beyond in the depths of the cellar. He could see numbers of doors, some open, some closed, and in front of him a wide arched corridor.

"Who's there?" he called with a bravado at which he could have laughed. "You might as well show yourself. I'm armed and I'm going to find you."

His voice had sounded as if he had been speaking in an empty church. The silence rang in his ears.

Then, as he started back toward the room where the light must be, it went out, and for an instant he was almost dazzled by the darkness.

He cursed himself for not having thought to bring along his flashlight. The cellar was obviously huge; it must cover the whole area of the house; there were many rooms, and in the pitch dark it would be impossible to find anyone who wanted to keep hidden. He might feel around to see if he could discover a light switch, but there was small hope of that: he could search for a half hour, an hour, without happening to find one. Or better, he might return to the kitchen, look for a candle, a lantern, a flashlight, keeping his eye all the time on the cellar door. No one could escape into the house. If this strange prowler, as seemed likely, knew the way out to the yard, there was nothing John could do.

He turned around and walked back toward the foot of the stairs down which there came a murky beam. Above, the door was sharply illumined, and suddenly a shadow moved across it.

John stopped and drew in his breath. That shadow had filled him with a sick horror, as if it were the sign of all evil, of something unimaginable, unhuman. Suddenly he realized that the light he had seen down here must have been turned on, and then off, by a switch somewhere in the kitchen. Its purpose had been to lure him down these stairs while perhaps whoever had cast that shadow crouched in one of those deep closets into which he had barely glanced.

With the poker clutched in his hand, his blood singing in his ears, he rushed up the stairs, but before he had gone half way the door swung closed, leaving him in such thick darkness that he groped for the wall. Then, above his own harsh breathing, he heard the click of a lock.

12

John swore half aloud, just to have an excuse for hearing the sound of his own voice; for he could imagine waves of silence crowding in upon him from the blackness, rising like a cold tide up the shaft of the stairway, engulfing his feet, his knees, and still rising until it would close over his head to sweep him away into that dark limbo of which Ronny had spoken.

He climbed the rest of the flight slowly, turned the knob, and pushed; but, as he had known it would, the door held fast. Should he pound on the panel and try to rouse someone? If the kitchen doors were closed, it was doubtful whether anyone would hear him, in this big house with its massive walls. At least he could try.

He knocked briskly and waited. The door, he remembered noticing, was an exceptionally heavy one and the stairs were so steep that it was hard to get a good stance. After a couple of minutes' pause, he knocked again, this time as loud as he could, but the rapping even to his own ears sounded muffled and ineffectual. Again he waited and then for the third time he knocked, now with an almost hysterical violence, so that he hurt his knuckles; but already he knew it was useless. No doubt the door at the top of the back stairs was closed. Possibly a person already awake might hear a faint disturbance, though even then he might think it was something outside banging in the wind; but John knew he could pound away all the rest of the night without rousing anyone from sleep.

He had better explore the cellar and see if he could find his way up to the yard. He started down the stairs, very slowly, because the steps, which seemed to be of stone or cement, were so worn that the treads had each one a different and incalculable slant and all of them were slimy. It would be the easiest thing in the world to lose his footing and plunge downward headfirst as you might plunge into a well.

It seemed to him that he had been going down and down for at least five minutes. He wished he had counted the steps. Then suddenly the floor came up to meet his foot, and he knew that he had reached the bottom. Where to go now? He remembered the arched corridor that divided the cellar in two; the light had been burning somewhere around a corner to the left. That light would be the best thing to aim for, because even if it was connected with the kitchen it could doubtless also be turned on at the bulb itself.

Then as he groped for the wall, so that he could be sure he was walking straight, a chilling idea occurred to him, bringing with it an aftertaste of panic: until now he had assumed that the person he had been chasing had tricked him into the cellar in order to make an escape. Suppose it were for another and deadlier reason. Suppose more than one person were involved, and the second one were here crouching in the dark, quite aware of where he must be standing, ready to spring upon him!

He moved as quietly as he could to the side of the passage. Then he stopped once more, listening intently. The damp cold was penetrating his clothes, even his woolen sweater; he wondered whether there were greasy smears on his hands where they had touched the slime of the wall.

For a moment he was reassured: it had just struck him that the person on the stairs could not have expected to be overheard and pursued; but this thought did not comfort him long. Perhaps that was just what *had* been expected. It may have been intended that he should explore that sound, that he should be decoyed into this black and moldy labyrinth, that his last taste of life should be this foretaste of the grave. He remembered Ronny's warning, repeated in one form or another by Ellen and

Fran and Douglas. Fran and Ellen, at any rate, had told him that they knew of no definite danger, and he had believed them at the time; but now even their faces, as he recalled them, seemed tainted by this corroding darkness: perhaps they had simply not dared to tell him what they knew; and as for Douglas, his handsome bold smile seemed a kind of infernal mockery. But it was Ronny's face that he could see most clearly—the terror in his glazed eyes; he could hear his words, hardly more than a whisper: "Go away! You must get out of here before it is too late!"

Well, he had not gone, and perhaps it was too late already.

Then John felt ashamed of his nerves. I'll count to a hundred, he thought, to steady myself, and then I'll start a tour of exploration. If someone is here to get me, he's apt to get me no matter what I do; he must have a light that he can flash whenever he wants to. If nobody is here, I'm wasting time and probably catching pneumonia.

He began shuffling along the passage, touching the wall every few seconds with his hand. In this way he discovered several closed doors, but for the time he passed them by. Every now and then he would stop to listen. There was still not the faintest sound from within the cellar; but now his ears could make out, as if from another world, the billowing of the wind about the house. After an immeasurable interval his fingers, as they reached for the wall, felt nothing. This must be the corner around which the light had been burning. He turned to the left and slid his foot cautiously along the floor.

The next instant he drew it back, with a thrill of horror; it had been poised over empty space. He thought of *The Pit and the Pendulum,* of the dungeon in the French chateau (wasn't it Loches?) into which political prisoners had been thrown during the Middle Ages: in the blackness they would begin to explore the place, just as he was doing now, and sooner or later would plunge into a curbless well.

With his hand gripping the corner of the wall, he lowered his foot an inch at a time, half expecting at any moment a violent push from behind. It was a vast relief when his toe touched something firm: it was a deep step—perhaps there was another flight of stairs. Again he felt ahead, but apparently this step was the only one. This wing of the cellar was about ten inches lower than the main corridor.

It was also, he began to realize, faintly warmer, and as he advanced the warmth increased. It did not take the chill from the air. It seemed rather like some distinct and, as it were, contradictory flavor which stood out all the more sharply because it did not blend with the coldness and the damp. Then, so dim that at first he thought it was just an hallucination—the kind of ruddy shapeless spot that may swim across your closed lids if you press with your fingers against your eyeballs—he noticed a glow ahead of him, a few feet from the ground. It must be the furnace.

He walked straight toward it, leaving the wall. Yes, he could see a line of rusty light, which would be either the top or the bottom of the furnace door.

Suddenly the whole atmosphere changed: it was now so dry and warm that he felt as if he had stepped from a cold pool on to the bank. He took out his handkerchief to protect his fingers and reached for the metal handle. He found it at once, and as he pulled the door open, the dimensionless chaos through which he had been groping disappeared like a puff of smoke and he had emerged into a world of shape and form.

A network of glowing veins pulsed through a bed of coals; he could make out the cylinder of the furnace itself; and as he stared around him he could see, a few feet away, a column of masonry against which some dark objects were leaning—no doubt a shovel and a poker. It came over him that if anyone were stalking him down, he had for the last couple of minutes been a perfect target, standing there beside the open door. Since nothing had happened yet, there was now every chance that nothing would.

As his eyes grew accustomed to the glow he made out a bulb hanging from the ceiling, almost within reach of where he stood. With only the slightest hesitation, he turned it on, and the whole room took shape: there was a large bin at his right; a pile of screens was stacked against one wall, and beside them, neatly folded, lay half a dozen garden chairs with canvas seats, which no doubt spent their summers on the porch. Just under the ceiling, well out of his reach, were two oblong windows, not more than a foot high; he wondered why not even the dimmest light shone through them, and then he realized that they must be blocked by the snow.

There was no sign of steps leading up into the yard. He glanced at his watch. It showed quarter past three.

In this sudden warmth and light, in this relief from tension, he felt a mist of drowsiness close around him. He could not bear the idea of returning to that cold and darkness, of searching through room after room for a door which when he found it might be padlocked, or frozen shut beneath a foot of snow. In a few hours Dorothy or Mrs. Chardwicke would be down in the kitchen getting breakfast. He took one of the chairs, unfolded it, dusted it off with his handkerchief, and set it up about a yard from the furnace. At any rate, he would rest here for a little.

But he had hardly stretched himself out when he fell asleep.

"Well, for crying out loud! If you didn't scare me!"

Opening his eyes, he saw Dorothy standing above him; he noticed that she wore a denim apron black with coal dust, and remembered where he was.

"Hullo, Dorothy," he said, and tried to stop a yawn. She gave him a keen look which, as usual with her, suggested a squint.

"What in hell are you doing down here?" she asked.

"I was after someone," he said. "It couldn't have been you, by any chance?"

"Let's get this straight," she said. "Were you drunk last night and stumbled down these stairs, and the door swung to on you? Is that it?"

"I might almost think I had been," he said. "But I wasn't. I heard someone prowling about the house. I thought he might be up to no good—a burglar perhaps. I thought he went down here. Perhaps the door did swing closed. It closed at any rate."

"Hmph!" she exclaimed. "That may be true. Just about anything might happen in this God-damned house, I guess. Or again it may not. However, it's none of my business."

John had never seen her in better humor and thought he could guess the reason.

"Now that you're here," she said, "you might stoke that furnace for me, and then we'll have some nice hot coffee."

When they came up into the kitchen, Mrs. Chardwicke in a white smock that covered her to her feet was standing beside the stove. John wondered whether it was a relic from her nursing days. It struck him then that the place where she would seem most natural was the ward of a hospital, as one of those vague but efficient head nurses that you couldn't imagine out of uniform, that you couldn't think of with a personal life of their own, and whose glances gave the impression of never being focused on anything, simply because, no doubt, they were taking in everything at once.

She looked at him now with only the faintest surprise, and before she could speak Dorothy exclaimed:

"Here's a perfect gentleman for you! What do you think he's been doing? Actually stoking the furnace! You don't get service like that every day. I told him he deserved an extra cup of coffee before his breakfast."

Dorothy's remarks had so completely the effect of explaining his emergence from the cellar as something quite natural that John thought she must have spoken deliberately. He was grateful to her for her tact. If his Uncle Paul thought he had better tell Mrs. Chardwicke, or anyone else, of his adventure, he could do so later.

Mrs. Chardwicke gave him one of her undirected smiles.

"You seem to be quite a lady's man, John," she said. "I shouldn't have thought it, to look at you. You never can tell, though, can you? Sometimes when they are, they want to make you think they're not, and sometimes when they're not, they want to make you think they are; so I guess no one's much the wiser."

Though you could not describe as kind a tone so completely without warmth, it seemed to John that it was meant to register kindness. It occurred to him, for the first time, that in her own way she might like him. What had seemed to him rather offensive in her references to Fran and Ellen yesterday afternoon might be merely her awkwardness when she tried to unbend; it struck him now as even somewhat pathetic, like the advances of some large-boned and unattractive dog.

"I'm getting started on a batch of my special little plum cakes," she said. "We'll have them for dinner. I don't believe you've had one yet. The Doctor is very fond of them, but he shouldn't eat too rich food, so I don't make them as often as I used to do. I hope you'll like them."

13

Just before five that afternoon John knocked eagerly at his uncle's door. It would be the first time since his report of Ronny's death that he would have something new to tell him.

"I was hoping you might turn up today," Professor Hatfield said. "Let me see. . . . It must be at least three days since you've come round."

"I've been quite busy," John said. "Quite a number of things have happened."

After the professor had poured a couple of drinks and then settled down behind his desk, John described everything he could remember, trying to relive each scene as he reported it, so that nothing would slip his mind; his talk with Douglas night before last and the tense moment with Fran immediately afterwards, the picnic yesterday and Mrs. Chardwicke's greeting on their return, the doctor's ill-humor that had driven poor Ellen from the table, his own conversation with Fran in the evening, which Douglas had interrupted, and finally his adventure of the night and its peaceful aftermath, when he had sat drinking coffee in the kitchen fragrant with the odor of baking cake. Occasionally the professor would ask him a question, or John would recall something he had left out and go back to describe it. When at last he had finished, his uncle looked at his watch.

"Do you realize, John," he asked, "that it's quarter past six and you're supposed to dine at half past? There are a number of things I'd still like to discuss with you; so I suggest that you call up the Chardwickes and tell them you're dining with me. I must

315

congratulate you on the account you've just given me. It has been most vivid and enlightening. I'd be careful of those third-story stairs, by the way, if they are as dark and steep as you describe them. No more bolting down them as you did last night. We can't be sure what that tapping may mean, but I doubt very much that anyone was signaling in code."

"What do you think it was then?" John exclaimed. "And why should anyone have wanted to lock me in the cellar?"

"As for your first question," Professor Hatfield said, "my hunch would be that someone was trying to convert those dark stairs into a death trap by some simple device. I may be quite wide of the mark. Even if I'm right, I think that particular scheme will be abandoned, after the scare you gave the murderer. The answer to the second question is obvious. You were close on the prowler's heels. He was lucky to escape unseen. Had you discovered him he would have had to give some explanation; he would have been in a most awkward position. I've no doubt that, as you thought, he hid in one of the food closets after he had turned on the cellar light from the kitchen. He must have held his breath as he heard you wandering around. Then there was silence. Of course he hoped, though he could not be sure, that you had gone down cellar. After waiting for a couple of minutes, he would have cautiously come out, heard you in the cellar, and locked the door with a sigh of relief. He would now be quite free to go up to his own room in safety, and also to remove any traces, if such there were, of the work he had been engaged in when you interrupted him. But now you had better let the Chardwickes know that you're dining with me."

John stepped into the hall to telephone, and was relieved when it was Ellen who answered; he had rather dreaded having to tell the doctor or Mrs. Chardwicke at such short notice that he wouldn't be there for dinner. When he re-entered the room he found the professor pacing the rug.

"Sit down, John," he said. "Don't mind me!" And for several minutes he continued his walk.

His face had a closed, an almost blank look, except for his eyes which seemed to be focused on something far away: John could imagine that this was just his expression when he was on the track of some particularly rare bird. Suddenly he stopped and stared straight at John. His smile was as controlled as ever, but John could see that he was excited.

"I'd like to ask you one or two more questions," he said briskly. "Not about facts; I'm sure you've told me all of them you know, and told them remarkably well; but just about your own impressions. Would you say that the relations between Ronny and Douglas could be described as a really intimate friendship? Ronny brought him to see me once or twice, but that was early in the fall before they had had much chance to know each other. Of course you never saw them together, but Douglas has talked to you of Ronny, and Fran or Ellen or the Chardwickes, not to speak of Dorothy, may have made remarks in passing that would give you some lead. I realize from what you've said that in a way they were rivals, which probably created some strain in their relationship, as it might between two brothers, for that matter. But I'd be curious to know just what was there to be strained."

"I don't think so very much," John said slowly. "I don't think that Douglas disliked Ronny in himself though I guess he was jealous of him. Apart from that, my idea would be that he felt friendly enough and probably a bit condescending. About the way he feels toward me, I should imagine. Of course I don't know Ronny except from what you and the rest of them have told me, but I'd be very much surprised if he took Douglas any more seriously than Douglas took him. I doubt if there was anything on either side that you could call real friendship."

"Hmmm!" the professor said. "That would have been my own opinion. I'm glad to have it confirmed. And now, what would you say about Ronny and the Chardwickes? He never spoke very much about them to me. Have you heard anything from anyone to make you think that he felt toward the good doctor and his wife at all the way he might have felt toward his own father and mother? Or that they, one or both of them, felt toward him any of the affection they might have felt toward an actual son of their own?"

"You would be better able to judge Ronny's feelings than I," John said. "I've no idea what either of the Chardwickes thought of him, but I can say this: neither one has shown any signs, since I've been there, of having been through a really tragic experience. I don't mean that they have seemed callous, but they definitely have not acted as if they had lost their own son."

"Hmmmm!" Professor Hatfield said again. "You know, John, I think it's barely possible that I may have the faintest glimmer of what has happened, of what still is happening, in that ill-fated house."

The professor looked very serious, and yet in his voice, John thought, there was a hint of exultation that was slightly ghoulish.

"You mean you think you suspect who killed Ronny?" John asked eagerly. "And why?"

"Suspect would be too strong a word," his uncle protested, "and it's not unlikely that I'm completely mistaken. But I do have, as I said, just a glimmer—perhaps it will prove a mere will-o'-the-wisp—of what the situation is."

"You think you know what that person was looking for in Ronny's room the night he died?" John asked.

"I think I do, in a general way, yes," his uncle admitted.

"What is it?" John asked quickly. "I can't wait to hear!"

His uncle gave him a long look. "I'm afraid you may have to wait for a time," he said, "that is if, as I assume, you'd like this mystery to be cleared up. It's not, I may say, merely a question of avenging Ronny's death. That would, after all, be dealing with something that, most regrettably, has already happened. If I am not mistaken—and again I can't emphasize too strongly the fact that I may be—the most important thing now is not avenging the dead but protecting the living. The danger is still actual."

"Danger for whom?" John asked. "You mean for me?"

"For you, certainly. You've been warned to leave the house by Ronny, Ellen, Fran and Douglas. By me, too, for that matter; and I'd warn you again now, except that, from what you've said, I'm sure you would pay no more attention to my warning than to the others."

"But do they know?" John asked. "Do they know what the actual danger is?"

"It would be hard to tell," the professor said, "exactly who knows how much. But I shouldn't be surprised if some of them, at any rate, suspect."

"But I'm just a newcomer," John exclaimed. "Why should anyone in that house wish to harm me?"

"Ronny was a newcomer last fall," Professor Hatfield said, "and you know what happened to him. If, as we've both thought for some time, and as Fran's remarks to you would tend to confirm, the motive for his murder was not financial, the chief thing that placed you on a different footing from Ronny no longer exists."

For a moment John saw once again Ronny's face as it had floated before him in the seething blackness of the cellar, the fungoid pallor of the cheeks, the haunted eyes. He glanced at his own fingers and could imagine them plucking at a weight of fever-drenched blankets.

"Uncle Paul," he asked, "do you mean that I'm the only person for whom that house is dangerous?"

His uncle looked grave. "Anyone in that house may be in danger," he said, "if it is thought that he knows, or even suspects, the truth."

"But certainly *I* don't!" John exclaimed. "I wish I did. Why won't you tell me now? If I knew, I'd surely be able to keep a better guard."

"If I wasn't sure that's not the case," his uncle said, "I'd tell you my suspicions immediately, deluded and fantastic as they may very well be. But John, if they are not deluded, if they are even somewhere near the truth, it would not be the slightest safeguard to know who the murderer is. His methods, as before, will be devious and circumspect. But by all means, keep on watch. You say you know nothing, but after all you have observed enough to give me this theory of mine. Be on guard against everyone. That is the only safe thing. If I told you a name, the name I should now choose, it might be the worst thing I could do, by giving you a false sense of security in regard to other people. You have a sophisticated mind, John; you are not ingenuous; but you are, I'm glad to say, frank and sincere by nature. Suppose, for example,

that you knew at this moment, or even that you strongly suspected, the murderer was myself, could you sit here comfortably now
and sip your drink, could you talk to me as you have just been
doing, and not reveal to me at once that something was wrong?
I very much doubt it."

John looked at his uncle. As he met his eyes, he was struck by
the coldness, the hypnotic fixity of his glance: that face, usually
so friendly, so reassuring, seemed at this instant almost reptilian.
Could his whole impression of his uncle be wrong? John recalled
his half-joking reference to blackmail during their first conversation. It occurred to him that much of his sense of what was
sinister in the Chardwicke house had been the result of suggestions first planted by Professor Hatfield. The house was strange
enough; yet perhaps this man whom, after all, he had known for
a bare two weeks, was himself just as strange.

John tried to smile naturally and raised his glass to his lips.

Professor Hatfield smiled too, and became himself once more.

"You see!" he exclaimed. "That's what I mean. I have only to
give you a fixed stare and arrange my face as if I were struggling
with a toothache, and you become self-conscious. The most dangerous thing you could do would be to reveal your feelings to the
murderer as clearly as you did to me a minute ago."

"But you mean," John asked, a little embarrassed by the way
he had fallen into the professor's trap and eager to change the
subject, "that whoever it is might deliberately try to murder any
one of us in that house?"

"I mean just that," Professor Hatfield said, "if the provoca-
tion were sufficient."

"But it sounds completely mad!" John exclaimed.

"Not completely mad," his uncle corrected. "Few people, unless perhaps congenital idiots, are completely mad; and perhaps
even fewer—not even the most lucid geniuses, the most commonplace Babbitts—are completely sane. What is a normal motive for murder? Gain, revenge, lust, fear, ambition? But where,
in any case, do you draw the line? It would seem an insane act
for a wealthy man to murder an acquaintance for twenty-five
dollars. At what point would the sum be large enough to make

his action sane? Twenty-five hundred? Twenty-five thousand dollars? Would it be sane to murder a friend for that amount? A brother? A son? You may murder in blind passion, which to all effects is temporary madness. Such a murder, indeed, would be in a sense, more mad than this one of ours, because it would be accomplished while the murderer was, as the expressive phrase goes, 'beside himself.' It would have little in common with the emotional texture of his daily life and would be, to that extent, unpredictable. Whereas Ronny's murder was the result of slow and careful planning; its motive, unless I am wrong, evolved from the very core of the murderer's personality: it was a true act of self-expression. More mad or less, you murder because only in that way you can get something you want, or you can avoid something you dread, or perhaps by the one action achieve both those ends. The madman, you say, acts under compulsion: he may shrink with horror from what he does and yet he cannot help doing it. And yet do not most normal men find themselves at times acting in just that way? Or again, one might say that the madman does not understand what he is doing: he thinks his action is something quite different from what it is. But which of us fully understands all of his own actions? At just what point of incomplete understanding does the act pass beyond the limits of sanity?"

"But surely. . . ." John began.

His uncle smiled at him. "Of course there is the question of degree," he admitted. "There is the great majority of human actions which the great majority of people consider natural and understandable—in other words, sane. The human mind is a very sensitive thing—wonderful, yes, but also mysterious and terrible. We can, after all, draw a working distinction between sickness and health, even if none of us is wholly sick or wholly well; and I would not deny that in this case we have to do with a sick mind, a personality that is ravaged as a face might be destroyed by leprosy. And the most awful thing about it is that the personality, the face, is still recognizably human. Before we have finished with this case we will have had to go far afield into the chilling and terrifying outer regions of the human consciousness.

Before we can understand it we will have had to look down into the frozen depths of an inferno, a desert so remote from our normal experience that if in the deepest sleep we should step across its borders we should struggle to wake up as from the most awful nightmare. That much warning I do give you, John. But finish your drink and we'll go out for dinner. I think by now the club dining room is closed, and I know a place just off the square where one can get a meal that is not too unappetizing. And by the way, I don't believe I told you that, since I was sure you would not move out, I've planned to move into Dr. Chardwicke's house myself."

"You're going to move in there too!" John exclaimed.

Few things he could have heard just then would have given him so much pleasure. As Professor Hatfield had been talking, John had felt more and more the shadowy coldness of the house gripping at his heart; he had felt that he might open any one of its doors and find himself lost among those interminable rooms in which poor Ronny had been trapped. But if his uncle was there in the house, he somehow could be trusted to break the spell, to destroy the black magic.

"That would be wonderful, Uncle Paul," he said, "but I thought you told me the doctor wouldn't take you."

"I didn't think he would at the beginning," his uncle explained, "but at that time I was at least half-convinced that he was contemplating murder. I'm sure now that even if such were the case he would not dare raise any objection. He knows I know that there is a room vacant. He knows there is a question, as he had feared there might be, of his losing his laboratory. He may even welcome my arrival at this particular time as a guarantee of his soundness, his responsibility."

"But won't it put the person you suspect on guard?"

"I doubt it very much, but that is a risk I must take. I must endeavor to make myself appear as innocuous as possible. It's true I may have been some help, in a small way, in exploring on one or two occasions that border region which lies between crime and madness, and thus discovering the diseased—or if you prefer, the guilty—person. But I don't flatter myself that my connection with these cases has made much of a stir. In fact, once the police

has appeared on the scene, I've always withdrawn as discreetly
as I could. I should like you, however, tomorrow at lunch, when
everybody is in the dining room, to mention to the doctor that I
shall call on him that afternoon and would like if possible to move
into Ronny's room that very evening. Then you can tell me what
reactions, if any, you noticed among those present. I shall be surprised if you see anything unusual. But my dear John, after what
you have told me just now, I should no more think of letting you
stay on in that house without my being there to keep an eye on
you—and an eye on everyone else—than I should let you go alone
and unarmed into the deadliest of jungles."

If John had expected his uncle's presence in the house would change the atmosphere, he was not disappointed. The professor arrived in a taxi with numbers of bags and packages just before dinner and would not hear of delaying the meal by being shown to his room. He was seated on Mrs. Chardwicke's right, John's former place; and John's seat was moved along nearer Ellen's, so that now he sat between Ellen and his uncle. When he had told the Chardwickes at lunch that Professor Hatfield would like to take Ronny's room, he had done his best to observe the way his announcement was greeted; but so far as he could see there was, as the professor had predicted, nothing in the least suspicious.

"I should feel proud to have Professor Hatfield with us," Dr. Chardwicke had said, "though I'm sorry, John, that you will still have to keep that tiny room upstairs. It seems so out of the way and I'd looked forward to your moving down into our little community on the floor below. However, I must admit that you seem to be thriving up there. As my dear mother used to say whenever she thought I looked especially well: 'Darling, you've got roses in your cheeks!'"

Mrs. Chardwicke had seemed especially pleased. "Tell your uncle that of course we can take him in today," she said. "The doctor and I used to see him occasionally years ago, before the doctor's health began to keep us so much to ourselves. He's just the type of person I should like to have, but warn him that he mustn't expect too much. Just plain simple cooking."

"I've told him about your cooking," John said with a smile. "He'll know what to expect."

"Oh, I hope you haven't told him too much!" Mrs. Chardwicke exclaimed, though she dimly returned his smile. "I'm sure a man of his position must be particular and I should hate to have him disappointed."

Fran, Ellen and Douglas had shown the friendly interest one would expect. Though Dorothy was in the room at the time, he forgot even to glance at her; but he was sure she was the one person in whose reactions his uncle would not be interested.

John had never seen his uncle more charming, though he was amused at his air of innocent cordiality. Professor Hatfield expressed in the most gracious terms his regret that circumstances had interrupted for so many years his acquaintance with the Chardwickes. Somehow he managed to appear completely himself and yet to suggest that that self was merely a good-natured unworldly professor, a shade old-fashioned in his manner and always ready to smile at his own absentmindedness. He spoke of Ronny's death and the shock it had given him; he showed the deepest interest in Dr. Chardwicke's recent work, so that before the meal was over the doctor had offered to take him through his laboratory; he treated Fran and Ellen and, in the most tactful way, even Dorothy, with a kind of grandfatherly courtesy, scolded John for not having brought Douglas around to have a drink at the club, and would have been almost fulsome in his praise of the cooking if his remarks had not shown that he was himself an expert cook.

"My dear Mrs. Chardwicke, who was responsible for that delicious souffle?" he asked as they rose from table. "Should the award go to you or Dorothy? I suspect that such an exquisitely homogeneous result couldn't have been a work of collaboration."

To John's surprise, Mrs. Chardwicke almost bridled.

"It was Dorothy's tonight," she said, "but I claim some credit too, because I taught her. I'd be glad to give Mrs. Hatfield the recipe when she comes home."

"I should feel guilty in accepting it," Professor Hatfield protested, "because I know how people treasure their recipes; but I see you're one of those generous people who make no mystery of their cooking."

"On the contrary," Dr. Chardwicke said with a jovial air, "as a rule my wife guards her culinary secrets like a Gorgon. You don't realize what a hit you've made with her!"

"I'm always glad to share my recipes with people who I think will appreciate them," Mrs. Chardwicke told her husband serenely. "It's not often one meets such a connoisseur as Professor Hatfield."

The professor bowed and glanced over his shoulder at Dorothy who was standing near the doors that led into the kitchen.

"My dear," he said, "if you should ever be looking for a husband, though in your case, quite obviously, the main difficulty would be in trying to make up your mind among a dozen candidates, you have only to let him taste one of your meals. I'm sure there would be no escape for him after that. I might add that such tactics would be quite unnecessary unless the young man were blind."

In spite of the quaintness of his phrasing, he managed to put such warmth into his voice (as if, twenty years ago, he would himself have found Dorothy irresistible) that she gave him a smile John would not have imagined her wasting on a man over fifty.

While they were drinking their coffee in the parlor, Professor Hatfield showed the liveliest interest in the old furniture, especially the pictures. Dr. Chardwicke took him the rounds of both rooms. They began with a large oil landscape, a clump of willows with some wooden-looking cows standing near a pool, which hung in a monstrous gold frame above the sofa.

"Of course it's pretty terrible as art," the doctor said, "but I confess I take a kind of pleasure in it . . . a kind of amusement, perhaps. It belongs so completely to its period, like the vaudeville acts we used to see as young men, Professor Hatfield. They were often atrocious, and yet I should love to see them now."

If Professor Hatfield had never been more cordial, certainly the doctor had never been so benign: he seemed almost to bloom as the professor talked to him, and if John had not been on the alert he would not have noticed the ingratiating persistence of his uncle's flattery.

After they had looked at several landscapes and genre pictures, Professor Hatfield inquired about the portraits. The doctor seemed to take even greater pleasure in describing the eccentricities of this or that one of his ancestors. John was surprised that with the professor he became really amusing, even charming; perhaps because he felt for the first time since John had seen him that he was talking with an equal. It struck John in a way as rather tragic: as if the doctor had become once more, for a short while, the man he had been before his collapse; and it was as such a man, a brilliant and respected colleague, that Professor Hatfield treated him.

"Are there none of Mrs. Chardwicke's family here?" he asked finally. "So far, if I'm not mistaken, doctor, these have all been relatives of yours."

"Not a one," Mrs. Chardwicke told him before the Doctor had a chance to reply. "My family were all plain people. They couldn't afford to have their portraits done, and I'm sure there was nothing interesting about them."

"I'm sure at least that *that* is not true," the professor exclaimed gallantly.

John was surprised that when Professor Hatfield said good night it was nearly half past ten.

"I wonder if you'd help me up with my books, John," he asked. And John was even more surprised when his uncle turned blandly to the Chardwickes. "What do you think of this nephew of mine?" he exclaimed. "Here he has been in Woodside for more than two weeks and I've hardly seen anything of him. He has dropped in at my room a couple of times, and I've tried to lure him to stay by offering him a drink, but it doesn't take that young man long to down even the stiffest highball. I'm afraid he may think I've played a rather unsportsmanlike trick on him by moving into his own quarters, but now that I'm here, John, I expect to make up for lost time. I warn you, young man, that I shan't let you go from my room tonight until you've told me every bit of family news."

Then, as if he feared that even his obvious jesting might be interpreted by John himself, or by the others, as a real reproof, he added: "Of course I know the boys are so busy they can hardly turn round, these first weeks of medical school; and when I see such a collection of charming young women here, I can't blame him if he doesn't want to spend his spare time with his aged uncle. But I'm sure, Doctor, with your lodgers, you must know by this time what young men are like, and you too, Mrs. Chardwicke. John tells me that your treatment of him has been almost parental."

The professor shook hands with everyone before he left the room. It was the first time that Fran, Douglas, and Ellen had all stayed downstairs so long. John took two suitcases, Douglas a pile of books tied together with string; Fran and Ellen each took a package or two, so that everything could be carried up in one trip, leaving the professor with only a moderate-sized bag.

As soon as they had put their articles of baggage on the floor and left his room (which John would always think of as Ronny's) Professor Hatfield went to the door, locked it, and hung his handkerchief over the knob.

"Uncle Paul," John exclaimed with a grin, "after that last exhibition, how do you expect me ever to believe anything you say again? I've never seen a more brazen display, when you know I've spent hours in your room. And the worst of it is, I could feel you were positively gloating in your deceit."

The Professor gave an almost impish smile but raised a finger to his lips. "Sssh!" he said. "These doors are thick, but it might be well to speak softly."

He walked with the same stealthy speed to the long window, looked at the fastening, and drew together the curtains of faded brown rep. Then he stared in a leisurely way about the room, and sniffed the air with his head raised in an attitude that reminded John of a bird that has just taken a drink.

"Hmmm!" he said. "Still a trace of the carbolic smell you mentioned. I'm sure Dr. Chardwicke, to do him justice, took every precaution. If our landlord, John, may sometimes act foolishly, as which of us does not, by the way, it would be a mistake to assume that he is a fool. I thoroughly enjoyed our talk this evening. I must acknowledge once more, John, your powers of description. The house, the atmosphere, is just what I expected. And this room . . . as you told me, it is on the whole rather grim. If I had a fever I should not care to have to gaze at those singularly dreary medallions. No, it's not a very cheerful place to die in."

The big room was shadowy now, because the only light turned on was the reading lamp beside the bed. As John watched the professor, it occurred to him that one might assume, from the deft way he moved, that he was an experienced burglar.

"The noise you heard," he suddenly asked, "the night of Ronny's death: could you say at all, John, from what part of the room it seemed to come? From the direction of the closet, of the bed, of that big chest of drawers?"

"No," John said, "I shouldn't have the slightest idea. I turned the knob at once and then, as I told you, it stopped. I didn't think until later that perhaps I should have listened first and tried to locate it."

"Naturally not," Professor Hatfield said. "With this heavy door, you were lucky to hear it at all. The fact that you did, suggests that whoever was in here must have been rather desperate and in quite a hurry. He must have passed an unpleasant moment when you tried the door. And now, John, Dr. Chardwicke said that you would show me the bathroom I am to use—the same one that you do, he told me. Perhaps you would."

The professor followed John through the hall and then into the deep, narrow bathroom next door.

"And which of the household use this bathroom?" he asked.

"All of us except Dr. and Mrs. Chardwicke," John said. "The one they use connects with their bedroom, I think. Of course we all keep our towels and washcloths in our own rooms. You probably noticed the towel rack beside your bureau."

"An excellent idea," the professor said. "In that way there can be no confusion. Quite an array of toothbrushes, I see. Evidently some of you use more than one, which is a splendid habit. I think I'll keep mine in my own room, and John, I'd rather advise you to do the same with yours. And now good night! I can't tell you how pleased I am with my new quarters!"

15

The next two weeks were the strangest that John had ever lived through. His life had been queer enough since he first entered the Chardwicke household; but now overlaid upon the atmosphere of gloom and tension was a kind of incredible cheerfulness. Sometimes it was even hard for John, knowing what he did, to believe that his uncle was always acting a role. Because not once since that first evening had the professor talked with him confidentially: anyone might have overheard their few private conversations, perhaps in the parlor before dinner, or sometimes—though not often and then only for a few minutes—in the professor's own room. On these occasions, in contrast to the first evening, John noticed that his uncle was apt to leave the door slightly open. If he gave any sign that things were not as they seemed, it was only by a kind of twinkle in his eye, as if to mark approval of the way John played up to him, or by the excitement John fancied he could make out beneath the alertness of his movements, the briskness with which he rose from his seat when any of the ladies entered the room, the intensity of his brief tight smiles.

Everyone in the house seemed in his own way to unbend, to respond to the professor's cordiality. The one exception was possibly Douglas, who was drinking more than ever. He had moments, it is true, of a rather wild gaiety, but there were also evenings when he sat through dinner in a mood which John thought must be a kind of alcoholic depression. He was apt to arrive late for meals; he was out of the house more than anyone else, and often did not wait to have coffee with the others.

John was sure that he had gone up to Dorothy's room at least once more. When he had spoken of it to his uncle, the professor had shrugged his shoulders.

"After all," he said airily, "youth will have its fling, and Dorothy strikes me as a young woman who can take care of herself. I can't quite imagine you, John, if you were as desperately in love with Fran as Douglas seems to be, seeking consolation in the arms of a girl like Dorothy. And if our friend Douglas thinks that his behavior, which Ellen, as you told me, suspects, and of which Fran herself must be aware, will arouse her jealousy and hence her interest, he is simply making the mistake that a great many young men, who were not fools either, have made before him. It might work with some girls but not with a girl like Fran. In the meanwhile, then, let us not grudge him what meager consolation he may find. As you must have learned, it takes all sorts to make a world."

At moments John would be amazed to catch himself laughing heartily at some of Dr. Chardwicke's anecdotes. Encouraged by Professor Hatfield, the doctor showed a shrewd gift for imitations, and could take off some of John's professors with such malice and gusto that John felt he might have missed his calling. Often, though, as he lay in bed, listening to the mice in the attic or the wind among the branches of the elms, it struck John that he was taking part in a Dance of Death: at any moment the laughter might be frozen, the whole phantasmagoria might vanish like the moving pictures from a screen, and the horror which must still be lurking in this house would stalk once more through its desolate and haunted rooms.

Meanwhile even the weather helped keep up the illusion of innocent and normal cheerfulness. The morning after Professor Hatfield moved into the house was the beginning of a thaw. The drifts along the edges of the sidewalks, which had suggested in their angles, their peaks and ridges, a chain of miniature Himalayas, were smoothed down and rounded off, as if a geological change requiring thousands of years had been accomplished overnight. The upland fields beyond the lake gleamed among the woods with a pearly brightness. Water flowed through the gutters with a rush and tinkle that seemed the very sound of spring.

Then one morning, as John started out for Science Hall, he saw that it had frozen again: as he looked into the sun the streets were ablaze with reflected light, and the treetops glowed like a mesh of white-hot wires against the sky. Winter had returned. There was no longer anywhere the noise of water, but instead the creaking of the icy twigs as they knocked against each other.

Though during the week he had had no time for picnics, he had, while the fine weather lasted, been walking several times with Ellen and Fran. He loved to watch the pleasure that both girls took in the beauty out-of-doors. Fran was still very quiet but he could see that she was sensitive to each note of color, each delicate sound, with the kind of aesthetic appreciation that one feels, heightened to the pitch of genius, in the music of Debussy. Sometimes now there was a frosty glow in her cheeks, and John hoped that she was beginning to get over the first dreadful shock of Ronny's death.

Ellen was far more exuberant. The sunlight, the sparkle of the fields, the delicious air, almost made her drunk. If she had dared, he suspected, she would have loved to roll over and over in the snow like a young dog.

She seemed to adore Professor Hatfield.

"I just love your uncle!" she told him. "I think he's about the nicest man I've ever known, except Father, of course." And John blushed as he realized how little she suspected the cold eye that the professor's joviality concealed.

Then on Saturday, at lunch, two weeks to a day after the professor had come to the house, he asked Dr. Chardwicke if he would not show him his laboratory that afternoon.

"Of course I'd be delighted to," the doctor said, "if you really would like to see it." He spoke with the guarded eagerness of a stamp collector asked to show his albums to an intelligent amateur.

"I suppose you have a whole menagerie of living germs," Professor Hatfield exclaimed. "It always makes my flesh creep to look at those tiny colored rods or chains or whatever they may be and realize that they are just as deadly as the fiercest tiger or the most venomous cobra."

The doctor chuckled. "Oh, you get quite used to them," he said. "But you mustn't raise your hopes too high. I do have a most interesting collection of slides that cover pretty much the whole field. Of late years, however, I've been limiting myself to only a few living colonies. The room they allow me is very small, as you will see, and I haven't the energy I used to have."

"I'm sure I shall be fascinated by your slides," Professor Hatfield said, "but I hope you will give me a peep at the living germs too. Just what have you got at present, if it's not indiscreet to ask?"

"By no means," the doctor said graciously. "Just now I have typhoid, paratyphoid, tuberculosis, tetanus, African sleeping sickness, leprosy, and that I think about completes my list."

"No bubonic plague!" Professor Hatfield exclaimed like a disappointed child. "However your collection should be quite gruesome enough to satisfy even my morbid tastes."

He turned to Ellen. "I suppose you've seen them all," he said. "I imagine you're quite blasé about them by this time."

"I hate them," she said. "Cousin Clarence only showed them to me twice. I hate to look at them."

John spent the afternoon working in the library. As they were sitting down to dinner that evening, Professor Hatfield exclaimed:

"You know, Dr. Chardwicke, it's just occurred to me! You recall how earnestly we were talking as we left your laboratory. I'd asked you about the way they were fighting sleeping sickness in Tanganyika and you were giving me a most interesting account. You had left the room just ahead of me, you remember. Dr. Macfarlane was standing by the bulletin board in the hall and had called you over to ask you a question about something. You had left the key in the door and of course I should have locked it. But it's just crossed my mind that I pulled out the key before closing the door and left it unlocked. It was very careless of me."

"Oh dear," the doctor exclaimed. "I suppose that means I should go up there tonight."

"Not at all," Professor Hatfield said suavely. "If anyone does that, it would of course be myself, or I might send John. But really, doctor, I don't see that it makes the slightest difference. Nobody goes up to that fourth floor unless they have business of their own, especially at night. Even if anyone wanted to pry, he'd have no reason to suppose it was unlocked."

"But I feel responsible . . ." the doctor began.

Professor Hatfield gave a good-natured chuckle.

"You're thinking now of our little talk a month ago," he said. "My dear fellow, I'm afraid you took it too much to heart. I'll go on record as assuming full responsibility for my own negligence. You have nothing whatever to do with it. If you'll give me the key, I can lock it Monday morning when I go to my classes, if you're not planning to be there tomorrow. Douglas happened to mention that "Fighting Lady" is at the Orpheum. He saw it yesterday and was quite enthusiastic. The reviews have been excellent. I hope you and Mrs. Chardwicke will give me the great pleasure of attending it this evening as my guests. You'd better come along too, John. As a Navy man, you should be interested."

The doctor protested once more, but again Professor Hatfield waved aside his objections. The next minute Douglas entered the room, late as he so often was now, and a trifle glassy-eyed.

"We're talking about 'Fighting Lady,'" the professor told him. "I'm insisting on carrying off Dr. and Mrs. Chardwicke and John, partly on your recommendation."

"Yes, I enjoyed it," Douglas said. "It's good, clean, healthy fun."

16

When John looked out of his window the next morning, he saw that the trees and the lawn were covered with clean snow. In the air was what he at first thought was mist. Then he noticed that it was everywhere flickering like an old motion-picture film, and realized that the snow was still falling. He was sorry, because he had promised Fran and Ellen to take them on a picnic this noon, and now he was afraid that Fran, at least, would not come.

He was surprised, therefore, when he spoke of it at breakfast, that it was Ellen and not Fran who backed out.

"I'd love to go, John," she said sadly. "You know I would. But I've got a little cold, I think. And I have lots of things to do. I ought to go to the university library and look up some notes for my next history topic."

When Fran and he both urged her, she only shook her head.

"I thought I could count on you, Ellen," he said with mock reproachfulness. "I admit I felt a little doubtful of Fran."

"I don't see why," Fran exclaimed. "It's very beautiful today. I've been out already. It's not cold, and I love the snow."

"I'll put you up some sandwiches," Mrs. Chardwicke promised, "and give you some coffee in a thermos bottle. Then you won't have to bother to make a fire. It might be pretty wet."

At half past eleven, when Fran and John stepped out-of-doors, the almost invisible snow was still falling. The drifts which during the thaw had grown grayer and grayer were now a stainless white on top, but you could see on the more vertical slopes and in the

hollows the dingy snow underneath, as if in some careless clean-
ing job nature were merely covering up the old dirt, hiding it, as
it were, under new carpets. Fran, in a black coat and small fur
cap, had never been livelier. As they walked along, blinking at
the flakes on their lashes, there was a look of eagerness, almost of
expectation, on her face: today she might not be thinking of the
past, might not be seeking escape in the transitory present, but
admitting, if only for the moment, that there might sometime be
a future in which life would again be worth living.

"Where shall we go?" he asked. "Ellen took me to the quarry
at the end of the lake, but that's quite far. Have you any special
place in mind?"

"No," she said, "I don't care where we go as long as it's in the
woods. I love the deep woods when it's snowing. It seems almost
as if you were out of the world."

They followed the main street to the edge of town, just as Ellen
and he had done, but then instead of turning to the right, toward
the lake, they took a path to the left into the thick woods which
had given the town its name. John thought he had never known
such silence; but soon he became aware of the faintest rustling,
as of fine silk being crumpled: it seemed hardly a sound at all,
but rather an innate quality of this softly tumbling air, which you
could perceive only through some special sense far more delicate
than hearing. Snow now lay thick on everything. It filled the boles
of the trees, the interstices of the bark; it clung to the fur of Fran's
cap and frosted her hair.

"If we could only be lost in it forever," she exclaimed, after one
of the long silences which with her seemed so natural, "and not
have to go back to people!"

Her tone was sad but it was not merely sad, and John felt his
heart pounding.

They ate their lunch in a campers' shelter several miles from
town in the depths of the forest.

"Ronny used to bring me out here," she said. "It was one of his
favorite places."

Though there was nothing to cook, he foraged for wood and
built a small fire; and it was while they sat here watching the

flames, scarlet in the midst of the quivering grayness, that she told him for the first time something about her life. She spoke of her brother, three years older than she, whom she had adored and who had been killed in a motor accident the day before his sixteenth birthday, of her father now overseas.

"He's a fine man," she said, "but somehow we were never intimate. Perhaps it is because after Mother's death he has always been in love, and always with a new girl. Most of them lately have been just about my age. I remember how shocked I was the first time I realized what was happening. It was only a few months after Mother's death and I was ten years old. I know it's wrong to make moral judgments. It's a thing I've tried to break myself of. But in spite of everything it has put a kind of wall between us which has made both Father and me unhappy."

John remembered that his uncle had said Fran's mother had killed herself, and wondered whether Fran did not suspect that her father's affairs had begun before his wife's death.

Fran walked to the door of the shelter and stood looking out through the trees. During their lunch the snow had stopped, and now the silence of the woods was no illusion. While John collected their things and put out the fire, neither one of them spoke. Then she said, as if there had been no pause:

"Yes, John, you have no idea what a lonely person I've been!"

John was standing close beside her. Her tone was filled with such a desperate melancholy that he could hardly bear it; and without planning, without making even the swiftest decision, he put his arms around her and kissed her lips with a sudden brusque ardor. He had never been so surprised at anything he had done in his life, and the next instant he had never regretted anything more.

She pulled herself away from him violently, as if she were angry; but when she turned toward him so that he could see her face once more, he realized that it was not anger that had made her draw back: he only wished it had been. Her eyes looked startled, disappointed, almost shocked. He could imagine that at that moment he actually repelled her.

"Oh no, John!" she said. "You shouldn't! Not now! I didn't dream you would. If it were Douglas, yes, but not you!"

As he remembered that it was Ronny who had first brought her to this place, that it was not much more than a month since Ronny's death, he felt bitterly ashamed.

"I didn't mean to, Fran," he said. "That's my only excuse. It isn't an excuse at all, but you must believe that I didn't mean to. It was just that you were so beautiful—so beautiful and so sad."

Then all at once the shock went out of her eyes, and she smiled at him kindly, even affectionately, as if she were his sister.

"It was my fault," she said. "If a girl tells a young man she's lonely, especially if it's a young man she likes, he naturally thinks she wants to be consoled. I should have known better."

"But it wasn't that," he protested with a deep flush. "I didn't think at all. I just couldn't help myself."

"Let's not talk of it any more," she said. "It's not important enough. Come on, John. We should be starting back. And you mustn't worry or I shall feel terribly guilty for acting like such a prig. It hasn't spoiled anything."

It was the muted happiness of these hours in the woods that John was to think of later as at once the climax and the end of this the most fantastic period of his life. Because on their long walk home through the stillness of the afternoon Fran really convinced him that nothing had indeed been spoiled by his unforeseen and passionate blunder; so that at moments, even, he would catch himself incorrigibly tempted to interpret her reproachful "Not now!" as another way of saying "Not yet!" Whenever he realized the trend of his thoughts he would check them as being both vain and indecent; but by the time they reached home he felt he had rarely spent a happier day.

At seven o'clock the next morning as he was crossing the hall in his dressing gown for a bath and a shave before anyone else should want the bathroom, his uncle's door opened a few inches and Professor Hatfield, without a word, beckoned him into his room. He was wearing an old gray wrapper. His eyes, his whole face, looked sharp and tense.

"I've been on the watch for you," he said, "for the last half hour. Of course there was no need, really, because you would have discovered soon enough that your razor blades were gone. But I was afraid you might ask someone about them—someone else than me, that is."

"My razor blades!" John exclaimed in surprise. "They're gone? Where are they gone to?"

His uncle smiled. "Not far," he said. "In fact they are safely wrapped up in a neat package inside my briefcase. But before I tell you anything more, you'd better put these back in their place. You'll see there are only three of them, just as there were before. I'd rather counted on something like this happening, so I've had these on hand for the last week. Of course they are quite all right, but it's just conceivable that the razor itself may have been tampered with; so I'd feel easier if you didn't use it this morning. You can borrow my electric one, if you like, or stop in at some barber shop."

His uncle handed him a partly used package of blades, which John would certainly have taken for his own.

"But what do you mean?" he asked, still a little drowsy. "I don't understand what it's all about."

"Just put these back first," Professor Hatfield said, "on the little glass shelf above the wash basin where the others were. Put one of them in the razor, as if you'd used it this morning. I noticed that you had thrown away the last blade and were going to open a fresh one today. Be careful not to cut yourself, though I'm sure that now there's no danger."

With a queer feeling that all this was still part of his dreams, John did as his uncle told him, and in two minutes was back in the professor's bedroom.

"On second thought," Professor Hatfield said, "you'd better not stay here now. Go and take your bath as usual. Needless to say, you won't mention our little interview at breakfast. I'll walk up with you afterwards to the campus. As a matter of fact, I have a ten o'clock myself and should be going before long. I'll explain everything on the way."

It was an effort for John during breakfast not to show his curiosity, his sense that something strange was happening, but he felt that on the whole, with his uncle to inspire him, he did fairly well. Professor Hatfield drank his coffee quickly and rose from table before any of the others were finished, in order, John suspected, that he might be sure the two of them would be joined by no one else.

"I'll be running along now," he said, "if you'll excuse me, Mrs. Chardwicke. I have an experiment I'd like to set up before my ten o'clock."

John gulped down his own coffee and took a last bite of toast. "I might as well go with you," he said.

He could hardly wait until they were outside to question his uncle.

"Now tell me what it's all about," he asked eagerly, as they walked down the path in the gray neutral light. "Of course I have a vague idea."

"I suspect you do," Professor Hatfield said. "No doubt, knowing just why I came into this house, you have an idea that my leaving the laboratory door unlocked and announcing the fact at table was something in the nature of a ruse, or perhaps I should say a trap. As I told you, I knew after my talk with the doctor, the day of Ronny's funeral, that he would be especially careful about locking his laboratory and keeping track of the key. I felt that under these circumstances you, and all the other inmates of the house, would be reasonably safe from any attack by germs. Even were the doctor himself the guilty one, he would not dare to repeat his crime—at least not for some considerable period. Then, day before yesterday, when I felt I had safely established my residence in the house, as it were—I allowed myself exactly two weeks—I announced that the bacterial supply was again available, and only for a limited period: it might be now or never."

The Professor gave a short chuckle. "The hardest thing," he went on, "was arranging to keep the good doctor's attention so occupied when we left his lab that he would forget to lock the door. Of course I planned to have Terry Macfarlane waiting by the bulletin board ready to pounce on him the moment he appeared. Poor Terry had to hang around there for nearly half an hour, because when I got the doctor started on sleeping sickness, I could hardly budge him from his chair. The game was to get him to move on without stopping the flow of his talk."

"And you are just assuming that germs of some sort have been put on my razor blades," John asked. "Isn't that a pretty long shot?"

"At any rate, we will know by this evening," Professor Hatfield said. "And it was not such a long shot as you may imagine. I had my special reasons, which you will know in good time. One of them was the fact that as I examined the package last night, I could see that each of the blades had been taken out of its wrapper and then put back. I'd looked at them the night before, and they had not been touched."

The professor bowed cordially to an elderly goat-faced man with a brief case, who joined them as they were crossing a street near the University Club.

"John," he said, "I'd like you to meet my old friend, Professor Glautz. This is my nephew, John Frazer."

For the rest of their walk the two professors talked together about changes in the management of the university pension fund. Only when John left them in front of the club did his uncle turn to him again.

"You might meet me at five o'clock," he said, "at Dr. Macfarlane's office in the hospital, Room 107, and we can walk home together."

John felt that today he did not learn much from his classes. When he knocked at Room 107 at five o'clock sharp, it was his uncle who opened the door. Dr. Macfarlane was there too—a large-boned man, with rather crowded features, red hair and bushy red eyebrows. The moment he spoke he put John at his ease.

"Well, young man," he exclaimed heartily, "your uncle and I have got a little exhibit here, arranged for your special benefit. Somebody is interested in you. There's no getting round that fact. Since you're a med student I don't have to ask you if you know how to use a microscope. Just take a peek at those babies."

John put his eye to the microscope that stood on the doctor's desk. In a circle of the palest blue, like a summer sky, he could see a pattern of small dark-blue objects: they were rod-shaped but

enlarged at one end so that they suggested the most ethereal drum-
sticks or perhaps baseball bats. They would have made an attractive design for a piece of silk.

"Do you recognize them?" his uncle asked.

"I probably ought to," John said, "but I'm afraid I don't."

"They are the bacilli of tetanus. From one of your razor blades.
We found enough on each of the three in the package to kill a
dozen men."

John lifted his eye from the microscope, looked around him
desperately, and the next minute vomited into Dr. Macfarlane's
wastebasket.

17

"The whole thing is most gratifying," Professor Hatfield said. "I was counting on tetanus."

Dr. Macfarlane had already given John his first shot of toxoid, as an extra precaution. He had then brought out some whisky, and now John, the professor, and he were sipping highballs and smoking cigarettes.

John had never felt more the need of a drink. Though he had been warned for the last month to be on his guard, nothing had prepared him for the shock of knowing, without the chance of doubt, that someone in that house, a person with whom he must have talked every day as a friend, had plotted to kill him in this cold-blooded manner. It is a ghastly thing to learn that you have been chosen as the victim of the most malignant and unprovoked murder; and John, hardly as yet able to realize it, felt that he could understand the horror which must shape the lives of those who suffered from the mania of persecution.

Dr. Macfarlane's whisky was now very comforting; but he knew he must drink it slowly to avoid being sick again. He suspected, too, that with his shaken nerves and his empty stomach, it would take very little to make him drunk. His eyes kept straying to the microscope, as the glance of a criminal reprieved at the last minute might be fascinated by the electric chair. He knew that he must still look pale and hoped he could keep his hands from trembling.

"I don't see how you could be so sure," Dr. Macfarlane said, "but of course you haven't told me very much about the business as yet."

"Well, you see," the professor explained, and the quiet precision of his voice had a soothing effect on John's nerves, "Dr. Chardwicke had living colonies of typhoid, paratyphoid, sleeping sickness, t.b., leprosy and tetanus. That was the only choice. The first two were ruled out because everyone in the house knew that they all had been having shots. Of the other diseases, all except tetanus, even supposing infection were obtained, would take years to prove fatal, and our murderer could not wait. Anyone, moreover, who had even a smattering of bacteriology, such as you could read up in the most popular manual, would realize the extreme difficulty, perhaps the impossibility, of secretly infecting a person with leprosy or tuberculosis. I don't know about sleeping sickness, but that would be so exotic, it would so certainly point to a laboratory infection, that even if it were an acute instead of a lingering disease, I'm sure it would have been ruled out. Whereas anybody may develop tetanus at any time. The germ, or at least the spore, is notoriously long-lived and the manner of infection as simple as can be. One has only to cut himself with an instrument sufficiently infected, and then, if he doesn't take the shot in time, there is an excellent chance that he will get the disease and that it will prove fatal. Correct me if I'm wrong, Terry. Now what is the way in which a man most often cuts himself? Shaving certainly. Even with a safety razor. I don't mean a real cut, but a nick, a scrape. Before I got my electric I suppose I drew a suggestion of blood at least once a week. Mere trifles, of course; but that might be all the better, because no one dreams of getting a tetanus shot after such an accident; no one pays the faintest attention to it. I had noticed, John, that your skin seems very sensitive in this cold weather, especially the skin of your throat and beneath your jaw, and of course you never allow yourself a reasonable time to shave carefully. If I had observed the pink smears on your neck, somebody else, on the lookout for such things, might well have done so, too. I was delighted, when you first showed me the bathroom, to see that you kept your razor there, on that glass shelf, in sight and in reach of everyone."

"I wondered why you seemed so pleased," John said with a wan smile. "I remember you spoke of my toothbrush but you didn't mention the razor."

"Naturally no one could be sure the scheme would work," Professor Hatfield went on, "but if at first you don't succeed, try, try again—perhaps with different means. We have no way of knowing whether poor Ronny succumbed to the first attempt. I think the chances are he did not. I remember the account that Mr. Lawes, the warden of Sing Sing, gives of Dr. Arthur W. Waite, who murdered both his parents-in-law, and planned as well to murder his wife and her wealthy aunt. Mr. Lawes writes that Dr. Waite told him, in discussing his attempts to murder his aged father-in-law, Mr. Peck: 'I gave him large doses of everything I had—diphtheria, pneumonia, typhoid and influenza germs, but they did not affect him. I then tried tuberculous sputum, soaked his sheets and opened windows, but everything failed to do serious harm.' Dr. Waite, however, was admirably persistent and at last succeeded in killing the old gentleman by a combination of arsenic, chloroform and smothering with a pillow."

The professor paused a moment while Dr. Macfarlane poured a little more whisky into their glasses.

"But what made you think the murderer would try germs again?" John asked. "Why not some other way?"

"Well, in the first place," his uncle said, "murderers who do not stop after one crime are very apt to use the same method over and over again. This is most fortunate, because it has led to the capture of very many who might otherwise not have been discovered. Mr. Smith, to mention only one example, might have succeeded in killing half a dozen more wives and building up a substantial fortune to retire on, if he had not always drowned them in their bathtubs. In this case of ours, the fact of your mentioning at lunch the day after Ronny's death, as you told me you had done, that you had not yet had your Navy shots, including tetanus, would tend to call attention to that means once more. It would also suggest the desirability of speed, since you might be given your inoculations at any time."

"But Ronny's death aroused so much suspicion!" John exclaimed.

"In my mind, yes, and in yours," the professor admitted, "but otherwise, apart from Ellen's half-hysterical outburst and Douglas' suggestion that anybody could have stolen the germs, neither one of which was followed up, the event was outwardly accepted as a natural death, or at worst as an unfortunate accident. And with a disease like typhoid or tetanus, it is impossible to prove, by examination of the body, that murder is involved, no matter what suspicions one may have; while poison is always poison. If a body is found full of arsenic, it's a pretty safe bet that it did not get there by innocent means. Perhaps you may have noticed, John, that I've made a number of comments on the food and the cooking. I hoped to suggest, without being too obvious, that I was very sharply food-conscious; or if anyone, through my own clumsiness, should come to suspect that *I* suspected foul play, it would be assumed that what I was looking for was poison of some sort in the food. This would tend to make him veer away from that particular method. Of course your strange adventure in the small hours of the morning, John, convinced me that the tapping you heard on the stairs was an attempt to trip you up by stretching a string or wire across. You remember I told you to be careful. At best those stairs are dangerous. But I was confident if this was the case that your scaring away whoever was there that night would prevent a repetition of the attempt; and later it occurred to me that since Dorothy often comes down in the mornings before you do, such a method could not be counted on for any one chosen victim. No, all in all, I was pretty confident that when I told the household that bacteria were once more procurable, someone would avail himself of the chance."

"But Uncle Paul," John exclaimed, "I've just remembered! Douglas wasn't in the dining room when you told us. He didn't come in until afterwards. And then of course you took Dr. and Mrs. Chardwicke off to the movies with me. That would leave only Fran and Ellen and Dorothy."

John could not tell whether his uncle's glance contained approval or affectionate irony.

"That would seem to narrow our field of suspects considerably," he said, "wouldn't it? Though you forget there was also Sunday morning. So far as I know, Dr. Chardwicke didn't go to his laboratory until around noon."

"If I understand the setup," Dr. Macfarlane said, "there was nothing to prevent Douglas' getting wise before he stepped into the room. That would have been all the better for him, because he could always say he hadn't known the laboratory was unlocked."

"I must confess that had occurred to me," Professor Hatfield admitted demurely, "though of course I couldn't have planned on his arriving just then. It would have been quite accidental."

"Uncle Paul!" John exclaimed suddenly. "You're a regular devil!" The whisky had taken its effect at last: he felt all at once interested and gay. "I think I see now why you dragged the Chardwickes and me off to the movies. Suppose Dr. Chardwicke went up at any time Sunday to lock his lab, he'd know we'd remember that anybody left in the house Saturday evening would have had a perfect chance to rummage. The Doctor could carry away whatever he wanted, and always say it had been stolen while he was sitting between you and his wife watching 'Fighting Lady.' "

"My dear John," the professor said with a twinkle, "how Machiavellian you've become! I trust it's not my influence. No, all I'll admit was my artless statement that the season for germs was again open. One thing I was a shade doubtful about was the proper timing: I didn't want to make my announcement too soon, because I felt the murderer would like a rest period, to collect his energies and to avoid the suspicion that too quick a repetition might arouse. On the other hand, I didn't want to postpone it too long, lest finally he might switch to some other method. But as I said, I was pretty nearly one hundred per cent sure that if bacteria were available at the right time, no other method would be used, unless the germs, so successful in accomplishing the first murder, had failed with this second one."

"Unless they'd failed with the second one!" John repeated. "They did fail, thank God! Or thanks to you!"

"Oh no indeed!" the professor contradicted. "This second one will have been a brilliant success."

For an instant John's faintness, his nausea, returned. He thought he could not have understood his uncle.

"What do you mean?" he asked with an attempt at a smile. "Did you say this last one was a success? Have I been infected with something I don't know about, or am I just too drunk to catch what you're saying?"

His uncle was immediately all concern.

"How stupid of me!" he exclaimed. "I should have remembered that you've just had a nasty shock. You've been infected with nothing, my dear John, unless perhaps with the colds that have been going around Woodside. And you certainly are not drunk. You are merely relaxed, which I'm sure Terry will say is by far the best state for you to be in just at present."

"I shouldn't blame him," Terry said, "if he wanted to get absolutely cockeyed. Go ahead, John, help yourself. You'll be doing it on the doctor's prescription."

"But then what is it that you meant?" John asked. "I still don't understand."

"I only meant," Professor Hatfield said, "that under my management, and with Dr. Chardwicke's help, you're going to develop within the week a typical and fatal case of tetanus. But don't be alarmed. It will cause you no discomfort, except the possible boredom of passing several days shut up in your room—or rather in my room; because I shall insist, when the symptoms start, on your taking that one, while I move up into yours. Normally, of course, one might expect you to be taken to the hospital; but your case will be so rapid, so fulminating, that Terry will decide that to move you would be needlessly cruel. Tetanus should have complete quiet in a darkened room, with the attendance, preferably, of only one person. The hospital just now is so crowded that you would have to be placed in a ward, where conditions would be not nearly so favorable. The incubation period in your case will be five days, which is under the average; and as a rule the shorter the incubation the more violent and hopeless the case. Once the disease has actually manifested itself, I think we could kill you off in three days at the most, without seeming to rush things unduly. Would that be possible, Terry?"

"Oh yes," Terry said, "a really good case of tetanus might kill a man in three days."

"But what about my classes?" John asked. "What about the medical school and the Navy?"

"You don't realize what a distinguished person our friend Terry is," Professor Hatfield said. "He just about runs the medical school, and he's an intimate friend of Commander Neagle's. You may be sure that with Terry in charge neither the medical school nor our local branch of the Navy will raise the least objection to our little experiment. I have felt rather guilty in the knowledge that I have certainly been diverting you from your studies since your arrival here in Woodside. Now you will have several good days to catch up on your reading."

18

From now on John's life, for a time, was to become a nightmare. He could find no consolation in his knowledge that the mind that had schemed to destroy him was not normal. "It is ravaged," the professor had told him, "as a face might be corroded by leprosy, and the most awful thing is the fact that it is still recognizably human." That was the most awful thing: it was not so much the madness, the latent obsession, as the smile, the greeting, the clasp of the hand, that he must be exchanging each day with someone hungrily alert, like a beast in its ambush, for signs that he was doomed. As he looked about the, table, he would have the sense that everyone, even his uncle, was wearing a mask which might conceal, as in some primitive legend, the most loathsome and terrifying face. At moments it would even occur to him, since everything was possible, that all these people might be sane and that he was himself the madman.

He did not yet understand his uncle's purpose, except that obviously he hoped in some way to get the murderer to betray himself. Since the grisly farce must be gone through with, John would have liked to act it out as soon as possible; but his uncle would not allow him to appear at breakfast with a bit of plaster on his throat until the fourth day.

"Of course it is true," Professor Hatfield said, "that a person waiting for his plot to succeed will tend to be credulous of signs that point to its success. That is what he had planned would happen; he would not have planned it in that way if it had not seemed plausible. Moreover he had been through the sequence of wished for events so often in his mind that it seems only natural to see them materialize outside it. But even so, we don't want to seem to make fate play into his hands too quickly. We'll assume that you used the first blade three days in succession without injury. Then, on the fourth morning, you will have thrown that one away and put in the second. With this blade you will not have been so lucky; you will have given yourself a nick and put on a sliver of plaster to stop the bleeding. Of course one is far more apt to cut himself the first time he uses a new blade."

John could only admire the naturalness with which his uncle called attention to the cut that evening at dinner.

"You ought to allow yourself more time for shaving," he said. "I've noticed that you and Douglas both will do anything for five or ten minutes' extra sleep in the morning, no matter how much it makes you rush around once you're out of bed. Personally I'd far rather get up half an hour sooner and then have plenty of time to dress and eat in comfort, but I confess that was not my habit when I was your age. I think for your next birthday I'll have to give you an electric razor."

John hoped that his own reply, his admission that he had indeed cut himself while shaving, did not ring too false. At any rate there was the satisfaction that one more step in the drama had been enacted, which meant that the end was that much nearer.

The final rush of events, however, with its shocking climax, did not begin until five days later. In the meanwhile the coldest spell of the winter had struck Woodside as it was apt to do in mid-February. The mercury sank to ten below every morning and there was a blast from the lake. In bed John would listen for hours, it seemed, to these gusts swooping down across Canada from the endless night about the pole; he would brood upon the thought that heat, without which there could be no life, was something exceptional and transitory: you would find it in the sun; you would find it, unbelievably intense, in the depths of the giant stars; but even such molten worlds were mere flecks in space. Life, with all its warmth, was like the line of foam, blade-thin, along the crest of a wave. No matter how cold the day, tomorrow would be colder.

On the evening which Professor Hatfield had scheduled for the next scene there was for the first time that winter a fire in the dining room. The rest of the house was so chilly that as John stepped through the portieres he felt an incongruous sense of coziness and cheer; the coals cast a glow over the walls and ceiling, which re-enforced the candle flames. Professor Hatfield had presented Mrs. Chardwicke with a pepper plant, covered with scarlet fruits, to take the place of the poinsettia in the middle of the table; and as Dr. Chardwicke stood up in the firelight to carve the roast (for which, Mrs. Chardwicke explained, she had been saving points for days), he made John think of some benign character in a Christmas story by Dickens.

As he watched him hand the servings of meat to Dorothy to be passed first to the ladies, John felt a grim kind of stage fright; although the professor had told him that the business about the razor five days ago was far more tricky and that he had carried it off brilliantly. But now John knew, when the doctor asked him how he would like his beef, that he certainly must look disturbed.

"I don't think I'll take any tonight," he said. "Thanks just the same."

"Not take any!" Dr. Chardwicke exclaimed. "What's got into you, boy? This is roast beef. Don't tell me you don't like it!"

"Usually I love it," John said, "but I don't feel hungry tonight. I seem to have sort of a stiff neck."

"A good meal won't hurt a stiff neck," the doctor said heartily. "You just chew on that slice of beef, my boy, and it will limber it up for you. You haven't been eating so much lately as you used to do. I've noticed it. You must be in love!"

"I've had a headache today," John said, "and it seems to hurt me a little to chew and swallow. It doesn't seem worth the effort. But I'd love some mashed potatoes and gravy."

Before the doctor could protest again, a surprising thing happened. Dorothy who had taken the plate the doctor had handed her, dropped it on the floor. Everyone turned at the crash, to see Dorothy clutching the back of Dr. Chardwicke's chair, as if she might be going to faint.

"Dorothy," Mrs. Chardwicke asked severely, "what is the matter with you? Are you not well?"

Although it was hard to be sure in this ruddy light, John thought that Dorothy looked pale.

"I'm just a butterfingers," she said. "Excuse it, please. I've got a jumpy tooth and it gave a twinge."

"I hope it won't give another when you have one of my dinner plates in your hand," Mrs. Chardwicke said.

"I'll pay for the plate, if that's what's bothering you!" Dorothy exclaimed, and her voice had recovered its pertness.

As they were rising from table, Professor Hatfield said:

"John, I shouldn't wonder if you were coming down with a touch of flu. If I were you, I'd go right up to bed. I've got some old-fashioned pills which seem to be able to ward off such things when I'm threatened with them. No doubt it's just my imagination, and I'm sure the doctor here would laugh at them, but I'm going to give you one just the same."

"I'm sure I shouldn't laugh at all," Dr. Chardwicke said. "A number of those old-fashioned remedies have proved their usefulness. Look at chaulmoogra oil, for example, an ancient oriental specific for leprosy before our Western medicine took it up."

John knew the doctor would have enjoyed continuing his discussion of primitive remedies, but his uncle intervened.

"Come along, John," he said, "the sooner you're in bed, the better!"

He took him by the arm and led him at once toward the stairs.

"Beautiful!" he exclaimed, when he had closed Ronny's door. "You couldn't have done it better! Uneasiness and depression are among the early mental symptoms, and your portrayal of them was masterly."

"Unluckily," John said, "it wasn't acting. I've seldom felt more uneasy and more depressed."

"I mustn't keep you long now," his uncle continued. "I feel just a shade worried about Dorothy's impulsive action. I hope that it will not give anyone the alarm. At least she recovered herself admirably—and if the damage is done, it is done. But you must promise me this, John. You have told me that you couldn't listen at

Dorothy's door when Douglas is with her, but if he goes up there tonight, as I think he may, to discuss her strange behavior, you must lay aside your scruples for once. I can almost guarantee that you won't be listening in on any love-making. Will you promise?"

"Yes," John said reluctantly, "I suppose so. It would be silly not to go the whole way when we're in as deep as we are. But you have no idea how much I hate it!"

"I think I do," the professor said, "which makes me appreciate your compliance all the more. If you would not keep on watch for Douglas, I should have to. And it would be far more difficult for me to track him up those stairs from down here than it would be for you to take a few steps along the hall outside your room. At this stage, I simply can't afford to be discovered, particularly after Dorothy's performance. But whatever you hear, John, wait until morning before letting me know. No matter how sensational the news, it can wait until then, and I doubt very much if it will be news to me. It would create as much suspicion if you were found coming down to me during the night as if I were discovered lurking in the passageway."

"But why," John asked, "should anyone be on the lookout?"

"I hope they won't be," the professor said, "but it's possible that they, too, may be curious about Dorothy."

As John sat in his frigid room, with the light turned off so that Douglas, if he did come up, might think he was asleep, he was reminded of his first evening in this house when he had waited to prowl down the stairs on his quest of Ronny. That had been a cold night too, but tonight, though the wind had dropped, was even colder. At first he had climbed into bed, because it was the warmest place; but then as his thoughts began to move in more and more eerie circles, he was afraid that through nervous exhaustion he might fall into a doze; so he got out, put on his dressing gown, wrapped himself in a blanket and sat by the table in front of the window.

Through the frost on the panes he could see the jagged blaze of stars. The red lights of the radio masts across the lake were dimmed by the constellations. It seemed to him that his jaw ached, that his neck was really beginning to feel stiff. He had difficulty in swallowing some saliva. What an ironical twist it would be if the little gash he had deliberately made had become infected! Of course he had had his first tetanus shot, but he thought he remembered reading that even so the disease might develop. Wasn't this whole pretense, this acting out of symptoms, a tempting of fate? There was something malignant in the silent windless cold. This corrosive air, which could burn like hot metal, might be the very breath of whatever spirit of destruction, of annihilation, was lurking in the universe, to be horribly incarnate, now and then, in the mind of man.

Then, after nearly two hours, he heard Douglas' steps. The night was so still they sounded louder than usual. It was clear Douglas was making little effort to keep quiet, and John suspected that between now and dinner he must have had a great deal to drink. He opened and then closed Dorothy's door so carelessly that John could even hear it from where he sat.

John got up, flung the blanket on his bed, and stepped out into the hall. By standing not more than a yard from the top of the stairs he could hear the voices in the room quite clearly. If the door should open unexpectedly, he could always pretend he was on his way down to the bathroom.

But at once he was so interested, so shocked, that he almost forgot the risk of discovery.

"It's too much!" Dorothy was saying in a tense, frightened voice. "I just can't stand it! Lockjaw, that's what it is! It came over me all of a sudden when he said he couldn't chew. It was bad enough to kill Ronny. I never said a word, but don't think I didn't suspect, with you acting so queerly! I never would have said a word, even to you. But now, if it's going to keep on. . . ."

"You little fool!" Douglas' voice was savage and thick. "You're telling me that I killed Ronny? I never heard anything so crazy! Perhaps this is tetanus. I doubt it, but if so, it's accidental. I have nothing to do with it. But don't you dare go talking to anyone, do you hear me? or perhaps I *will* do something."

"It's all for the sake of that coldhearted bitch!" Dorothy exclaimed. "That's what gets me! She takes up with Ronny and you can't stand that. Now she's just beginning to take up with John . . . just beginning, mind you! It might have come to nothing. If I know her, she'd just about as leave be eating peanuts as sleeping with a man. I know the type. But you couldn't wait. You couldn't take the chance, you were so damned jealous!"

"You're crazy, I tell you!" Douglas growled; and from the gasp Dorothy gave, John was sure that he had seized her arm or her shoulders. "I've never killed anyone and I never intend to, but if you want me to start, you're going about it in just the right way."

"It's because he's such a decent kid," she said. "He seems so young and innocent, kind of. But I wouldn't care, I wouldn't tell, if you'd only be nicer to me, Doug, if you'd only keep away from her. You're so wonderful, Doug! I'm just wild about you! And she treats you like the dirt beneath her feet. Look at me, Doug. Don't you know I'm crazy about you?"

Douglas chuckled deep in his throat. "Why you depraved little thing," he said huskily. "I believe it gives you a thrill to think your man's a murderer!"

"Yes, yes," she said, and her voice now was something between a gasp and a sigh, "you give me a thrill . . . you don't know what a thrill. . . ."

There was the sound of kisses, and John, half sick with disgust, crept back to his room. He had heard more than enough.

19

The noise penetrated John's dream as the caving in of vaults deep underground: he had been lost in some catacomb or cellar; the cold bit to his very bones, which was not strange, because when he glanced at his hand and wrist through the green phosphorescence which was here the only light, he saw that the flesh had been dissolved and what he was looking at was the hand of a skeleton. It was then that the vaults crumbled to trap him there forever, and the dust which at the moment of the explosion had swirled about his body like a spiral nebula puffed out into twinkling darkness. The malevolence of that darkness was so terrifying that his struggles, with spine bent backwards so that his body rested only on his heels and on the top of his head (in this, the final spasm of tetanus), would no doubt have roused him; but the first thing his waking mind was aware of was the knocking at his door and then the desperate voice which only after a minute he recognized as Dorothy's.

"John," he heard her saying, and the next instant her hand was shaking his shoulder, "John, come quickly! Douglas has fallen downstairs. He's unconscious, and the funny way his head is bent I think his neck is broken, or it may be his back. I think he's dying!"

John opened his eyes. All he could see in the lighted room were Dorothy's cheeks rising like two slabs of dough to fill up her eye sockets; then her whole face took shape, distraught and bloodless, as she leaned over him, and he grasped the meaning of her words.

He jumped from bed, put on his dressing gown and followed her to the stairway. In the light which shone down the shaft he could see Douglas' body sprawled headfirst to block the foot of the stairs, his head twisted into a position that made John think of a contortionist. He did not move and John could not hear him breathing.

"Have you told anyone else?" he asked sharply.

"No," she said. "I heard him fall just a minute ago. I rushed down there and saw he was unconscious. I didn't dare to step over him for fear I'd move him and do some damage."

Then she continued with a question which reminded John once more, now that he was fully awake, of the part he must still play:

"But how are *you* feeling, John? Are you all right?"

It would have seemed to John, after what he had overheard earlier in the night, that now the whole thing was over and there would be no need to continue the pretense of his own illness; surely his uncle had suspected no such ending as this; but he did not quite dare not continue with the professor's scheme until he had consulted him.

"I've got a pretty bad headache," he said, "and my neck seems to be worse, but that's all right. I can jump over Douglas without disturbing him. We ought to tell Dr. Chardwicke and my uncle. If his spine is injured he should be got to the hospital at once."

The next half hour seethed with confusion. John wakened first his uncle, then the doctor; the noise, the coming and going in the hall, aroused both Fran and Ellen; in a short time Dr. Macfarlane appeared, summoned by Professor Hatfield, and an ambulance drove up not five minutes later. Perhaps for John the most ghastly thing was the sense of repetition: in so many ways it was like the hushed midnight turmoil at the time of Ronny's death.

As two orderlies were carrying Douglas, still breathing, downstairs, Professor Hatfield said to Dr. Macfarlane:

"Terry, I wish you'd drop in tomorrow to take a look at John. He had a stiff neck last night and felt generally miserable. He's got a splitting headache now, poor boy, and he says his neck feels worse. I imagine it's a touch of the flu that's been going the rounds, but I'd feel more comfortable if you'd look at him. Don't think of stopping now. This is of no consequence, and I'm afraid Douglas is in a bad way."

"He's in a bad way all right," Terry Macfarlane said. "I doubt if he'll make the grade to the hospital. If we can get him to the operating room, he might stand a slim chance; but it's pretty damn slim."

At this point Dorothy broke into hysterical sobs, and Mrs. Chardwicke put her arm around her and took her up to her room. John was about to follow them, after a muttered good night to the company, when his uncle seized his arm.

"You're going to sleep in my room for the rest of the night," he said. "I'm not going to let you sleep in that drafty little hole, the way you're feeling. We'll switch rooms until you're yourself again. Don't you think that's a good idea, Doctor?"

"An excellent idea!" Dr. Chardwicke exclaimed heartily. "But if John is coming down with the flu, as seems most likely, I don't think you should sleep in his sheets."

"I'm not nervous," Professor Hatfield said. "Still, I can't afford to be missing classes; so perhaps, Doctor, if your good wife will give me some clean sheets I'll make up the bed myself. I don't want to put her to any trouble, and Dorothy is in no condition just now. I'll go back to my room first to collect a few things and see that John is comfortable. If Mrs. Chardwicke will lay the sheets in John's room, I'll see to them when I go up."

"I'm sure Althea won't dream of your making the bed yourself," Dr. Chardwicke said, "but I'll give her your message."

Then with a most scrupulous gentleness, which almost gave John once more the sense that he was really ill, Professor Hatfield led him into the room where Ronny had died.

The moment he had closed and locked the door, however, he was all alertness and curiosity.

"Now tell me at once, John," he said, "what you heard, if anything. What has happened to Douglas was a shock to me. I feel I should have been prepared, I should have forestalled it, but I suspected no such sudden action."

"But wasn't it an accident?" John exclaimed. "Douglas had been drinking before he went up, and it's likely both Dorothy and he had more to drink in her room. It would be the easiest thing in the world to fall down those steps if you were cold sober. You warned me about them yourself."

"It was no accident," Professor Hatfield said grimly. "Look at this, John."

He took out of the pocket of his dressing gown a piece of picture wire with a knot at each end, in one of which there was still a large tack.

"Where did you find it?" John asked in surprise.

"I found it under Douglas' legs on the stairs. It was the first thing I looked for when he was moved."

"But who put it there?" John felt completely bewildered. "And why? Was it to trip me? Weren't they content with the tetanus? From what I heard in Dorothy's room, I thought Douglas was the person we're after."

"Tell me exactly what you did hear," Professor Hatfield said. "It may clear up a few doubts in my mind."

Then as John talked to him he began packing things neatly in one of his smaller bags.

"Hmmm!" the professor exclaimed, when John had given him a complete account of Douglas' and Dorothy's conversation. "That of course explains Dorothy's reaction to your illness: she suspected Douglas and not the real murderer. That means, at least, that she will not interfere to complicate matters now that Douglas is safely out of the way. 'Safely,' I mean, from our point of view. For him, poor lad, I'm afraid it's the end."

"Then Douglas did not kill Ronny?" John asked. "He was telling her the truth?"

"He was telling Dorothy the truth," Professor Hatfield said, "when he said he had killed no one and was planning to kill no one, though luckily for our little scheme, she did not believe him. He was not telling her the truth when he said he was doubtful whether you had contracted tetanus and that if you had, it must be an accident. He must have been convinced that you were coming down with tetanus, and if you were, he was certain it was murder. That is why an attempt, and I'm very much afraid a successful one, was made on his own life."

"You mean Douglas knows who the real murderer is?" John asked.

"He either knows, or suspects so strongly that it amounts to full knowledge. I was sure he suspected to some extent. That was why I took care Douglas was out of the dining room when I mentioned I had left the door of Dr. Chardwicke's laboratory unlocked: I feared he might keep watch to prevent anyone's going up there. It gave me quite a start when he came into the room so soon afterwards. I realized I had been careless, but luck was with me. As a matter of fact, when I came in after the movies, Saturday night, I managed to chat with him for a few minutes and he told me that no one had left the house during our absence. I kept discreet watch myself for the rest of the night; no one went out; so that I knew your razor blades could not have been touched by Sunday morning. I wondered whether our trap was going to fail; so I was delighted when on Sunday I had reason to be convinced it had succeeded, though of course I couldn't be sure until Monday when Terry examined the blades. What I should have realized is that the first attempt to put a wire across the stairway, the attempt which you interrupted, was not aimed at you but at Douglas. On that particular night it was of course he, neither you nor Dorothy, who would be the first to come down those stairs. With this as a warning, I should have been prepared for the swift attempt to silence Douglas tonight: the murderer must have reasoned that if Dorothy suspected foul play, Douglas also would suspect—the difference being that Douglas was not mistaken in the criminal."

"But if you know it was murder, or attempted murder," John exclaimed, "oughtn't you to tell the police? Oughtn't you to show them that wire?"

"All in good time," his uncle said. "Three more days, John. Tonight is Tuesday. Your death will occur at about ten thirty Friday evening. After that certainly, if we need them, the police will be called."

"But won't they be angry with you for not telling them at once that you found the wire?"

"Unless you care to betray me, my dear John," Professor Hatfield said with the briefest smile, "they will never know I did find it until Friday night, after other startling events had aroused my suspicions. And now good night. I mustn't be lingering here with you too long, or conceivably the suspicions of someone else might be aroused."

The only things that made the next three days at all bearable for John were the almost constant company of his uncle and the visits of Dr. Macfarlane. Douglas had died just after reaching the hospital without regaining consciousness. Professor Hatfield had told John this as he stopped in on his way down to breakfast. He would not allow John himself to appear.

"My dear John," he said, "you're far too ill for that already. Terry will drop by during the morning and diagnose your case. Since the hospital, as I told you, is crowded and since private nurses are almost impossible to obtain on short notice, I shall have the pleasure of being your attendant. It won't be for long."

The first morning John had asked if, now that there was no risk of his betraying his knowledge, since he would be seeing no one, his uncle would not tell him what it was all about, and who it was he suspected. But Professor Hatfield on this point was firm:

"You'll know everything before long. This is not just perverseness on my part. It's not the childish wish to spring on you a theatrical surprise. That's the last thing I want to do, but I have my reasons. When I tell them to you, I think you'll admit that they were entirely valid."

Each time the professor returned to the room in which now he ate all his meals and which he left only for the briefest intervals, during Dr. Macfarlane's visits, he would relate to John the progress of his symptoms.

"I was just telling Mrs. Chardwicke," he said on the second afternoon, "that the lockjaw is so extreme Terry brought a nasal catheter when he called an hour ago and we now have to feed you through the nose." That evening he announced that Dr. Chardwicke and he had been discussing the *risus sardonicus,* a lifting of the eyebrows, a pulling down of the corners of the lips which gives the sufferer a characteristic and macabre expression. "In your case, I regret to say, John, it is especially pronounced, in fact quite harrowing. I almost promised the doctor I'd let him take a peek at you. I felt we could put on a very interesting little act, but on second thought, I imagined that you would rather not be bothered."

John was at any rate thankful to be spared this. Professor Hatfield would allow the reading light by the bed but no other, and the curtains were kept drawn day and night. Dr. Macfarlane from time to time poured a little chloroform on a handkerchief ("It's sometimes used," he explained, "to control the spasms") so that the faint sweet smell was always present in the room and no doubt, as was intended, spread through the hall.

It was the nights that were the longest; and as John dozed and woke up and dozed again, he would find himself, in a region between dream and waking, identifying himself with Ronny. Like him, Ronny must have counted the medallions of the grimy brown paper; he must have found the nights, night after night, even more unending; his delirious mind must have wandered into even more remote, more fearful realms.

It was a relief when at ten thirty on the evening of the third day Dr. Macfarlane pronounced him dead.

"Only a few hours more," his uncle told him encouragingly, "though they may be the worst, because I shall have to let them see you. It's only friendly and natural. However, all you'll have to do, John, is to lie completely still. The light will be dim, and I won't let them stay long. In a few minutes then you may expect visitors. I shall be here at that time with them. Then later, John, after several hours, perhaps, you must be prepared, if all goes well, for one final lonely visitor."

"And that will be the murderer?" John asked. "But how will you know? What proof will you have?"

"You remember the person you heard moving about in this room, when you came downstairs to get your coat, the night of Ronny's death? I think that tonight, John, after all this waiting, we shall find out what he was after."

20

The first wait was not long. Perhaps ten minutes, perhaps half an hour after his uncle had closed the door to announce his death to the family, the door opened again and John, with his eyes tightly closed, not daring even to peek through his lashes, heard the footsteps of several people, he had no idea how many, on the carpet. He remembered having watched actors whose parts required them to feign dead and to lie for minutes on the stage in full view of the audience, and having wondered whether they were not seized by a compulsion to move, to sit up, to make some noise. He must not think of that, or next thing he would be moving, himself: he must relax absolutely; he must hardly breathe—though in the thick shadow the rise and fall of his chest could not be observed.

"It's terribly sad," Dr. Chardwicke exclaimed after a minute, and surprisingly there was a suggestion of tears in his voice. "John was a sweet boy."

"At least it was quick," Mrs. Chardwicke said, and her tone was quite as usual. "He didn't suffer long."

For a minute or two there was silence except for the sound of faint movements in the room. Then he heard his uncle say in a voice which would have done credit to the most expensive undertaker:

"I thought you'd like to have just a glimpse of him. I'm sure he would have wanted it. He was so happy here. And now, perhaps. . . ."

John could hear the shuffle of feet as people went out into the hall. It was a minute later that something happened which might have ruined the whole scheme.

There was a sudden burst of low sobbing, and the bed shook as if someone had flung himself on his knees with head and arms resting on the edge of the mattress.

"Oh John, John!" he heard in a passionate and heartbroken whisper which he recognized as Ellen's. "You never guessed how I loved you, did you, John? How could you bother with me when Fran was there? She's so beautiful and she'd been so unhappy! I was glad, really I was, for her and for you. But now it doesn't matter. You'll never know, and it doesn't matter!"

As John recalled this afterwards, he was sure that if he hadn't realized how it would frighten her, he would have sat up at once and taken her in his arms to console her. He could catch now some hint of the struggles she had been through in mastering her jealousy of Fran; he knew why she had not gone on the picnic with Fran and him: she had thought that he asked her only through kindness and that she would be in the way. Cutting through his sense of the unreality of all that had been happening was a robust thankfulness that he was not dead, that he was young and healthy, that life was before him.

He heard Ellen rise to her feet, as if suddenly aware that his uncle stood behind her. "I couldn't help it," she said. "It was the truth."

"You're a good girl, Ellen," Professor Hatfield said, and his voice had never sounded so kind. "I hope that someday you will be very happy."

Then together they left the room. John heard the door close; but the key was not turned in the lock. He raised his eyelids and saw that his uncle had pushed open the curtains and turned out the light.

The window gleamed frostily in the midst of the darkness, and an oblong of moonlight fell across the floor. John shifted his position, though he knew that he must remain lying on his back. He tried to recapture in his mind the sound of Ellen's voice, because it was so warm, so full of the stuff of life; but it seemed to dwindle away so that he could not imagine it. He could not even picture her face distinctly. Instead he had the vision of himself as he stood at the foot of the stairs in the dark cellar and looked up at the light in the kitchen; only now the stairs reached up and up indefinitely; his uncle and Ellen were climbing them side by side: John knew it was they, although they had gone up so far already that he could not recognize them.

The room was growing colder and colder. His uncle had not locked the door, so that it could be opened in almost perfect silence without the turn of a key. But there would surely be some faint sound. When would he first notice it? What would it be like? He would see no strip of light on the carpet as the door opened, because the hall would certainly be dark. Let's hope that his uncle arrived not too long after the murderer!

He must have lain here for several hours surely. Did he dare to close his eyes? It would do no harm if he fell asleep. Ah, but if he slept he might sink down into those interminable rooms that Ronny had spoken of, into the depths of that dark swirling cloud, and wake up screaming.

The square of the window hypnotized him; he could imagine its leaving its place and floating around in the darkness. It *was* moving surely: the frame itself was still but something was moving in the dim moonlight beyond it. This was no sharp outline, like the shadow on the cellar door: it was wavering, almost transparent, as if it were a condensation of the frost.

He blinked; his eyes must be playing him tricks. But it was not only his eyes: he could hear a number of short breathless jerks as the sash moved upwards. Someone on the roof was opening that window. He must close his eyes now, if he was ever going to!

Then as he stared into the blackness of his lids, the thought came over him with a feeling of cold nausea that his uncle would not know the murderer was here: Professor Hatfield must be waiting somewhere in the hall, perhaps in Douglas' room, and would see or hear nothing. John held his breath, but that was wrong because sooner or later he would have to let it go with a gasp. For now he was not alone in the room. Someone was moving across the carpet toward his bed. He could hardly distinguish the steps: the sound was more like the faintest brushing of dead leaves over frozen earth.

Then he knew that the murderer was standing beside the bed looking down at him: the slightest move, the least breath, might mean that he was really dead, without the chance of return, before anyone could come to his rescue.

Now that the footsteps had stopped, he heard another noise: it was the sound of breathing, fierce and rapid but still soft, like the panting of a desperate animal heard at a distance in the forest, like the noise he had heard through the door the night that Ronny died.

A wave of cold lapped around his body as the bedclothes were swiftly pulled back and the murderer slipped into the bed beside him.

The next instant there was the clatter of someone jumping in on to the floor, and through his eyelids John could see the glow of light.

"Fran," his uncle said, and his voice did not sound severe but gravely impersonal, "it's all over now."

When John, in horror, at last opened his eyes, he saw Fran standing beside the bed in her silvery kimono, facing Professor Hatfield. Her head was flung back; her hands, close to her sides, were tightly clenched.

"No," she said in a breathless voice, "no, you can't do this! Tomorrow perhaps. Later. You can do with me what you like. But you can't come between John and me! No one can do that! Douglas would have interfered; so I had to kill him. This is our wedding night—the only one, because they will take him away; they will put him in the earth. So you must go!"

Professor Hatfield's face was expressionless, but he shook his head.

"You can get up now, John," he said. "You must be tired lying there so long."

As John sat up, Fran turned with a cowering movement, as if she had been struck by an arrow. For the first instant, as her eyes met his incredulously, he saw that her cheeks were glowing as they had never been. Then her face froze into a look of repulsion, of horror, which reminded him of the moment, in the snowy woods, after he had kissed her lips; the blood was drained from it, and shuddering violently she covered it with her hands.

"Yes," she moaned in a voice that suggested Ronny's when from the depths of his fever he had spoken of the horror in the cloud. "It's over! It's all over."

21

"I must admit," Professor Hatfield said to John, "that I hoped Fran would do just what she did, if I gave her the chance. Death from bichloride of mercury is not comfortable; but for her it is better, I'm sure, than spending the rest of her life in an asylum."

It was a bright afternoon nearly a week later. As they walked along the woodland path, they kept brushing snow from the twigs.

In spite of the sun warming his back, John shuddered. "She was really mad then?" he asked. "Of course she must have been."

"You remember my saying how hard it is to draw the line," his uncle said. "She was what is called a necrophile, a person who is attracted only by the dead, and with her the compulsion was so strong that she could not struggle against it. One can fancy it was people like her who gave rise to the legends of the ghouls, the haunters of graveyards, or the evil spirits, whether of the water or of the forest, who would appear to young men as women of un-natural beauty and lure them to their doom. The inner world she lived in is so remote from ours that to us it seems a land of pure nightmare. Doubtless it often seemed such to her, but she could not help herself. When the urge was upon her she could only kill to obtain what she wanted, and kill she must. Such an urge, I'm glad to say, is rare, and to all normal people utterly horrible, so that we think of it as mad; yet the planning of each murder was lucid and deliberate. She killed Ronny because in her own ghastly way she loved him; she tried to kill you because you reminded her of him. With Douglas it was quite different. He filled her only with repulsion, the more so, doubtless, because he was forcing upon her his all too human and passionate attentions. Douglas suspected the nature of her aberration, but he was nonetheless desperately in love with her. After Ronny's death he tried to use his half knowledge as a kind of blackmail, or at least of persuasion; so she killed him out of self-protection. She doubtless felt, and probably with good reason, that if he had kept silent about Ronny's death, your death from tetanus would be too much for him, and he would speak, and that is why she acted so quickly. From the killings themselves she derived no pleasure. They must have been terrible experiences for her: she was merely driven to them as a means to an end."

"Are you just guessing about Douglas?" John asked. "Or do you really know?"

"I'm not guessing," Professor Hatfield said. "She left me a letter, John—or really she left it, as you will see, for you. I haven't mentioned it until now, just as I haven't talked to you about the case, because I wanted to leave a few days for the shock to wear off."

He felt in the pocket of his overcoat and pulled out an envelope. "It was written hurriedly," he went on, "under great strain. In places it is almost illegible. Would you like me to read it to you as we walk along?"

"Yes," John said, "but there are a few questions I'd like to ask before you begin. First of all, how is Ellen? I'm thankful you arranged for her to move out to Dr. Macfarlane's. The Chardwicke house would be so awful for her, now that you have moved out and Dr. Chardwicke is in such a state of depression. But I haven't heard from her or seen her since she left."

His uncle gave him one of his dry smiles. "Perhaps I should have told you that we're bound for Terry Macfarlane's at the present moment," he said. "His house is just beyond this wood. I think at first poor Ellen was ashamed to see you, because she felt she had given herself away. She thought that you might not like to see *her*, after what you heard that night. I dared to assume, however, that this was not the case. Was I wrong?"

"No," John exclaimed, "you certainly were not."

He stooped, gathered some snow which he molded into a ball and flung it as far as he could through the branches.

"And there's one thing I'd like to ask *you*," Professor Hatfield said after a minute. "I'd like to get it off my chest, because it has worried me a great deal. You remember I spoke to you of the nice question of timing our experiment. I wasn't entirely frank with you, however, in explaining the real difficulty. The problem was to wait long enough for Fran, who obviously, from the start, was attracted by you, to feel that attraction sufficiently strong to drive her on to a new murder; and yet not to wait so long that you would have fallen seriously in love with *her*. I do hope, John, that I didn't wait too long."

"No," John answered slowly, staring ahead through the bright branches, "no, you didn't, Uncle Paul. I was fascinated in a way. If you had waited much longer some damage might have been done, though now I can only think of her with a kind of horror which seems all the worse somehow because she was so beautiful. Perhaps there were two things that saved me: in the first place my realizing that Ronny had died so recently, and in the second place my fondness for Ellen. From the very start she seemed almost like a younger sister—almost, but I'm beginning to see now, not quite. And always, compared with her, because she was so natural, so very warm and loyal, Fran, even when I felt her charm most strongly, seemed a little cold and exotic."

"Well," Professor Hatfield exclaimed, and John could hear his relief, "I'm delighted if that's the case. But perhaps now, John, you realize why even at the end I wouldn't tell you the murderer was Fran: it seemed to me not inconceivable that if you knew it was she, you might refuse to enter into my plot. As you will learn from her letter, she told Ronny the truth before his death, and yet he did not speak, to accuse her. And then I felt, too, that great as the shock of discovery might be, you would have been far more wretched, during those last three days, if you had known it was Fran I was expecting and for what purpose she would come."

"But how did you happen to suspect her in the first place?" John asked. "That's what I don't understand."

"Since my conviction was arrived at only gradually," Professor Hatfield said, "perhaps the simplest thing would be for me to give you the complete evidence pointing toward her by reviewing events and impressions in chronological sequence. From the first we knew that her heredity was deplorable. Her uncle, Dr. Chardwicke, had never been quite normal and had lost his job because of a nervous breakdown during which he had been confined in an asylum. Her other uncle, as I told you, had died in an institution. Her mother had killed herself. You may recall some of the amusing anecdotes Dr. Chardwicke told us about the subjects of his family portraits—incidents amusing only from a distance and suggesting a long line of eccentricity. When I called on Ronny in the early days of his sickness, it was Fran whom I saw. She gave me the impression of continually wanting to glance over her shoulder, as if she were afraid that someone would appear. I had thought it was her uncle that she dreaded, but it was just as plausible to guess that it might be Ronny himself; because if I saw him I might realize how very ill he was and persuade him to go to the hospital, where his chances would be infinitely improved. Later of course, on your first evening, she urged her uncle to consult other doctors; but she must have known that he would not be so easily persuaded. If she was as doubtful of his abilities as her talk seemed to suggest and if she had really wanted to save Ronny, she could have overridden the doctor's somewhat vain and pettish objections. What she hoped to do was to throw suspicion off the track, should anyone suggest foul play. She had you as a witness that she had asked for a consultation and that Dr. Chardwicke, who was Ronny's heir, had refused to call one.

"And then came your vivid account of your talk with Ronny, which, as I said, was what first made me think of Fran. It struck me so much that I asked you to go over it with me several times. My impression was that Ronny must have received some shattering psychological shock which had made him turn his face to the wall. He was more or less delirious when you saw him, but it seemed as if his wandering was centered about some special horror, something unspeakable, something in fact which had been so horrible that he managed, with the help of his fever, to wrap it around in the swirling cloud to which he more than once referred. I felt, in other words, that the shock he had undergone was not only physical but moral.

"Now the chances are that an intense moral shock cannot be induced by someone to whom you are indifferent. The more you love and trust a person, the greater suffering he is able to inflict upon you, and the more dangerous he may become for your peace of mind. You may recall my asking you if there was any deep friendship between Douglas and Ronny; you said you were sure there was not, and I know you were right. I asked if you'd seen anything to suggest that the relationship between Ronny and the Chardwickes approached a true parental and filial relationship, and again you said that you had not. Apparently then, the only two people in the house that Ronny was deeply fond of were Ellen and Fran. I've said that I gave little thought to Ellen from the first; and obviously Fran was far more important to Ronny than anyone else. She was the person most able to produce the shattering effect that you described. But what could she have done? Unfaithfulness seemed not enough to account for Ronny's sense of something positively hellish. Moreover it had nothing to do with the element of danger with which Ronny felt you were threatened when he urged you to run away. It struck me suddenly, at first as something merely fantastic, that the knowledge that his fiancée, the person he loved and trusted most in the world, was the very one who was slowly murdering him would account for his feelings. I have, I think, a fairly lively imagination in the field of horror, but I can think of no situation more completely like a foretaste of hell, particularly when you consider the motive for the murder. No wonder Ronny, knowing what was to come, kept identifying himself, in his nightmares, with the dead.

"Next there was your account of her actions at the time of Ronny's death. She looked down at him for a moment and then walked over to the window. You had climbed out of the bathroom window (from which, by the way, I kept watch on that last night), looked into hers and then into Ronny's, which meant that anyone could climb out of hers, walk along the roof, and climb into Ronny's room, that is if the window was unlocked. That would be much the safest way to get from one room to the other if you did not wish to be seen; and it occurred to me that when she crossed the room it was not simply to withdraw from the rest of you, but

for the quite practical reason of undoing the clasp. When she returned to look once more at Ronny's corpse, she swooned. You
assumed that she was overcome by grief, but it was not grief. On
the night of your 'death,' by the way, she walked to the window
again; if she had not done so I was prepared to let her see me do it,
on the pretext of keeping the room cool by raising the sash a trifle.

"Of course it was she you heard in the room that night when
you came downstairs after your coat. I had racked my brain to
think of what anyone might be hunting for and could think of
nothing, unless a will; but what little money Ronny had was left
to the doctor, and if Ronny had died intestate it would have gone
to him anyway, as his nearest relative and his guardian."

"But she urged me to leave the house," John said. "Do you
think that was in a moment of comparatively normal feeling when
she wished to save me from herself?"

"I'm afraid not," the professor replied. "Judging from your account, she urged you very gently, and stated at the same time that
she herself was in danger, which she realized of course was the best
way of keeping you there. In fact that whole conversation struck
me as definitely suspicious. You may not have realized how she
simply followed your lead. She did not say she suspected murder
until you had already said that you did. She did not say Ronny
had warned her until you had told her that he had warned you.
In other words, she was putting herself in the same boat with you
as a possible victim and thus removing herself from the field of
suspects. It was only natural and wise that she should refuse to
commit herself about either the doctor or Douglas: she knew that
investigation would prove them innocent and that the safest thing
for her was to leave the field as vague and mysterious as possible.

"Perhaps there is only one other thing I need mention—the
detail which would have clinched the case, if I had still been in
doubt. I told you that whoever obtained the tetanus bacillus must
have done so on Sunday morning, the day of your picnic with
Fran. We had breakfast that day at nine o'clock, as we always did
on Sundays. It was a mild snowy day. Don't you remember that
when you asked Fran and Ellen if they still wanted to go, Fran
told you that the day was beautiful and that she had already been

outside. She had left the house at a little before eight and been gone for three-quarters of an hour. That of course is when she took the germs."

John remembered how he had walked through the snowy woods with Fran; he remembered her look of eagerness, of quiet expectancy; he remembered above all her exclamation—"Not now!"—when he had kissed her. Fatuously he had interpreted it as meaning: "Not yet!" Perhaps his interpretation had been right; and as John thought of what this implied, he felt actually sick.

There was still her message. He could not bear to hear it; and yet it seemed to him that he must, or he would be always wondering what it had contained.

"The letter," he said. "Would you like to read it now?"

Professor Hatfield unfolded the sheets of paper in his hand, and while he read he would stop now and then for a moment, to move slowly on again.

> Dear Professor Hatfield:
> I am addressing this to you, although it is meant for John, because I know your curiosity will make you read it, while I can imagine John's destroying it unread. If you can get him to read it, I feel you will have done me a great favor. Why do I wish John to see it? Perhaps because never in my life have I been able to talk to anyone with complete sincerity, and I should like to do so once before I die. When I attempted to do that with Ronny, he was so overcome with horror that I could not go on. If John feels the same horror, at least I shall not be there to see it.
>
> Life has always been hideous to me. Some of my earliest memories are the various attempts my mother made to kill herself before my father had her taken off, screaming and struggling, to an asylum, where in a few months she at last succeeded. I had watched her being taken away, peeking through the curtains of my room at the top of the house.

I don't know when I began to realize my father's love affairs. I cannot describe to you the horror and repulsion with which they filled me. They seemed somehow connected in my mind with my mother's death and with the mysterious place to which she had been taken. I would dream of it night after night. I pictured it as a torture chamber in the top of a tower without doors or windows.

I have always suspected that my brother's death was not accidental. Before he went out in the car that night he had had a quarrel with my father. He had always adored Mother and blamed Father for her death. We talked of it often. I was thirteen years old when he died, and when his body was brought home, I felt that I could not keep on living. But the next night I came down from my room and kept watch as he lay in his coffin. It seemed to me that for the first time I really saw him. He was beautiful, with pale gold hair, like yours, John, and like Ronny's. I was suddenly thankful that he was not alive to know all the revolting uncleanness of physical love. I felt that we were closer together than we had ever been, that there was no barrier between us. The night passed like an unearthly dream.

Perhaps if I had not met Ronny when I did, I should have killed myself. The moment I saw him I realized he was meant for me; I knew at once after the lonely and frightful years of my growing up, that he was my brother and my bridegroom. I had the sense of his purity which I knew must never be corrupted. He thought I was cold; sometimes he doubted my love, because I could not put up with the vulgarity of kisses; but I could not blame him: I knew too well that no one can be completely pure, no one can be completely himself, in this loathsome madhouse which is life.

It was easy enough to plan his death. I did it quite simply, without hesitation, without fear. But then, when he became ill, a strange and horrible thing happened to me. One night I had the sense that I myself was mad. I had had it often when I was younger; it had haunted me for years; but I felt, I hoped I had outgrown it, left it behind me forever. No one will know the agony of those moments.

I went to Ronny's room. That was several days before you came to the house, John, sent me, I soon realized, to take Ronny's place. I told him that it was I that was killing him, killing him not because I hated him but because I loved him, so that he could be my bridegroom, forever pure. I asked him to forgive me if I was mad; but then when I saw the horror in his eyes I realized that I should not have spoken, and I left him. My speaking was the one mad thing: his horror was merely the incomplete understanding which is a part of life. But at least, John, he did not betray me.

I should have known that everything on earth is sure to be ruined. Douglas had been pursuing me with his attempts at love-making. To me he was the very essence of all the filthy heat and corruption of living. The night of Ronny's death, he came to my door, and from what he said I guessed he suspected something of my secret. Someone came to Ronny's door later that night, our wedding night. I imagine it was Douglas, but I lay perfectly still and he went away.

But then, John, on every occasion he urged me to come to his room. He said he could "cure" me, if I would give him the chance, he, a loathsome example of earthly lust. He even offered not to "give me away," if I should become his mistress or his wife. There was only one thing for me to do.

I have nothing more to say, except that I forgive you for betraying me. You think of me as a criminal, a murderer, but that is because you see things with eyes dimmed by the corruption of human desires. I should have known that the only perfect lover would be Death himself.

For several minutes John and the professor walked on in silence.

"If it will make it seem any less of a shock," Professor Hatfield said at last, "I think that Fran's infatuations were, in a measure, what I might describe as platonic. She refers to Ronny as her bridegroom but also as her brother. She associated him with her real brother who was killed. Apparently you and Ronny both suggested him. The dark depths of her mind will always be a mystery, but I imagine that her communion with the dead, with her bridegroom 'forever pure,' was more than anything a perverted kind of mystical experience. Had it been merely sensual, she might have chosen other means than illness to get rid of her victims. I don't pretend to know."

John wondered whether his uncle really believed what he said, or whether he was just trying to diminish, in some small way, his sense of horror. He heard off in the woods the notes of a chickadee and was thankful for this sign of life in the midst of the stillness.

The snow was growing more and more dazzling, as if the sun were moving nearer. He could imagine the whiteness dropping from the branches, and buds appearing against the blue sky. They stepped out of the woods. Across a road stood a pair of white gateposts beyond which the lawn of a white-pillared house blazed in the sun.

"That's Dr. Macfarlane's," Professor Hatfield said.

As they walked up the drive, the door opened and Ellen started out. She was wearing a red sweater and no hat. As soon as she noticed them, she stepped inside quickly and closed the door.

"You see," Professor Hatfield said, "she's still a little afraid of you."

"We'll have to fix that in short order," John exclaimed, and in a moment he was running at full speed up the snowy drive, leaving the professor far behind him.

COACHWHIP PUBLICATIONS
CoachwhipBooks.com

ANITA BOUTELL

DEATH BRINGS
A STORKE

CRADLED
IN FEAR

COACHWHIP PUBLICATIONS

COACHWHIPBOOKS.COM

A JUDGE MASSIE MYSTERY

THE CORPSE IS INDIGNANT

DOUGLAS STAPLETON
and HELEN A. CAREY

COACHWHIP PUBLICATIONS
CoachwhipBooks.com

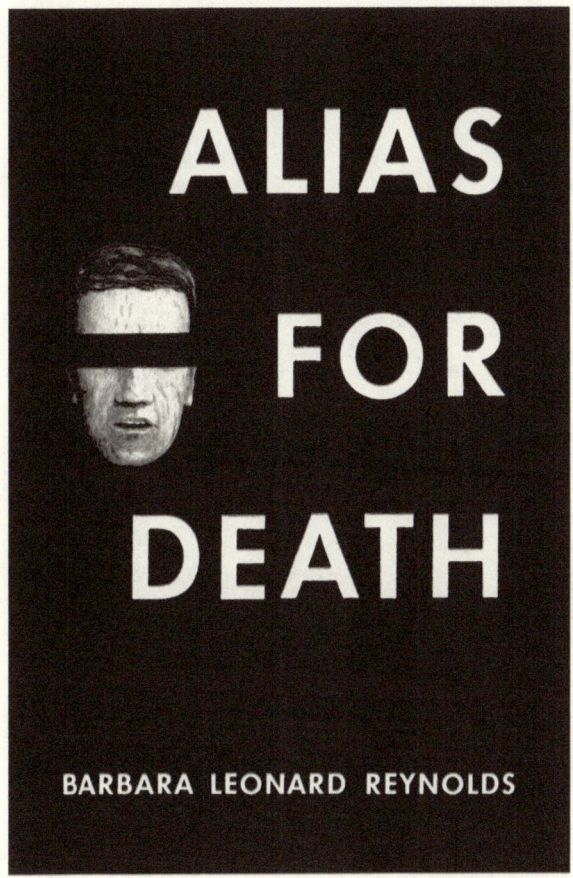

COACHWHIP PUBLICATIONS
CoachwhipBooks.com

DEAD
WEIGHT

ADDISON
SIMMONS

COACHWHIP PUBLICATIONS
CoachwhipBooks.com

COACHWHIP PUBLICATIONS
CoachwhipBooks.com

DEATH SAILS
THE NILE

F. Burks McKinley

COACHWHIP PUBLICATIONS
CoachwhipBooks.com

DEATH
SERVES
AN ACE

HELEN WILLS
AND
JOHN W. MURPHY

COACHWHIP PUBLICATIONS
CoachwhipBooks.com

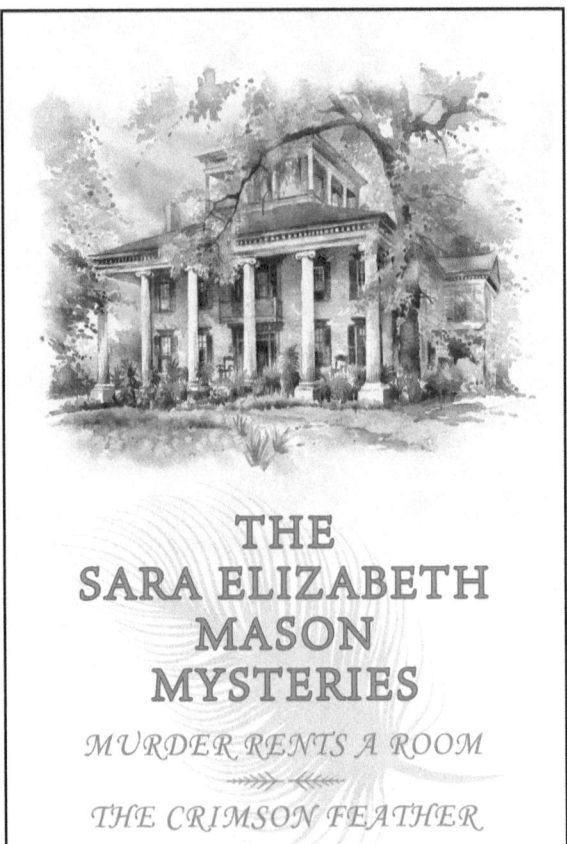

THE
SARA ELIZABETH
MASON
MYSTERIES

MURDER RENTS A ROOM

THE CRIMSON FEATHER

COACHWHIP PUBLICATIONS

CoachwhipBooks.com

THE
SARA ELIZABETH
MASON
MYSTERIES

THE HOUSE THAT HATE BUILT

THE WHIP

COACHWHIP PUBLICATIONS
CoachwhipBooks.com

THE
RUMBLE
MURDERS

Henry Ware Eliot, Jr.

www.ingramcontent.com/pod-product-compliance
Lightning Source LLC
Chambersburg PA
CBHW030628020726
47493CB00006B/1617

* 9 7 8 1 6 1 6 4 6 4 5 9 2 *